# PLAYTHING

*Also by Bea Setton*

Berlin

# Plaything

## BEA SETTON

doubleday

TRANSWORLD PUBLISHERS
Penguin Random House, One Embassy Gardens,
8 Viaduct Gardens, London SW11 7BW
www.penguin.co.uk

Transworld is part of the Penguin Random House group of companies
whose addresses can be found at global.penguinrandomhouse.com

First published in Great Britain in 2024 by Doubleday
an imprint of Transworld Publishers

A CIP catalogue record for this book
is available from the British Library.

ISBNs 9780857528001 (cased)
9780857528018 (tpb)

Typeset in 12.5/14.5 pt Adobe Garamond Pro by Jouve (UK), Milton Keynes
Printed and bound in Great Britain by Clays Ltd, Elcograf S.p.A.

The authorized representative in the EEA is Penguin Random House Ireland,
Morrison Chambers, 32 Nassau Street, Dublin D02 YH68.

Penguin Random House is committed to a sustainable future
for our business, our readers and our planet. This book is made
from Forest Stewardship Council® certified paper.

For Noa Amson and Sally Tulaimat

Two different things wanteth the true man: danger and play. Therefore he wants woman, as the most dangerous plaything.

Friedrich Nietzsche, *Thus Spoke Zarathustra*

# PART I

# I

## Pulp Fiction

I T HAPPENED IN CAMBRIDGE. But don't get excited. This is not a campus novel, not an exploration of the dark timbres of an impressionable mind. The cloisters of King's College, the velvet lawns strewn with Snow-White-red apples? Forget those fairy tales. We couldn't eat the apples anyway, as the grass was out of bounds to students.

To find the setting of my story, you must leave the university and follow the river north. Keep going until the water grows troubled with shopping trollies and undetonated World War Two bombs. Take care; the pavement beneath your feet will begin to undulate, and bicycles will give way to cars and the Travellers' grand old pony traps. You'll know you've reached the place by the happy stink of vinegar and the line of grandpas outside the working men's club. The tourists, the black-gowned students and their avuncular professors? They do not come here. I should not have either, but fate and circumstance threw me a line, and I followed it.

I didn't ask my parents to drive me at the start of term. I didn't want to be stuck in the car with them, as I knew I'd feel obliged to put on the 'Anna Show' – to make jokes,

3

lighten the atmosphere, to squeeze my mum's hand conspiratorially as my dad complained about the soggy homemade sandwiches. And I didn't ask my little brother for a ride. We had been close as children, but at some point he became a man. The chubby warm paw that had clung to mine was replaced by strong, monkey-delicate fingers which inspected my own hands coolly: 'Why don't you let me pay for a manicure?'

'If you were a guy,' he liked to tell me, 'not having a driver's licence would be sexual suicide.'

My ex-boyfriend Jamie had initially refused to give me a ride. Jamie had a sweet nature, but he had been led to believe this was a sign of feminine weakness, and he sometimes fretted that he was *too* nice and needed to learn to put himself first, because 'people have walked all over me and taken advantage. My *whole* life.' The oblique reference to 'people' didn't fool me; I knew he meant 'women', and more particularly, *me* – but hand on heart, this accusation was false. It was *him* who overdrew on my time and kindness; I was his agony aunt, his life coach and, very occasionally, his sex therapist. Admittedly, I was more qualified for some of these roles than others.

Our break-up was amicable – I think we were both relieved we didn't have to keep the boyfriend-girlfriend charade going – but he'd been having a major I'm Too Nice phase the week I was heading to university, so I had made plans to take the train. I was dreading the journey from Dorset, trying to figure out if I could subject the other passengers to the sulphur pong of my iconic egg and cress sandwiches, and whether I should pack Mango Bango Jambo Banana or if it was wholly ridiculous for a graduate student to bring a cuddly toy to university. But then the coup that Selfish Jamie had mounted on Kind Jamie failed, as it often did, and he offered me a lift.

We drank coffee; we listened to music; we sang along to Leonard Cohen's *Hallelujah*. Neither of us had much stamina for long journeys, so we stopped at a Drive Thru McDonald's on the A505 outside Royston. We chewed off the corners of plastic packets and squeezed tangled strings of ketchup over chips, tarried over chicken nuggets whose cloud-like shapes resolved into dinosaurs and other fantastical creatures. Jamie was choked up and proud: 'You deserve this more than anyone, honestly.' We relived the moment I had found out I had been admitted to Cambridge, how Jamie had whisper-screamed into my ear while I tried to play it cool, because we were at the checkout in Tesco; there were people around.

By the time we started driving again, the sky was becoming overcast, white clouds lining up in neat rows like nurses waiting for the casualties of some disaster. Jamie pulled off the main road on to a small country lane. He wanted us to arrive in Cambridge via 'the scenic route'. I was drowsy and drifted in and out of sleep, but the smell of Jamie's Filet-O-Fish made me nauseous. I tried to focus on the road in front of me.

The horizon was flat and uninterrupted save for the occasional solitary tree standing sentry over mustard fields, the neon yellow no more restful for the eye than the too-bright headlights of the car approaching from behind. I glanced up, and for an instant I thought the rear-view mirror had transformed into a TV, and I watched with interest as the car spun across the narrow road and crashed into the ditch.

'Jamie!'

He was already pulling over, and in a matter of seconds we were both running towards the car behind us. I was shocked at how far we had travelled from the crash in so little time, and though I tried to run faster, I was barefoot, and the soles of my feet stung as they slapped against the tarmac. Ahead, the driver's door opened and a man staggered out, bare-chested and shoeless. He was swaying, clawing at something in the air – but he was on his feet, not dead.

My breath was ragged in my ears. I was starting to slow down when a black car pulled up beside the wreck. *Thank God*, I thought, *we won't have to deal with this alone.*

A man got out. He grabbed the bare-chested man by the shoulder. At first I thought he was trying to steady him, but then he drew back and hit him across the face. The man spun to the ground, and the other fell on to him, tearing into his body with such savage fury that I came to a stop, hallucinated a dog mauling a child, felt the same helpless terror at the idea of intervening. Jamie, braver than I was, ran on.

'Hey!' he shouted. 'Stop!'

The attacker looked back and, noticing our approach, got to his feet and ran back to his car. He reversed – almost ramming the man still lying in the road – and then tore off in the direction of Cambridge.

The scene seemed to recede from me like a mirage into the distance even as I reached the wreck, even as I saw the man's ravaged face up close. Was I dreaming? No, here was the material evidence: the emergency smell of burning rubber, blood from his nose dripping heavy and metallic as coins on to the asphalt.

'Are you OK, mate?' Jamie asked, bending over and touching the man gently on the shoulder. He was still sitting on the ground, cradling his face in his hands. 'Do you need to lie down?'

He didn't answer. Another car slowed down to take in the accident, and I half expected someone else to jump out and attack the man again, but it soon sped away. Smoke was coming out of the wreck. Jamie went to turn off the engine, while I bent down to talk to the man.

'Should I call an ambulance?'

He looked up at me. He seemed young, in his twenties perhaps. Half his face was covered in blood; there was a deep spurting cut across the bridge of his nose, which was so swollen and knocked out of shape that it hurt to look at it. His eyes searched my face for something. He staggered to his feet, pulling on my forearm to heave himself up.

'He'll kill me.' The high falsetto strain of someone trying not to cry. 'Please help me, please help me.' Teeth startlingly white against the blood in his mouth. His fear frightened me. Who was he? What had just happened? I looked around for Jamie, wiped the back of my arm on my shorts; it was covered in blood. I swallowed, tasting the iron in my mouth.

'We can call the police. Or give you a lift into town?' Jamie said. The man seemed not to hear. Instead he began to stumble away from us into the nearby field. 'Wait!' Jamie shouted. 'You could go into shock!' He did not turn back, but hurried on with the awful, limping urgency of a wounded animal, until he disappeared from view. My legs were buckling; I had to sit down. I held Jamie's hand while he called the police. 'Don't worry,' he said, after he had hung up. 'They're on their way; they'll be here *really soon*.'

A van pulled over. The driver rolled down the window and asked if we were all right, inferring from how pale and shaken I looked that I had crashed the wrecked car.

'We're fine,' Jamie explained. Half an hour passed; forty minutes. No sirens, no ambulance, no police.

'Why aren't they coming, Jamie?'

He tried them again, and they assured him that they were on their way. We sat beside the smoking wreck, the sun above a red contraction that gave no warmth. Its colour

7

seemed to correspond to the blood clotting on the road. I was sick in heaving waves. I kept thinking of the man's face, the intensity of his distress, the feel of his fingers on my arm, and the odd intimacy of encountering someone in such a primal state of fear. Jamie brushed back my hair and gave me a tissue to wipe my mouth. After an hour had passed with still no sign of the police, we drove on to Cambridge – very slowly, bracing ourselves for an attack that never came.

'Why didn't the police show up?' I asked, looking into the rear-view mirror to check no one was following us.

'Austerity.' Jamie smiled to reassure me, but I noticed his hands were trembling at the wheel.

'Well,' he said, as we pulled in at the college's car park, 'the bad news is, I think we just had a close shave with the Cambridge Mafia. The good news is, that's most definitely the worst thing that will happen to you here. Cambridge is very safe. It *is*! Really, Baby A. I checked on Crime Stats.' He kissed the back of my hand, forgetting, in all the drama, that we were no longer together.

'You can eat the apples that fall on to the path,' the college porter had said, as he showed me to my room once Jamie had left, 'but you can't pick them directly from the trees. And they're very sour.'

I took stock of my room the next morning: no over-head lighting, only a tiny desk-lamp, contorted like an injured centipede. A free-standing wardrobe with a door that swung open of its own accord, full of wire hangers that jostled and clicked. The narrow bed with its plastic mattress cover gave a springy moan as I sat down to lace up my Converse. Not really what I'd expected. I tried to take a photo to send to my mother and to Jamie, but I couldn't hide the room's menacing impersonality. Instead, I went outside and sent them a picture of the facade of the building. Florence House was a sweet red-brick cottage for graduate students, and its English quaintness disguised the depressing motel-style rooms within.

The wind was cold, and it shooed me along with the fat September clouds. I followed signs to the Porters' Lodge down a path lined with bright autumn flowers: tall euphorbia, their heads nodding heavily like a cluster of pale green butterflies; red hot pokers in scarlet and yellow, spiky and compact as undetonated grenades.

Automatic doors emblazoned with the Newnham College crest opened on to the Porters' Lodge, a modern space with a plush blue carpet and pink Bauhaus lamps dimmed low. It looked like the White House Oval Office would have looked had it been occupied by Hillary Clinton, or any other powerful woman with taste. One of the porters was sitting at the desk.

He introduced himself as Stan and offered to escort me to breakfast. He had a bald head so shiny it looked as if it had been polished, and a magnificent circus moustache. I followed him down a long corridor covered with William Morris wallpaper, a yellow design of robins and orange trees. The corridor smelled, strangely enough, of orange blossom, and the confluence of sight and smell made me think of Willy Wonka's lickable wallpaper.

The dining hall was quiet apart from the great steam exhalations of the samovars. The room shimmered white with the milk jugs on every table. Only a dozen women were up, most of them in their pyjamas and dressing gowns, their phones propped against sugar bowls and teacups. I sat in a bay window overlooking the garden. I felt self-conscious, sitting by myself in such a grand room, and all my movements felt a little unnatural, stagey. *Is this how I drink coffee normally when I'm at home? Or is this my new affected Cambridge way?* I sniffed my arm. No trace of blood; only my own coffee-breath. I wondered if the police had ever turned up, and whether the man in the accident had made it home or was still hiding out in the mustard fields.

I got out my phone and typed in 'accident Cambridge', but the only recent traffic news had involved a collision between a car and a horse trailer outside Ely. The details were gruesome: six horses had died. I searched 'Cambridge Mafia', but all that came up was an article about the Conservative Party, and a stage adaptation of *The Godfather* put on by the Amateur Dramatic Club.

I looked around, feeling uneasy. I'd come to Cambridge looking forward to starting a new chapter in my life, but I felt as if I'd arrived in the middle of someone else's story and been handed a script without understanding the character I was supposed to be playing. There was an unpleasant feeling of irresolution, an unsettling list of questions troubling my mind, which ought to have been blank, because this was the beginning of my story, day one.

I had a meeting that morning with my PhD supervisor: Professor Crabwell, MA, MPhil, PhD (UC Berkeley). He was a bigshot in my field – reproductive physiology – and I was excited to meet him. It was largely thanks to his enthusiasm for my research project that I had received the Meyer Lansky Award, one of the most prestigious four-year scholarships in science. My supervisor at Exeter had cautioned me against working with him, as he had a reputation for being tough on his doctoral students. But I had found my lab at Exeter too cushy, and was never quite sure if the praise heaped upon my research was merited. My supervisor there acted as though every student she taught was a future Nobel Prize winner. I wanted a real test.

I had an hour to kill before we were due to meet, so I went for a walk and wound up in the Sidgwick Site. It was as though the humanities faculties had entered into a bad architecture contest. The philosophy department looked like a rubber tyre on stilts; the designer of the law building seemed to have tried to fuse a cruise ship to an untethered marquee. It appeared that the divinity faculty had decided to divest from this God business altogether and to convert their premises into an oil refinery plant. I turned right on to West Road, past the Caius College Stephen Hawking Building, which I hoped for his sake was consecrated after his death.

All this ugliness in the city I had imagined to be a kind of Valhalla was an unwelcome surprise. But I was soon to discover that Cambridge is a jarring mix of beautiful buildings and horrible ones. Amongst students, there is a tacit omertà on the subject, perhaps out of loyalty to the collective Oxbridge fantasy. No one ever mentions the unsightly things.

So we learnt to avert our gaze, to look intently at what we wanted to see, and then not at all. This selective myopia, which I rapidly and readily adopted, was to cause me much grief; it meant I was focused too narrowly on certain things, unable to see the whole picture.

I got a bit lost in the maze of streets and arrived at Crabwell's office five minutes after the appointed time. I knocked on the door, and when he opened it he gave me a reproachful look.

'Ah! She finally shows up!'

Crabwell dressed like a stapler would if it were granted sentience. His face was extraordinarily strange. He had glossy, almost juicy eyes, spindly translucent lashes that fluttered like flies hovering over blackberries, and an unnervingly white, all-American smile. His office smelled of peanut butter and disinfectant.

'I hope our little morning meeting didn't interrupt your beauty sleep.' It was hard to tell if he was joking or not.

He opened the door a little wider, and I saw that two men were already inside.

'Take a seat. Anna, meet Charles and Leonid. Everyone else got here right on time, so you've missed some of the niceties, but Charles has brought us some cookies!'

Charles, BA, MSc (Cantab), offered me a tin of Turkish Delight. He looked like the caricature of a Cambridge student: auburn hair combed into a neat middle parting that formed two waves around his face like the droopy ears of a spaniel; lips as blood-red and pouty as the Queen of Hearts'.

I spluttered as I inhaled the confectionary sugar.

'You're not allergic to nuts, I hope?' Crabwell asked.

'No, no,' I coughed, turning red as I felt all of them staring at me. 'Swallowed wrong.'

'We have to watch out for nut allergies' he said, looking reproachfully at Charles. 'We've banned them from the lab. And obviously you'll be dealing with even more hazardous substances. That's what we were just discussing, Anna: safety protocol. You all have safety and ethics training this week, but I wanted to re-emphasize some things . . .'

Crabwell went over the protocol, demonstrating the safest way to put on gloves, and how to prevent injury when using 'sharps'. Afterwards, he asked each of us to describe our research: 'Briefly, please. If I'm passionate about anything, it's concision.'

We were all first-year PhD students working on similar projects, investigating how obesity affects foetus development in rodents. Leonid, BPhil (Oxon), was researching the inflammation process in the womb of guinea-pigs. He relayed this information in a monotone, and I couldn't tell if his indifference was feigned or genuine. He was by far the best looking person in the room, but in a mass-produced kind of way; he came with the standard set of sinewy arms, broad shoulders and periwinkle-blue eyes,

Dumbo ears offset by a *Top Gun* moustache. He seemed bored, nonchalant, as if he was already over the whole 'PhD thing'. I wondered if he'd look so cool after three years of decapitating guinea-pigs and pulling their still-live foetuses out of their stomachs.

Charles, on the other hand, described his research as if recounting the plot of a thriller. 'Insulin-like growth factor 1,' he began, 'is one of the most understudied hormones in the intraplacental gestational cycle.' He paused for dramatic effect. 'This *crucial* protein . . .' He smacked his thigh for emphasis, and his foot shot up like a counterweight. His shoes were long and pointy, like something a court jester might wear.

The only distraction to this gripping tale was Crabwell's verbal tic. Every few seconds, he would clear his throat so loudly that it was impossible to hear anything. When it was my turn to explain my work, I paused each time he did it, waiting for him to interject. Babies of women with diabetes are sometimes born underweight or overweight, and the mechanism for this outcome is not well understood. I was investigating whether there is a link between birth weight and the production of insulin-like growth factor 1, a hormone which regulates foetal growth.

I soon found myself losing my train of thought. The image of the car crash kept flashing into my mind: blood speckling the tarmac, the imprint of the man's fingers on my skin; details that seemed more vivid than they'd been the previous evening, as if my memories were bathed in the too-bright car headlights. I tried to concentrate, to focus on the project proposal – I knew it by heart, had practised this speech so many times before the PhD interview – but I rambled and rambled, until Crabwell interrupted a final time.

'Ahem. That all sounds good. You've already published in *Reproductive Physiology*, haven't you?'

'Yes,' I said. And then, before I could stop myself, I added, 'Twice.'

The corners of Crabwell's mouth quivered, hinting at the remote possibility of an encouraging smile. 'Gentlemen, you'll have to catch up with Anna! I expect at least *three* publications from you by the end of the doctoral programme.'

Charles and Leonid's faces were carefully neutral. *God*, I thought, my heart sinking. *They're going to hate me after this.*

Crabwell stood up and opened the door, which we understood as our cue to leave. I shook his hand, but his own remained limp as a rubber glove in mine. He did not return my grasp, nor my smile, and I was disturbed by the coldness of his expression.

Well, I would win him over. Work hard, get results. I would help out Charles and Leonid whenever I could, too, but I would not let them catch up with me. I was not intimidated by their Oxbridge degrees.

That's an important thing to know about me. I'm likely as smart as you are, if not smarter. I'm not bragging. I know there are other qualities I lack, like sound moral judgement and courage. But I'm clever and ambitious, and I'm not going to pretend otherwise.

I took the long way back to Newnham, walking down narrow Laundress Lane and over the bridge at Sheep's Green. The brook had spilled and flooded the meadows, and the grass stirred greenly beneath the water, which stood perfectly still, unblemished as quartz. I took a selfie to send to Jamie, but the sun was behind me so half my face was in shadow.

I might as well say what I look like now.

I have curly, dark blonde hair that is difficult to style, so I mostly tie it up. I have a permanent blush in my cheeks that does nothing to reveal my interior state. I'm not a shy person, nor even a prude. My eyes are green, like my mother's. The dark green of a mint leaf. A mojito cocktail in my very English face. They're the best thing about me.

The worst thing is my nose – it has a prominent bridge, giving it a hawkish curve. The description of Severus Snape's nose in the Harry Potter books bothered me when I was a child. His abnormally large, hooked nose sounded rather like mine. 'Yours is aquiline, not hooked,' my mother would assure me. 'You'll grow into it.' This is what all mothers tell their daughters: you will be beautiful, eventually. I never grew into mine.

I am very tall, with broad, powerful thighs and shoulders. I have large breasts that sit high, and I have a habit of yanking up my bra straps for extra support. They make me attractive to a certain kind of man and threatening to another.

I don't own much jewellery, but I used to wear a pair of earrings – two diamond studs barely bigger than a grain of sand. My brother is a jeweller and made them for me for my twenty-first birthday. But they went missing for a large part of this story, so it's better to imagine my earlobes bare.

I'm twenty-two, and well past the age of hoping that I will one day grow up to be a great beauty, or that a better haircut or eccentric diet will make any significant difference to how I look.

I had lived most of my life convincing myself these things didn't matter, that 'interior beauty' – kindness, intelligence – counted as much as the real thing, and I pulled it off with some success until I met a man who possessed a rare and grave beauty. Then I had to accept that all of this – my face and my body – mattered a great deal.

But I was weeks from that yet. This was the very start.

## 2

## The Great Attractor

I WOKE AROUND MIDNIGHT with an urgent pinch in my stomach. I rolled over, willing my body to let me wait to pee until morning, but realized that someone in the hallway was shouting. I sat up, frightened, my heart beating in my chest, groping in the alien darkness, but my hand closed upon nothing; I couldn't find the light switch.

'Shut the fuck up!' A woman's voice. 'You're gonna wake my housemates!'

'Get them up!' the man replied. 'Get them all in here!'

I heard a door slam, followed by the clumsy percussion of drunkenness, something heavy dropping on the carpet, the mechanical whine of bedsprings. I remembered where I was. In my new room, in college. The relief was such that I could have cried. The man from the crash did not know where to find me; he didn't know who I was. But then: an unpleasant twist in my stomach. *Help me,* he had said, *please help me.* And I hadn't done a thing, hadn't even offered him words of comfort. I had clung to Jamie's hand like a little girl, a coward.

Through the wall, the sound of glasses clinking, the jingle of a belt. Then a taut, erotic silence I tried my best not to listen to.

'Can I film this?' the man gasped. 'So I can keep it for later?'

I couldn't contain myself and spluttered, and it seemed they heard me too, because the man fell silent. But then the woman burst out laughing – a baboon-like, manic chatter that swung through the wall that separated our rooms, and the sound was as close and warm as a handshake. I lay back down, still laughing, even as the mattress groaned again and music came on, some awful, trumpety smooth jazz. It was so loud that I was sure it must have been an accident, that they would lower the volume, but after a few minutes had passed I realized they were not planning on turning it down at all.

I went out into the hallway and located the music coming from the door adjacent to mine. I stood there, hesitating. I hadn't met any of my housemates, and worried I'd be seen as a killjoy if I complained. This was ordinary uni fun after all, and it was only midnight, not all that late. But I had to be in the lab early the next morning, and I was anxious about getting enough sleep. I balled my fist, getting ready to knock, but was saved by the sound of footsteps. A woman wearing large slippers shaped like chicken feet and a white fluffy dressing gown appeared at the top of the staircase. She peered at me short-sightedly.

'Ah! You're new?' She sounded American.

'Yeah. I'm Anna.'

'Ji-woo.' She shook my hand, then gestured towards the door. 'It's Vicky. She's special. I mean, she's great but she's a bit . . .' She waved her hands, as if trying to communicate something she didn't dare say aloud, and then pounded twice on the door. The music grew fainter.

'That usually works.' She turned back towards the staircase. 'Sweet dreams.'

I got back into bed, but it wasn't long before the music seemed to grow louder, or perhaps it was only that the house grew quieter, so still it felt deliberate, as if it too were trying to listen in. I dreaded hearing what was happening underneath the music but felt my curiosity straining to detect it. I waited for Ji-woo to pound on the woman's door again, to shut them up, but she probably thought it was my turn to intervene. I imagined us both lying there in a stalemate, willing the other to get up and deal with it, like exhausted new parents waiting for their partner to attend to the screaming baby. At last I slept.

I went to breakfast early the next morning, doctoring my exhaustion with tiny medicinal gulps of coffee. I concentrated on tracking the trickle of liquid from my mouth to my stomach as one follows a train of thought, an exercise designed to give me a look of concentration, to make it seem like I wasn't too desperate for company. I was, but I didn't want anyone to feel obliged to sit with me.

'Vicky. That chick.'

Ji-woo plonked her tray down beside me, tore open two packets of brown sugar and emptied them into her porridge bowl. I hadn't really seen what she looked like the night before. She was chubby, with a long squarish face and hair that glistened like a rook's feathers. But her constituent parts had little to do with the impression she gave; she was so dynamic and spry, the emotion on her face intense and elastic, creating the effect of a blurry picture, more shimmering movement than fixed image. She ate with gusto and spoke quickly between spoonfuls.

'I hope it didn't give a bad impression. I actually really like Vicky.'

'No, no. It didn't,' I said, semi-truthfully. 'I felt bad for intruding.'

'Oh, don't feel bad. I once walked in on her when she

was with this chick. In the kitchen. On the *table*.' She shook her head, as if trying to dislodge the image from her mind.

'Oh God!' I was genuinely shocked by this – not the act, but the location. The kitchen of Florence House was as cold as a meat storage fridge, not ideal for a steamy encounter.

'She wasn't even embarrassed! That girl does not have healthy boundaries. She's cool, but she's kinda weird.' She waved her hands as she had the previous evening, making clear that the word 'weird' was a euphemism for something else.

It was the first time I had spoken to anyone properly since arriving in Cambridge, and I considered telling her about the crash and the fight. But I didn't want to cast myself as someone to whom bad things happen, and the story seemed so extraordinary that I could barely believe it was true. I was worried she would think I was exaggerating. So I let her talk.

Ji-woo was from Los Angeles ('But I'm not some Crazy Rich Asian from Beverly Hills – I grew up in Koreatown. The ungentrified bit') and was in her second year of a PhD in physics, doing research into Dark Matter.

'I'm studying something called the Great Attractor. Stop me if I'm boring you.'

'Is that the actual name?'

'I kid you not. OK, so imagine you have two objects in space. We understand from Newton's law of gravitation that they should be moving towards each other, attracting each other.' She brought her fists together. 'But sometimes they move in a totally different direction, towards a third thing.' She extended her arms towards me until her fists almost touched my chest. 'But that third thing is dark – it does not interact with photons. The gravity is so powerful that it swallows the light. So while we can see this thing's effect on the objects – its gravitational pull – we can't see the thing itself. It's a blind spot.' She picked up her spoon. 'This thing is called a "Great Attractor". The Milky Way – our galaxy – is being pulled towards the Great Attractor at a speed of about 2.1 million kilometres per hour. That's what I study. Well, at least in part. And it's crazy, because it means we on Earth are likely moving toward something we can't see. Imagine that: being pulled toward something huge and dark, but never being able to tell it's happening. So freaky.'

She swallowed another spoonful of porridge.

'That's the PG version of my research. I can take you all the way to R-rated, but you already look like you wanna die. More coffee?'

Those first three months in Cambridge were the happiest time I spent there. This was my innocent phase; even my dreams were straightforward, my subconscious having very little raw material with which to concoct any nightmares.

I bought a bike for getting around town, and a blue beanie embroidered with my college crest, and I became used to the Cambridge horizon; there is only one. No endless iterations as in a mountainous or hilly place, where there are as many perspectives as in a multi-angled crystal; the land is flat, everyone in sync with everyone else, sight tethered to sea-level. I grew accustomed to the menace of the fighter planes from the nearby air-force base howling overhead, so low in the sky that I winced as they flew over the roofs of King's and John's colleges, fearful that the spires would slash their iron bellies.

I installed Mango Bango Jambo Banana on my bed and worked hard to tame the unfriendly atmosphere in my room, to flush out the exam-stress sweat of its previous occupant and replace it with my own particular fragrance: lab disinfectant and the lavender oil I used to mask it. I polished the desk until it shone, grew animate with reflections which seemed to follow me around the room like a vigilant parent.

I put the mystery of the car accident out of my mind, though sometimes the drone of motorway traffic – which I could hear even in the deepest recesses of college – made me think about the journey, about the man disappearing into the mustard fields. But Jamie had been right: my close shave with the 'Cambridge Mafia', as he had called it, would not be representative of my first term. A *Pulp Fiction* trailer for an *Emily in Paris* type of story.

After our midnight encounter, Ji-woo and I became good friends. She was always happy, constantly cheerful. Most of the women I met in college traded in anxieties and miseries, lying on their backs to expose their tender bellies to each other like submissive dogs, giving a fresh meaning to the term 'suffrage'. I didn't like this; I wanted to be happy at Cambridge, and I wasn't interested in pretending that I hated myself or thought myself stupid. Nor was I interested in revisiting painful episodes of my past to garner people's empathy. I'd left all that behind, and Ji-woo's sunny nature was a welcome change, though I knew that others found her 'toxic' and thought her positivity was a facade. It was true that she was prone to cliché; she had decorated her room with posters of motivational slogans: 'Self-Care Is My Superpower', 'Keep Going You Got This', and above her desk a large photo of Coco Chanel with the quote, 'Beauty Begins The Moment You Decide To Be Yourself'.

At first I thought this must be some kind of act and that, over time, I would manage to excavate the foundations of Ji-woo's Hollywood exterior. Surely no one studying theoretical physics could be so basic? But that was the remarkable thing about her: Ji-woo was exactly who she appeared to be, as honest and forthright as a mirror.

It was thanks to her that I got to know Vicky. I'd been a little anxious after the episode on my second night, but our shared laughter set the tone for the complicity that developed between us. She, too, was American, though from a small town in Ohio. She had long golden hair, a tiny retroussé nose and dusty freckles. She had the looks of an innocent Bambi, but she was wry, savvy, outrageous. Frequently tipsy on weekday evenings – something unusual for Cambridge students, who were far more uptight than I'd anticipated; the kind of people who wake up early and go to the gym and take fish-oil supplements, more aspirant Elizabeth Holmes bio-hacker types than indolent Sebastian Flytes.

In comparison Vicky was reassuringly dysfunctional, and at first I thought she was a good influence on me, as she tried to make me relax about my work, to take everything less seriously. She was brilliant – she'd received a Gates Scholarship and was already supervising a handful of second-year undergraduates – but unlike Ji-woo and me, who were always staying late in the lab, she never seemed to do any work towards her theology degree.

'It's like philosophy,' she'd explained, 'except every time something gets hard or you don't get it, you just say, "God dwells in the unutterable, ineffable infinite and transcends our concepts and language." End of.'

She watched a lot of Netflix; she drank from pouches of wine that she left lying around her room looking like squashed, blood-engorged ticks; she invited all kinds of strange people into her bed. She liked men, she liked women, she liked neither; she liked souls and was indifferent to the physical form in which they alighted.

True, Vicky irritated me at times: she came into my room without knocking, and I often found her eating other people's food in the communal kitchen; a chunk of someone's cheddar in her mouth, her spoon thrust deep into my jar of peanut butter. But she compensated for this with her generosity, often leaving notes in the kitchen encouraging everyone to help themselves to cake, cookies or whatever else she had. One day she treated us all to champagne.

'Are you sure? It's awfully good stuff!' said one of our housemates, examining the label.

'Yup,' Vicky said, filling a mug with champagne and passing it to the girl. 'Special ingredient . . . crime!' She smiled when she saw the girl's expression. 'Just kidding!'

Stolen or not, many of the other women in Florence House felt uncomfortable with her largesse. 'Those tight-ass bitches,' Vicky would complain. 'Why is it that the posher the accent, the meaner the broad?'

I didn't spend much time with the posh girls, and they certainly weren't interested in being friends with me. I had not gone to private school, was not from London or Sussex, and my father was not a gentleman farmer. Therefore I was not someone they felt they could invite to the Union, to hang out with Spunky or Dingo or Piggers. I didn't mind. I got along better with the international students: the Americans, like Ji-woo and Vicky; the Europeans. It was thanks to them that Newnham was not like Exeter – a cliquey outpost of the London elite.

Vicky, Ji-woo and I spent many Saturday afternoons baking together in the communal kitchen. They pricked pie crusts and nibbled on chocolate chips as I folded blueberries into yoghurt and rolled thick wedges of cold butter into belching dough. The smell would waft through the house and the other women would venture in one by one, timid until I told them to pull up a chair, there was plenty for everyone. The kitchen grew crowded and chaotic, and then we'd have Whisky Macs as we waited, watching through the oven door as the sugar crackled brown on the muffin-tops.

I inherited my love of baking from my father. He was a pastry chef by training; a '*maître pâtissier*', he would say when trying to show off, which was often. My mother had met him in the high-end bakery he worked at in the Bristol docks, where she lived while studying for a degree in psychology. Their relationship seemed so improbable to me that for a long time, I viewed my birth as a kind of mythical origin story, as strange and fantastical as Eve being cleft from Adam's rib.

He liked his children quiet and his women slender as bells. I remember one day when he scolded my mother as we sat at the kitchen table, spooning up the gooey heart of a camembert.

'Babe! You've had enough.'

Her spoon clattered on the plate, and she left the room. I looked at him, frightened. Perhaps the cheese was poisonous.

'Camembert is safe for little girls,' he'd said, noticing my concern, 'but it's dangerous for big girls.'

Our only common interests were Arsenal football club – my father was a season ticket holder and regularly took my brother and me to games in London – and cooking. But even that shared pleasure was complicated. He struggled to let me learn. He would set me up with sugar and lemon, but then just as the meringue was stiff, he'd snatch the piping bag out of my hands: 'Squeeze and *then* lift! Here, let me show you.' He studded a perfect strip of white beads along the baking parchment beside my own attempts, which cavorted and smirked like Dr Seuss characters.

Inevitably I abandoned him in the chaos of drooling eggshells. He'd call after me, but I hid in the toilet when he came looking. He'd knock at the door, beg for forgiveness.

'I didn't mean to take over. Come back, we can finish it together.'

I'd ignore him, hating myself more with every passing minute until my anger was drowned by my self-reproach. Then I'd feel guilty for having upset him. For I was always protective of him; my dad was naive about the damage he did to those around him, like a toddler with a loaded gun.

I couldn't ever bring myself to hate him, no matter what he did, though I longed to excise him from my life, to pluck the strands of his DNA out of every one of my cells. I assume all children are like that, tethered to their parents by a useless vestige of evolutionary history – as pointless and painful as wisdom teeth, but far harder to extract.

Loving my mother was a more straightforward experience, especially when I was little. I was allowed to wake her at any time of night, and she was never cross; she'd sit at the foot of my bed, thread her fingers through my toes, and explain that yes, while the Texas chainsaw man and the Florida skunk ape were terrifying, they lived in the United States of America, which was a long, long way away from Dorset, and she doubted they had passports.

While she had understood how to shepherd me through the trials of childhood, she did not know how to advise me as I got older. She was one of those women who resent feminine norms but conform to them entirely. She went for her monthly wax; she ate only cabbage soup for weeks and wore shoes that tortured her feet. So when she had a daughter, I think she was conflicted. *Do I teach her to rebel, as I never have? Or show her the ropes of 'good' feminine behaviour?* In the end she did neither, preferring to leave me to my own devices, which was a blessing because I didn't develop her complexes, her poor self-esteem – not until later.

But sometimes unpleasant comments would slip out:

'Do you want me to take you to see a dermatologist?' she would ask in the middle of a conversation about university applications, making me wonder if I should be more worried about my skin. Or, 'Don't worry, darling, plenty of men like tall women,' she would say, apropos of nothing.

But overall, I was not unhappy as a child. My parents' flaws are nothing out of the ordinary, and my childhood isn't the missing piece of the puzzle that explains how I've turned out. They are not to blame for anything.

I got used to my Cambridge work routine. We were expected to show up at the lab at 9 a.m. Everyone who worked in Crabwell's lab had to sign a check-in sheet upon arrival, so I was able to see that Leonid was always late, while Charles and I always arrived exactly at nine. We'd often see each other from a distance, race down the street and through the door, wrestle over the sign-in sheet, vying to be the first one in.

We became fast friends. We spent our lunch hours together, usually at Market Square where we bought halloumi wraps from Mamoun's trailer, or else huge cheesy scones from the old Welsh man at the Earth's Crust bakery. We'd eat while wandering around the market, taking free samples of juice from the Brazilian smoothie lady and looking at the stalls of flowers, fruits, books, candles and precious stones. Charles often bought me things – goat's-milk soap, paper bags full of peanut butter fudge. His generosity was compulsive, anxious. He seemed to think he needed to work extra hard to make people like him. I learnt that he had been bullied at boarding school.

'I honestly loathed it. Loathed it. I was terrible at sports, and my voice didn't break till I was seventeen. That didn't help.'

'But you're funny, Charles!' I said, trying to buck him

up. 'You probably would have been fine at a normal school.'

'You're wrong. I would have been *pulverized* at a state school.'

Despite my protestations, I secretly sensed that he was right. There was something vulnerable about him that was a provocation even to me. I would sometimes imitate him ('You would have been puuuhlverized, would you, Charles?') and enjoyed saying things that I knew would shock him: 'I haven't had sex in so long I think my hymen has regenerated itself.' He would snort with embarrassment and blush like a Victorian lady. He *was* funny – I had been sincere in telling him so – but he probably would never learn to appreciate what others found comical about him. His entire persona amused me: his foppish clothes, his prudish sensibilities, the gushing enthusiasm for everything – 'Costa coffee? I simply *adore* it!'; 'Your hair? It looks *fabulous*, don't do a thing to it.'

My other lab mate, Leonid, was too blasé to take an interest in Charles and me. The little I knew about him was speculative and second-hand. He sold drugs; he sold his underwear; he was a professional kickboxer; his father had died playing Russian roulette. He'd disappear from the lab for days on end, only to show up with love bites on his neck and a dozen Chelsea buns in a greasy paper bag. He gave us these to buy our silence, in case Crabwell showed up and enquired why he was missing.

He needn't have bothered. Crabwell was practically never in the lab. He would sometimes pass through on Monday mornings, to ask everyone what they were working on, but apart from that he was largely absent. Despite this, he would occasionally send out a reproachful email about some safety protocol he had witnessed one of us violating, or to scold us for a chaotic workstation ('Messy lab, messy mind!').

I was disappointed, though at the time I couldn't admit to myself how lost I felt without a mentor – nor could I allow myself to acknowledge that it might have been wiser to stay on with my kind-hearted supervisor in Exeter. I did my best to get on with my work without Crabwell. The main issue was that I needed someone to teach me how to euthanize and dissect mice before I could make a real start on my PhD work. In the end, I came to rely on the help of an Italian postdoctoral researcher, the only other woman in my lab.

Rosa. White-blonde eyebrows, white-blonde eyelashes, front teeth protruding timidly on to her lower lip. She ran me through the ethics training required to euthanize animals. She was a practising Catholic and maybe that is why killing the mice affected her so deeply. Before each dissection she would follow the same ritual: a murmured prayer, a bow of the head, and the sign of the cross.

'You shouldn't laugh,' she'd say, when she caught me looking at her with a faint smile. 'This isn't something you ever want to get used to.'

If you are squeamish and need to skip the next three paragraphs, I will understand. I don't want to refer obliquely to my 'lab work' and for you to imagine some abstract world of bloodless precision; the choreographed whirling of test tubes in the centrifuge, time marked only by the regular click-click of pipettes spiriting infinitesimally small volumes between invisible reagents. That isn't what this kind of work is really like. But don't worry if you need to skim over it. The takeaway is that I was initiated into a kind of daily brutality in Crabwell's lab.

I had never killed a mammal before, so Rosa taught me. She would say her prayer and then we would get dressed, hairnets over our hair, dark blue gowns covering our clothes, looking like futuristic nuns. We would choose a mouse from the 'sac rack' as the cages were called ('sac' short for sacrifice). I'd look at them, tiny carefree things trotting around the sawdust, and think about which one I ought to pick. I worried about separating two mouse friends, taking someone's special person away. I hated the arbitrary cruelty of choosing. Sometimes, if one of the mice struggled too much, I would let it go and take another.

Once the mouse was caught, we placed it in a sealed plastic box, and filled it with anaesthetic which smelled like magic markers. The mouse soon fell asleep and curled up into a ball, or else rested its little head on its front paws like a dog. We would lift the slumbering creature out of its box. I would lay it on its back on a Styrofoam tray, spread its limbs and stick them down with Sellotape.

Then, I used a scalpel to cut down from the neck to the pubis, and horizontally across the bottom of the ribs. This was a very delicate process, because I had to be careful not to dig too deep. It felt like cutting through stretchy chicken skin. You lift the flaps of skin and expose the organs. It isn't gory. The organs of healthy animals are beautiful; glowing red, rosy with blood. The smell, however, is strong, and very particular, like that of a bedroom that has stood empty for a few days: something muggy, wet; a little sweet, like foetid fruit. The impression that someone lives here, but they're not in right now. The heart is a tiny, fluttering thing smaller than a fingernail. You extract the mouse's blood with a syringe and then collect the other organs, starting with what you can see: the intestines first, then the liver, the pancreas and the fat. Finally the brain is harvested, the head cut open with a scalpel.

'It's easy with mice,' Rosa explained, 'the bone isn't too thick. But you'll see when we dissect guinea-pigs. Opening their skull is like trying to crack open a walnut.'

I can't say I was unmoved by this. At Exeter, I had experimented on fruit flies and dissected a frog, but I had never killed something so undeniably sentient before. Sometimes I was filled with a kind of paralysis, the scalpel poised in mid-air. Could I really do it? I had never been made to feel violent before, never thought of myself as an agent of any irreversible action. You may upset someone, but you can always say sorry; you might shatter a teacup or a plate, but you'll find a replacement in IKEA. Everything is replaceable, redeemable. But once you've killed something, you cannot take it back.

# 3

# The Eagle

'Look, it's an elite sport. How often in your life are you gonna get to do a vigorous activity with the British elite?'

'I don't care, Vicky! The elite in this country do all kinds of mental shit. Like badger-baiting and molesting foxes and stuff.'

'But the boat club is where all the gays hang out! I'm sick of you and your aggressive straightness. And look at your arms.' She dug her fingers into my bicep. 'I could break your bones with a karate chop. Come on. Do it for your health. Or do it for me.'

Rowing season started at the end of October. Four days a week, we woke at six. We drank tea before leaving, huddling over our cups, letting the heat rise into our faces. It was cold in Florence House, so cold that I wished I could crawl into the teacup or wrap my arms around the tepid ribs of the radiator. But I enjoyed the early morning mist, the ride through Jesus Green and along the river to Midsummer Common, the light from Vicky's bike slow-blinking at me like a sleepy firefly. Cows loomed out of the fog like ghosts, startling us. The grassy fields and path ahead were just as dark as the sky, and the lack of contrast made everything look flat and one-dimensional, as if the city had folded itself away at night and not yet reopened for business.

Vicky and I were always a little late – her fault, not mine – and the other rowers would be waiting for us, jumping up and down and slapping their hands together to keep warm. They wore neon beanies, silver Lycra unisuits and tinted cult-leader sunglasses, and I always had the impression that we'd walked into a Seventies disco-party; but no one was talking, stunned by the cold and the hour, as if the ravers had taken a vow of silence.

We manhandled the heavy eight-person boat onto the water and climbed in, balancing precariously with one leg still on the bank. I was in the bow with Vicky directly in front of me, and we were always being told off for getting in out of turn, tightening our shoes before locking our oars, or otherwise messing up the military precision of the whole operation. We shed jumpers, put on our sunglasses against the morning glare reflecting off the water. We counted down our seat numbers from stroke to bow, then used the oars to lever ourselves away from the bank, pushed past a sleepy squadron of white swans and headed north.

The first few minutes were always the worst, my body moving gracelessly over itself, out of sync with the others. I had a tendency to plunge the oar too deep into the water, slowing the boat and making it judder, as if I'd thrown in an anchor.

'You're not digging for gold!' the cox would call. 'Two, take a stroke. Five, take a stroke.'

But by the time we reached the railway bridge, I had usually found my rhythm. I fixed my eyes on the horizon, the words 'SUNSHINE POSHO' spray-painted in giant black letters on the green bridge. What was it supposed to mean? I wondered aloud to Vicky. Was it a drunken scrawl?

Or a searing social critique of the whole Cambridge establishment?

'If you can talk, bow pair,' the cox shouted over us, 'you're not pushing hard enough.'

I came to know the River Cam: a many-faced Janus whose character changed as it flowed north. Picturesque at first, lined with boathouses painted in pretty Easter-egg colours. Gold-leafed Goldie was the loveliest of them all. This was where the elite rowers trained for the Boat Race. The rap they blasted every morning – even in the quiet of dawn – pulsed all the way to the Sunshine Posho bridge. There the river widened into the yawning mouth of the Reach, where there were no trees and the wind made you gag for breath. A tight turn at Grassy Corner led into the sinuous twist of the Gut. Here it was mercifully windless, but it was a stagnant kind of peace. Strange objects loomed beneath the water. I often saw men magnet-fishing from the bank. They dredged up supermarket trollies, forever-locked safes; sometimes, if they were lucky, rusting muskets from the Civil War. The river went on for hundreds of miles, all the way to the sea at King's Lynn, but I never explored further than Baits Bite Lock.

I came to know the riverboats: some well-kept crafts with names like *Mayfly*, *Rise and Shine* and *Gypsie Scholar* carved in curly script on the prow, dogs sleeping in the bow; others dishevelled carcasses rotting away in dark eddies, man-like shadows moving around them like a skeleton crew. On those autumn morning outings with the rowing team, the mist rose like breath from the water, or like the steamy exhalations of the untethered horses that ran wild along the bank, beating us in every race. I saw the embers of bonfires lit by the Travellers, the rising smoke like a reflection of the coiled mooring ropes.

\*

I loved the speed of the sessions, the push of power, the click of the oars at the catch, the cox's calls. Hypnotic, semi-sexual, they sent me into a kind of agonized trance.

'Long and LOOSE! Long and LOOSE! MOVE NOW, MOVE NOW! Stick the knife in, murder those footplates, MOVE NOW, MOVE NOW!'

By the end of November, my stroke had improved so much that I was moved into one of the higher boats, leaving Vicky – whose diminutive height was a disadvantage – behind.

That brought a new intensity to my life. The top crews trained five days a week, with double outings on Saturdays and two indoor sessions, and we had our own coach. Kayla had blonde hair extensions and fake nails that seemed only to lengthen the reach of her power. She was from Oklahoma and had grown up training horses for the Kentucky Derby. She instilled the same animal obedience in her crew: 'Eyes forward,' she yelled from the bank, when she caught me throwing a sideways glimpse at my oar. 'Next time I'm going to make you wear a blindfold.'

And she did: the next morning, she tied a scarf around my eyes and forbade me from taking it off until we were back in the boathouse. I was glad no one could see my tears of humiliation. But it helped; I stopped looking at my oar. I came to see her impossibly high expectations as a gift, for it takes a certain kind of generosity to reject mediocrity, and a certain kind of respect to think someone ought to do better. It was what I'd hoped to get from Crabwell. He couldn't even be bothered to tell you when you were a failure.

I developed a painful click in my wrist from feathering my oar. I was constantly famished, and carried roast potatoes wrapped in silver foil to snack on at any time of day or night. My thighs rippled with muscle; I could no longer fit into my jeans. But I didn't care. I was tall, I was strong, and soon I was one of the best. I felt Kayla's eyes on me, saw her pride in me. She made me feel like her new prize stallion making true on early promise.

By the last week of term I was tired all the time, from the rowing and the long hours in the lab. What was more, Charles was struggling and had taken to asking me regularly for help. I had almost finished my western blots – a process used for separating out all the different proteins in the blood samples – while he had barely got started. His problem was that he was disorganized. Whenever we ordered new antibodies, we needed to test them to figure out the optimal concentration and incubation times. This was a long, tedious process, and Charles always forgot to take notes. So he would get confused, forget the concentration of protein or antibody he had just used, and be forced to start all over again.

'But how can you handle all this going on at the same time?' he moaned at me, when I showed him my own neatly laid out, optimized protocol.

I didn't admit it to him, but I found the work relatively easy. I was precise, manic about details, and I was dexterous – the same quality that made my brother a good jeweller and my father a good chef. As a child, I'd loved going into work with him in the restaurant kitchen: atomizing chestnuts, cutting seams in vanilla pods, tweezering herbs with a surgeon's steady hand. It was a pleasure to watch him, to see the rising chaos around him as the tickets came in and the chefs shouted out the orders – 'Four soufflé all day! Five soufflé all day!' – and his imperviousness to it all. His eyes shining and focused as a steel blade, the tap of his knife on the board more regular than a metronome, and after everything, the spare elegance of the food on white plates. The lab wasn't so different from the kitchen. You had to learn economy of movement, to glide by others working in a tight space, to handle sharps, to work cleanly, to prepare your mise-en-place perfectly so that you wouldn't falter as you ran through the protocol. I loved the feeling of order imposed on the fizzing frenzy of things that are alive, blood cells transformed into readings on a graph. My father and I revelled in it: the feeling of mastery over entropy, of beauty and sense extracted from chaos.

I realized quite quickly that the men in the lab were not even worth competing with. But I did not want them to resent me, so I often helped them prepare buffers, or locate their samples in the fridge – trickier than it sounds, as samples were sometimes spread out through several boxes in the freezer. They were rubbish at looking for things and gave up too easily.

'I'll find them for you,' I'd say, laughing at their disgruntled faces. 'Just give me your list.' I didn't mind too much, and my goodwill – at least towards Charles – was not feigned. I suppose I enjoyed being asked for help – it felt like a tacit acknowledgement that I was the best, that they looked up to me somehow. The problem was that Rosa expected me to assist her with her research, too. I stayed later and later at the lab and got little sleep. Things got more and more difficult to manage, until on the last day of term, I botched two dissections.

I wasn't really to blame for the first mistake. Rosa had asked me to help her harvest mice embryos, but I had never done this before, and when I tried to prise the mesometrium away from the uterus, my forceps damaged some of the tissue.

'Don't worry,' Rosa said. 'I should have showed you. I'm sorry.'

But then, only a few minutes later, I made another error; when I went to suck up the mouse's blood with my syringe, I missed the heart by an inch, stabbing though the flesh beside it. The pain seemed to wake it, and despite the anaesthetic, it began to thrash around. I stood there, paralysed by shock, and Rosa shoved me aside and broke the mouse's neck with a deft snap.

'Take a pause,' she threw at me, but her advice was redundant as I was already running out into the break room. I ripped off my gloves, then sat with my head between my legs, hating myself, wishing I could at least faint. I shut my eyes and felt a memory flare like a white ribbon of burning magnesium in the dark of my mind.

In the park with my dad. He's trying to get me to play football with him. He kicks the ball to me and I lunge for a pass, fall over. Cold thump of earth; it had been winter then, too, and my leg had buckled beneath my weight when I tried to get up. Head between my thighs then, too, as I almost fainted from the pain.

'Come on, Sporty Spice,' my dad had said. 'You've only bruised it.'

It's always like this: whenever I feel humiliated and inadequate, my mind casts itself back to that memory, to the Big Bang of humiliation and inadequacy in my life.

Eventually, Charles popped his head around the door and offered to take me for a drink at the Eagle. 'Just a nip,' he said, 'to steady your nerves.'

It had become a tradition to go there a few times a week. Ji-woo's lab was not far away, so she would drop in on her way home, and Vicky would bring her reading to the pub, usually already dead-ending her second pint by the time we arrived. After a few weeks, I asked Charles if he could bring some of his other friends along.

'Ji-woo is desperate to meet more men,' I lied, hiding my own sly motives. 'We never get to meet any at Newnham.'

It wasn't that I was desperate to meet men in particular, but I wanted access to Charles's social circle, which was substantial given that he had been at Cambridge for his undergraduate degree, and before that had attended a private school which operated as a cradle-to-Oxbridge conveyor belt.

For the first time since I'd left school, I was socially ambitious: I wanted to be invited to parties, I wanted to go to May Balls. I worried that I was missing out on the fun of Cambridge; the friendship circles where cocaine circulated as freely as beer, hot rooms stuffed with people, an amorphous tumble of glittering bodies. I knew this scene existed, had seen evidence of it: the girl walking barefoot down King's Parade one morning, a cowboy hat on her head and her high heels dangling from her finger-tips; the looks that would pass between people in pubs and on the street, the kind that make you understand you're on the outside of something.

I had been popular enough at school until the sixth form – part of a 'cool' group of girls. We were easy-going, happy to sit on park benches and watch the boys play football for hours at a time, their hair slick with sweat, the sky like wedges of coloured glass in the puddles.

Looking back, I cringe to think of how we acted around the boys. We were their little handmaidens, fetching their JD whiskey from the supermarket because girls were not often ID'd. I don't think any of us were even that inter-ested in them, only lured by their new fascination with our new bodies. I got less attention than my better-looking friends, but I had a large chest which provoked some interest. I was flattered at first; how the merest glimpse of my cleavage would reduce them to a state of animal long-ing. It took me a while to understand that I didn't wield any power. A siren was singing through me, blowing through my body as if it were a conch shell, reeling the boys in and bringing them crashing against me like

38

wrecked sailors. They heard the music, but I didn't. There was nothing about them that called to me at all.

There was one particular boy – we'll call him Nate – who was known to be a little fragile; a bit 'emo', as we used to say then. He was skinny and had nostrils that flared like sails in a high wind. He was prone to crying, to posting melodramatic Facebook statuses about how much 'lifesucks' and 'can't w8 2 get out of this place'.

I agreed to meet up with him one day during the free week we had before our GCSEs began. I assumed he wanted to talk about how lifesucks and how he couldn't w8 2 get out of this place. I was pleased when he singled me out. 'Wanna go park after school?' *Why not?* We ate Skittles and smoked a cigarette, sitting in the bushes to avoid the rain. I was innocent then; he was so sad and soft and sensitive, so wimpish. It seemed outside the realm of possibility that he should push me over and crush my body into the dirt.

The phone and keys in my back pocket dug into me. It was my first kiss, and it felt so biological, like a kind of vivisection.

I could hear my mother's voice in my head. 'What are you doing?'

I gritted my teeth. His hand reached under my shirt. The Skittles turned to gravel in my mouth. I watched as he tried to pull up my bra. It wasn't my body between his hands, not really. It was anyone's, anything. His desire was so generalized that even as he looked at me I felt myself evaporate.

'You should open your mouth more,' he instructed. 'But you're really sexy.'

He lay on me again. What had I expected? Part of me must have known this was the deal. He pulled my hand down towards his crotch, moaning. I snatched it away; he moved it there again. I said nothing. His lips, smooth and

39

hard as a stepping stone from my mouth to chin to neck. He gripped my wrist hard, tried to stuff my hand down his trousers, his eyes rolling in his head.

'Hello? Darling? Hello?'

This time he heard it too. I pushed him over and scrabbled for my phone. I had pocket-dialled my mother by accident.

'Darling? Is everything OK?'

'Hi Mum.' I was shaking, felt sick with shame. How long had she been listening?

'Darling, you've been calling me.' She laughed in a hollow, embarrassed way. 'I suppose I should have hung up, but I was worried. Who are you with?'

'I'm with Louise.' She was my best friend, and I was always at her house. But what had I done? It was my first kiss. I'd remember it for the rest of my life. What a waste of a precious memory!

'Louise just called, darling, so I don't think you are with her. I thought you were going to the cinema. Where are you? Outside? I hear birds.'

'We were, but the film was cancelled. I'm in the park.'

'OK, darling. No problem. You know you don't need to invent excuses. You're entitled to privacy. But don't be out too long.'

I hung up. Nate stared at me. He flared his nostrils. He probably thought it made him seem pensive. It made him look like an angry donkey. Why can't you throw up bad memories as you do bad food? Every bad decision is tattooed on your brain for ever. No lasering it off.

'She's so angry I'm not at home doing revision,' I said. 'I have to go home right now.' He smiled. He didn't seem to believe me, and tried to kiss me again. 'She knows I'm with you,' I said, moving away. 'She's calling your mum.'

I got away thanks to that lie. He brushed the leaves and dust from the back of my jumper so tenderly, and of course

40

it was that gesture that troubled me the most. The perversity of it, like crushing cyanide into a baby's milk bottle.

I phoned Louise from the bath that same evening and told her I had 'crazy' news. I was shivering in the hot water. 'I didn't want it to happen,' I admitted. 'I said no. But I guess that's it. I've got my first kiss over with. That's a relief.'

A few weeks after our GCSE exams, Nate raped Louise at a party. Though of course we didn't use that word back then. She called me straight away. 'I said no,' she admitted. 'I said no. But I guess I'm glad I got it over with. Now when I meet someone I like, it won't be so awkward.'

I wasn't traumatized by the whole business, not at all. It felt like one of the many routine bereavements of female adolescence, and the fear faded as rapidly as the bruises on my wrist. But I promised myself I would never let a man have power over me again.

In any case, after that day, I became serious about my academic work. I didn't socialize after school any more, and I spent breaks working in the library. Sometimes Louise would join me, but she was upset by the superior attitude I took towards our old friendship group. She said I had become a snob, but I didn't care. Nate and his crew – they weren't going anywhere. They would sink into their nice and pleasant mediocrity and eat from the plate they'd been given. I wanted to be a great mind. I wanted to have a great life.

In my final year at school I started going out with Jamie, who was Louise's twin brother. We installed ourselves in each other's lives with the unobtrusive gentleness of nitrogen in air. We breathed each other in and out, hardly even noticing the other was there. Jamie had the sexual drive of an endangered panda, and a neutral energy that I found reassuring. Our relationship was almost entirely chaste.

41

We both applied and were accepted for bachelor's degrees at Exeter University, and moved into a freezing flat near the Ship Canal. We spent most nights working late, and I resented the laughs and shouts of the women outside propping each other up on their way home, the drunken stutter of their heels on the pavement. I promised myself I'd have fun again at some point.

I wanted to be popular at Cambridge, as I had once been at school. I wanted to be at the centre of things.

Charles did as I asked and started inviting some of his friends to join us at the Eagle. Most of them sang with him in the Queens' College choir. They would show up in their brilliant red cassocks, drink beer and stout at record speed, and run off to Evensong looking like a bunch of tipsy cardinals. He was also friendly with a number of men who belonged to the tight clique of alumni from Harrow. They were polite enough to me, but they'd often piggyback on my gentle teasing of Charles with their own sharp little digs, remind him of embarrassing incidents from their school days. Looking back, it seems cruel that I didn't tell Charles to stop inviting these bastards out with us, but I was drawn to one of them – a philosophy student and poet called Ian.

The ugly name suited him. He had a large, egg-shaped head that sat on narrow sloping shoulders; he was pale, practically luminescent. When I imagined him bare-chested, I pictured being able to make out his heart beating and his organs pulsing underneath the skin like the belly of a newborn fish.

Against all odds, this man had incredible charisma. The first time I met him, he shook my hand. His was clammy, but something in his grip surprised me; the juxtaposition of softness and power, as if he were half in mind to pull me into his body, but he wouldn't do it now, not in front of the others. He sat next to me and mostly ignored me, though at one point he turned and said: 'Your eyes are green, but there are flecks of brown in them. It's very unusual, you know. I've not seen eyes like yours before. They're as luminous as your earrings.'

'Thanks, Ian,' I gushed, my fingers tugging at my earlobe. 'I guess I've never heard them described so precisely!'

I felt from then on that there was a special understanding between us. I overinterpreted all of our interactions, each quantum shift in his tone and the trajectory of his eyesight, finding as much meaning in his silences and his absence as in his presence.

On the evening of the botched lab experiments, the already precarious group dynamic of our pub gatherings dissolved. Angus, one of the Old Harrovians, took the Charles-baiting too far. Angus was funny at times; he'd act like a caricature of the posh boy he was, snapping his braces when he wished to emphasize a point in conversation, and referred to all of us as 'chaps'. But he had a nasty side, and was jealous that Charles was so pally with the women. Never mind that Vicky, Ji-woo and I did not see him in a sexual light at all, and as a result treated him like more of a team mascot than a man.

That night Angus was in a malicious mood. He turned up already drunk from a college Christmas party, wearing a paper crown. It was cold even inside the pub, our hands red and bony against the icy pints. Angus was looking under the table, complaining that he'd lost his Harrow scarf.

'It was hanging on the back of my chair!' he grumbled. 'Who took it?'

'You can have mine,' Charles said, unwrapping the blue-and-white striped scarf around his neck.

In response, Angus flicked a crisp at him.

'I don't want yours, Charlie boy. I know about your devious little habits.'

Charles brushed his red hair out of his face, ignoring him.

'Come on. Tell them what Bates made you do!'

No response from Charles.

'Come on, it wasn't even that bad. Just a matter of going to the toilet with—'

'Angus,' I interrupted, feeling that I had to stick up for Charles. 'Stop being such a wanker. You're embarrassing yourself.'

'*I'm* embarrassing myself? What about you coming on to Ian? You look so desperate.'

'Shut up,' I said. But I knew I was blushing, and there was no conviction in my voice.

'And you're fucking ugly,' he added, the corners of his mouth tightening upwards. 'Your nose is nasty. Your whole face is nasty.'

Charles leapt forwards and slapped Angus. We all looked on in amazement. Charles himself seemed taken aback by what he had done, and stared at his hand as if it didn't belong to him. I felt Angus hesitate; Charles had not hurt him, but he had embarrassed him, and that seemed injury enough as he grabbed Charles by the collar and pulled him over the table, sending the pint glasses scattering like bowling pins.

Angus's knuckles were white against Charles's blue shirt, and as the shock washed over me I thought how ugly a fight is in real life, none of that choreographed violence you see in movies; there was no grace in how Angus punched Charles once, twice, went in for a third – but was pulled away. A man had grabbed the back of Angus's jumper, so abruptly that he almost fell over, and in his attempt to regain his balance, he let Charles go. The stranger forced him into a headlock and frog-marched him out on to the street.

We watched them through the fogged-up window. The stranger's lips were moving. He seemed to be trying to reason with Angus, who was still bent over, trapped in the crook of the man's arm.

I don't remember what I thought of the stranger's face, if I noticed his looks. It was the scene that caught my attention, the setting that seemed to become artificially vivid and cinematic: the slow drip, drip, drip of the beer on to the stone floor, like thawing ice; the way the lamppost shone through the last autumn leaves, projecting their dainty silhouettes on to the two men; the impression that they were on fire as the orange light and dark shadows licked their bodies.

The stranger released his grip on Angus, who straightened up. He moved towards the other man, and I flinched as I thought he might be going to hit him, but instead the men embraced; a masculine hug, their bodies arching away from each other.

The men separated, and Angus pushed his hands deep into his pockets and walked away. The stranger came back into the pub and went to the bar without a glance in our direction. Facing away from us, he put his arm around the waist of a girl sitting on a bar stool. Her dark hair was French-plaited in two perfect braids.

Ji-woo fetched us some drinks while Vicky and Ian inspected Charles's face.

'Was that your first fight?' Vicky asked.

'Yes.' Charles was pinching his nose and trying to smile through the blood.

'You're lucky it wasn't your last.'

Charles pressed the cool pint glass against his eye, his face distorted in the liquid. I reached over to squeeze his hand. Ian looked at me, mouthed, 'Are you OK?' He seemed to know Angus had been telling the truth. He smiled into my eyes. But lust, like shame, dies when it is brought out into the light. Ian's charisma looked like a tealight candle beside this bonfire, this man who had made all of us look like children.

I ignored Ian, and looked over his shoulder at the stranger and the woman beside him. Their backs were still turned. They were both wearing leather jackets, dark jeans. I considered going up to the bar, using the pretence of buying everyone a shot to get a better look at them, but before I could build up the nerve, they moved towards the door together and left. I stared after them through the window as they made their way down the cobbled pavement. *Turn around*, I wanted to say. *Turn around.* They looked like the couple on the cover of the Bob Dylan album: his hands thrust deep into his pockets, her arms entwined around one of his, their breath rising in mysterious white contortions. So intimately conjoined, so intent on one another, that in comparison everything else – the castle battlements of the colleges, and the moon burning cold and alien above it all – seemed to belong to a sad and impersonal world.

'Who was he?' I asked, as they disappeared.

'Who was *she?*' Vicky corrected me.

# 4

## The Heart Wants What it Wants

I WOKE UP WITH the kind of hangover that is easy to confuse with a bad conscience. I must have committed some transgression during my dreams, as I'd done nothing wrong the previous evening. Maybe it was what Angus had said about my looks. Perhaps I was anxious about Charles, confused as to why he had reacted so violently when Angus had insulted me. I worried he had feelings for me, and that he had misinterpreted my affectionate manner.

Or maybe it was only my dread at having to return home. It was the start of the Christmas holidays, and I was due back in Dorset that evening. Waves of nausea rolled through me, and the floor seemed to tilt beneath my feet as I packed. I was about to leave when I realized I was not wearing my diamond earrings. I couldn't find them anywhere. I always took them off before rowing, but was careful to put them in a saucer on my desk. I went through my pockets, becoming more and more agitated. I tore the covers off my bed, went down on my hands and knees looking for something twinkling on the carpet. I texted Vicky and Ji-woo, but neither could remember whether I was wearing them in the pub the previous evening. I was distraught – my brother would be sure to notice they were missing. Finally I gave up and took the bus to the station.

The Penzance train was full of young people carrying trekking backpacks and tote bags stuffed with dirty laundry, every student from London and the North going home for Christmas. I walked the length of the train but found only a free patch of floor. I took a bite of the pasty I'd grabbed on the platform at Paddington. It worked on me like liquor, the starch and sting of the peppery potatoes loosening the white-fingered migraine gripping my temples.

I was not looking forward to Christmas. As a young child I would get upset because my father was never around; he was always busy at the restaurant. My mother would pressure him to take me on special father–daughter trips in the build-up to Christmas to make up for his absence on the day itself. We went skiing in Italy or Austria, wherever had the best rates.

What I remember most from those weekends were the long dinners, balled-up greasy napkins, the fondue, and the booze my father drank with concentrated greed. He always chose a table in the middle of the dining room. This was in order to have a good view of the waitresses. They interested him more than mountain peaks and snowy crags. My father was fantastically obsessed with 'girls', as he called them. He was like a birdwatcher, taking a scientific interest, wanting to add yet another specimen to his collection.

My father stood out from the other patrons – ruddy-faced men in brown corduroys – and the waitresses often returned his attention and flirted back. It was odd to see how they responded to him, but then I stopped looking at him as my dad and saw the man he was through their eyes; a lean livewire body, deeply grooved cheeks, a rich masculine vitality. He'd pull up his sleeves, showing off his sinewy forearms and scarred hands, the cuts and burns from the kitchen suggesting a bad-boy lifestyle. The waitresses fussed around our table, bringing him complimentary glasses of schnapps.

Sometimes they mistook me for his girlfriend.

'Another glass for you? And your wife?'

'She's my daughter,' he would growl, appalled at the idea he should be with a woman as plain as I was. For before she started drinking, my mother had been a beauty; a redhead with the fire and fervour to go with it. My father had been proud of having her on his arm, and he was pleased that at least his son had inherited his parents' good looks. When my brother started bringing home girlfriends, he derived second-hand sexual satisfaction from this proof of his son's virility.

'Your little brother's snogged another girl,' he'd inform me, smiling, and I shrugged, because what else could I have done?

*Well, no more father–daughter bonding trips ever again*, I thought, stuffing the pasty wrapper into my back pocket and swallowing an ibuprofen. Neither he nor my mother could force me to go any more. At Reading I was able to find an aisle seat opposite two men who were taking up much of the room with their legs and iPads. I put on my headphones and had just laid my head on the table between my arms, when the man sitting opposite me spoke. His lips moved, but I couldn't hear him over my music, and I asked him to repeat himself.

'Where are you getting off?' he said.

It took a second for me to understand what he was asking me, but when I did, I felt uneasy.

'Why?'

'In case you fall asleep. I'll wake you up.'

'Oh, don't worry. That's nice of you, but I can manage OK.' I hesitated. 'Plus I'm not telling you where I get off, you might be a murderer.'

He gave a low chuckle and shook his head very slightly, as if surprised that I'd managed to make him laugh.

'You go to Newnham?' he asked, his eyes flicking from my face to my crested beanie and back, as if showing me the evidence. He had a long grave face. His hair and his eyebrows were dark. Lustrous olive skin, shadows under his eyes that gave him an Al Pacino kind of beauty. I thought he looked Italian, perhaps Greek.

'Yeah, I do. Were you in the Eagle last night?' It had just occurred to me that there was something familiar about him.

'No,' he said.

'I'm sure I saw you. Two of my friends got into a fight? You came over?'

He frowned slightly and shook his head. 'I wasn't out last night.'

'Really? I swear it was you. You were with a girl?'

'No. I'm not your guy.' He tapped his fingers on the table. Was he lying? I tried to imagine what he would look like in a dark room, how his face would appear beneath the shadows of the lamppost. But his clothes threw me off; the man from the night before had worn a leather jacket, whereas this man wore a camel-hair double-breasted coat, with a woollen scarf and gloves in the same colour. The styles seemed incongruous.

I noticed a flicker of alarm in his eyes as the train gave a rattling lurch.

'It's always bumpy like this, don't worry,' I said, assuming that this was what had disturbed him.

He didn't return my smile.

'Are you a Cambridge student?' I asked.

'No, but I work at Goldie. The university boathouse?'

'Oh, so you're a rower?'

'No, I'm a physio.' He spoke rather slowly, evenly.

'Oh, cool.'

He nodded. His long eyelashes lent his expression a dramatic sort of nonchalance that verged on indifference.

'I actually hurt myself rowing.'

I swivelled my wrist to demonstrate, and it creaked and whined like a rusty door.

'How the pain?'

'Pretty bad,' I said. In truth, it was excruciating, but I didn't want to sound like a coward.

He asked me to point to exactly where it hurt. I thought for a moment that he might touch my wrist, but he didn't.

'It could be intersection syndrome,' he said, probing his own wrist with his other hand as if to demonstrate the mechanics of the injury. 'Maybe your grip is too tight on your oar?' His glove slid up his wrist a little, and I noticed he wore a beautiful watch with a blue dial and a black leather strap. It struck me because none of the young men I knew had watches like that – they wore the neurotic, footstep-counting-sleep-monitoring kind.

'That makes sense,' I said, nodding. I was always getting terrible blisters, and the cox kept telling me that I should loosen my grip.

'You can rehab it.'

'I might make an appointment with you after Christmas.'

I hadn't meant to sound forward, but my words embarrassed both of us, and he looked down at his phone.

'Do you want a mint?' he asked after an awkward silence, reaching inside his breast pocket.

'Do I need one?' My tone wasn't flirtatious; the question was sincere. I could still smell oniony billows of air from the pasty each time I exhaled.

'Uhm, no,' he replied, and gave a slight smile. 'It's just that I can't stop eating them, and they're going to give me a stomach ache.'

'In my line of work, we call that an oral fixation.'

'Are you a therapist?'

'No, sorry.' I shook my head, instantly regretting my attempt at humour. 'I was joking. I'm a PhD student.'

'What kind of stuff?'

'Reproductive physiology.' This time I *was* flirting. 'I will have a mint, thanks.'

He tapped a Fisherman's Friend into my palm. The train was still rocking, and we almost touched as we swayed towards each other.

'Where are you headed?' I asked, the mint burning against my tongue.

'Torquay.'

'Oh.'

We returned to our phones. I wondered if he knew my dad's restaurant. It was a fancy place: waitresses in black aprons, threading through the cracks between the tables thin-waisted and efficient as ants, carrying twice their weight in trays and plates of stupid amuse-bouches, post-modern smears of protein and galactose. No, I couldn't imagine him there.

My eyes ran a relay between my phone and his face, information passing like a baton from his body to my mind. Theatrical, Cleopatra eyes. His expression was not warm. There was something icy about his elegance. But I felt an almost overwhelming heat when he looked at me. He was like a bonfire I wanted to get close to but that burned too hot. I was sure he was lying about not being the person who had broken up the fight. Some kind of false modesty, perhaps. I wanted to know his name but couldn't ask. It would have seemed odd for me to take such earnest interest in a complete stranger. It was odd that we had spoken at all.

I got out at the next stop, and he nodded and gave a brief, tight-lipped smile. My wrist clicked as I waved.

*

I arrived home in the interlude between thunder and lightning. All the signs were there – my hair standing on end, the house crackling with current – but no one told me what was going on.

It was the week before Christmas. My little brother was visiting from Manchester and had brought home his new girlfriend Megan, pronounced 'Mee-Again'.

'What is she *like*?' I whispered to my mum, as she hugged me over the doorstep.

'Like me forty years ago.'

I found them sitting in the kitchen. My brother looked good, swish as ever in his Ben Sherman shirt, his immaculate fade cut and diamond studs. His girlfriend was tiny. Behind the surrealist shock of her make-up she was freckled, dusky-eyed and glossy as a newborn calf.

'Mee-Again, Anna. Anna, Mee-Again.'

She hugged me. She smelled of apricots and pastry crust. The bald white of her skin peeked through her red hair.

'How did you two meet?'

'At work,' he answered for her. 'We're colleagues.'

My brother – who had struggled at school, and whose confidence had been crushed by the same teachers who predicted that I would split the atom – turned out to be a wonderfully gifted jeweller. He was able to do with silver and gold what my father could do with pastry, to pull and solder pieces as fine and delicate as spun sugar. He trained under a master diamond cutter at Graff in London before moving to Manchester to work in the Jewellery Quarter, where he had met Megan.

She was not, I found out from my mum later, his colleague – she was his apprentice. Worse still, she was only sixteen, barely past the age of consent.

'Is this normal?' I asked my father.

We were sitting at the kitchen table, watching football.

Our TV was in the kitchen because my mother had turned the front room into a consulting room when she had given up her NHS job and set up her own private psychotherapy practice. We were never allowed in that room, which meant there was nowhere comfortable for the family to gather, no curling up on the sofa together in front of a film. Most of the time we all sat in our own rooms watching stuff on our laptops, but my dad had called me down for the Arsenal–Everton game and a pot of tea. He didn't drink it himself, but he liked to dunk his biscuits, so I let him use my mug for his McVitie's. He would often soak them for too long, and the biscuit would crumble into my tea just as he lifted it to his lips.

'What's normal anyway?' he mumbled, his mouth full, sending crumbs flying.

'She's only just done her GCSEs. Don't you think it's a bit weird?'

He swallowed. 'The heart wants what it wants.'

'Right. Funny how the heart always wants young, pretty and inexperienced.'

'I'm sure she's capable of making up her own mind.'

'Can't you see why it's problematic?'

He shrugged. 'It's not really any of your business, Anna.' He turned back to the TV and swore as Martinelli toe-balled a shot and sent it flying over the crossbar.

'Is this normal?' I asked my mother. She was in the bath and I was lying on the floor beside her, enjoying the delicious cold of the tiles in anticipation of my turn in the hot water.

'No,' she said.

'Why don't you say something?'

'Your dad thinks I'm jealous of her.'

'Don't fall for that bullshit. It's got nothing to do with jealousy.'

But over the next few days I felt my own tingling of envy. It was impossible not to notice how much better my father and brother treated Megan. Seats given up, glasses refilled, shopping bags carried, pampered like a little pet. My mother and I had never received such treatment; we lugged our own suitcases, sat at the table's right angles and refused the last slice of cake. They did not fuss over us. I had never minded before, because I had assumed my brother and father were like that with all women. But seeing the way they treated Megan, it was hard not to feel resentment and wonder: if this was a woman, what was I? What did they make of me, with my big hands, my big nose, my lack of grace?

Thankfully she and my brother mostly hung out in his bedroom, or drove to spend afternoons together in the studio flat my dad owned above the restaurant in Torquay. My brother had bought a two-seater sports car, a good reason for me not to be able to tag along – but I would have loved to get out of the oppressive atmosphere of the house. He drove Megan around, showed her where we'd gone to school, the youth club where he'd played football. On Christmas Eve, they went to the carol concert in Exeter Cathedral and came back with a box of oysters and champagne. My father was an amazingly efficient oyster shucker; he even had a protective glove made of chainmail like a knight's armour to protect his hand. My brother and I had loved playing with it as children, and now when our father's back was turned he threw it at me across the table. The memory of happier times flashed between us like distant lightning.

Jamie and Louise were away visiting their grandmother, so I had no one to hang out with. I spent a lot of time lying in bed, staring at the ceiling. When I was little, I would see whole worlds and mythologies in the cracks of the paint. I'd forgotten many of the old patterns, but one jumped out at me. A woman's face. A large L-shaped nose, a wide-open mouth, and a strip of hair behind her head. I always thought of her as the Howling Woman. Pareidolia, my mum called it. The tendency to find patterns or faces where there are none. A cat's silhouette in the scratches on the car; a horse in the mayonnaise. I was prone to that, as a child. Back then, it was as if everything in the world had a distinct personality and could speak. This phenomenon had sometimes frightened me, but now I found it oddly comforting that it was still there, that old innocence, that I could still find Howling Woman's face in the cracking paint.

I thought from time to time about the man on the train. I did not fantasize about him exactly – he was like a Classical statue, too beautiful to be erotic – but something about him had moved me. The grave face, the elegance. I hadn't ever seen anyone like that, other than in a film. And he had spoken to me.

On Christmas morning my brother and father slept in, and Megan braved the kitchen alone and offered to help my mother and me with the cooking.

I set her up with a knife and chopping board, showed her how to cut a cross in the Brussels sprouts.

'Why do we need to do that?' she asked.

'Because Jesus Christ died for us on the cross,' I said, in a deadpan voice. My mother snorted.

'My parents are Jewish,' Megan said, biting her lip. 'We don't really do Christmas.'

'It's a joke,' I reassured her. 'It's just so they cook faster.'

I went back to the stuffing, crumbled chestnuts into breadcrumbs, but I could not concentrate. I felt my per-spective segment and double like a fly's. I saw Megan magnified through my mother's contempt; how she hadn't a clue how to help in the kitchen, couldn't walk anywhere with her spiked heels, couldn't grasp anything with her long nails. My mother plucked stray feathers out of the turkey, tugging at them with such force that Megan winced, as if she were enduring a painful eyebrow wax.

I imagined how she must see us: our unmanicured hands, our unbleached teeth and ungenial topics of conversation. I tried to include her. 'I'm at Sylvia Plath's old college in Cambridge. You know, the woman who wrote *The Bell Jar*?' She shook her head. ' "Lady Lazarus"? No? Oh, I'm sure you'd love it! Hang on.'

I ran up to my bedroom to fetch her my copy, set it in front of her. She smiled politely, but she looked at the book as if it were a helping of broccoli she had to finish before she would be allowed to get down from the table. I remembered what Louise had said to me when we had been applying for university: she was right, I had become a snob.

Christmas lunch was uneasy. My mother was quiet and chastened. I suppose she'd argued with my father. He was skittish about the food: the mashed potatoes didn't contain celeriac; the chestnut puree lacked salt. He spent much of the meal checking his phone ('in case they need me at work'), snapping the black points off the burnt parsnips and placing them reproachfully on my mother's plate. He looked at Megan – who was wearing a shimmering translucent shirt over tight-fitting trousers – with more appetite than at the food.

I put on the Anna Show. I told them about the accident and fight I'd witnessed with Jamie; I told them about Crabwell, the college, all the details they hadn't asked me about. My family was generally not interested in my life, nor my research, but I went on talking despite their lack of encouragement. My mother poured herself yet another glass of wine, and I saw my father noticing. He ate steadily, the turkey and potatoes distorting his throat like a rat in an anaconda's gullet. I talked on and on, impervious, spinning and spinning, a whirling dervish lost in a private rapture. No one responded to what I said. My mother's disapproving gaze was fixed on my brother, who had draped his arm possessively around Megan's shoulders, as if to ward off the fervour of my father's stare. My mother caught my eye, raised her eyebrows slightly as if to say, *Aren't men pathetic?*

I didn't return her conspiratorial glance.

You reap what you sow. For that was the contradictory thing about my mother; while she resented my brother's macho behaviour, she had cultivated his masculinity from the time he was a baby. She told him to toughen up when he cried, to answer to playground bullies with his fists. She gave him toy guns and football boots and fed him James Bond and *Top Gun* and Indiana Jones, raised a son more masculine than my father, her father, all the fuckers out there. *You think you're a man? Here's a man!* I thought of pictures of him as a baby: the beautiful boy, gleaming like a weapon in his crib. He didn't stand a chance of ever becoming anyone but who he was.

My poor brother. The least I could do was to talk, smile, fill Megan's glass till it overflowed to give us something to laugh about, eat all the Brussels sprouts so no one would realize they were inedible. By the time pudding rolled around and the brandy was distributed, the general mood had lifted. Even my mother laughed when my father took a spoonful of Christmas pudding and said: 'Looks just like a blood clot. But rather less appetizing.'

Megan left on Boxing Day. I made a play of saying goodbye affectionately to her, but she didn't seem fooled by this show of sisterhood and pulled away early from my hug. My mother stayed in bed, nursing an alleged flu, while my brother, father and I watched TV in the kitchen. First the races; it was a Boxing Day tradition for my father to put a hundred pounds on a horse, usually chosen because he liked the name.

'Pie-O-My,' he said, looking at his phone. 'Evens for her to win and a place in the first three.'

'And they're off. Seven furlongs, seven hundred metres today on the December course.'

We watched the horses bolt out of the starting gates, the commentator's voice trembling on the edge of non-sense as he spoke in machine-gun double-Dutch. 'It's Persian Force in the lead, Black Beauty in second, Pie-O-My coming on strong in third.' My dad – who'd been pacing backwards and forwards, his hands folded on top of his head – ran towards the TV. 'And Mischief racing up the dip, and now Pie-O-My brings it up to Persian Force, and now Pie-O-My is in the lead!' My brother and I exchanged laughing glances as my dad smacked his own thigh, as if whipping the horse on. 'And they're in the last stretch. Persian Force being attacked by Black Beauty. Pie-O-My pulls away by half a length! But Black Beauty is on after him! Black Beauty is starting to clear! Black Beauty is over the line! Pie-O-My in second!'

'Fuck!' my dad shouted. He sat back on the chair, deflated. Checked his phone. 'Well, I net fifteen quid. Better than last year.'

He switched over to the Arsenal–Bournemouth game. It had been a horrible season, but we were hopeful, as this was the first game with Arteta as manager.

'Why isn't he starting Pépé?' I asked, sipping a biscu-ity tea.

'He wants a team that plays with the badge in mind,' my brother replied, fiddling with his studs, something he always did when he was tense or excited. 'Pépé's not hus-tling enough to make it into the starting line-up. And he can't defend for shit.'

The game was tense: at first Arsenal dominated, with

Saka and Nelson looking dangerous, but Bournemouth scored near the end of the first half. My father rushed to cook bubble and squeak – my favourite – during the half-time break. I watched as he chopped chestnuts and mixed the leftover potatoes with roast carrot and cabbage. The popping and whistling of the buttery mess in the pan drowned out the commentary. We ate in front of the second half, screamed and high-fived when Arsenal equalized. It was the happiest I'd felt all Christmas.

But then the game ended, and rather than joining in our post-match chat, my dad became absorbed with his phone, turned inwards.

A feeling of dread spread from my full stomach to my chest. I tried to stop it, but it was like damming a river with my hands. I kept talking to my brother but felt his attention had shifted to my dad. He was glancing at him and his phone, trying to figure out who he was writing to. Dad got up, and without saying anything, walked out of the room. My brother twiddled his studs as we watched the TV in silence. Then I heard the zip of a suitcase from upstairs and I understood at once.

'He's leaving, isn't he?'

My brother shrugged, crossed and uncrossed his legs.

Footsteps on the stairs, and my father bounded in wearing his leather jacket and the Newnham beanie I'd given him for Christmas.

'They need me at work,' he said. 'I'm off.'

My brother shot me a warning look, but I followed my father into the corridor. He was stuffing his feet into his trainers, a duffel bag under his arm.

'Why do you need that?' I said. 'If you're just going to work.'

'Might need to stay over,' he replied, without missing a beat. 'It's chef's day off tomorrow.'

'Dad,' I said. 'I know where you're going.'

I went to snatch his car keys, but he caught my wrist, the one that was injured, his grip so strong that I shouted from the pain. He let me go and I took a step backwards. As much as I tried to control myself, humiliating tears seeped out of me like blood through a bandage.

He said nothing, only shot me a glance full of cold disdain before closing the door quietly behind him.

It was my mother I cried for. It was her life he was ruining. Not mine. I had hardened myself against my father long ago. But I see now that I was wrong, that I should have cried for myself that day too. Because my father leaving my mother again made life at home unbearable. And some months later, when I desperately needed somewhere to go, home was the last place I wanted to be.

# 5

## Pandora's Box

I DID MY BEST not to carry the dark seed north to Cambridge, but there was an unfamiliar pressure lingering in my chest as I boarded the train. I looked through my lab notes and out of the window as we passed through Stevenage, Hitchin, Letchworth Garden City; a disheartening landscape of flat, mud-clotted fields, the febrile January sun reduced to a narrow streak of neon-yellow marker pen along the horizon.

The last week at home alone with my mother had been difficult. Alternating stretches of day and night that seemed to show no forward progression, the passing of time marked by the thawing of the ice in her glass and the level of gin in the bottle.

On our final afternoon together, I found her sitting in front of her bedroom mirror, plucking out the white strands from her mane of red hair, laying them on the dressing table like fishbones on a dinner plate. Our eyes met in the glass. 'She's like me, twenty years ago,' was all she had to say about my father's affair. Later, we sat in the garden as night fell. The cigarettes wouldn't light at first, match after match breaking against the box like unkept promises. I tried to make conversation, to cheer her up, and I shivered in the cold she couldn't feel, the red tip of her cigarette burning like a votive candle against the dark.

The carriage rattled. I thought of the man I'd met on the way home, how he'd started when the train shook. His Christmas couldn't have been worse than mine. He probably came from a normal family.

Vicky met me as I stepped off the train. I started laughing the moment I saw her, and she laughed back at me while I struggled to pull my bag through the ticket barrier, shaking her head as I approached.

She hugged me, and I rested my chin on her head and breathed in her lemony, bourbon smell.

'What happened to you?' I said. 'You're so much smaller than I remember. Did they shrink you in the wash?' I felt the nightmare of the past month recede, as if each gulp of her perfume were a waft of incense banishing the sulphurous spirit of home.

'You lost weight,' she said, turning her face up to me. 'Have you been fucking? Or have you been unhappy?'

'I've been fucking unhappy.'

The best days of Cambridge were soon to end, and like the precious last golden minutes of light as night approaches day, there is something softly radiant about the memories I have of that January. I loved being there. Loved Stan the porter, whom Vicky and I teased by saluting every time we entered or left the college. Loved the gardeners, who always had time to talk to me about what they were planting, what was budding that month, which plants were suffering from the frost. I loved dinners in the dining hall, the sight of all the women, their necks swan-like as they stooped over their bowls, blowing on spoons to cool their soup. I even loved the food, though it was a little chastening, a little grim.

'Everything they serve is white,' Ji-woo complained. 'It's like a weird racist cult.'

She was right: the cafeteria rotated cauliflower soup, rice pudding, boiled eggs, white risotto differentiated from the porridge gruel only thanks to the presence of green peas. But I didn't mind. It was bracingly Dickensian. I even loved the cold, the mist, how it backed away from me, an ever-receding ghost on the horizon. It hung low over Newnham, hemmed us in like drapes hanging from a four-poster bed. The morning frost lingered long and showed up again early, while we were still having dinner: sparkling ice ferns unfurling on the window panes as the night fell around us.

Most of all, I loved my friends. Not more than I loved Jamie and Louise – but my affection for the twins was trimmed by ambivalent feelings towards my past and my hometown, and thus was as muddled and fickle as self-love. It was easier with Vicky and Ji-woo because they came from a different planet and reminded me of nothing. And they revealed new parts of me to myself. They thought I was funny, resilient – they admired how I dealt with my family – and my intellectual curiosity was something they appreciated and nourished. My friends back home had always thought I was a bit up myself. 'It's not that you're annoying,' Jamie said, when I asked if he found me irritating. 'It's just that you're mega intense, sometimes. Which is a good thing!' he hastened to add, when he saw the expression on my face. The truth is he never listened to me closely, and he and Louise had a way of changing the subject whenever I brought up anything 'serious' or 'deep'.

Whereas Ji-woo and Vicky loved those kinds of conversations. I never tired of asking them about their research. What astounded me most of all were the unlikely similarities between their two projects. Ji-woo's work investigating gravitational anomalies and dark matter was – in its most abstract, conceptual form – not so distinct from Vicky's PhD research into the limits of knowledge.

'It's easier to define dark matter in terms of what it isn't,' Ji-woo explained one night as we were sitting on the floor, huddled against the radiator in the kitchen of Florence House. 'We know it isn't a black hole, we know that it probably isn't anything resembling normal matter. There was a theory for a long time that it could be made up of something called MACHOs, these huge neutron stars. But basically nothing we have so far really fits. There's this unknown matter and it makes up the vast majority of the universe. Like 95 per cent of it.'

'Right, that's kind of like in theology. God is defined by what he's not, because he cannot be reduced to linguistic or rational concepts. No, no, wait,' Vicky insisted, anticipating that we were about to interrupt her. 'Think about it like this. Many theologians conceive of God as being infinite. And all these logicians – Russell, Cantor, Gödel – have tried to fit the infinite into mathematical frameworks. But it doesn't work. Because like dark matter or God, the infinite resists human knowledge.'

'But the difference between you and me is that you think there's something fundamental about the nature of reality or our minds that means we can't ever understand this stuff.' Ji-woo was lying on her back now, her feet pressed against the radiator. 'Whereas I don't think that. Dark matter, quantum weirdness, all of it. We're going to figure it out. It's only a matter of time.'

'I think you're wrong. Though obviously I think the nature of unknowable things is that we don't know they're unknowable.' Vicky stood up and went over to the stove, turned it on and opened the oven door. It gave out a sad garlicky smell, but also some heat. It really was that cold.

'Don't you ever think' – Vicky was opening the fridge

now, looking at the jars on the top shelf – 'there's some things that we shouldn't even try to know. Like the atom bomb? Or AI? There's a whole area of philosophy which examines the proper limits of knowledge.'

'The peanut butter's on the bottom shelf,' I said. 'You mean Christian philosophers, don't you? Like the people who wanted to torture Galileo?'

'No,' she said, irritated. 'Not only Christian philosophers. The Greeks as well. Like Pandora's box. She was too curious, and opened it and fucked everything.'

'Knowledge isn't inherently dangerous. It's like a hammer. You can use it to build a house or to crack someone's skull. As long as people don't do anything bad with it, I don't think there's stuff we shouldn't try to know.'

Vicky unscrewed the jar, scooped up some of the peanut butter with her finger. 'Yeah, but that's the problem. They always do something bad with it.'

I never tired of talking to them. The girls didn't deflate me. They didn't think I was boring or 'too deep' or snobbish. I was intellectual, I was curious. There was nothing wrong with me.

January was a productive month in the lab. I knew my way around, and so lost no time digging for reagents, looking for samples or preparing buffers. Plus, Rosa was away visiting her family in Italy, so I wasn't interrupted by her requests for help. I finished processing my maternal organs, and found there were highly inflated levels of IGF-1 – the protein that signals inflammation – in all the mice that had gone on to produce underweight offspring. I knew this was a significant result, and I reported the news of my progress to Crabwell, delivered in person with flapjacks I'd bought from the Earth's Crust bakery stall at the market.

He had spent the holiday in Mexico, but he looked paler than ever, as if he'd recently donated blood. He was wearing a large new Fitbit watch, which ticked and buzzed and twitched like a black beetle trapped on his wrist. He accepted the flapjack, but squeezed some disinfectant gel into his hands before touching it.

'You're following the coronavirus, I guess,' he said, pushing the gel towards me. I rolled the cold viscous liquid between my fingers. 'Even more important to stick to our protocols.' He took a bite of the flapjack, and a scattering of syrup-coated oats collapsed on to his desk. 'Wow, these things are messy.'

I nodded, struggling to conceal the fact that my entire flapjack had crumbled into my lap.

'But – nice result,' he went on, as if my success in the lab compensated for the slovenly confectionery. 'Now you're going to have to analyse all the foetal tissue. You can do that next.'

'There was just something I wanted to mention, Professor Crabwell.' His expression was not encouraging, but I went on. 'I understand I'm meant to be assisting Rosa, but I feel like I'm the only PhD student she asks . . .'

'Mmh-hmm?' He tapped himself over, as if looking for a light, but I knew that he didn't smoke.

'Yes. I was wondering if maybe we could find a way of distributing the work more evenly between Charles, Leonid and myself . . .' I trailed off, disheartened by the look on his face.

'You don't seem like the kind of girl who needs someone to come to their rescue, Anna.'

'I'm not.'

'I think it's best if you deal with this between yourselves. It's your responsibility to manage your work commitments.' He stared at a point to the left of my chin, as if I had a second pair of eyes dangling down there. 'You seem more than capable of defending your interests. You're not a damsel in distress.'

I left the room without closing his door, my paltry attempt at retaliation.

From then on I avoided Crabwell as much as I could, and when Rosa returned from Italy at the end of January, I tried to stand my ground. I told her that I was at last feeling some momentum in my own work, and didn't have time to help with the new batch of dissections.

'I'm never even going to work on guinea-pigs,' I said. 'You should ask Leonid instead of me – the training would actually help him.'

'I need you. You're the best, and I want you to be comfortable with as many protocols as possible,' she replied. 'You'll thank me later,' she added, as I resignedly pulled on the lab coat, hairnet and gloves.

I hated handling the guinea-pigs. Mice are intelligent animals, but they are not particularly expressive. It was easy to see them as extensions of pipettes and test tubes and microscopes: tools fitted for purpose. But the guinea-pigs were different. They squeaked merrily whenever I approached, trusting that I meant them no harm. I developed insomnia, and came to dread the nightly rehearsals of sleeplessness, feared the day appearing like a rotating stage I'd have to stand on, and smile and recite my set of bright, meaningless lines: not too bad, how about you?

In February the rowing season started. The cold that winter was drastic, dangerous. The fog did not lift as the sun rose but froze to our clothes, so that we all shone like silver gilt. I had missed it over Christmas; the deliriously early mornings, the pull and recovery of each stroke, every tug of my oar sending whirlpools sucking downwards into the water, tiny bright wells carrying the day into the depths. But after only a few sessions my wrist began to twinge, and by the end of the first week I could barely hold the oar.

'Let me see,' Kayla said, grabbing my arm. My pulse throbbed between her fingers as she inspected my wrist. Sharp, long nails, eyes boring into mine as she watched for a reaction, a sign of pain. I saw the horsewoman in her; her rough care, the brusque affection. She moved my fingers, and I had to grit my teeth not to scream, but she noticed anyway.

'Go see the physio at Goldie,' she said, tearing a page out of her training notebook. She scribbled something on the paper. 'This guy really knows what he's doing.'

# 6

## Sporty Spice

B Y THE AFTERNOON OF my appointment, I had interrogated my recollection of the meeting on the train so thoroughly that I no longer trusted the meaning I extracted from it. Had it been him in the pub; did he really go out of his way to make conversation? Or was that all my own invention, a kind of false confession I had obtained by torturing my memory for details I wanted confirmed?

I had planned to walk to Goldie Boathouse along the river, but as I approached I saw that the footpath was barred by a policewoman on a motorbike.

'You'll have to take Victoria Bridge,' she said.

'What happened?'

'A magnet fisherman pulled up a grenade,' she said, looking ludicrously nonchalant. 'Bomb disposal's on the way.'

'A grenade?' I asked dumbly. 'You mean the thing that explodes?'

She nodded.

'Are they evacuating?' I said. 'Should I leave?' She did not answer, intent on the mantra-like murmuring of her radio.

'Hello?'

'You'll have to take Victoria Bridge,' she repeated.

I walked in the direction she had pointed to, feeling my heart and stomach clenching in on themselves, two gripped fists squaring up for something unpleasant. What if there was an explosion close to the boathouses? Was it safe being so near the river?

It was too late to cancel now.

I was used to Cambridge's anti-climaxes by that point, so I was not surprised when I found that the beautiful facade of Goldie Boathouse was badly let down by the interior. As I opened the door, I was met by an oniony stink of perspiration, and the sight of damp concrete walls and neon tube-lamps weeping an infected yellow over a group of men grunting under weights. Their sweat speckled the floor. One of them, who had been standing in front of the mirror watching himself do biceps curls, let his dumbbells fall to the ground, and turned towards me.

'You're lost,' he decided. He had blue bloodhound eyes and a face so sun-weathered that it seemed surgically grafted on to his young, muscular body.

'Yes, I'm sorry to interrupt, but I'm looking for the osteopath.'

'He's not an osteopath.'

'Oh, sorry,' I said, flustered. 'I'm looking for the guy I made an appointment with for a rowing injury.'

'Yes, I know who you're looking for. I work with him, and we are not osteopaths. We're physiotherapists.' He took a sip of a fluorescent blue sports drink. 'They're not the same thing.'

*Thank you for educating me, you knobhead*, I wanted to say, but I just smiled, and he pointed to a staircase. 'Up there.'

I reached the landing and saw that the door was ajar.

'Anna? Come in.'

He was sitting with his back to me, doing something on his computer.

I looked around the room. It was immaculate and impersonal. Rows of black filing cabinets; a high blue massage table and a skeleton, slowly revolving on its axis, with a perfect, toothy smile. No framed diplomas, no plants, no photos.

'Take a seat,' he said, indicating the chair by his desk. He was still looking at his screen.

I watched him in profile. He had a curl of dark hair falling down over one eyebrow. He frowned as he typed, leaning forwards, as if he were short-sighted.

'Sorry,' he said. 'All done. But if I don't write it down, I'll forget it. We've met before, haven't we?' he said.

'Yeah, I think we did,' I said. I thought he might shake my hand, and wiped my palm on my jeans, but he turned back to his screen.

'Bear with me a second. I'm gonna open a file for you, and then you can tell me what's been going on.'

I nodded. I was glad he remembered seeing me on the train, and glad that he admitted remembering. I wondered if I should tell him about the grenade in the Cam.

'Remind me of your surname?'

'Anna Mead.'

'Date of birth?'

'The fifteenth of June, 1997.' I crossed my legs to hide the fact that they were shaking.

'Height?'

'Six foot,' I said, and then waited for him to make the usual comment about how gigantic I was for a woman, but he said nothing.

'Weight?'

'I'm not sure. I haven't weighed myself in ages.'

'Do you mind being weighed? I can estimate, if you'd rather not.'

'You can estimate.'

He nodded and wrote down a number I tried to make out but couldn't. I glanced towards the window. Still no explosion.

'Are you OK?' he said. He must have noticed something in my expression.

'All good.'

'Do you menstruate regularly?'

'Uhm.' My voice was a little high, as I strained to sound casual. 'More or less. Can I ask, why do you need to know this?'

He nodded gravely at the question.

'With female athletes we always ask about menstruation. We need to make sure your periods are regular, because certain injuries are linked to bone density issues.'

'Ah, that makes sense. Yeah, they are regular,' I said.

He had asked me another question, but I hadn't been paying attention.

'What, sorry? What did you say?'

'Have you had any other injuries?'

I tapped my left leg. 'Fractured my tibia when I was eleven.'

'How did that happen?'

The grainy loop of my memory played in my mind like an old film. *Come on, Sporty Spice*, my dad had said. *You've only bruised it.*

'Football,' I said. 'A bad tackle.'

'Football?' he said. 'Do you still play?'

'No.'

'Ah. Shame.' He turned back to the computer screen. Why was it a shame? Why would this disappoint him?

'I follow it though,' I said, keen to hold his attention.

Eyebrows raised, eyes still on the screen. 'Who d'you support?'

'Arsenal.'

'Ugh, you're a Gooner?'

'Don't tell me you're Spurs!'

He shook his head. 'Chelsea.'

I pretended to gag. 'That's not much better.'

He turned back towards me, a look of private amusement on his face. 'So what's been the issue with your wrist?'

I showed him how the bone seemed to jut out, and moved it to demonstrate the creaking noise it made, but he snatched my arm and held it still.

'Whoa, easy! Don't jerk it around like that. May I?'

I nodded, and he took my arm in his hands. Long fingers, bitten nails like mine.

'You're shaking,' he said. His eyes danced all over my face, like a flame. 'Are you OK?'

'I'm fine. I'm just cold.' The strong fingers, the feel of my own soft skin beneath his hands. The whole thing felt uncomfortable and a bit sordid. Paying an absolutely beautiful man to lay his hands on my body. *Poor guy*, I thought. *How many sad cases come here just to have you touch them?*

He was looking at me expectantly, and I realized that again he had asked me a question.

'What, sorry?'

He looked concerned and spoke slowly. 'Can I get you something? A blanket? A hot tea?'

'No, no.' I felt myself blushing, hating how needy his offer made me seem. 'I'm fine, really.'

He started manipulating my hand, asked me to resist the pressure he applied against my fingers, rotating it from side to side, leading me in a painful, slow-motion dance.

He frowned, his dark eyebrows giving a melodramatic intensity to his face. 'This really hurts, doesn't it?' He poured some oil into his hands. He started rubbing his thumb along my arm, and I felt a current of pain running up from my wrist to my neck, flickering for a heartbeat behind my eyes. Pain, again, along with a much sharper feeling of desire.

'Don't worry, it isn't serious, just painful. You have intersection syndrome. You're gripping the oar too tight – that's why you have so many blisters and why you injured your wrist. I've got some exercises you can do to rehab it, but the main thing will be resting and icing it.'

'How long should I rest it?'

'A month.'

'A month?'

'Minimum.' His eyes were stern, frowning into mine, quashing any dissent. 'I'm going to stabilize it, OK?'

He taped up my hand so that my index and middle finger were stuck pointing upwards, like Christ's gesture of blessing.

The sky was so flat and low above the colourless meadows of Midsummer Common that I felt both vertigo and claustrophobia, as if the landscape and sky were folding together like the pages of a book and I was trapped in between.

There were a few boats on the water, the rowers shivering in the freezing February drizzle. One month off. That would mean Kayla would have to replace me. I dreaded letting her down.

I tried to attribute my sadness to the disappointment of having to miss the rest of the rowing season.

In truth, I was depressed because my physiotherapy appointment had been just that: an appointment. Nothing had happened. He hadn't even offered me the student discount I was owed, and so it had cost me sixty-three pounds. I hadn't dared bring it up. I paid the full amount without saying anything, and nodded awkwardly as he told me to tell the next patient to come in.

A sinking in my chest, a deflated balloon sensation. I

don't know quite what I had hoped for. I knew nothing romantic would happen. I didn't even really desire this man. His beauty made me sad, in the same way the pastel loveliness of a sunset made me sad – there was a feeling of not wanting to enjoy perfection that was so ephemeral, which slipped through your fingers before you could really take it in. But I wanted to grasp it and hold on tight. I wanted him more than I'd ever wanted anyone.

I took the long way home past the ADC Theatre and Emmanuel College, glimpsed a fire burning through the porter's window. I couldn't go back to finish the day at the lab. Couldn't do anything with this stupid hand, anyway. It began to pour with rain; people were taking shelter under the awning of Wetherspoons and in doorways, groups of undergrads laughing and screaming as they ran for cover. I didn't want to be alone.

I called Vicky, but she didn't pick up. Ji-woo always had her phone on airplane mode when she was working. I tried Charles.

'No, Anna, no! I just got back from lunch break. I've just started running a gel. I can't. Oh. OK, OK. Fine. Just one then. Give me half an hour. Fifteen. I will hurry!'

Ten minutes later we were in the Eagle, sucking the foam off the top of our Guinnesses.

*I feel like shit. Did someone spike our drinks?* I wrote to Charles, when I woke the next day.

*Which of our many drinks? Bottle of wine one or two? Or the round of sambuca shots you bought for the entire pub?*

I groaned aloud as my phone pinged with the pictures: a whole night's worth of drunkenness. Charles and the barman; me and the barman. The lighting was so yellow that we looked livery and strange, our faces bloated like the puffer-fish monsters in a Hieronymus Bosch painting. A few of Charles and me looking awfully cosy. God, had anything

76

happened between us? Charles didn't seem the kind to make a move on a drunk girl, but you never know. I might have made a move on him! Drunk Anna was more than capable of doing something rogue. I felt sick with shame at the thought. I considered sending him a probing text, but then realized I would rather not know. Oh, and the shots! Insane! I didn't dare check my account to see how much I'd spent.

I tried to stand up, but the room spun and the floor seemed to rise up to greet me. I rested my cheek against the carpet, grateful that it had cushioned my fall, and ran my hands along its smooth surface. I wouldn't be able to make it to lab that day. My stomach felt like it was trying to migrate to my mouth. But I had never missed a whole day of lab before, never even been late. What if Crabwell actually made an appearance? He'd think I was never there, that I was a slacker like Leonid. I wrote to Charles:

*Please tell them I can't come in today. Don't say hangover. Say it's my wrist. Make it seem serious.*

Wrist. Oh God, oh God. I remembered the night before, each disjointed memory like a crime-scene picture illuminated in painful moments of camera-flash lucidity. Slumped against a toilet stall, dabbing at my phone, squinting to focus. The physio. Caden. I'd sent him an email. Then Charles holding me up at some point, leaning in close. Could I have let that happen? My phone trembling in my hands, I checked my emails.

Anna to Caden (01.07)
Hey Caden, I'm sorry to ask this and please don't worry at all if the answer is no, but would you like to go for a drink some time? No worries at all if not, have a lovely evening and thank you for the session today! It was so helpful!!!

Caden to Anna (08.13)
That's fine. How's tonight? I finish work at six. X

A rabbit-thump of alarm in my heart, and the flaring shame cooled into something harder, more unpleasant. 'Fine' was so bland, so unenthusiastic. A rejection would have been more welcome than half-hearted acquiescence.

'Vicky!' I pounded on the wall that separated our bedrooms. 'Vicky, I need you!' A minute later she came storming into my room in her silky pyjamas, shielding her eyes from the light.

'The fuck is wrong with you? It's not even 9 a.m. yet!'

'Vicky!' I said, holding out my phone, my voice pathetic, pleading. 'Look.'

She snatched it away from me and read the message, cross, blinking sleepily.

'So?'

'Does it seem like he really wants to go out with me?' I said, twisting in the blankets.

'Yes!'

'No! It sounds like he feels obliged.'

'Dude.' She pushed the phone into my face. 'Didn't you see he put an X?'

'Yeah. But only one!'

'One X means he likes you. More than one X means you're his crazy auntie or some shit.'

'Are you sure?'

'I'm going back to bed.'

I tried to fall back asleep but couldn't. I was shaking, just as I had been in his office. Finally I answered him, said yes, I would see him at the Maypole, and I got out of bed and ran into Vicky's room. She rolled over and patted the space behind her.

'But no talking,' she said.

# 7

## The Maypole

WE SLEPT UNTIL MIDDAY, and then I spent the afternoon alone walking around the Newnham gardens, watching the skinny bees hovering over sprays of wintersweet, the yellow buds dripping from the branches like beads of maple syrup. There were tiny sparrows scudding in the underbrush, and I dug the heel of my shoe into the hard ground to try to dig up some of the soil for them, but there was nothing, no worms.

'Sorry, guys.' They looked happy enough.

I put my nose into the wet blossoms of a Daphne bush. A deep, cold, sweet scent. As a child I would cry for my mother to lift me up to smell the flowers I couldn't reach. She loved winter gardens. I thought about the lab, and regretted not forcing myself to go in.

Now there was nothing else to occupy my thoughts. Why did I have to write to him? Why could I not have just enjoyed the fantasy? I could have added him to the collection of men who nourished me without causing me any pain; the Benicio Del Toros and Idris Elbas and Tony Montanas of my imagination, my secret stokers in lust. But at that time, I didn't know the wisdom of self-denial. I was like Pandora with her box, unable to exert any self-restraint.

It's funny to me now that I did not spend more of the

day worrying about what to wear, that I didn't even shave. In part I think I was protecting myself; I did not dare to hope that smooth legs would be relevant. But a part of me was also truly clueless. I didn't really understand what was expected of me, didn't know how to seduce men. I guess I'd smeared and sparkled my face with products on occasion before going out with Jamie, but he had often helped me to apply it. I didn't even have any make-up with me in Cambridge.

In the early evening, I went over to Ji-woo's room. I found her sitting at her desk, her hair a slick oily comma down her back, her green clay face-mask cast in an anxious frown as she scrolled through BBC News.

'Dude, my supervisor is freaking . . .' She trailed off.

'Why?'

'The outbreak? The Wuhan virus? SARS? Remember bird flu?' She frowned as she saw my expression. 'Why do *you* look so freaked out?'

'I'm about to go on a date with the most beautiful man in Cambridge.'

'Show me!' she demanded. We tried to find him on Google, but while he had a profile on the Goldie Boathouse website, there was no picture of him, only a stock photo of a dark silhouette where he might have uploaded something.

'Oh!' she said. 'Mysterious! Like the Great Attractor! So the date is tonight?' She looked me up and down, appraising me. 'What's going on with your hair?'

'What do you mean?' I went to look in her mirror. I suppose she was right. I looked like a mad scientist, my hair more frizzy than curly.

'I wish I wasn't going. He's way too good looking.'

'You're beautiful! And anyway, it's what's inside that counts.' She would have sounded more convincing if she wasn't still eying my hair with such a worried expression.

'We can solve this,' she said, turning to her computer, her ringed fingers flashing as she typed.

We lost ourselves in a whirlpool of YouTube videos: get rid of split ends by setting your hair on fire; the pigtail method; the hatchet method; the mayonnaise mask. We decided my dry ends were beyond the help of condiments and instead went for the chop. I lay down on the floor, fanning my hair on to a wooden cutting board. Ji-woo combed it out, hovering over me, knife in hand.

'Just get it over with!'

The knife made a dull thwack as it hit the wood, a disappointing anti-climax that was reversed when I shifted and we saw how much had been cut; a sickle of curls.

'It's so short on the top! You've given me a mullet!'

'It looks great!' she said, but she looked panicky, and then relieved when I burst out laughing.

I set off in my Docs, a short kilt, and a yellow seersucker jacket that I'd bought for rowing.

'I'll take it off,' I said, when Ji-woo shook her head in despair. 'I'll take it off as soon as I'm inside.'

The haircut had edged my mood from panic to a kind of amused hysteria, and as I walked down Trinity Street, in the deep shadow of the ancient colleges, I felt my mouth spread in a huge smile. There is no place lovelier than Cambridge at night, and it was a particularly lovely night: the stars in cahoots with the old-fashioned lampposts; the bare trees arranging themselves to let the moonlight through. I was walking fast – the ground seemed to roll under the thrust of my heel; the statues of saints and the gargoyles of John's and Trinity seemed to bend their mild, blind eyes on me, to watch me pass with benevolence. I was so stupidly happy.

I strode into the Maypole and passed through a succession of tiny, wood-panelled rooms full of men, but I couldn't see Caden. My pocket buzzed: *You walked straight past me.* I retraced my steps and saw him in a corner by the entrance. He was staring into his phone, and its light illuminated his face from below, casting a long box shaped-shadow on to the wall behind him. He was so absorbed that I stood and watched him, unwilling to interrupt.

But then he saw me, and the corners of his mouth turned upwards.

'What can I get you?' I asked, without even saying hello.

'No,' he said, sidling out from his chair. 'It's on me. What do you drink?'

'What will you have?'

'I'm a bitter drinker. But you don't have to do as I do. I can get you a cocktail if you like. Wine. Anything.'

'No, no,' I said, feeling flustered. 'A pint would be great.'

He went to the bar. He was wearing the camel coat with a pair of faded blue jeans and dark New Balance sneakers. I watched him interact with the barman, fumble for his wallet. It reassured me to see him do something so banal.

He carried the pints over to our table, then hung his coat from a hook on the wall. He did this with great care, smoothing out its creases, and I felt self-conscious in my ugly rain jacket. I quickly shucked it off.

'How long have you been a physiotherapist?' I asked, before he could speak. I was scared he would make reference to the drunken email I had sent him.

'Nine years since I qualified.'

I took a sip of my drink, suppressed a shudder. Why had I let him order me an IPA? Guinness was my drink. I hated all other beers.

'How did you end up in Cambridge?' I asked.

'My girlfriend wanted to move here. So we came about three years ago. My ex, I mean.' He shook his head, closed his eyes as if in pain. I rushed to fill the silence, pretending the word 'girlfriend' hadn't snagged like a stray nail.

'Oh, cool. And do you like living here?'

'Yes.'

'A lot?'

'Yeah. I like being near the river.'

I kept firing questions at him, to which he gave perfunctory answers. It felt more like an interview than a date. As he spoke, I made a panicked run-through of all the topics I might bring up, the stories I might tell him. But I couldn't think of anything he'd find interesting. I was quite incapable of putting on the Anna Show for him. He sat there, staring at the pint between his hands, his eyes hard and shining and unfocused.

'Do you want another drink?' he asked eventually.

He returned with two pints and two vodka shots, which I accepted without question, grateful for the anaesthetic against the unbearable pain of his proximity. Several times, during longer, more awkward silences, I was on the brink of saying something like, 'I'm too nervous to actually enjoy this, are you having a good time?' or 'Why did you come out with me?' but I didn't dare. I was not nervous to the point of nausea, though the conversation improved when I changed the subject to football.

'Do you think they're going to fire Lampard?' I asked.

'You don't hire a manager still figuring out his job and expect short-term results. Frank's signing was always a long-term project.'

'Right, but I mean, Chelsea's never been a "come here to grow" type of club, has it? Especially not under Abramovich.'

'Yeah,' he agreed. 'You know a lot about football, don't you?'

I shrugged, falsely nonchalant, and reached for my beer. As I did, I knocked over his pint. The glass bounced once, twice, and came to rest without shattering, its vibration against the floor ringing out in a long, sombre note. Beer trickled slowly off the table. The blood dripping from the man's nose on to the asphalt. I winced, thinking of the accident, the smell of iron.

'Ignore them,' Caden said, misinterpreting my expression as the men on the next table gave a mocking smatter of applause.

Eventually, the alcohol created a stand-in for closeness. We bonded over our shared irritation with the other people in the pub: the drunken actors who threaded in from the ADC Theatre and screamed for service; the barman who pulled a foamy pint full of air; the call of 'Last orders!' and the stuttering brightness of the lights that came on at eleven thirty.

'It's late,' he said, as we stepped outside. 'Let me get you home safe.'

'Cambridge is really safe,' I said, zipping up my yellow raincoat. It was freezing.

'You never know,' he said. 'Shady characters everywhere.'

I thought again about the car wreck and the fight, considered telling Caden about it, but the incident still frightened me too much to be turned into an anecdote.

I looked down. We were standing far apart, but our long thin shadows overlapped.

'I have to be up early tomorrow,' I said.

'So do I. Don't worry, I just don't think girls should walk home alone in the dark, even in Cambridge.'

The cold was sobering, and as we made our way to Newnham it robbed us of the closeness we'd felt a few minutes earlier. Our breath hung in the air like empty speech bubbles that seemed to mock our silence. I could not understand why he was walking me home. The evening had not gone well; I felt it had been stressful for both of us. He had seemed withdrawn. He hadn't asked me a single question about myself or my degree. A generous reading of his behaviour would have been that he was shy. A franker one would be that he was disinterested. So why was he walking me home? And why wasn't he trying to make conversation now? It didn't make sense.

I led him on a shortcut across the college gardens. The moon was so bright that we didn't need our phones to navigate, but I took mine out anyway just to give myself something to do.

'This is it,' I said once we reached Florence House. 'Thank you for walking me home.'

He smiled, teeth white in the night. An image flashed into my mind: the bloody teeth of the beaten man. I swallowed, felt my heart beating in my neck. He was looking at me with an expression I couldn't read.

'Thanks for the drinks,' I stammered.

He took a step towards me. His eyes were darker than the night around us because they contained no stars. He said my name. I said nothing. Our faces touched; our lips touched. It was like falling through ice, an exhilarating shock. The yearning was painful, and I thought, *This man will ruin you*, and I thought, *If I must be ruined, I want to be ruined by him*. His lashes against my cheek. I stroked the fabric of the coat between his shoulder blades.

He broke away. 'Can I come up?'

I crossed my arms, shivering. 'You want to come up?'

'Yes.'

'But I mean, *why*?'

'I don't want to say goodbye.'

'But did you enjoy yourself tonight?'

He laughed, shook his head at me. 'I did. I guess you didn't.'

'No, I did. I just didn't really get the feeling you were having fun.'

'I'm sorry about that.' He ran his hands through his hair, looked down at his shoes. 'I'm just awkward. I guess I've not been on a date in ages.'

'Really? But I mean, don't women throw themselves at your feet?'

He laughed again, but I hugged my arms tight to my chest, too cold to relax.

'You're not throwing yourself at my feet,' he said.

'Only because I'm cold.'

My mouth was buzzing, as if I'd been stung.

'You can come up, but I don't want to sleep with you.'

'I didn't mean it like that. I just meant I don't want the night to end yet.'

I let him in, hurried up to reach my room before him, and threw Mango Bango Jambo Banana under the bed just in time.

'I thought it'd be fancier.' Standing in the doorway, he was a dark silhouette against the brightly lit corridor. He shrugged off his coat.

'I know, so did I. Cambridge is beautiful on the inside, ugly on the outside.'

He let the door swing shut.

'I think you mean the opposite.' The voice came to me across the dark room, coiling out of the shadows like a rope. We fell on to the bed. I pulled off his fleece and inhaled his smell at the crease of his neck; a single clear note that I couldn't name. I closed my eyes and breathed it in, but the more it enveloped me the more its nature eluded me, and I thought, *This is enough, this is enough, I could swim in this moment for all of my life.*

And I said things then, things I'm embarrassed to repeat, the kind of words you only say to someone you are convinced you will never see again – that he was the most beautiful person I had ever seen, that he should take pride in it, that being as beautiful as this was a form of genius.

86

Mouth smiling into mine, a gruff chuckle in his throat. I ran my hand from the top of his shoulders and stroked his bicep, his back, arched and strong as a taut bow. He unzipped my skirt. Kissed my neck, my stomach, sure and soft. I felt his curly hair against the top of my thighs. Then my mind split in two: half of me accelerating, galvanizing speed; the other half tugging me back, trying to stay the momentum. I went to press my legs together, but he held them and stroked the terror out of me – *Everything's fine, breathe.* Part of me wanted to stand up, to regain control, but another – a less familiar part of me – was on its own journey, revelling in everything he did. A swath of moonlight drifted in, and I looked at the shadow our bodies cast and then I closed my eyes. I focused on my breath, trying to slow myself down, but it felt as futile as trying to pin the peak of a wave to prevent its fall, and I came in a few minutes. Caden sat up on the bed and turned towards me. His dark eyes were calm, infuriatingly calm.

I straightened up, ran my fingers up his thigh, but he put his hand over mine, steadied it.

'You said you didn't want to have sex.' He enclosed my fist in his hand. 'But I'll stay over?'

'Of course,' I heard myself saying before I could stop myself. What I really wanted was for him to leave, so that I could be alone. I needed to analyse what had just happened. I felt the fizz of pleasure running through me diluted by doubt, by the feeling I hadn't quite mastered the situation. But he cuddled up to me so sweetly when we lay down, pressing his stomach up against my back, throwing his arm over me so that his fingers curled in front of my face. He was asleep in minutes: I could feel his breath against my scalp.

# 8

## Sandwiches

*I hope you slept well. Green Dragon, tomorrow night, at seven? X*

STRANGE HANDWRITING. HIS ES were like the letter C cut horizontally through, and his capital G was curly and old-fashioned, almost Gothic. Each letter was thick and dark, as if he'd pressed down hard with the pen; as if he really meant it.

I filed the note in one of my work folders, tidied my room. I retrieved Mango Bango Jambo Banana from under the bed, hesitated before smoothing down the sheets. I smelled the pillow where he had lain but could detect only the faintest trace of that single clear note. I was tempted to leave the bed unmade as evidence to myself it had really happened. The memory of him in my room seemed almost like a hallucination, as though a dark-haired angel had fallen into my bed. And – probably like those visited by holy apparitions – I was quite disturbed. Why on earth had he chosen me?

The stuff I liked about myself – my brain, my wit – were irrelevant. He hadn't asked about my PhD, and I hadn't even had the opportunity to prove my intelligence.

I suspected that he was not my intellectual equal, that he wouldn't be able to grasp how clever I was. I couldn't imagine what he saw in me. I guess that's what fascinated and unnerved me. And I wanted to know. To see myself through his eyes.

Vicky and Ji-woo were in our usual spot in the dining hall, next to the bow window with the curving radiator. Ji-woo was wearing satsuma-coloured mittens and a matching woolly hat, and Vicky had a hot water bottle on her lap.

She was reading aloud.

'If you have travelled from Wuhan or anywhere else in China to the UK in the last fourteen days, you should immediately let the college know.' She took a sip of coffee. 'Stay indoors and avoid contact with other people . . .'

'Oh Em Gee!' Ji-woo said, shaking her head, her eyes roaming vaguely over the dining hall.

'Don't worry,' Vicky said, putting down her phone. 'They're always freaking us out about something. Remember SARS? Swine flu?'

Ji-woo seemed about to say something to Vicky, but then she slapped her hand down on the table and pointed at me.

'The guy! How did it go?'

She was incredulous when I told them that Caden had gone down on me, and even more so when I explained that he hadn't let me reciprocate.

'Straight women are too easily impressed,' Vicky said, scraping her empty bowl and eyeing mine hungrily. 'It's like you want to give a man a Nobel Prize for oral sex. It's not that ground-breaking.'

I spooned some golden syrup on to my porridge, swallowed a mouthful. My lips were sore from his stubble.

'So, are you going to see him again?' Ji-woo asked.

'He's asked to meet up again tomorrow. But I don't know. I don't really get it. I didn't get the feeling he liked me all that much.'

'Of course he likes you!' Ji-woo replied.

'He didn't ask me a single question. He didn't ask about my PhD.'

'Thank God he didn't,' Vicky said. 'Who wants to hear about the vivisection of baby animals?'

I tried to give her the finger with my bandaged hand, but it just made her laugh.

She accepted the remains of my porridge, which I pushed towards her. I wasn't hungry. I had just spotted Kayla, demolishing a stack of toast in the corner of the hall, and remembered I would have to tell her I couldn't row for a whole month.

'So what did you guys talk about?' Ji-woo pressed.

'Nothing. The weather. Football. Like, really the most basic stuff. He mentioned his ex, and actually referred to her as his *girlfriend*!'

'That's a red flag,' Ji-woo said.

I massaged my temples, feeling a hangover coming on.

'It means he is not emotionally ready to leave his baggage behind,' Ji-woo continued, nodding at her own assertion. 'If someone brings up an ex, it's a sign they're trying to create toxic triangulation.'

Vicky rolled her eyes at me. All the wisdom Ji-woo dispensed had a similar, Instagram-ish flavour. 'A negative mindset will never give a happy life,' she would say. 'Let your inner child breathe.' One of her favourites was, 'Put on your own oxygen mask before helping others.' I nodded politely, but I never listened to her.

'It's a sign of narcissism,' Ji-woo went on. 'People often bring a third person into the relationship in order to remain in control.'

'Everyone our age has a past,' Vicky said, pouring

packets of sugar on to the table and picking the granules off with a moistened finger. 'After twenty-one, everyone has a fossilized heart.'

I was happy to find an empty lab. Rosa and Crabwell were in the break room, having some kind of meeting. I expected them to ignore me as I started to set up my gels, but Crabwell beckoned to me through the glass door. I went in, smiling but a little wary.

'Good morning, Professor Crabwell,' I said, pleased he'd seen me arrive so early.

'Anna, nice of you to show up,' he said, not returning my smile. 'It's a shame you were too hungover to come in yesterday.'

I felt as if he had thrown boiling water in my face.

'It was my hand.' I held up my bandaged wrist. 'I hurt it rowing.'

'Charles had a different story.' He took a pencil from his breast pocket, clicked it distractedly. He watched me. I was unable to think of a reply. He tapped his lower teeth with the pencil. I swallowed, lowered my gaze.

'In any case, you missed my lecture on the ELISA protocol,' he said, holding his nails close to his face, frowning as if he found something wanting there. 'You'll have to ask Rosa to go through it with you.'

'Oh, I've done the ELISA sandwich before,' I said, brightening a little. 'I did it loads of times at Exeter.'

He pursed his lips. 'It's better if you go through it again. The protocol is expensive. Exeter is Exeter; Cambridge is Cambridge.'

I nodded, unsure if I should stay or go, and then turned and went into the lab. I buttoned my white coat, smoothed it down, tried to focus, to stay the tears I felt welling up. Why the hell had Charles told him?

He arrived a few minutes later, but it was impossible for

me to confront him because Rosa was there, watching me set up the workstation.

'I know you know it,' she said, her voice reasonable, diplomatic, 'but there's no harm in going over it again.'

The process involved 'sandwiching' growth hormone between two antibodies; one held the hormone in place and the other created a fluorescence used to measure the hormone concentration. Rosa spent the whole morning going through the instructions with me – despite the fact that they were written clearly on the kit.

At lunchtime, Charles tapped me on my shoulder, expecting me to go to Market Square with him, but I only shook my head.

He came back from his lunch break with a falafel wrap for me, but I ignored him, working steadily through the afternoon, the only sounds in the lab the rumbling of my stomach, the buzzing of the test tubes as I pressed them against the vortex machine, and Rosa's whispered prayers as she sacrificed her mice alongside me. The light faded; I switched on the neons, my eyes flinching at the glare from the plastic well-trays. Vortex every sample for homogenization, then pipette the contents into the wells. Buzz, click, buzz, click. I was lost in my work, so I didn't notice Rosa leave and jumped when Charles clapped me on the shoulder.

'It's seven,' he said, 'and you haven't eaten. Let me take you to the Eagle.'

'You're not *taking* me anywhere,' I said, shrugging his arm away.

He was taken aback by the anger in my voice, and he winced as if I'd struck him.

'Wh-what?' he stuttered. 'What's wrong?'

'You told Crabwell I was hungover,' I said, my voice cold and harsh. 'He had a go at me this morning.'

'I'm sorry, Anna,' he said, in a feeble, quavering voice.

'I didn't mean anything by it.' I shrugged and turned back to my bench.

'Why did you?'

'I just . . . I feel . . .' He started saying something but then trailed off.

'What? What did you feel?'

He shook his head.

I let the silence hang between us and began to tidy up – I spritzed the bench with three neat squeezes of Vigor, felt the ammonia prickling my nose. In truth, my anger was starting to abate, but I wanted to make him suffer a little longer. I went to check that the fridges were closed, and was about to ask him if we could get a takeaway rather than pub food, when I heard a sob, and turned to find him hiding his face in his hands.

'I really didn't mean to,' Charles said, hanging his head, his long auburn hair covering much of his face. 'I didn't mean to,' he said again. His voice cracked. He was really crying now. I put down my cloth and bottle.

'Oh, Charles! I'm sorry. I wasn't even that angry!'

I put my arms around him. He stood rigid for a moment, but then melted into my hug.

'It's OK,' he cried, his mouth hot and wet on my shoulder.

There was something weirdly familiar about this closeness, the satiny feel of his cheek against mine. Had something happened between us at the Eagle? I felt only the vaguest lurching sensations as I cast my mind back, a generalized feeling of guilt that flapped around but found nowhere specific to land. Perhaps I had done or said something that night to hurt him. Maybe that's why he had ratted me out to Crabwell.

'Wanna go get dinner?' I said, desperate to ease my guilt. 'My treat?'

He pulled away from me, his shoulders still shaking.

'Yes,' he said, smiling feebly. 'I should like that very much.'

We got takeaway from Gardies, then walked with our tin-foil wraps to Queens' College, and up a winding Gothic staircase to Charles's garret room. Sloping ceilings; his red, hooded choir cassock hanging from the back of the door. Windows with glass so thick it warped the view of the gardens and river beneath. The distortion made the wooden Mathematical Bridge look like a pile of logs, a pyre waiting to be set alight.

I perched on the stone window seat while Charles sat on his bed, one foot balanced on the opposite knee, offering a flash of thin, green-socked ankle. I put on the Anna Show and did my best to cheer him up, to make it seem like we hadn't argued. I talked and smiled and teased as I knew he liked to be teased, the hot aluminium bundle radiating a searing heat into my lap.

I was ill at ease, though not because of our argument. Although I'd been in his room plenty of times before, something had changed between us. Now, I felt nervous at the intimacy, at the nonchalant way he let his knee knock against mine, how he offered me a bite of his lamb kebab, a string of his saliva stretching across the mouth of the sandwich, and how wet it felt against my own mouth – because I did not say no; it seemed somehow important that I accept it, so I did, and I chewed and swallowed and smiled at him, even as I felt the meat churning in my stomach, bumping around inside me like shoes in a dryer.

I left Charles's room that night with the knowledge our friendship was compromised, that I could not trust him as I had before. I had not told him about my first date with Caden in the Maypole, nor my plan to meet him in the Green Dragon the following day. I'd like to think I wanted to spare his feelings – that I was trying to protect him from the pain of knowing that I liked someone else and that he didn't stand a chance with me – but the honest truth is, part of me likely enjoyed his attention. Charles was clever, and his respect for me flattered my intellectual vanity. I did not want to give that up, though if I had, I would have spared everyone a great deal of misery.

# 9

## The Green Dragon

THE GREEN DRAGON – ALONG WITH the Sunshine Posho bridge, Grassy Corner and the Gut – was one of the many landmarks used by rowers to navigate the River Cam. Until my date with Caden, I'd thought the moniker 'Green Dragon' had something to do with the willow trees that grew along that stretch of river. Their long limber branches – like the claws of some beast – often ensnared the boats of less experienced crews and dragged them into the bank. But I learnt that day that the trees had nothing to do with it; the Green Dragon was a pub only a few metres from the river, which had been blocked from our sight by trees and bracken.

I left the lab a little early, but then I lost my way in the dark. I cycled along the river for a while, then turned into the darkness. The streetlights petered out, and the roads gave way to a confusion of narrow lanes that all seemed to insist that no, *they* were the right way. The road and trees were glazed with a fine sparkling frost, which made everything look exactly the same and disoriented me still more. I found it at last: a many-chimneyed corner house with a wooden sign with a painted dragon, creaking in the wind, like a saloon in the Wild West.

The pub was full of woodsmoke and a few men, and I

felt some of them give me the once-over, but I wasn't concerned as they were the kind that would ogle a dog if it was wearing a skirt. I looked around, but Caden hadn't arrived yet. I dropped my shoulder bag on a corner table near the fire, then went to fetch something to drink. An Alsatian was prowling near the bar, and it growled as I approached.

'Quiet!' the barman said, with a kind of gruesome fierceness.

He turned to me, still scowling.

'What do you have on tap?' I asked.

'Water,' he said, and laughed at his own joke.

'I meant, what beer do you have?'

He ran his hand along the top of the taps.

'I want something that doesn't really taste too much like beer,' I added, remembering the horrible IPA.

'You want a beer that doesn't taste like beer?'

'Yes.'

'Is that some kind of riddle?'

Eventually he poured me two Estrellas, and I carried the drinks back to the table, everything made awkward with my bandaged hand. I checked my phone. Nine minutes late. *But you're always early, or too exactly on time.* I sat and checked my appearance in the mirror on the wall opposite. I'd washed and combed my hair, and it certainly looked better than the last time we had met. Black polo neck, and aubergine-coloured cord dungarees which Ji-woo said made me look like a giant toddler. The lipstick she'd applied so carefully had already been swallowed away. How do they do it, those women who manage to keep their lipstick intact all evening?

I sipped the foamy head of the beer and watched the dog snap at invisible flies. My legs and cheek on the right side were hot from the fire, while my left side was cold. I felt like an unevenly cooked Sunday roast.

Caden was now twenty minutes late and had ignored the text I'd sent him when I'd arrived. I was anxiously nursing my drink, but it was already almost finished. I kept noticing my reflection in the mirror, and all my movements seemed unnatural. I thought about the lab, the list of things I wanted to get done before the weekend. I had to compensate for the day I had taken off, and for the day Crabwell had made me waste relearning a protocol I already knew. I felt like I was getting behind, and I wished I had brought a journal to read.

Thirty-three minutes late. I felt the entire pub knew I was being stood up. I took a sip of the second pint, cracked my knuckles.

When could I leave? Should I leave?

I thought of the cheerful evening I would have had at Newnham with Vicky or Ji-woo, or even with Charles: wine and Sainsbury's luxury ravioli; stupid arguments about what music to play and who was meant to have bought the parmesan. But then the chain of association led my thoughts to our drunken evening together, then the memory of the fight at the Eagle – to Angus, and what he'd said about me. I looked over at the mirror, watched the ugly distortion in my throat as I swallowed. Of course Caden didn't want to see me again. I was nasty as hell.

Flies filed over the table, over my hand, as if I were not there at all. Thirty-five minutes late. I got up to leave, feeling a crushing humiliation that would erupt into tears once I was safely outside. I was nearly at the exit when the dog jumped up at me. I screamed, or the scream was dragged out of me, the long leash of sound pulling the men's attention in my direction as they turned to stare.

'Down, girl!' the barman said, giving a broken, wheezing laugh. 'She won't hurt you!' The dog got down, and I wiped the moisture of its hot breath off my face just as Caden came through the door.

He looked far too nonchalant for someone so late, his walk almost swaggering.

'Hey, sorry,' he said, stuffing his phone into his back pocket. 'Have you been waiting long?'

'Yeah.' The relief was overwhelming my anger, but I couldn't keep the hurt out of my voice.

'Didn't you get my text?'

'No,' I said.

'Are you sure?'

I checked my phone, my anger faltering. 'Yeah – nothing.'

'I'm so, so sorry,' he said. 'My colleague Kieran came in to talk just as I was getting ready to leave, and reception is awful on the river.'

This, at least, I knew to be true. We were always running into problems when someone was late for rowing, as messages wouldn't go through.

'It's OK,' I said, trying to smile as we sat down. It was only half an hour, nothing to cry about.

'Can I buy you a drink?' he asked.

I looked at his profile in the mirror. It felt wrong to be sitting so near to him, like peering too closely at a painting in a museum. I saw myself nod, but then felt daunted when I saw him approach with two more pints, as I was already quite drunk.

'Cheers,' he said, clinking his glass against mind. 'And thank you for waiting.'

'It's not a big deal.' I took a cautious sip. It tasted strong and salty, like liquid Marmite.

'Was your colleague OK?' I asked, trying to dispel the silence settling around us.

'Yeah, he's fine. Just girlfriend trouble. His ex is crazy.' I took another sip. I was so full of beer that I felt it sloshing against my ribcage. I watched him in the mirror. Rolling up the cuffs of his long-sleeved green T-shirt, absentmindedly coiling his fingers through a lock of dark hair.

He asked me about my wrist, whether I was following the news. I told him about the email that had been sent to all students. I found the conversation difficult. He kept repeating how terrible his hangover had been the day before, and the more he emphasized it, the more worried I became. Had he been too drunk? Did he not remember what had happened? Or worse, did he regret it?

'Have you had dinner?' I asked. I felt a bit sick.

'Are you hungry? Let's see what they've got.'

The barman nodded at Caden as we approached. 'See you've moved on,' he said, with a wink.

Caden didn't acknowledge what he had said; there was not even a flicker in his expression.

'Is the kitchen still open?'

The barman made a theatrical show of checking his watch. 'Closed twenty minutes ago, mate.'

'Oh,' Caden said. He turned to me. 'Shall we have another drink? Or do you want to go?'

'Go,' I said. Was this where Caden brought all his women?

'Can't I make you dinner?' he asked, as the pub door swung shut behind us. 'Come to mine?'

'I've got to be at the lab early tomorrow.'

I unlocked my bike and made to say goodbye, when Caden put his hand on my shoulder. It was the first time he'd touched me all evening.

'I'll see you home before midnight. I *swear*.'

I didn't look at him, only at the hand on my shoulder. There was warmth in it, but it made me shiver.

'It'll be fine.'

I don't know why he said that – perhaps I looked frightened – but as he did, I felt a kind of tremor go through me, an aftershock of the night we had together.

*Breathe*, he had said. *Breathe. You're fine. You're perfect.* I caught sight of our reflection in the window. Next to him I shone a little brighter. Like the moon borrowing light from the sun. I nodded, and followed him in the direction of what I guessed was north. We had met on the train, then my injury had led me back to him. The coincidences were too neat, too pressing to ignore. I let myself go with it, out of a curious deference to chance.

The bar of light from my bicycle swung back and forth over the proximate blackness, picking out odd fragments: the cobbles sweating black in the cold; the right angle of a yellow skip; a scatter of silver canisters.

'Laughing gas,' he said.

We passed a few shuttered shops, a pet store called Woofmeister, and a pub called the Golden Hind. We stopped in at a Tesco Express.

I waited for him outside, my breath visible in the cold, unsure if the ache in my stomach was from hunger or alcohol. There were several carts parked outside, the horses waiting docile as cars, the sweet smell of hay cutting through the traffic fumes.

I shivered, watching Caden struggle with the self-service machine. He bought pantry staples and a jumbo packet of condoms, which he slid into the bag surreptitiously, looking over his shoulder to check no one had seen.

I wasn't pleased by the thought that he knew I wanted to sleep with him. As if this, too, was inevitable.

Caden lived on Sherwood Close, a narrow curving dead-end street in an area in the north of Cambridge called King's Hedges. The houses were identical and seemed squashed tight together, like a neat row of front teeth. A few boarded-up windows, and one decorated with a red-and-white St George's Cross. Caden's house stood out a little because of the front door. It had been painted in crude red-and-blue stripes.

'I didn't pick the colour,' he said, fumbling with the keys.

Most of the front room was taken up by a black, L-shaped sofa which curved around a large TV. The floor was vinyl wood which crackled beneath my feet. Save for a large sunflower-shaped picture frame above a bookshelf, there were no decorations. It was sparse and functional to the point of being impersonal. I followed him into the kitchen, which had a glass door that led to the garden. He dropped the shopping bag on to the counter, dug in his fridge, and opened two cans of Camden Pale Ale. The yeasty-burp smell turned my stomach.

'Do you live alone?'

'Yeah.' He took a sip. 'Would you mind if I had a quick shower? I had a really full-on day.'

'Of course not.'

'I won't be long.' There was a door past the kitchen sink that led into the bathroom. I heard the scream of a hot-water tap as the shower came on.

The man had made me wait all evening.

My irritation faded as I looked around me. I love being left alone in other people's homes; it gives you access to so much information about them they would never tell you themselves. I knew, for instance, that Ji-woo had not been raised in a culture of shame like I had, because she kept a huge box of tampons on her bedside table in plain sight; and I knew from the well-thumbed and densely anno-tated Bible I once found in Vicky's bedroom that, for all the jokes she made about her theology degree, she was actually pretty devout.

And Caden?

Harder to figure out, to draw any obvious conclusions. Some things were impeccable: his knife collection was stacked in order of size against a strip of magnetic steel. The plastic bags beneath the sink were twisted into elegant eights, the tea-towels neatly folded. The fridge was immaculate, and empty apart from a few gleaming bottles of designer water, craft beer and white wine. But otherwise, the kitchen showed odd signs of neglect: the basil and rosemary plants in the window were withered; the counters were covered with a fine, sand-like substance I couldn't identify. And the strangest thing: there was a fist-sized hole in the plaster wall next to the light switch. I looked at it closely, but it was impossible to discern if it had been punched through or if it had been caused by something more benign. It frightened me a little.

I unpacked the shopping, except for the condoms, which I left in the bag. Caden had bought a bottle of red pasta sauce, parmesan and some Napolina spaghetti. The fruit bowl contained a shrunken onion, which I peeled and diced as finely as I could. He kept his knives nice and sharp. I simmered the onion in the last of a bottle of good olive oil, crushed some garlic with the flat of the blade, and threw it into the pan. While it softened, I went back to the living room to inspect the picture frame above the bookshelf.

There was a large, central circle, surrounded by five smaller circular frames. These were all occupied by photos: a few of a white cat, a teenage Caden in Chelsea strip outside a stadium – presumably Stamford Bridge; another of a man and two curly-haired little boys smiling and holding hands. But what drew my eye was the centre frame. It was empty. Clearly it had once contained a photo, but now the white space stared blankly out at the room, like a blind Cyclops eye. I wondered why Caden had left it empty. Surely, everyone who came over would notice and ask him about it? Perhaps that was what he wanted. To arouse curiosity.

I went back into the kitchen, flicked on the kettle and continued with dinner.

By the time Caden had finished his shower, I'd prepared the sauce and put the pasta on to boil.

'Oh God, and I said I'd make you dinner.' A cloud of shampoo-soap smell, creamy and fruity. Dark hair dripping on to his white T-shirt. Wristwatch, jeans, bare feet. They were godly feet, the kind Mary Magdalene might have washed.

'It's OK,' I said, tearing my eyes away. He spooned some parmesan over our bowls. I could imagine my dad rolling his eyes, making some cutting remark: *Pre-grated cheese is sawdust. No Italian would ever eat it.* There was no dining table, but Caden set us up with two wooden trays, and we ate side by side on the sofa, the trays perched on our laps.

He chewed slowly, curling his pasta on his fork into neat little bobbins. The pasta sobered me; I felt the nausea recede as I chewed and swallowed.

'So you're a cook,' he said.

'Adding garlic to a supermarket sauce hardly makes me a cook.'

'You like your food, don't you,' he said.

I shrugged. 'Who doesn't?'

'Many women don't.'

He leant over and shook my empty can of beer. He made to fetch another, but I stopped him.

'Do you have anything else to drink?'

'White wine?'

'Perfect.'

'I can make a Kir.'

He returned to the table with two full glasses of wine, and a squat brown bottle with a pretty blue label: *Crème de cassis*. He poured a few drops into my glass, and the liquid curled into the wine like blood in water.

'What's this?' It tasted like Ribena.

He didn't answer. He was staring at the bottle intently, turning it over in his hands.

'Where did you get it?' I tried again.

He placed it on the table and looked at me, glancing up dramatically from under his long lashes.

'My ex. She was French.'

I nodded.

'Where from?'

'Paris.'

'Cool. Have you been?' I asked.

'Yes, a few times.' His voice was even and inexpressive but his mouth had tightened, and I noticed that he had pushed away his bowl, though his dinner was only half eaten.

'So have I,' I said, and I picked up my bowl and stabbed at the spaghetti with my fork.

I hated Paris. I'd been there once, on a school trip. A tick-box tour of the Eiffel Tower, Notre-Dame, the Louvre. The ammonia stink of piss on the Metro; the men who fixed you with the thousand-yard stare of a firing squad. Then a cruise on the Seine. Freezing, joyless, the guide's voice unintelligible over the microphone. And the women: sour-faced, exasperated, superior in their chic little out-fits. But I didn't want to say this to Caden; it would seem like I was being rude about his ex-girlfriend, as though I was trying to talk her down. I took another sip of the Kir, and was trying to think of something to say, when I heard a sound, a scratching at the kitchen door.

'Pringle!' He leapt to his feet, opened the door to let in a large cat. It had a cream-coloured body and a dark, vel-vety face, as if it had been dipped in hot chocolate. Extraordinary eyes: green, but with swirls of blue and speckles of brown, like two tiny globes.

'Is it yours?'

'It's a she,' he corrected, cradling the cat in his arms. 'No, she's a neighbourhood cat, but she comes over all the time.'

He plopped it on my lap. I stroked it, as it pommelled my knees and thighs. It smelled of piss and some kind of chemical.

'They don't like it, if you stroke their fur the wrong way.'

'Sorry,' I said awkwardly, trying to figure out what he meant. The cat leapt back to Caden. He held it in his arms and rocked it like a baby.

'Who's the prettiest kitty-cat?' He kissed the underside of the cat's paws. *Is he going to kiss me with that mouth?* I thought. *Surely it must walk all over shit and stuff?* But Caden was obviously one of those people who adore animals. I didn't say anything. He put it down, and it gave a luxurious arching stretch.

'Do you want to go upstairs?' he asked, just as I took a huge mouthful of pasta. I pointed at my face, exaggerating the chewing to make it clear he'd have to wait for an answer, and – to my complete surprise – he reached over and tickled my neck. I batted him off, but already he was poking my ribs, grabbing at my foot.

'Shtop,' I laughed, my mouth still full. His eyes were shining and intent, full of happy mischief like a little boy, an expression that transformed him. 'Stop it!'

'Is that a yes?'

'Sure,' I said, wiping my eyes with the back of my hand, 'but no tickling.' I felt the first pang of fondness for him, something deeper than the raw desire I'd experienced before.

'After you.'

He followed me up the stairs, and I was aware of his gaze on my back. We reached a landing which had two doors, one open and one closed. He took my hand, led me towards the one that was open. He turned the light on. I got a glimpse of a blue duvet, a neatly made bed, flowerpots on the windowsill, before he seemed to think better of it and turned the light off again, though it was not entirely dark as the light slanted in from the corridor.

I moved towards him warily, carefully, as if he were an animal I'd come across in the wild, something I didn't want to scare away. Our eyes met and we were both still, and it was utterly silent. A breath-held, exquisite moment.

His expression was tender, and I felt moved by whatever it was he saw in me that evoked that tenderness. *Why do I feel like crying?* I thought. *Don't cry.* I closed my eyes, and when I opened them he was closer. His eyes were dark and still. He stroked the hollow of my neck, watching my face, and he was so solemn that I wanted to laugh to dispel the tension, but I didn't dare. And then he put his arms around me, and I held him close. We stayed like that for a while. I felt like I was holding a whole universe between my arms, and I thought the convolutions of his neurons and organs were like network of galaxies I was going to get to explore, and then I thought of the 95 per cent of the world that is unknowable dark matter and I held him tighter, and he kissed my forehead and moved away.

He began to undress, and I did the same. He was oddly meticulous: he unstrapped his watch, folded his jeans carefully, and hung his shirt in the standing wardrobe. I did the same, making a neat pile of clothes that he took from me and placed on top of his chest of drawers.

He sat on the bed and reached out his hand for me.

I gently kissed his chest, his stomach, following the V of muscle downwards. I covered it in kisses, but I felt him tense up slightly. Perhaps I was being too tender. I stopped the kissing and took him in my mouth, tasted the slight salt before he pushed me gently away from him, and pulled me down beside him. He said my name. I wanted to ask him to say it again, and again, but I couldn't bring myself to speak.

He moved away from me and used the torch of his

phone to rummage through his bedside table. *The condoms are in the Tesco bag downstairs!* I wanted to scream. At last he found one, a shiny red square, and his solemn air was replaced with neurotic intensity as he put it on.

His ribcage swelled against my chest. I felt I was surfing on his breath. I became very still; an expectant intensity, listening for the sound of something drawing closer, wanting it to and not wanting it. I covered my eyes; I couldn't bear his gaze on my face.

'Everything's fine,' he said, unpeeling my hand from my eyes. I turned my head to one side and watched our shadows, how they moved freer and lighter than us, sad angels unmoored by the real weight of things, unable to feel the weight of him on top of me, or to grasp the shared insight we gained as we moved together, slow, slow, stopping to breathe each other in, to kiss each other, and smile as if to say, *Isn't it amazing? And it's just us, it's you and me, it's we who are doing it.* The tense and muscular drum of my heart, each beat growing closer and closer. One part of me holding back and another urging me on, digging its heels in to hurry me. I held my breath, straining against it, but it came anyway.

'Christ,' he whispered, pleading, into my ear, 'Jesus Christ.' I pushed him off me and turned my back to him, and he did the same, each sequestered on the inside of our own sensation.

He got out of bed, pulled on his jeans. He leant over to kiss my forehead, and then went downstairs. I watched him go – watched the movement of his shoulders like the slow liquid roll of a leopard climbing down from its perch.

I got up to switch on the light. A plain, drum-shaped lampshade that threw a narrow cone of light on to the bed. Bare white walls, white carpet, the only colour the blue bedspread and four pots of orchids lining the windowsill. Their pink petal-lips trembled very slightly in a phantom breeze. I'd always thought orchids looked out of place indoors, trapped like tropical butterflies under glass, their wings pinned and mounted in unnatural display. They were more pornographic than beautiful.

Caden returned with a bar of chocolate and the cat.

'Does it stay over?'

'She. Yeah, sometimes.' He broke the chocolate into squares. 'Four for me, six for you.'

'That seems fair.' I finished my share in seconds.

'Oh, you're still hungry. Next time, I'll cook a proper dinner.'

'I'll make pudding.' I was thinking of all the elaborate dishes I could come up with to impress him.

'You're the pudding!' he said. He smiled, and watching him I smiled as well. He leant in close.

It was too late for me to go home, and I slept poorly in Caden's bed, my mindless fantasies never attaining the status of dreams. Caden frowned in his sleep, looking very severe with his dark eyebrows. The cat couldn't settle either, but clambered all over us, and I felt it was a projection of my mind, searching all night for a comfortable place to rest. I found myself obsessing over my work, wondering if I'd left the sample fridge open, if there would be enough tissue in the foetuses for a proper growth hormone reading, whether I'd have to go in on Saturday to get it finished.

The alarm went off at seven thirty, and Caden jumped out of bed before I had time to blink. I heard grunting, and I followed the sound on to the landing. I found him in a small box room next to the bedroom. It was empty apart from a tall stack of transparent boxes and a yoga mat, on which he was doing push-ups.

'Sit on my back,' he panted.

He lowered himself inch by slow controlled inch

towards the floor. His olive skin glistened like the fur of a wild animal.

'I'm too heavy!'

'I'm really strong.'

He looked as if he could keep going for ever, his shoulder a continuous spinning wheel for the axle of his body.

'I need to shower.' I felt self-conscious in the too-bright daylight, and vaguely anxious at the thought of the full day ahead after so little sleep.

'Just off the kitchen. Clean. Towel. In. Cupboard.'

The shower was over a bath, the ledge of which was lined with plastic bottles of every imaginable shape and colour, like our store room at the lab. There was everything: detangling shampoo for long hair, face scrub, cleansing oil, clay face mask, pomegranate cleansing soap, self-tanner, glow-in-shower lotion. I counted eight different conditioners: restorative, shine, moisture, thickening, protein, heat-damaged hair, leave-in, Olaplex. How could anyone take the specificity of these products seriously?

I dried myself on a towel, awkwardly because of my injured hand, and – curious to know the brand of the perfume he wore, to identify that mysterious singular note – I opened the cupboard under the sink. It contained hair straighteners, a million hairpins, and something called Glimmer Goddess body lotion, shining with particles of glitter as tiny as asbestos.

I changed back into my dirty clothes, and when I opened the door I almost bumped into Caden, who was in the kitchen.

'Hi.'

He was topless, grinding coffee beans with a hand-held grinder, which he handled forcefully like a sexy car mechanic.

'Bathroom's free,' I said.

'I'll shower in a minute. I want to smell like you a little longer.'

No one had ever said something like that to me before, and I felt myself blushing. I focused on the toast, buttering it while he poured the grounds into a French press.

'Wow,' he said, picking up the toast, examining it closely. 'What the hell is this?'

'What?'

He pointed. 'You've literally left a foot of unbuttered bread on these!'

He was right. I'd left the edges bare.

'I don't want you to get your fingers greasy! I was being considerate.'

'Isn't your dad a chef? And you can't even make toast.' He rolled his eyes in mock consternation.

'I bet I'm a better cook than you are,' I said.

'We'll see about that, Pudding.'

## 10

# Hello Kitty

W HILE I FOUND PUDDING to be an unflattering
nickname, a nickname is always a victory of sorts.
Soon I was signing off my texts to him with the pudding
emoji and suffering from a urinary tract infection.

My GP came straight to the point:

'Are you sexually active?'

'Yes.'

'Do you have multiple partners?'

'No,' I replied, almost affronted. How could I have
time for multiple sexual partners? Between Caden and
my work, I was barely sleeping. Even the nights spent
alone in my own bed were exhausting, as I would replay
the last time I'd seen him in my head, the things he'd
whispered to me – *Do you think about this when you're
alone? You taste so good* – things that mortified and elec-
trified me.

'Are you in a new relationship?'

This was a good question. We had been seeing each
other regularly in the month since we'd met at the boathouse, but we hadn't ever spoken about whether this was
a relationship, let alone an exclusive one. At first I had
assumed Caden wouldn't be able to find the time to sleep
with other women, so there was no point even bringing it

up. But then one day, while he was showering, I found a tiny, blood-smeared Hello Kitty plaster in his bed.

I tried to picture him wearing it, but it was impossible to even imagine it. It must have come from someone else. The blood was rust-coloured, not fresh, so I couldn't be sure that he had had someone else in his bed *recently*. I hoped that it belonged to his previous girlfriend, that she'd left it behind. But I made his bed every morning when I slept over, and had never seen the Hello Kitty plaster before.

'Um, yeah, we've only been seeing each other for a few weeks.'

'It's very common to get UTIs at the beginning. When the frequency of sex dies down, you won't get them so often.'

'Fantastic!' I said. She didn't catch the irony.

I'd never really understood sexual obsession before. I hadn't come close to feeling that way with Jamie. But then, I had not been turned on by him at all, only by how much he wanted me. It hadn't been desire, really; only a form of narcissism. Plus, he was too self-conscious, always trying to hide his body beneath the sheets. He had been so faltering, scared of doing something wrong, that I felt I was leading a workshop every time we slept together.

I thought of Caden all the time. The only thing I had ever been dominated by was fear – mainly fear of failure – and curiosity. Never desire. But memories of things we'd done together – things he'd done to me – would flash constantly into my mind throughout the day, even while I was in dissection, even while I was talking to my lab mates. His fingers running along my lips, fingers in my mouth, kissing for hours and hours, pressing each other in turns against the front door. By the end of the day, my body was cavernous with longing, and I could barely bring myself to go and hang out with my friends, to eat dinner with them, when all I wanted was him.

At times, when I held Caden in my arms, I felt a rush of yearning and anguish – for what? For more of him? I couldn't get close enough to him, even as I kissed him, his ears, his mouth; even as I scratched at his skin and strained against the bounds of my own. It was almost cannibalistic, my desire for possession, for him to become a part of me.

But the power balance was tilted in Caden's favour. The Hello Kitty plaster led me to believe that he was still fucking other women, while I spent my spare time googling 'how to give better blow jobs' and 'aphrodisiac dinners for two on a budget'.

Meanwhile, the coronavirus spread across Europe. On the 28th of February, the Vice Chancellor of the university had sent out an email claiming that 'there is no reason to feel unduly worried. We are aware that the majority of those who contract this virus experience only mild symptoms, not unlike the flu'.

But people were tense. At the very start, we spoke in terms of individual cases: a sixty-four-year-old in Perugia; a forty-eight-year-old in Milan. But the dots of individual cases on a map became whole swaths of colour, especially in Italy. Rosa was tracking the numbers closely, concerned about her family. She always had the radio on in the lab, and while I didn't understand Italian, the bubbling eloquent anxiety of the newsreader was clear enough.

I'd like to say we were worried. But in truth, we treated it like a bit of a joke. Italy seemed a long way away from Cambridge.

Crabwell was at that time never in the lab, though one day he summoned us all to his office to review our first term's work. He was wearing a mask. It was the first time

I had seen someone wear one, and privately I thought he was being a bit ridiculous. He handed the disinfectant around.

We shivered in the breeze from the open window, while he went on. He was pleased with me and with Charles, but he blasted poor Leonid.

'I'm unclear what exactly it is you've been doing. The progress report you've handed in is based on your project proposal from last summer, before your PhD even began. And the writing' – he turned over a piece of paper – 'is poor. Your write-ups are more *chronological* than logical. And the language is too flowery. This is science, not a lady's journal. Read Anna's papers; she gets it.'

After the meeting, Leonid asked me to look over the draft of his write-up. I agreed, and at the end of the day we hung back, waiting for Charles to leave.

'Staying late?' he asked, eyeing us both as he wiped down his bench. He looked put out, but I couldn't tell if it was because he suspected something was going on between Leonid and me, or whether it was only because Charles hated the feeling of anyone working harder than he was.

'Yup,' I said vaguely, not meeting his eye.

We went to the Free Press pub, a tiny place in a narrow alleyway behind Christ's Piece. We found a cosy nook near the empty fireplace and struggled to make room for ourselves on the bench.

'You're big, for a woman,' Leonid said, staring down at my thighs. 'You've got the legs of a rugby player.'

'And smart for a woman, too?'

'Sorry.' He blanched. 'I didn't mean it in a bad way. I love strong women!'

'Don't worry. I'm just exhausted. Lab killed me today. Do you have your paper? Want us to go through it?'

'Forget it.' He shook his head, signalling to the barman we were ready. 'Let's just have a drink.'

He ordered us Guinnesses, the foam catching in his *Top Gun* moustache. And Leonid, who I had dismissed as sexy but stupid, completely surprised me. He was hilarious, able to give spot-on imitations of Rosa, Crabwell, even Charles:

'Come on, chaps, we can do it. Steady the buffs!'

I laughed despite myself. 'Don't make fun of Charles, he's my friend.'

'How can you be friends with him? He's so jealous of you. It's so obvious.'

I faltered for a moment. I didn't know if he meant romantically jealous, or only that Charles was competitive about work.

'I can't stand him and the Harrow guys. He's such an Old Boy.'

'Well, maybe I'm an old girl. And I don't want beer,' I added, when he went to order another drink. 'G&T, please.'

'Oh, sorry dahling, I should have known,' he drawled.

It got late – too late to have dinner in college – so we ordered food. I stuffed my face with a steak made out of cauliflower, while he ate a worryingly pale pork roast.

'I'm sure it's fine,' I said, as he took a timid bite. 'Maybe the pig was anaemic.'

My arm brushed against his as I leant over to steal a chip from the enormous Jenga-mound of fries on his plate. Perhaps it was the alcohol, perhaps I wanted to get even with Caden, perhaps it was just blind lust, but I let my arm linger there. And in a second I sensed my advance was uninvited. He drew back, looking uncomfortable.

'Uhm, so can I ask you some stuff about the write-ups? I don't have my paper, but I have a notebook.'

We discussed his protocol and I gave him some pointers, but the shame burnt through me like a flare.

'Let me pay,' he said, when the bell rang for last orders. 'It's the least I can do. You've helped me so much.'

That made me feel even worse. He had wanted me to help him with academic work, and I'd made a pass at him like some creepy male professor. He hugged me as we parted, and I imagined he felt sorry for me. *Poor, desperate, nerdy Anna.*

I ran through Christ's Piece park because it was dark, and because I wanted to burn off some of my humiliation. My breath smoked out in front of me; it was cold for March. It felt as if the winter had dragged on for ever. I slowed my pace when I reached Regent Street, which was too brightly lit, too crowded, too drunk. There was a long queue of people waiting to get into Wetherspoons. Women in open-toed heels and tube-top dresses, their hair tied up in buns frosted with sparkling hairspray. They seemed immune to the cold. Their eyelids blinked slowly under the weight of false lashes, like moths beating their powdery wings.

Two men walking on my side of the street had noticed them, too, and began calling out to the girls and wolf-whistling. 'You girls are fit!' They burst out laughing.

The men gave lemon-wedge grins and walked past without noticing me.

The day after I made a pass at Leonid, Caden suggested we visit a stately house near Saffron Walden called Audley End. His own car, he told me, had been at the garage for months, but we could borrow his friend Kieran's. I was excited to get out of Cambridge and sang in the shower. I came out to find Caden ironing.

'You know what I love about you?' he said, his eyes still on the crease of the trouser leg.

I shook my head, blushing for the compliment, at the co-occurence of 'love' and 'you' in the same sentence.

'What?'

'You don't take long getting ready at all.'

'Oh?'

He looked up, a lock of hair obscuring his eyes. 'My ex-girlfriend took ages choosing her clothes, doing her make-up. It was so annoying.'

'Right . . .' I nodded, trying to figure out how this might translate into a compliment.

'You're much lower maintenance.'

I thought of the ugly waxen plants Jamie had bought me for my last birthday: dragon lilies, spider plants, nubby succulents. 'They're so low maintenance!' he'd said when I objected that they had no scent. 'They don't need any looking after! They're basically impossible to kill.' I wasn't sure how I felt about being classified as the female equivalent of a succulent. If I was low maintenance, what was Caden's ex? A beautiful hothouse orchid? Something complicated and delicate. But I supposed it was better than seeming needy and demanding.

We walked to Kieran's house. Caden took my hand. I glanced at his profile, at the almost solemn eyes, the dramatic lashes. He was wearing his long camel coat, and he looked so elegant, like a movie star. The joyous, singing mood returned: I was so happy, though a little physically uncomfortable. My arms were longer than Caden's, and they hung below his, baboon-like. But I clung on tight until we arrived at Kieran's place, a ground-floor flat in a block behind Goldie Boathouse. Caden knocked on the door, and I recognized Kieran as the knobhead I'd seen when I'd gone in for my appointment.

'I think we've already met,' he said. Tombstone-white teeth, his face greasy as an oiled herring.

'Have we?' I said, but he looked as if he didn't believe me.

The car was disgusting. The smushed food on the floor and under the seats was so bountiful and varied that it no doubt contained several civilizations of bacteria. We drove through the curiously perspective-less landscape of Cambridge, through flat fields so identical that it was hard to believe we were moving forward at all.

I had not been in a car since the accident with Jamie, and I glanced at the rear-view mirror from time to time to check it did not flicker, to make sure the reflection remained benign.

'You seem a bit tense,' Caden said. 'Are you scared?'

'I'm never scared,' I lied.

Eventually we turned off the motorway, on to a narrow road. We passed through two iron gates to a path that wound its way through a birch wood. The white trunks were covered with black spots, and the light gliding over the trees made it seem like the forest was moving around us, stretching and pacing and elastic as a snow leopard. At last Audley End came into view.

'Doesn't it remind you of Devon?' I said. The limestone was so luminous and white that it looked more like a sea-cliff than a house.

'No,' Caden said. 'At least, not the Devon I'm from.'

He paid for our tickets at the entrance, and we made our way into the house. It was cold and smelled spicy, like fresh paint. There didn't seem to be anyone else visiting. We walked through the dining room, with panelled walls and a Gothic plaster frieze. We looked at the portraits in a long, narrow gallery, our footsteps echoing in the silent room. One painting of a young woman caught my attention.

She wore a green velvet dress and her eyes were green too, a shimmer like sunshine dancing on their surface. There was a spark of curiosity in her expression, and her lips glistened as if she'd just moistened them to speak. What did she want to say?

'Caden,' I called. He was ahead of me and had almost reached the exit. 'Come and look at this painting. Doesn't she remind you of me?'

But he threw only the most cursory glance over his shoulder and wouldn't slow down.

'I want to show you something.' He hurried me out into the garden.

'Look,' he said, as we stepped into the greenhouse, 'aren't these carnivorous ones sick?'

He was pointing to a gourd-shaped plant hanging from a purple leaf. It had a shiny red opening that looked like a gaping mouth, lined by crenulated teeth. The inside of the plant was pale, swollen, and threaded through with tiny red veins, like a pregnant stomach.

'Horrible.'

He didn't answer; he was intent on the flowers.

'Have you been here before?' I said. My voice sounded thin, distant.

'A few times, with my ex.' His lids were lowered, and his long black lashes made his gaze seem melancholy and theatrical. 'She loved these,' he added. He glanced up at me, but I felt him looking beyond me, as if he were staring through a piece of coloured glass.

I walked ahead, unable to bring myself to say anything. The greenhouse was humid and airless. I hated these kinds of plants: long purple grasses, flickering like devil's tongues; pink orchids; peace lilies, their yellow pistils caressing my arm, strangely odourless. Caden had his phone out and was aiming it at me. I reached out my hand to block the camera.

'Just one?'

'I hate having my picture taken.'

I hurried through the sea of plants, circle after circle of mouths in ecstatic Os, the scent like sour breath, a zooey pungency, something reptilian, and I found myself going faster, not even pretending to look at things.

I'd thought we were discovering a place together, but this wasn't a voyage into mutually uncharted territory; it was a retracing of steps, a revisiting of memories he shared with another woman. Mixed in with the predictable feelings of jealousy and sadness, a prickling of curiosity about her. Had she let Caden take her picture?

'The toilets are over there,' he said, pointing, as he followed me out into the cold.

'I don't need to go.' I shivered. The sky was darkening. I zipped up my coat.

'I love that you never need to pee. My ex needed to go all the time.'

'Brilliant, Caden. It really makes me feel so good about myself to know I have a stronger bladder than your ex-girlfriend.' I pulled at the car door, but the passenger seat was locked. Caden was reaching for the keys in his coat pocket. He looked at me in surprise.

'I meant it as a compliment.'

'Well, I wish you'd shut up about her.'

The door clicked beneath my fingers like a pulse as he unlocked it, and I slammed it shut without waiting for his reply.

He got into the driver's seat. He didn't look at me, but stared at the steering wheel. 'I won't mention her again.'

We drove in silence through the woods, the birch trees still stuck at high noon, but there was no sun playing on the snow-leopard tree trunks; the sky was almost the same colour as the tarmac. Caden switched the headlights on. After a few minutes, he turned off on to a small country road next to a posh-looking farm shop. We parked along the low wall of an old graveyard.

'I'll be back in two secs.'

I kicked off my shoes, watched the rain speckle the windshield. The car hummed and ticked, and the heat fogged up the windows so that I could barely see outside. It occurred to me that Caden hadn't left the lights on. If another car came down the lane, it might not see me. The rain was heavy now, making an irritating scratching noise on the windows.

Caden returned with two grey-pink roast beef and horseradish sandwiches. I wondered if his ex had enjoyed roast beef. Usually I bloody loved it, but now it tasted like dust, a relic, Miss Havisham's wedding cake. I was sure he'd been here, in exactly this spot, eating exactly this food, in the same dirty car, with her.

A flash of lightning made me jump. Caden looked at me over the mouth of his sandwich and smiled.

'You're scared?' he asked.

'No,' I lied, bracing myself for the thunder.

'No?' His smile was a little cruel. 'You look scared.'

'I'm not,' I said, but then the darkness flashed again, so bright that it seemed as though someone out in the fields was firing tracer rounds at the car. My hand fluttered over my throat. Caden put down his sandwich, placed his hand on the door handle. Slowly, with his eyes fixed on my face, he opened his door.

'What are you doing?'

He got out, and when I saw that he was coming towards my side of the car, I locked my door.

He pulled on the handle. 'Open up!'

'Why?'

He didn't answer, only knocked on the window.

'Come on!'

I didn't move, but he reached for the keys in his pocket and unlocked the door himself. He leant in close, and I thought he wanted to kiss me, but he just reached for my seatbelt and unfastened it in one deft click.

'Come on!' he said again, and when I didn't move, he grabbed my arm and pulled me towards him out of the car. 'Get out!'

'What are you doing?' I winced as my socked feet found the ground. 'My shoes!'

But Caden didn't give me time to put them on; he pulled me along, past the farm shop, down the country lane with its mossy walls. The stone path dug into my feet. *What's he doing?* I thought. *God, I shouldn't have come here.* The rain was so intense that there was no point flinching, no point even narrowing my eyes. I let it wash over me. Epileptic flashes of light in the vaulting dark overhead. The only warmth came from Caden's fingers on my arm. His grip was too tight, but I was scared of shrugging my arm away and finding out that he really wouldn't let go. *No thunder – when will the thunder come?* My feet were hurting and raw and slipping on the stones, and I was about to cry out when Caden led me through a little gate and into a graveyard. Tombstones at every angle, jutting and bucking.

Caden's face was turned up to the sky, squinting as if he were looking for something. Then he looked at me. He seemed not to feel the cold or the wind. There was immeasurable meaning in his dark eyes, in the dark shadows beneath them. My heart hammered in my chest.

'What's the matter? Why are we here?'

He looked as if he were about to speak, but he shook his head. Raindrops streamed down his face that could easily have been tears. It occurred to me that he might know someone who was buried here. Maybe his girlfriend had died, and he had come here to show me there was no rival.

The wind was cold and hurt my ears. I was about to speak again, frightened by his silence and the strange light in his eyes, but he stepped towards me and his lips pressed into mine.

'We can't do this.'

He drew back and looked at me, strangely merciless and strangely tender, and then kissed me again. His hand cupped my chin, falling to my collarbone, the fingers hooking into the neck of my T-shirt, the top of my jeans.

'We can't do this here,' I said, taking a step back. 'It's a graveyard.' But he moved towards me again, and he was sinking to his knees, bringing me down with him.

I showered at home, did my best to wash the grit out of my hair, to tend to the grazes from the tombstone. I thought that I might find the name and date of death from the engraving traced on to my back, but nothing showed up in the mirror as I towelled myself dry. This time I looked at all the products more carefully. Her hair must have been straight, very different from mine. I applied her shimmery asbestos cream. Caden had promised not to mention her again, but she was everywhere, hanging over the house like a sad moon.

I spent the rest of the afternoon trying to play with Pringle. Caden had bought her a numbers of toys, and her favourite was a sort of fishing rod with a bell and feather at the end of a long string. But as much as I jostled it up and down in front of her, she ignored me.

'Caden.'

He was watching something on his laptop, absorbed.

'Mmm?'

'Why won't the cat play with me?'

He took the toy, dangled the end behind the back of the sofa. Pringle became alert, her eyes watchful. He kept flicking it in and out of sight, until she jumped down from the sofa and went careening round the side after it.

'See,' he said, letting her catch it. 'She likes it when you hide the toy. You have to tease her with it, put it just out of sight and out of reach. *That* drives her crazy.'

And he was right; if I bounced the string behind the sofa she would prick up her ears, lunge and lunge until she had the feather in her claws. *That's just like me*, I thought. *That's Caden's method. Dropping those hints about his ex-girlfriend. He's jiggling a fishing line, and I hear the ringing of the bell just out of reach around the corner. He knows what he's doing.*

Caden went to return Kieran's car while I got started on our dinner. His promise of cooking had never materialized but I didn't mind; I liked to be left alone in the kitchen. I took his sharpest knife and sliced through three onions and six large potatoes until I had them in soft heaped piles. I cracked some eggs into an oily pan, and grated pepper on to it until the yellow was black. While the fritters warmed, I went into the front room to look for something to read in Caden's bookshelf.

There were mainly textbooks from his degree – *The Physiotherapist's Pocketbook*, *Essential Anatomy for Physiotherapists & Osteopaths*; a few history books – *Britain at War*, *The Longest Day*; the kind of novels I expected Caden to own – *The Da Vinci Code*, *The Godfather*; and a few surprises – *The Kite Runner*, *My Sister's Keeper*. There were also some books on sailing and travel atlases – *Britain's Coastal Towns* and *The Old Ways: A Journey on Foot*. I pulled out *Cambridgeshire & the Fens*, and as I leafed through it, a photo fell face-down on the floor. It was perfectly spherical, with tape stuck to the back.

I held it up to the empty sunflower picture frame and realized, yes, this was the missing picture.

A smell of smoke. Had he hidden it because he couldn't bear the sight of her? Or was it because he didn't want me to see her?

She seemed to rise up from her image like the genie from the lamp, so that we faced each other there in the front room. Red cat's-eye sunglasses pushed back on her head.

It looked like it had been taken somewhere hot. Greece or maybe southern Italy, that kind of blinding white stone. That alien sort of beauty. The pan was hissing.

I thought about taking the picture. But I slipped it back where I'd found it. At that time I was still able to rein myself in.

And anyway, it wouldn't fit into my pocket.

## II

## Men Are Dogs

THE LAST NEWNHAM FORMAL dinner of the Lent term was spring themed. Though it was already past the equinox, it did not feel like spring at all. The moon was spindly and jaundiced, the sun entirely absent. While a few crocuses and sweet snowdrops had pushed through the soil, the buds of magnolia and narcissus were still shut tight like fists balled against the cold, their cream-and-pink knuckles the only hint of fairer days to come.

Ji-woo and I had biked to the thrift shop in Mill Road for an emergency shop. She had found a million 'cute' and 'adorable' items, and I tried on the entire rack of dresses, all of which looked like distended, woolly placentas. My mood was steady enough. I put on the Anna Show for myself and was able to convince myself that I was happy. But despite attempting to sequester the picture into the deepest nuclear vaults of my brain, I was struggling. As I pulled the clothes on and off, dropping them into a depressing pile on the changing room floor, I felt the image rising to the surface of my mind, radiating the truth. *You're ugly, Anna. You're ugly.*

I settled on a caftan-shaped green velvet dress with a low neckline.

'I love how you feel you can just wear anything,' Ji-woo said, as I modelled it for her.

'I look terrible.'

'You know nothing about fashion.'

She was right. I didn't really have any style and didn't usually bother to dress up for formals. But that day she had promised to help me get ready. I had invited Caden.

Afterwards, we went to Tom's Cakes. Ji-woo turned down my offer to treat her to a cupcake. It had been a while since I had spent any real time with her, and I was shocked by how wan she looked. I knew that she was fretting about her father's poor health and the coronavirus. We had received an email from the Vice Chancellor that morning, explaining that 'the outbreak is likely to have serious consequences for the daily lives of our students and staff'.

'They're gonna kick us out,' she said, worrying the rings on her fingers. 'I guarantee you that in a week, none of us will be here.'

'They didn't even shut the university during World War Two.' I took a bite of my cupcake. Too much icing as usual; hard as mortar. 'Have a bite of this. Go on, just a small one.'

She glanced at a group of students on the table behind us. 'People are being super weird with me,' she whispered, leaning in close. 'I thought Cambridge students would be smart enough to know the difference between Korean and Chinese.'

She explained that her lab mates had been making jokes about how she might be a carrier, that they'd better all wear masks when she was around.

'You should complain,' I said, shocked. 'Tell your supervisor. Or someone in Newnham.'

She shook her head. 'I'm just in a funk,' she said. 'I need to manifest something more positive.'

By the evening of the formal, she had cheered up. She bought a bottle of Disaronno, and we passed it around, became flush-faced and hilarious as we changed. We were getting ready in Vicky's room. It had been a long time since I'd last tidied up for her. The bed was overflowing with carrier bags full of tat and open sleeves of Oreos, and the contents of disembowelled make-up bags were strewn across the floor.

'You look so *Downton Abbey*,' Ji-woo said, trying to flatter me. 'But stop hiking up your bra straps like that – it looks like they're going to pop out.' I regretted wearing a push-up bra. Fecund, fertile, overblown. Not even sexy. *Don't think about it. Look at these friends of yours. Look at how they love you.*

Ji-woo straightened my hair; my curls steamed between the hot tongs and fell limp and shiny on my shoulders. Vicky, meanwhile, was dabbing foundation on to my face.

'I'm contouring your nose. To make it look narrower.'

*Your nose is nasty. Your whole face is nasty.* Angus's face; the feel of the beer dripping on to my lap.

'Stop moving!' Vicky said, holding my chin. She tweezered on a pair of fake lashes, smeared my eyelids with green glitter. She did everything carefully, with only a light pressure, but as she put powder over the foundation and bronzer on top of the powder, I felt something close to claustrophobia, as if I was being walled in.

'Look towards the corner,' she said, holding an eyeliner pencil in her hand. 'A little more to the left . . .' And as I did, I caught sight of something shiny in the ashtray on the windowsill.

'Vicky,' I said, jerking my head away.

'Did I poke you?'

*The earrings.*

'No. It's nothing.' I closed my eyes as she traced the

pencil over my upper lid. Her hand was trembling against my skin, and I wasn't sure if it had been a moment before. Perhaps she'd realized what I'd seen. My earrings. The pair my brother had given me, the diamond studs I thought I'd lost.

'Kiss this tissue now. And again. Oh, I *nailed* it!'

I went to the bathroom.

I stared at the tiles on the floor, the white squares lined with black, like perfect graph paper. *Why is it*, I thought, flushing the toilet, *that my work is the least agonizing part of my life?* In the lab, I was in control of everything. If I messed up it was my own fault, and I could figure out how to solve it. My personal relationships felt unbearably complex in comparison. I could not bear the endless subtlety of it all, the ambiguity. Why would Vicky steal from me, her friend? What had I ever done to her?

I don't think I even considered confronting her. I probably convinced myself that our friendship was worth it. The truth was that I didn't have the guts.

I caught a glimpse of myself in the mirror. I looked unhappy. I felt sick from the smell of formaldehyde and artificial strawberries I had let my friends plaster on to my face. My eyes were so deep-set it looked like someone had hammered them into my skull.

Caden was waiting by the Porters' Lodge. He wore grey trousers with a black belt which matched his leather shoes, and a white shirt made out of some kind of knit-cotton, with the top button unfastened. I felt that multiplication of perspective I always experienced when I introduce people I know to each other. I saw him as my friends did, as if for the first time. He looked like an Italian prince, and while I could tell he was self-conscious, he was confident in his elegance. I saw his surprise as both my friends took his hand in turn – he was not used to shaking hands with women – and I watched him notice Vicky's upswept golden hair, how it revealed the ballerina curve of her neck, and saw through his eyes the perfection of Ji-woo's lucent face. I wondered if he felt he'd drawn the short straw, and then immediately hated myself for the thought. Because they were being so kind, chatting to him, doing their best to put him at ease as we made our way down the corridor.

'Have you been to a formal before?' Ji-woo asked. 'No? Don't worry. They try to make it intimidating, but it's not really a big deal. Newnham's all women, so you might get some stares. But men often come to formal. It's chill.'

'That sounds like an experience,' he said, smiling slightly. 'A load of gawking women?'

I cringed at that comment, and knew Ji-woo and Vicky had picked up on the chauvinist undertone. It was not the first time he had made that kind of remark. Only recently, he had told me that he had been pleased I hadn't wanted to go to bed with him on our first date.

'But did you want to sleep with me?' I asked.

'Yes.'

'So why are you happy that I didn't initiate it?'

He leant back in his chair, considering. 'My ex and I slept together on the first date, and it always bothered me.'

'But why?'

'She was too easy.'

'But *you* slept with her on the first date!'

'I know,' he shrugged. 'But I'm a man. Men are dogs.'

I didn't want to start an argument or ruin the atmosphere, but as we made our way down the orange-blossom corridor to dinner, I promised myself I'd call him out if he said anything like it again.

We reached the hall; rows of banquet tables set with symmetry so perfect that the room looked like a hall of mirrors. The glow from the candles caught in the mullioned windows and shimmered in each diamond-patterned square, just as light dances on fish scales.

'Don't sit yet,' I said, as he went to pull his chair from under the table. 'They say grace first.'

The Principal of College made her usual dramatic entrance, her green embroidered robe gliding along the floor as she strode to take her place at High Table. She was popular with the students, mainly because of an interview she'd had with the BBC. 'Over my dead body,' she'd said, live on air, in response to being asked when the college would start admitting men. 'Ask me again when the pussy-grabbers are out of office.'

She said grace in Latin and we sat down, the girls opposite Caden and me. He took his phone out to take a picture of the table, but one of the waiters intervened before I could.

'No pictures,' he said, 'or we'll confiscate the phone till after the dinner. And here' – he passed him a Halloween-orange tie – 'you have to wear a tie at Formal Hall.' Caden looked at it. For a moment I thought he might refuse. But then, with slow, deliberate movements, he hooked it around his neck and fastened it. His face was expression-less. I felt bad that I hadn't thought to warn him he needed to wear one.

'Cheers,' Vicky said, leaning across the table, clinking her glass against his. 'Don't worry, I'm constantly being told off for some breach of British etiquette.' He smiled, but I noticed his fist was clenched in his lap.

'You're a physio, right?' Ji-woo said.

'That's right.'

'For the Boat Race rowers?'

'Yes.' He spoke only when spoken to, like a polite child.

'You know, I love going to the physio,' Vicky said, tear-ing into her bread roll. 'I love it when they have your head in their hands. And they always say "relax" and then they crack your neck. And you know they could kill you if they wanted. Hot.'

I could tell he did not know what to say.

'Yes, really hot,' I said, 'knowing someone could paralyse you.'

'Who do you think you're kidding, Anna.' She was rolling the dough of her bread into little balls now. 'You spend your days breaking necks.'

Caden looked at me, waiting for an explanation.

'Oh, she hasn't told you what she does?'

I shot her a warning look.

Caden hesitated. 'Something in women's reproductive health?'

Vicky scoffed. 'Well, technically, yes. But she spends her days decapitating rodents.'

Caden choked on his wine, and I pulled a face at Vicky behind his back and mimed slitting my throat.

'She's exaggerating,' I said. 'A bit.'

I was grateful for the distraction of the first course, a chunky green minestrone. The portions were modest, and I found myself worrying that Caden would be left hungry. I passed him my bread roll, which he accepted without question. I don't know why I did this. I was hungry myself. I suppose he was my guest, and I felt responsible for him, but Vicky raised her eyebrows at me.

The groups around us were noisy and boisterous, making the silence that had descended on our part of the table more noticeable. Caden was running his hands over the tablecloth, smoothing the crumbs off.

I realized that he was intimidated, both by the setting and the intellectual all-female company. This was the first time we had socialized outside Caden's own territory, and while I felt protective of him, I also felt an odd sort of pleasure at his helplessness. For once he was in an environment he did not wholly master, and I saw him more clearly for what he was: a gorgeous boy. No less; but no more, either. He was like a bonfire in the middle of the day – still lovely, but less impressive. That evening I was able to put him into perspective, to cut him down to his real size.

'Do you cook, Caden?' Ji-woo asked.

'Sometimes,' he said. We waited for him to elaborate, or to return the question, but he didn't. He continued to run his hands along the tablecloth, sweeping up invisibilities. I knew it fell to me to make conversation – he was my guest, after all – so I launched into the Anna Show.

'It's funny, because even though my dad's a chef, my mum's the one who cooks. And he's always really rude about her food. He's always moaning about it and criticizing her. Even though she's quite a good cook actually. I mean, she doesn't have flair . . .' I talked on, following various threads, driven by a blind instinct to fill the silence, a spider weaving a walkway ahead of itself with no idea where it was leading. 'She's not creative, but she can follow a recipe. This one time . . .' With intense relief, I realized where this waffling was going to lead.

'One time he did something to annoy her. I mean, he often annoys her, but this was really bad. He came home and was grumbling about the fact dinner wasn't on the table. So she heated up some Pedigree. Do they have that brand in America?' Ji-woo shook her head. 'It's dog food. You know the kind I mean. The wet gross stuff. I don't know where she got it; we've never had a dog. I guess she went to buy it specially. Anyway, she tipped the cans over some pasta. Or rice, I don't remember. She told him it was a new Jamie Oliver recipe. And he ate the whole thing. And do you know what he said?' I made a dramatic pause. 'He said it tasted better than what she usually cooked. He said he'd like to have it again some time.'

I wasn't sure this last part of the story was true – it

seemed like the kind of thing my mother would invent to humiliate my dad – but I told it anyway, as I thought it was quite funny.

But they didn't seem to think so. They did not laugh, or even smile. Ji-woo was staring at me. Her eyes, softened by the candlelight, glistened with a kind of saintly compassion, and I realized she felt sorry for me, as did Vicky. She had been busy buttering her bread but had abandoned it halfway through, leaving the knife sticking out of the block of butter.

'What did he do to piss her off?' she asked. 'Your dad?'

'I don't remember.'

I did, but I didn't want to tell them. And I had also omitted another detail – the fact that my brother and I had been included in the 'prank'. She had fed the Pedigree to all three of us.

'A woman not to be fucked with,' Vicky said. 'And you were saying she never sticks up for herself.'

A flock of waiters assembled, arched arms swooping down in perfect synchrony. I looked at my plate. A rosy lamb chop, and potato discs sitting in a pinkish juice. Potatoes hissing in the pan that night at Caden's house, the night I found the picture.

I glanced in his direction. He was already cutting into the meat. He was always hard to read – his face seemed trained to indicate nothing – but I felt a flush of shame. What had possessed me to tell that story? It wasn't even funny. It was disgusting and abnormal. And now I'd contaminated his image of me. I pushed my plate towards him and did the same with most of the crème brûlée when it came. It was the best I'd ever eaten; I used the back of my spoon to tap the thick caramel top, like breaking ice on a puddle, and then scooped up the gorgeous eggy cream beneath. But I had no appetite. I kept thinking about the picture, about the wet slop of dog food.

'This is as good as the one I had in Paris,' he said, and gave me a dry peck of approval, the only one of the evening. One of my fake eyelashes came undone, and it wiggled in the corner of my eye whenever I blinked, like a black centipede.

He went home directly after dinner, as he had to be up early for work and had a football match straight afterwards. The feeling of power and perspective I had gained vanished with his absence. I wondered if he was really going home like he'd said, or if he was going somewhere else, meeting another girl, the girl in the picture.

Ji-woo and I went back to Vicky's. They complained about the tiny portions and moaned about how hungry they still were.

'I can't believe you gave him all your food,' Vicky said, sipping Disaronno. 'But I'd probably starve for that guy. God really does give with both hands.'

'He looks like Dustin Hoffman in *The Graduate*,' Ji-woo said.'

'He's tougher looking, though,' Vicky replied. 'Like Dustin Hoffman after some war trauma.'

I nodded, hoping I looked tired rather than annoyed. Their manner irked me. I found them too American all of a sudden, too loud, disingenuous.

'You guys make such a great couple!' Ji-woo went on.

'We're not a couple.'

'He definitely thinks you're his girlfriend,' Vicky said. She was fingering her eyelashes, pulling at the gunk of mascara.

'It's not like that.' I felt as if there was a bone in my.

'Whatever you say,' Vicky said, but Ji-woo reached over and put her silver-ringed hand on top of mine.

'What's wrong?'

It was the photograph, of course. The hidden picture. I couldn't admit it to them, barely to myself. But the moment I saw it marked the end of the illusion that my looks didn't matter. I felt sick with the unfairness of it, the realization that my one and only chance had been ruined in that clumsy shuffle of my mother and father's genes. I was plain; she was exquisite. An inalienable fact. For all these years, I'd convinced myself that my lack of beauty didn't matter. I thought people who cared about their looks were a bit stupid, and I looked down on them as superficial. I had learnt to take pleasure in what I saw in the mirror, tilting my chin so that the light would play in the mojito mint of my eyes, the honey and bark colour of my hair, which I knew was rare and lovely. The amused shock of recognition at seeing myself in photos: my big schnoz, my insane curls, the goofy smiling face.

There was no point telling Vicky and Ji-woo. Asking my friends for their opinion was like trying to see my reflection in a kindly distorted mirror. They'd tell me what I wanted to hear.

'It's nothing,' I repeated.

'It doesn't seem like nothing,' Ji-woo pressed.

'What's going on?' Vicky's voice.

'I hate myself,' I said, rubbing my face with my hands. 'I hate myself.'

'What?' Vicky prised my fingers from my face, an almost forensic intensity in her blue stare. 'What did he do?'

'It's nothing to do with him.'

'You're lying,' she said. She waited for me to admit it, but I didn't speak.

'Well,' she said, still examining my face. 'If he ever does anything to you, I'll scalp him with my bare hands.'

She returned to the mirror. I watched their reflections as they chatted about the formal, rubbed the make-up from their faces with wet wipes.

But I didn't see my friends, not really. The photograph stuck like grit in my eye, the image overlaid like a silk screen over everything I looked at: the room, my friends, the face of my phone. The curve of her upper lip as she smiled; the gap between her front teeth. And the beauty mark on her cheek: infuriating. Her eyes in the picture, like a statue that fixed a point through me and beyond.

# Not His Usual Type

I SUPPOSE YOU CAN guess where this is all heading. It was the 23rd of March. My personal story is going to intrude on the historical; or to be more accurate, the historical intrudes on the story. It was like that for everyone. Picture billions of little rock pools, each its own independent, lucid civilization; and then the pandemic washed over all of us, altering our lives, never for the better.

But this is not a Covid story. Think of the pandemic as you think of the Cambridge setting; a backdrop, a lighting effect, something that adds a little mood.

The make-up from the night before left an impression on my white sheets. It looked like the face of Jesus in the Shroud of Turin. I didn't have time to shower before heading to the lab. I was miserable. Dissection on a normal day made me feel nauseous, but with the added factor of the hangover it was almost unbearable. A fidgety squirming shame affixed to everything: the mouse in my killer's hand; the story about my mother; the fact that my own friend had stolen from me. As far as I knew, Vicky wasn't short of money, as the Gates Scholarship was generous. It is strange, the shame a person feels when they are wronged by someone they love. How one tries to smother the shame by taking responsibility for their actions. I felt revolted with myself, not with Vicky. I deserved this somehow, probably, just as I had deserved the Pedigree dog food.

I left the lab early to catch some of Caden's football match. The pitch wasn't too far, but I treated myself to an Uber.

The driver's car was a kind of emergency hangover pharmacy. I sucked on a tiny bottle of Spa and popped a paracetamol, accepted the chewing gum and an ethanol wet wipe, which I used to correct smears of eyeliner in her rear-view mirror. I noticed my bare earlobes, and felt a wrenching feeling in my stomach. Perhaps it was some kind of compulsion. Poor Vicky. Not her fault. But that was what my mother had always said about my dad's affairs. *It's a pathology, Anna. He can't help himself.*

We arrived at the pitch and I staggered out of the car, flinching vampire-like in the floodlights. There were a few other people watching from the sidelines – the subs; a handful of women, some with young children. I recognized Kieran and went over to stand beside him.

'How's it going?'

He smiled at me. 'Being a WAG?' His deeply sunken eyes with their down-dragged lids looked strange in the artificial light. They seemed to glow slightly yellow.

'Uhm, I guess so.' I felt myself blush.

'When did you two meet, then?'

'The day I came into Goldie for physio.'

'You're quite different from his usual type,' he said after a pause, still smiling to himself.

'Different in a good way?' I asked, unable to mask the hope in my voice.

He picked some dry skin from his lips.

'Depends on what you think is good, I guess.' He seemed about to say something else, but someone had come down in a bad tackle, and Kieran ran on to replace him.

What was I doing there? It was freezing, and I felt

entirely out of place. What should I do? Scream from the sidelines? Set up a cheer with the other WAGs? Remain detached and professional, arms crossed in a kind of Arsène Wenger stance?

Finally, to my great relief, the full-time whistle was blown and the men were shaking hands. Caden ran towards me, steaming like a racehorse. Had I seen him score? And did I mind going along to the Golden Hind for a pint to celebrate?'

'God, it's fucking rammo in here!' Kieran said, as we threaded our way through the crowd. He and I were getting the drinks, while Caden guarded the empty table. The men – all in yellow-and-black jerseys – were red-faced and stocky, clumsy on their feet and as cheerful as toddlers, but I sensed a certain volatility in the room.

'It's the Cambridgeshire derby tonight,' Kieran explained, nodding at the grainy TV. 'Peterborough versus Cambridge United. And full' – he leant in close – 'full of people from *down Fen Road*.' I nodded, pretending to understand what he was referring to. It was only later that I learnt 'Down Fen Road' was code for the Traveller community, the local scapegoats.

Someone bumped Kieran from behind and he slammed into me. He threw the offender a hostile look over his shoulder.

'Go sit,' I said. I was sure he'd start a fight. 'I'll buy you a pint.'

'I don't drink,' he replied. 'Didn't Cade tell you? I'm an alcoholic. But sober now.'

'Sorry,' I said, taken aback by his sudden confidential tone, 'but I mean, well done. For being sober. That's amazing.'

He narrowed his eyes and grinned at me, baring his tombstone teeth. 'Only joking. I'll have a Guinness.'

I turned my back to him so that he wouldn't see the expression on my face. In that moment my dislike for Kieran hardened into hatred, and I made an enemy of him. Which was a stupid decision, of course. He was Caden's best friend, and making an ally of him would have been much wiser. But I was proud, and so I left him to buy his own pint, as I carried mine over to the table where Caden sat with half a dozen of his teammates and their girlfriends.

'Do you play pool?' Caden asked.

'No.'

'I can teach you.'

'I'm scared I'll scratch up the cloth,' I said. I didn't want to make a fool of myself in front of everyone.

I watched him play with Kieran. I couldn't imagine these men watching women perform some amateur sport for hours on end. Unless it was amateur pornography. Funnily enough, there was something lascivious about how they played pool, how they gripped the long wooden cues and rammed their crotches into the table. It all looked a little *too* fun.

I was glad that Caden thought I was self-sufficient enough to be left alone amongst his teammates – the perks of dating a low-maintenance, self-watering succulent – but I felt very alone in this unfriendly sea of people. The other women all seemed to know each other and did not look interested in talking to me, and the few men who weren't playing pool were no more approachable. It seemed that 'socializing' for them meant sitting with your legs spread, scrolling through your phone, making accidental eye contact and saying, 'All right?'

'I'm great, thanks,' I said to the goalkeeper, when I finally managed to trick him into looking at me. 'What's your name?'

'Jay,' he said, looking surprised.

'Nice to meet you. How's the season going?'

'All right,' he shrugged. 'Some of our best players are off injured, but we're sixth in the league.'

'It's awful being injured, isn't it?' I said, seizing on a conversation thread. 'I used to row, but I hurt my wrist. I miss playing with a team. I should try football.'

'You could ask Caden's girlfriend. She used to play for us,' he went on. 'She was class. Though to be fair' – an amused expression brightened his playdough face – 'she was always being sent off. Quite a nasty game she had. Like the female Suárez.'

'Oh?'

'A real baller. I think she played for an academy somewhere. Caden!' he shouted above the chatter. 'Where was it your girlfriend used to play?'

Caden was bent over the table, directly under the green lampshade, his face glowing slightly viridescent. He kept his eyes fixed on the point of his cue.

'Paris Saint-Germain,' he said, and slid the stick through his fingers, knocking the ball into the pocket.

'But Anna' – he pointed his cue at me – 'is my girl-friend now.'

Our eyes met. His eyes were oddly hard, and I felt my cheeks flush. I looked down at my lap, unable to hold his gaze.

There was an awkward silence, interrupted by the *clack* of balls knocking against each other as Kieran took his shot.

'Oh, right.' Jay nodded.

I was relieved when he went back to his phone. I wanted to savour the joy in private. He wanted me. He'd said it in front of everyone. But how on earth had I managed it? I could never live up to his beauty. And he wasn't even clever enough to realize how clever I was. *He should be with a girl more like him*, I thought. *With his ex.* It dawned on me then that everyone there – the men, their girlfriends – had met her before. They were all comparing me to her now, I was sure of it. That's why he had asked me if I played football, when I went to see him in Goldie. 'Shame,' he'd said, when I said I didn't. What a stinking shame. And she had played for Paris Saint-Germain. I really shouldn't really have cared. It wasn't as if it was my sport and she'd beaten me at it. But watching football was my thing. It was a joy I shared with my dad and brother – my point of entry into a man's world. Even while I wasn't talking to my dad, he still texted me before and after every Arsenal game. It had been my wild card with Caden as well, and honestly one of the things I thought gave me an edge over other women. But it was nothing. I could talk football; she was a baller. She was class.

I took a sip of beer and felt as if I were swallowing soap. Why had Jay compared her to Suárez? Did she bite people? What kind of woman gets sent off in men's games? My thoughts buzzed like a nasty bluebottle, so loud I was surprised no one else could hear them. I took another sip, checked my phone. Charles had sent me a video of a child dropping ice cream and licking it off the pavement, and another of a cat in a tutu playing the keyboard, and then followed up with: *Have you seen the email?* I assumed it was something stupid from Crabwell, some complaint about the lab.

That's when I noticed a commotion near the bar, a jostling of people. Someone shouted. *Oh God*, I thought, rising to my feet. *There's going to be a fight.* I looked around for Caden, but he and Kieran were looking at something on his phone. And then someone called out, 'They're shutting down the schools! All of it is being shut down.' Someone switched the channel over, and we watched the Prime Minister's speech. There was a brief moment's silence when he finished announcing the lockdown, and then a rush towards the bar.

'No work tomorrow!' Caden and Kieran thew their heads back, drained their glasses.

I read the stream of messages flashing on my phone. Ji-woo had taken screenshots of the email Newnham had sent: *Leave college as soon as you can.* They could not guarantee, the Principal added in an ominous postscript, that they would be able to assist those students who remained should they become ill with the virus.

I fought my way through the crowd towards the door, but Caden caught up with me.

'Where are you going?'

'I need to go and figure out what to do.'

'I'll drive you!' Unfocused eyes, an unfamiliar thickness to his voice.

'You're drunk. I'm calling an Uber.'

He followed me into the dimly lit car park, spilling his pint on to the gravel. The kitchen vents were belching great waves of indigestion on to us, but Caden seemed not to notice as he leant towards me for a kiss. He tasted of salt. I turned away, feeling like I was going to cry with frustration.

'What's wrong with you! Why aren't you freaking out?'

'It's gonna be fine,' he replied, slurring a little. 'It isn't that serious for young, healthy people.'

His irritating cheeriness goaded me into saying what I had been frightened even to think. 'I'm going to have to go back to Dorset,' I said. 'To my family.'

He brushed his hair from his eyes, looking confused. 'Why?'

'Because they're closing down the university. And the lab. I haven't got anywhere to go.'

'Stay with me,' he said, shrugging his shoulders, his

palms splayed upwards, as if this was the obvious, sensible solution.

'I can't,' I said, pulling away from him.

'Why not?' His voice was gentle, not pleading at all, only infinitely reasonable. 'You can use the spare room,' he said, when I didn't answer. 'I'll move the boxes out of there.' He threaded his hands in mine, pulled me towards him. 'I want you to stay,' he said. His brown eyes were unwavering.

I hesitated. 'I just – I think you're not fully over your ex-girlfriend. I don't think you're ready to be with anyone else.'

For a moment he looked surprised, but then his face regained its neutral cast.

'I don't even speak to her any more. She was totally crazy.'

'Everyone says that about their ex.'

'Well, she was truly crazy. No woman will ever be able to hurt me as badly as she did.' The Uber pulled up, and he opened the car door.

'You are so welcome to stay, Anna. Really.' He kissed me and gave me a long, tender look before shutting the door behind him.

I watched him through the window as we pulled away. He stood completely still, his hands in his shorts pockets, looking after me with those dark impassive eyes. There was no chink of vulnerability in the armour at all, no discernible tender spot. I couldn't imagine anyone being able to hurt him.

It was the same driver as before. She offered me a cigarette and then lit one herself when I declined.

'I don't know what I'm going to do,' she said, turning to look at me. 'If I can't drive, I can't eat.'

'I'm so sorry,' I said, but I couldn't bring myself to comfort her. She was trying to exhale smoke out of the open window, but most of it blew back into my face. I felt almost seasick, like I might actually throw up. My mouth filled with saliva, each gulp like cold seawater. Caden's offer worried me more than it excited me. Being with him was exhausting and confusing. I could not figure him out, could not read him at all. But then I thought of Dorset. My old room, the Howling Woman, my mother.

I leant forwards.

'Can I have that cigarette, actually.'

I rolled down the window and lit up. I was truly unhappy, but I was not immune to the melodrama of the moment. I think I enjoyed it a bit, weighing the two options; the alternate fates I had the power to choose between. The known evil of home, or the spare room at Caden's. I blew a plume of smoke, enjoyed its cinematic elegance, how good it looked and how bad it was. *No woman will ever be able to hurt me as badly as she did.* I felt an unfamiliar and cruel resolve. *We'll see about that.*

This malice did not sit easy inside me, but flapped its feathers beneath my skin like a bird trapped behind a window. Why did his words feel like a challenge? Why did they excite me?

I found Ji-woo in her fluffy dressing gown and chicken-feet slippers, and Vicky in her pyjamas, sitting on the floor beside her. Ji-woo was speaking to her parents, and while I understood nothing apart from 'LAX' and 'Heathrow', the meaning was clear enough. After a little while she turned the camera around so that Vicky and I could say hello, and we waved and smiled as her parents invited us to visit them in LA.

'You're leaving?' I asked, as soon as she hung up. 'When?'

'Tomorrow morning.'

'Already?'

'Yes,' she said, biting her lip.

'And you, Vicky?'

She was picking at her golden hair. Her bourbon smell was stronger than usual.

'The college is letting me stay. I turned twenty-three this year,' she explained, seeing the look of incomprehension on my face. 'I'm not on my dad's health insurance. If I go there now and get sick, I'm going to bankrupt my family.'

'Thank God for that. I wish I could stay.'

'When are you leaving? Are your parents picking you up?'

'No.' I took a breath. 'I'm moving in with Caden.'

'Dude!' Vicky said. 'Seriously? I thought you guys weren't even a couple.'

'Yeah.' I shrugged, embarrassed. 'We only just agreed on that.'

'But he upset you,' she said, no longer laughing. 'You were so unhappy at the formal. And if you wanna know, I think the guy is kinda an asshole.'

I started to say something in Caden's defence, but Ji-woo spoke over me. 'You just seemed in a funk yesterday, Anna.' She spoke carefully, a diplomatic even emphasis on each word, in a way that made it clear she and Vicky had discussed my outburst of the previous evening, and had maybe been talking about it before I arrived. 'It seems he is not good for your self-esteem.'

'You know what's really bad for my self-esteem? My dad openly fucking another woman.' At this stage of my life, I frankly did not care that much about my father's infidelities. I was deflecting my doubts about Caden on to something that had ceased to trouble me, something that had faded into the background, but I knew it would placate my friends.

'Talk to the college,' Vicky said. 'Tell them you can't go home. Because of your domestic situation.'

'There's no way Newnham will let me stay here. Did you read the email they sent us? You think they're going to let me stay because my dad's a piece of shit?'

'The alcoholic mom angle might work.'

Ji-woo gasped, shocked by Vicky's flippancy, but I laughed.

We stayed up all night, packing up Ji-woo's room and finishing the last of her food from the communal fridge: her homemade kimchi, some steamed broccoli, and an enormous tub of chocolate mousse. At 3 a.m., Vicky hugged us goodbye and went to bed, while Ji-woo and I walked to the University Library in the dark to return her books.

The evening had been one of urgent anxiety about what was happening, overlaid with sadness about Ji-woo leaving. But there was something excitingly anarchic about that starlit walk; our previous concerns and constraints had become irrelevant. Our labs were shut, our research on pause. The stakes of our old life didn't matter. As we walked through that velvet pocket of darkness which had seemed particularly ours, I was filled with a feeling of violent nostalgia. The progression between different phases of our lives is usually so gradual we do not perceive the change; the present turns into the past surreptitiously, without our noticing. But in that moment, I felt the existence I had taken for granted was suddenly barred from me. I could not return to my previous life. And the future seemed terribly alien.

'We can use it as a mini-holiday,' Ji-woo said. 'I could do with some self-care.'

'Yes. A pandemic. Promises to be a really chill time.'

We laughed, but it was a harsh, frightened sound, and we fell silent as we passed Stan, his sleeping form sprawled on the front desk of the Porters' Lodge.

We stayed up talking, watching as the dark eye of the night contracted little by little, giving way to a bloodshot white as the sun came up. Finally the taxi arrived. Ji-woo and I struggled with her bags, dragging them behind us on the gravel like a pair of disobedient dogs. I lifted them into the back of the cab, and she threw her arms around me.

'I'm going to miss you so much, Anna,' she said, her breath loud in my ear, her voice a little hoarse. 'You're such a cool person. You're the best. Please be careful, don't get sick.'

I nodded, unable to speak.

'I'm too tired to cry right now, but I'm crying too, on the inside.'

I dried my eyes in her hair. 'We'll see each other soon.'

I spent the rest of the morning packing up my own room, numb with a kind of grief, though I wasn't entirely sure what I was mourning yet, wasn't able to feel around the edges of the loss. Mango Bango Jambo Banana, my lab notebooks, my yellow seersucker jacket and sports stuff and underwear. It took far less time than Ji-woo's room. The only thing I was missing was my diamond earrings, but I didn't have the heart to ask Vicky to return them. The room seemed to shrink around me as I emptied it of its contents, until I felt like I was sitting in a doll's house version of my room, already compressed to fit into my memory. At midday, Caden arrived in Kieran's car to help me move out.

I closed the door to Florence House. At the time, I was too preoccupied with immediate questions – what would happen to my grant money, whether I should sit Caden down for a stern talk about his omnipresent ex – to think about the significance of closing that door. I failed to fathom all the other doors slamming in its wake, and didn't notice that I was now standing in a dim corridor that would narrow more and more the further I advanced. I was like an anglerfish swimming through the blackness, guided only by its own light, with no inkling of what lay beyond.

# PART II

PART II.

# I

# Summer Camp

*0£/1br/CB4 1UX*
*ROOM FOR RIGHT WOMAN*
*I can help you out with a warm bed and house to sleep*
*in. I am a smaller white male in weight. Other places I*
*am bigger than normal! You can just play with it if you*
*want.*

I T WAS A WEEK into lockdown, and Vicky was spending a lot of time on SpareRoom.co.uk. She was one of the last students left in Newnham and was desperate to move out. The porters, she said, were being Covid Nazis. They didn't allow her to invite any guests into the college, and they waved her away whenever she tried to approach them.

*I haven't touched anyone for a week*, she texted me. *Can I come over? Or lend me Caden for an hour? I just need someone to lie on top of me. He can keep his clothes on.*

The issue was that private accommodation in Cambridge cost nearly double what we paid in Newnham. Mostly, the 'affordable' housing options she did find involved full-time care for a person with dementia in exchange for marginally reduced rent. In comparison to this, the option to 'just play with it' didn't seem too onerous to us. My phone pinged again, with a screenshot to:

> 0£/3br/Newmarket
> *WANTING TO SHARE A LIFE*
> *I am a very respectful male mid 30s. I have a small house looking for a woman that would like a good life with a good man . . . must be skinny and non toxic.*

*I guess you are skinny!* I texted back, shaking with laughter. *And technically non-toxic, at least from a chemistry perspective.*

Apart from texting Vicky, I was in regular contact with Charles, who was at home with his family in Wiltshire and having a 'rather stressful time'.

*My brother just told me off for swallowing too loudly*, he texted. *Apparently I have a stress-inducing swallow.*

I sent him pictures of Pringle to cheer him up.

*WHOSE CAT?* he texted.

*Local neighbourhood kitty!* I replied. I had not told him about Caden, nor about having moved out of Newnham.

*More pictures! ASAP!*

I obliged, though it wasn't easy to take good pictures of Pringle, because we did not get along.

I can't deny that she was a beautiful animal – her green eyes looked like sentient opals, and she had a powerful, mellifluous meow – but it was difficult for me to feel affection for her. She walked all over the kitchen counters, leaving gritty paw-prints behind. She harassed the birds in the garden. She licked herself constantly; loud, creamy licks that left her wet to the touch. I felt sick every time she wretched and gagged. She didn't let me stroke her.

'It's not personal,' Caden said. 'She's just not used to you.'

Despite my problems with Pringle, my living situation

was far better than either Charles's or Vicky's. Those first few weeks at his house were like an X-rated summer camp. We stayed up late fooling around and woke at midday.

I made maple syrup-glazed bacon sandwiches for breakfast, while Caden mixed us Bloody Marys. We'd toddle out barefoot into the garden, blinking in the unseasonable April sunshine. The next-door neighbour – an older woman with a flamboyant purple perm – would be out in the garden talking to Pringle over the hedge.

'Who's a lovely girl?' she'd say. 'Here, kitty kitty kitty.'

Then there were all kinds of loosely scheduled activities: sunbathing, bonfire building, river walks. We took turns going for provisions and bought picnic food, marshmallows, Magnum bars – except on Fridays, when we went to get fish and chips from the van outside the working men's club, keeping a safe distance from the grandpas in the queue. Caden often went running along the river and did some kind of workout every day: sit-ups, push-ups, weights, all to the tune of various national anthems. He called it his 'motivational' playlist.

'But this is ridiculous,' I said, the first time I walked in on him doing sit-ups to the tune of 'La Marseillaise'.

'It's MOTIVATING!' he panted.

*Aux armes, citoyens, Formez vos bataillons, Marchons, marchons!*

'You're crazy.'

At night, Caden mixed cocktails, the ice crackling and spitting like fat in the vodka orange.

I remember that first month of lockdown better than I remember any other phase in my life. Perhaps it was the eerie contrast between the gorgeous weather and the near-constant wail of ambulances. I kept thinking of the people who couldn't breathe, who were choking to death on the air of spring, beneath the bluest of skies. I dreamt often about drowning. I know that fear sharpens memory. I'm not sure if love does the same. Perhaps love only makes things seem more beautiful.

Spring in Cambridge. The grass full of egg yolk-yellow buttercups, so delicious-looking that I wanted to eat them. The leaves of the chestnut trees interspersed with cones of popcorn-shaped blossoms that gave off a strong, salt-sweet scent that reminded me of sex. And the daffodils running from Baits Bite Lock to Green Dragon Bridge, like a golden seam along the riverbank.

I had some difficulties adapting to my new life of leisure. I found it hard to relax. I read all the papers I had not had time to read during term. Then I went through my lab notes, and rewrote a draft of a paper I had finished in February. But after this there was nothing to occupy my mind. My sole obligation was to go into the lab twice a week to feed the mice and play with the guinea-pigs. Crabwell was worried that they would become depressed from a lack of interaction, so had organized a rota for those of us still in Cambridge to care for them.

This was the only time I had apart from Caden, and while the old Anna might have used it to analyse what was happening, to try to get some perspective on it all, the keen, scalpel quality of my mind had dulled considerably. I was languorous, sleepy, intoxicated by alcohol and sex – even when I went into the lab, cleaned out the cages, cut up the guinea-pigs' food. They blinked at me curiously in my voluptuous stupor, as if I were a total cretin. They were not happy. They were fighting. I often found gouge marks on their little bodies.

*It's because they're bored*, Crabwell had replied to my concerned email. *Make sure your games are really stimulating.*

It occurred to me that it was an odd thing to spend so much time playing with creatures I was destined to kill, but I didn't indulge in such facile philosophizing. I got on with it.

Caden would often come to walk me home from the lab. Once he arrived with a flask of G&T, and I had to laugh. It wasn't even noon yet, far too early for alcohol, but we'd been cut loose from such stringencies. We might die. We might as well enjoy ourselves. I took an icy gulp.

'I don't know how you do it,' he said, as we made our way towards the river. 'I couldn't.'

'Couldn't do what?' I shielded my eyes from the sunlight.

'Deal with it. Animals in cages. Killing them. All that.'

He took my bike from me and handed me the flask. Then, as an afterthought, he fumbled in his shirt pocket and handed me a pair of red cat's-eye sunglasses.

'Where are these from?'

I had recognized them immediately as the same pair she had been wearing in the photo, but I wanted to see if he would lie.

'They were my ex's.'

I nodded, glad my eyes were obscured by the dark lenses. The river path narrowed and I walked behind him, my eyes fixed on the back of the bike, watching the chain loop through the groove of the pulley over and over again, a snake swallowing its own tail into infinity. I shouldn't be annoyed, I told myself. I'd asked him a simple question and he'd given me an honest answer. And I needed sunglasses.

'Can't you rescue one of them, Anna?'

'What? A mouse? A guinea-pig?'

'Yeah.'

'Definitely not.'

'But I mean, isn't it horrible?' he said, manoeuvring the bike to the side to let a couple of bare-chested runners pass. 'It's so cruel.'

The flask was freezing in my hand. I didn't engage with Caden. His reasoning was so poor, so hypocritical – he ate animals; he took medicine. I knew I would win the argument, but I was worried that in the course of the discussion he would reveal himself to be less intelligent than I needed him to be. It was clear to me by then that he was not my intellectual equal – but I needed to think he was smart. So I went out of my way to protect that illusion, or non-illusion, about him. And the funny thing is, I never figured out what lay on the other side of that immaculate surface, whether it concealed an inner world of whirring activity or an empty tumbleweed town. I didn't want to know.

We sat on a bench in a nook between two weeping willows, not too far from the Green Dragon pub. He was frowning; preoccupied, I thought, by our conversation about dissection. I tried to think of something else to talk about, but he spoke first.

'Last time I sat on this bench,' Caden said, 'I was with my ex.'

I remained silent.

'This old guy came up to us. He seemed harmless, just a bit pissed. He asked how long we'd been together, about her accent and where she was from.' Caden was staring at the space between his legs as if looking for an escape route from the memory. 'And then he got weird. Starts saying, like, "You are so gorgeous. Such an amazing figure. You could be an actress." After he'd gone, she laid into me. Like, I wasn't man enough to protect her when someone came on to her right in front of me.'

I remained silent. For a few minutes we passed the thermos back and forth like divers sharing a scuba tank; to me, at least, each sip was as necessary as oxygen. *At least he's confiding in me*, I thought. *Isn't that a good thing in a relationship?* Caden never opened up emotionally. I couldn't shut him down the one time he did.

A sound tore through the silence as a group of aeroplanes in diamond formation shot across the sky.

'F-35 fighters,' he said. 'But don't worry, they're on our side. There's an RAF base near Newmarket.'

I shivered and took a sip of my drink. It tasted soapy from too much gin.

'I've never told you her name, have I?'

'No,' I said. He had only ever referred to her as his 'ex', as if she were entirely defined by that function. And this just inflamed my curiosity; like X marks the spot on the pirates' treasure map, it made me want to dig it up, find out what lay beneath.

'Don't you want to know?' A curious smile played on his lips, hovering somewhere between spite and amusement.

I thought about his name and how I savoured it, how it seemed like a special secret code word. Caden. Even saying it aloud felt intimate. I felt the trap of his question constrict around my throat. If I said no he would think I was jealous of her, and if I said yes I would be admitting I was curious.

'Sure,' I answered, trying to sound casual. 'Tell me her name.'

'Giselle. Her name is Giselle.'

After that, it was as if the genie was truly out of the lamp. I thought about her every day. I tried to find her on Google, Instagram, Facebook. But there was nothing under the name 'Giselle', even when I typed 'Giselle PSG football'. Caden and I were not friends on Facebook, nor Instagram. He had declined the requests I'd sent him a few weeks earlier.

'It's nothing sketchy,' he had said, which made me sure

it absolutely was sketchy. 'I just feel like social media really messed things up in my last relationship. All that performative stuff – posting pictures of each other, relationship updates. I feel uncomfortable with that.'

So I couldn't rely on the internet, only on what Caden told me about her. And while he did not talk about her openly too often, it felt like he was making constant veiled references. I found myself dissecting everything he said, placing his pronouncements under a microscope. I became an expert at subtext:

'Your shoulders are so broad. Like a rugby player's.'

*Subtext: My ex was so much more feminine.*

'You are so easily startled.'

*Subtext: My ex was much tougher than you are.*

'You seem tired. Want a break?'

*Subtext: You suck at this position. My ex was a rodeo champion compared to you.*

It wasn't only what he said; the physical vestiges of her existence were everywhere. Everything in his house – the bottle of ibuprofen (bad periods?), bobby pins (up-styled hair?), fake nails (how the hell did they stay on?), carved wooden chopsticks in the drawer (Sushi? Thai food?) – became a clue to help me solve the mystery, a hieroglyph from the lost world of their relationship. Before the cat's-eye sunglasses, Caden had given me a spare set of keys, which came with a silver keychain embossed with the words 'Rise and Shine' that I suspected belonged to her. And there was the pile of plastic boxes in the spare room that I did not dare examine more closely. At times there was something creepy about her absence, as if she was missing from her rightful place, like the New York skyline without the Twin Towers.

I would have liked to have been able to assuage my curiosity by asking Caden direct questions, but I was too much of a coward. I felt the trope of the jealous girlfriend hanging over me like a cloud of black flies. I would not make another woman into the enemy or a threat to my happiness.

Plus, Caden was unapproachable. There was something icy about him that prevented me from asking him anything. I'd often turn to him to find that his face had gone blank, his eyes unfocused, as if he were pondering something abstract and mysterious deep within. I liked that look, strangely enough. I liked the enigma of the man. It excited me.

But my resolve not to question him did occasionally break down.

One Friday we went to the fish-and-chips van, as usual. We stood in the queue that went all the way past Tesco, snaking round cars that had been illegally parked on the pavement.

'This is hell,' I said.

It was early evening, but it was implausibly hot. The scattering of clouds in the sky seemed to make things worse; they were like big, white fingers choking the heat out of the sun.

'Go home. Or go over there.' Caden pointed to an imperfect patch of shade on the opposite side of the street. But I waited beside him, holding his hand despite the heat. We were a good distance from the others in the queue, but our bodies cast long thin shadows which almost overlapped with the people in front of us, and that was enough to make me nervous. At last, we got to the front of the line.

'Cod or plaice?'

'Two cod, please.'

The man reached down and dropped a mesh basket of chips into crackling oil, snapped up two squares of fish with metal tongs. There was a scream of brakes, and a car rode up on to the pavement, dangerously close to the queue.

'Oi! We're standing here!'

Caden had been sorting through his wallet, but now he looked over his shoulder. He frowned. The man who had shouted – a tall redhead in a Cambridge United shirt – leant into the open window of the driver's side. Was there going to be a fight?

'Peas?'

'For me, yes,' I managed, though my heart was pounding in my chest. The memory of the crash jolted through me. I waited for Caden to give his order, but he stayed silent. He dragged his hand across his chest slowly, his eyes moving over the car. The Cambridge United guy straightened up, looking mollified. The driver of the car had apologized or managed to talk him down. The passenger door opened a fraction. Caden was watching, unnaturally still. And then the door slammed shut again. The car reversed off the pavement, and drove away.

'Peas, mate?'

But Caden was off already, his hands thrust into the pockets of his shorts.

'Caden?'

He didn't turn back. The fish-and-chips man was staring at me, holding up the two paper bundles.

'Vinegar?'

I grabbed the cut-glass bottle and shook its muzzle into each bag in turn, then fumbled in my pocket for money.

I didn't catch up with him until we were almost home. He stopped when he saw me struggling with the food, and reached over to help me.

'What's wrong?' I said.

'Nothing. Sick of the sun.'

I followed him into the kitchen. Wordlessly he began mixing himself a drink. But he did so in such an overt,

164

melodramatic way – slamming the ice tray on the counter, emptying half the bottle of gin into his glass – that it felt like an invitation for me to probe further.

'What is it? Who was that guy in the car?'

'Nobody.'

I reached into the paper bag and broke off a steaming chunk of fish. Its skin stuck to my fingers, my palate. He stood there at the kitchen counter, staring into nothingness. And then something occurred to me. A sinking feeling in my chest. I licked my fingers clean.

'Has this got something to do with your ex, Caden? Was she in the car?'

He didn't answer. We listened to the tonic bubbling in the glass as he poured it.

'Come on. Tell me. Is she still in Cambridge?'

He shot me a still, black glance. Then he took a long pull at his drink.

'Caden. Just tell me! What's wrong? I know you saw something. Please just say it.'

He put his drink down, closed his eyes.

'No offence,' he said, rubbing his eyes with his thumb and forefinger, 'but you really have this side to you that's difficult for me to handle. This' – he hesitated – 'nosiness. I need space. Don't harass me about my private business.'

The smell of vinegar was overwhelming in the hot little room. We stood there in silence. I opened the kitchen door, my gaze lowered. I couldn't speak. The cold equivalence in his voice, the complete lack of emotion, hurt me more than if it had been a burst of ill-temper.

Pringle came in then, carrying something in her mouth.

'God.'

Long, bloody cords dangled from her mouth. She sat and chewed, her tail curling limply behind her. The entrails made a wet rustling noise.

'Jesus fucking Christ!'

Then, quite abruptly, as if embarrassed by the attention, she dropped her prize and trotted past us into the front room.

We both stared at it for a moment. A curiously white coil, weeping blood on to the tiles.

'Well,' Caden said, picking up his drink and following Pringle into the front room. 'I'll leave you to deal with it. You're used to mutilating animals.'

## 2

# Bonfire

Don't think too badly of Caden. Truly, in those early spring weeks I spent at his house, I was mostly honeymoon happy, the evil eye of the ex dimmed in the red grin of the bonfires and the day-long drunkenness.

He took care of me. He massaged my still-tender wrist. He comforted me when I woke up with phantom-coronavirus symptoms.

'It's normal to have a dry throat in the morning.'

'But what if I do have it? What if I infect you, and you die?'

'Anna.' He took my hand, rested his forehead against mine. Big brown fawn eyes. 'We'll deal with everything that happens as it happens. I'm not irresponsible, but I'm not worried, OK? Neither of us is going to die of Covid.'

Despite his assurances, I sensed that he was anxious too. Before lockdown, he had been the kind of person who could command his body, even my body, to fall asleep whenever he wished. The minute he nodded off, I nodded off too, almost as if there was a switch within me that turned off with him. But since I'd moved in, he had been suffering from insomnia. He tossed and turned, and sometimes he had bad dreams; I'd hear him moaning in his sleep. I'd wake him then, and he would get up and pace the room while I watched, desperate to know what the dream had been about but certain he'd never tell me.

Mostly, though, he was in a good mood. He was funnier than I had thought at first. He set up a rotating fan in the sitting room and would shout, 'YEAH BABY!' whenever the breeze came his way. He'd fall at my feet to make me laugh, smear toothpaste or shaving-cream all over his chin and look at me with a deadpan expression: 'What you looking at?'

He was always checking that I was OK, bringing me coffee in bed, cocktails in bed. He'd carry my backpack, my keys, anything I had on me. I was surprised by how much I loved the way Caden behaved. It was as if I had been secretly craving this attention my whole life: with him I felt precious, delicate, like I needed to be handled with care.

It was true that Caden didn't really 'get' me, really understand who I was and how I thought. Or maybe it was only that he didn't notice the parts of me that I believed mattered: my intelligence, my empathy, the intellectual 'intensity'. He didn't want me for my brain; he wanted me because I was a *girl*: for my body, my long hair, my cooking. For the first time, I relished my femininity, felt it was real.

Most of the remarks about his ex were made in a context where I was failing as a representative of my sex; bitten unpolished nails, unkempt hair, un-made-up face. But little by little I was changing those things. I wore his ex's sunglasses, used her shampoos, her sparkly body lotion, and even her hair straighteners. I found the mechanics of hair-straightening puzzling, and I developed a newfound respect for people who did that sort of thing every day. I watched online tutorials to improve my technique, and my hair became sleek and obedient. It felt like a relief to finally do what was expected of me. I was almost grateful to Caden. He had gone some way towards making me into a real woman, taught me things my mother never had. He'd shown me how to appeal to a man, to go full object.

And don't forget that Caden was a beautiful man. It seemed outrageous that I was allowed to run my hand along the angular slant of his hip to play with his hair. To kiss his ear, stroke his back. Sometimes it was too much. I had to cover my eyes or turn away from him because his beauty exhausted me, and it felt like something I ought not to be experiencing, that I would have to pay a price for all this pretty soon.

In bed he would often look at me with such a serious expression that I would smile. He would smile back. Then he would kiss my neck, take my fingers between his teeth, one digit at a time until I couldn't smile any more. I would open my eyes to find him watching me, monitoring my progress, and if he felt I was getting too close, he would move away, reach over for a glass of water on the bedside table.

'Drink,' he would say. And I would do as he asked, and he'd shake his head. 'You should see yourself now. You're so beautiful. You should see it.'

There was no seeking assurance of whether this felt good or that felt good, no drawn-out post-mortem of how things had gone. Which was probably why it was so much better than sleeping with Jamie. We had discussed everything, and in doing so had banished the mystique, the dark matter, that was at the centre of mine and Caden's relationship. Our differences, the seemingly unbridgeable distance between us, was what made me so attracted to him; because every time I touched him, every time we went to bed, I felt like I was walking across a tightrope, a

dangerous narrow crossing, the slenderest support imaginable. Yet we managed it. We found each other.

I thought our sex life was practically perfect.

Caden was funny about my research. And when I say
funny, I mean that it revolted him. I had explained to him
many times why I was doing it, and its potential impact,
and all the ethical rules we followed – compared to the
meat industry, for example – but he didn't care. He was
always going on about how cruel it was, how awful he
found the thought of me doing something so violent, so
routinely. One day he actually hid my bike key so that I
wouldn't be able to go to the lab.

'Give it back,' I said. 'I'm going to feed them. Not to
euthanize them.'

He was intent on something on his laptop and he didn't
look up.

'Don't know what you mean,' he said, but I knew he
was lying.

In the end, I was forced to walk all the way there. I was
finding it increasingly depressing going into the lab. It was
always deserted – the care schedule had been deliberately
set up to keep us all apart – and apart from the hum of the
fridges, it was quiet. Everything was exactly as we'd left it:
Charles's beautiful fountain pens and sharpened pencils
lying in 3x2 phalanxes like marching squadrons of Roman
soldiers; Rosa's dizzyingly long to-do list sellotaped to her
desk. I examined these things as one might look at the
ruins of Pompeii. I looked at my workstation, stared at
my notes. I couldn't even remember the experiments I'd
been running. I missed using my brain, my interactions
with Charles and Leonid, even Rosa.

I went to the fridge, prepped the guinea-pigs' food. I
enjoyed watching them eat, how they chewed cucumber
sticks in the corner of their mouths, as if they were long

green cigars, and rubbed their noses against me when I fed them grapes, licking my hands with their tiny pebble-smooth tongues. There was a small ginger one who was especially friendly, vibrating with a happy purr when I stroked him. I dreaded having to resume dissections when the lab eventually reopened.

I speed-walked home, irritated that Caden had made me lose the whole morning.

'Caden?' I called, when I didn't find him where I'd left him in the front room.

He was not in the front room, the kitchen or the bathroom. I went upstairs to change out of my lab clothes, when I heard what sounded like a sob coming from the bedroom. I felt a pang. It was horrible to hear him sounding so upset. The door wasn't completely shut, and I pushed it open.

He was in bed, his legs under the covers, his laptop propped on his knees. I heard another moan and saw the frantic movement of his arm beneath the sheet, and too late, I understood. Too late, I tried to back out of the room, but he saw me. He looked furious.

'Christ,' he said, as he snapped the laptop shut. 'Why don't you fucking knock?' He fumbled with something under the blankets with one hand, and with the other, he yanked a red lanyard attached to a memory stick out of the laptop.

I went out on to the landing, gripped the banister. He came out wearing only his boxer shorts. When he saw me standing there, he put his head in his hands.

'Don't worry, don't worry,' I said, mortified, the colour rushing into my cheeks. 'I'm sorry I burst in like that.'

He walked past, his eyes avoiding me, and went downstairs. I heard the hot tap moan into action as he turned on the shower.

As soon as he'd gone, I opened the laptop. But the

screen was locked. I pulled the duvet off the bed and scrambled around the mess of clothes on the floor, looking for the red lanyard, but it wasn't there. He must have hidden it.

I made the bed that he'd mussed up, playing the scene in my head again. I was shocked to find out he was looking at porn. Which seemed perhaps naive, but there was something so archaic and beautiful about Caden, I just couldn't imagine him watching women getting rammed by huge veiny men. I couldn't picture him getting off on that kind of thing. And yes, I was aware that most men watch it, plenty of women. Probably you do too. But I never had. I looked down on people for finding pleasure in something so violent and degrading. So what if the women got paid; money does not make it moral. Shame on them. Shame on you.

That night, I got Caden drunk. I did this quite deliberately. I planned to ask him what he had been watching on the memory stick, and thought he was more likely to be honest with me if he was drunk. I didn't feel too guilty. I decided it was my role to get him to talk. To act like his subconscious; make him deal with things he didn't want to, make him face the subterranean dimensions of his life. He was often drunk anyway.

We both had wine with dinner, and I kept refilling his glass. I made us vodka cocktails, though my own glass contained nothing but water and the tiniest splash of crème de cassis. I watched the alcohol take hold of him and monitored the progress of his inebriation. He kept grabbing at me, kissing me, playing with my hair, beaming down at me with a glowing, warm affection that he exhibited only rarely when sober.

'You're lovely,' he slurred, as we made a plait of newspaper for the bonfire we were building in the garden. I quietly moved his drink out of his reach. I wanted him to be drunk enough to talk, but not so drunk that I wouldn't be able to trust what he told me. I went to fetch the matches, but he insisted on lighting the fire himself.

'Don't want you to get burnt,' he said, striking the match against his jeans, looking like a cowboy with the dark stubble on his face, his narrowed eyes, holding the flame aloft with a surprisingly steady hand. The fire roared. We sat on two garden chairs, my feet perched in his lap, his bare soles only inches from the fire. The Specials on the speaker. It was a clear night, I remember. Stars looming low, the air puckering all around us.

'Bats,' he mumbled. 'Watch they don't get tangled up in your hair.'

'Caden,' I said in a decisive voice, but then hesitated. How could I refer to the incident without embarrassing him? I didn't want to use the word 'masturbate', nor the word 'porn'. It had taken all afternoon for him to talk to me again. Before I could formulate the question, he grabbed his half-finished glass of Kir, took a greedy gulp.

'Too sweet,' he said, making a face. 'But you girls like sweet things.'

I didn't answer, waiting for him to elaborate.

'My dad liked sweet things,' he went on. 'He drank those flavoured beers. You know: Lambic, Desperados . . .' He broke off and turned to the fire, his eyes glassy. I felt anxious, wondering how I could redirect this towards the subject of the memory stick.

'Did I ever tell you what happened to him?' he said, lighting another match on his jeans.

'No,' I said, watching closely in case he set himself alight. 'You haven't told me anything about your family.'

'Well, he killed himself,' he said, in a matter-of-fact voice.

'I'm so sorry.' I took his hands in mine. He was still staring into the fire. 'I'm so sorry about that.'

He went on, ignoring me. 'I was already at uni. My mum couldn't bring herself to tell me, so she got my old football coach to call me up.' He gave a wan smile, shook his head. 'I thought he wanted to catch up. I was so happy when I saw it was his number.'

For a while we sat there, mute. The music switched over to Caden's national anthems motivational playlist. 'God Save the Queen'. I went to turn it off.

'You love it, don't you?' he said, when I came back from the kitchen. 'You love it when I tell you this kind of stuff.'

'No, I don't,' I said, shocked by the venom is his voice. 'I'm really sad for you.'

'Yeah. But you're happy I told you. You're always trying to dig stuff out of me. Asking me about my family. My ex, too.'

I didn't answer, though I thought he was exaggerating. I barely dared ask anything. 'You love that I just told you that,' he went on. 'You'll think how it's a good thing *he's finally talking about his feelings*.' This last bit he said in a cruel falsetto.

'I'm trying to get to know you, Caden. Not force you into anything.'

He went to add another log to the fire. And as he leant forward to stoke the flames, his face shone. He was crying.

# 3

# Spare Room

I SHOULD HAVE DRAWN him out of himself. I should have forced him to talk. Though in all honesty, I think Caden would never have unburdened himself to me, even if I had begged him; even if I had resorted to MI6 methods of interrogation, tied him down and broken each of his fingers, one by one. But I wish I had tried a bit harder, if only to sit a little easier with my bad conscience. That period of early lockdown was a missed opportunity, because at the end of May, Caden's physiotherapy practice reopened and our summer camp came to an end.

Now the time between Caden's departure for work and his return in the evening seemed to dilate into infinity. I felt lonelier than an astronaut cut off from his ship, traversing cold indifferent space, a dead emptiness with no landmarks to indicate how far I'd travelled, how much longer I'd need to go on. The days were recurrent, endless. My fears – about the lack of progress in my PhD, the possibility of catching Covid, the contents of Caden's memory stick – resurfaced the moment the door slammed behind him.

I took my lab notes out again; I reread the last few editions of *Reproductive Physiology* and *Human Reproduction*. I emailed Crabwell, hoping he would be able to tell me what I should work on. But I only got an automated answer in response. He was busy and not checking his emails regularly, it said. Call his cell in an emergency. But he had never given us his personal mobile number, and his departmental telephone rang and rang with no answer.

There were no further objectives, nothing to work towards. I was stuck in the present, and it was agony.

So I decided to keep myself busy by giving Caden's house a makeover.

I started in the garden, a long, narrow corridor of lawn leading to empty flowerbeds along the far wall. The old lady next door spent a lot of time outside, playing with the cat or tending to her garden, her purple hair standing out like a giant hibiscus flower. Caden was kind to her; he sometimes mowed the lawn for her, and always knocked when we were going shopping to see if she needed anything.

I smiled whenever I saw her, but I tended to keep my headphones on, and pretended not to hear when she spoke to me as she seemed pretty confused. She appeared not to have taken to me, rather like Pringle, and asked me probing questions.

'Who are you?' she'd ask, frowning, as if I were something unpleasant the cat had dragged in.

'I'm Anna. Your neighbour's girlfriend.'

'Are you foreign?'

'No,' I said, taken aback. 'I'm from Dorset.' *You fucking nutcase*, I thought.

'Didn't he say you were foreign?'

I smiled vaguely at her and went back to my manure.

I worked for hours in the sun. I hung bird feeders from the fence, and soon the garden bristled with robins, sturdy little things that waited for me to unearth wormy treats for them as I worked the soil. I pulled out all the weeds and crumbled clumps of dark manure until the earth was loose and loamy, dark and promising. Caden ordered bricks from a garden centre and helped me install pavers along the flowerbeds. After a few weeks of work, the garden looked better, neater. It still lacked colour, but I liked knowing that it was full of seeds, secrets that would detonate in a few months' time.

I moved on to the house. Our summer-camp antics had left an extravagant mess everywhere: forgotten cups of tea, the sour milk bobbing like cold rinds of fat; underwear abandoned on the sofa and chairs. I cleaned. I scrubbed the kitchen and bathroom tiles and threw bucketfuls of grimy water into the flowerbeds. I rubbed the sink until it shone and reflected my face, serious and concentrated, looming close like a fish rising to the surface of a pond.

As the days accumulated, and I spent many hours alone in the house, the ex's possessions started to exercise a charismatic pull on me. I knew on some level that most of the objects were ugly, mass-produced, meaningless. Part of me wanted to laugh at her trashy acrylic tastes, the naive credulity of a woman who'd buy 'Woman's Tea'. But I couldn't laugh at her. How right she was, to buy both smoothing and thickening conditioners, pantyliners for a more robust knicker, a bobby pin for a neater bun.

The objects were alarming, radioactive, but I couldn't resist them. I touched and handled her things very often. I put the tea strainer in my mouth. I kept one of the bobby pins in my back pocket. I wanted to consume and digest them. They were both a connection to her and a way for me to dominate her: I could have thrown them away or damaged them if I had wanted to – but I didn't. Not even the half-empty, leaking conditioner bottles. I scrubbed the edges of the bath but then replaced them carefully, as if they were precious ornaments on a holy altar.

Initially I had managed to keep my covert investigations in check, trimming my deviance with bona fide housework so that it might seem plausible that I had found a Victoria's Secret bra under the bed. *Caden, I'm sorry but you're careless. You leave things around and I find them by accident, like that Hello Kitty plaster, and these Hiphugger Pants, I think they're called.*

But little by little, I became bolder. When I'd cleaned every inch of the kitchen, bathroom, front room and bedroom, I turned to the spare room.

I began by reorganizing my clothes, folded them into origami piles of jumpers, socks, pants. I took out Mango Bango Jambo Banana and put him on my side of the bed. Then I looked at the plastic boxes full of his ex's belongings. I turned them over so that I could see inside, watching the shapes and textures revolve as if in the washing machine. Things resolved into identifiable objects: a shoe, a folder, a handbag. I couldn't spot the memory stick, though I was sure it was inside one of the boxes. It irritated me that they were so disorganized, and I longed to sort and rationalize their contents. But I didn't dare open them.

In the afternoon, after I finished my 'cleaning', I would blow-dry my hair, attempt to tame my frizz with her hair straighteners, and try to charm my drooping eyelids into taut lynx eyes with the flick of her pencil. I'd throw on a Beyond Meat burger and have it sizzling home-ily in the pan, pour myself a drink so that I'd be smiling wife-ily on the sofa in the front room by the time Caden came home, exhausted from my zealous espionage.

'The best thing about you,' he'd said, as I cleared away his plate, 'is that you always tidy everything up immediately after we've eaten.'

*Subtext: my ex was a slob.*

The morning after he made that comment, I called Vicky to complain about him. I confessed that I was becoming obsessed, that I'd been looking through his things when he was out of the house.

'Sounds like you should have stayed in Newnham with *moiiiii*!'

'I don't think you'd like it, Vicky. I don't do well when I'm bored. I'm going a bit crazy. I might start digging through *your* stuff.' With a pang I remembered her stealing, but she didn't seem to make the connection.

'Oh, that would be far more entertaining,' she said evenly. 'I'm way more interesting than Caden.'

'I'm not sure about that.' I told her about walking in on him, and the hidden memory stick.

'What do you think it is?'

'I'm pretty sure it's something to do with his ex.'

'The soccer player?'

'How did you know that?' I asked.

'I follow Caden on Instagram.'

That made me pause. 'Oh,' I said. 'He didn't accept my requests.' I looked up at the wall, at the blank picture frame. It seemed to be watching me like a gaping eye. The idea of spending an entire day alone in the house suddenly filled me with an odd kind of fear. 'Can you come over?'

'Too far,' she replied.

'I'll send an Uber?'

I paced around the kitchen as I waited for her, passing a wet sponge over the already immaculate surfaces, a cold, metallic taste rising in my throat. Who had added who on Instagram? It must have happened after the formal. I remembered with a sort of vertigo how beautiful she'd looked that evening. It was muggy in the house, and I felt like a caged animal, so I went to sit on the doorstep. But it was just as hot outside. I was still stuck indoors, stuck in the hot cell of my mind. *My brain is becoming this house*, I thought. *I need to get out.*

I watched the app for Vicky's Uber on my phone, tracking the car on its journey towards me, until I saw the real thing pull up. She made a running jump into my arms.

'We're alive!'

I had wanted us to remain socially distant, had planned not to touch her, but I clasped her to me and we stood like that for a while, her legs wrapped around my back, and I had to dry my tears in her hair, her neck.

She smelled of prawn crackers, as if she hadn't been showering. Her face was oddly puffy; from unhealthy food or too much alcohol, I couldn't tell. It had been nine weeks since I'd seen her, and she must have been lonely in Newnham. I reproached myself for not having invited her over sooner, though it would have been illegal to do so. I had always been a wimpy rule-follower.

'Caden is so neat!' she said, as I led her through the front room. 'But he has that control-freak vibe.'

'Don't give him the credit! I cleaned up!'

I poured us two Kirs and we sat in the garden, frowning against the relentlessly blue sky. She kicked off her shoes and wiggled her green-painted toes in the grass. Pringle popped up from under the neighbour's fence and jumped into her lap. She recoiled.

'Is this his cat?'

'No, it's a neighbourhood cat. But he looks after her. She's here all the time. Come here, Pringle.'

The cat ignored me, blinking on Vicky's lap. She took a sip of her drink. 'So, how've you been? Have you given yourself a haircut? It looks weird.'

'I've been trying to straighten it.'

'I like it more when it's curly. The eyeliner looks great though.' She picked at the ends of her own hair, inspecting them critically. 'So, what made you finally agree to break the rules, Little Miss Perfect?'

I sensed the reproach in her question, and I felt a childish kind of shame.

'I'm sorry. I'm just scared of getting sick. Or getting into trouble.'

'I didn't mean it like that,' she corrected herself hastily. 'I'm just wondering, are you OK? You don't look super happy. Is it Caden? Are you guys fighting?'

'No, it's not that. I don't know. He's still in love with his ex.'

'Giselle, you mean?'

I nodded. Hearing her name spoken out loud filled me with contraband excitement. It had been ringing against my skull for days. I wanted to hush Vicky, and to incite her into saying it again.

'How do you know her name?'

'His Instagram.'

'Can you show me?'

'No,' she said. She lifted the cat off her lap, plucked the hairs from her skirt and let them float away on the wind.

'Why?'

'Because I love you. And I don't want you to suffer.'

'But I'm already suffering.'

'In which case you should dump him.'

'I can't,' I said. 'I can't. I love him.'

There was a long silence. The sun was tilting slowly westwards, and the fire-pit and the chairs and our glasses threw slanted shadows that were still and sharp beside our blurry silhouettes.

'And I've already seen her,' I said. 'I found a picture. I know what she looks like.'

She glanced up at me. Her expression did not change. 'You are beautiful. You have nothing to worry about.'

I knew she was being disingenuous. Good friends generally are. They'd never offer you a true reflection, a true mirror. Perhaps that was what his ex gave me: a clear mirror, free from distortion. *This is who I am. This is who you are.*

'Caden's dating you,' she went on, recrossing her legs, squinting her eyes against the sun. 'Obviously he finds you attractive.'

'Men are dogs. They want meat. They don't care what kind.'

'Are you saying you're a low-grade sausage?' she said, trying to make me laugh.

'Please show me. Please.'

The sunshine was in her face, illuminating her eyes, which were cool and blue and empty.

'It's the past, Anna. She's his ex. Let sleeping dogs lie.'

'But it isn't. She isn't in the past.'

I told her how he had compared me to her, toyed with me when revealing her name. I told her about the photo I'd found, my suspicions about the memory stick, and about the stack of her possessions in the spare room.

'You think the memory stick is in there?'

I nodded.

She gave me a funny sideways look.

'Are you sure you can deal with the consequences of what you might find?'

'Yes,' I said. 'I want to know everything.'

'Well' – she drained the last of her drink – 'then let's do it.'

I checked the time on my phone.

'Caden will be back from work soon.'

She shrugged. 'It won't take long.'

We raced up the stairs, Vicky manhandling the banisters as if the house were a boat on high seas.

The room was a little musty. I went over to open the window while Vicky took in Caden's workout equipment: the neatly rolled mat, the pile of boxes. She didn't move, but stared at me expectantly.

'Well,' she said, 'what are you waiting for?'

I don't believe objects have spirits, but these boxes seemed to have an aura. I was like an archaeologist readying myself to unseal a pharaoh's tomb, terrified of King Tut's curse but unable to contain my curiosity.

*This is love*, I told myself. *Wanting to know someone intimately is a form of love.* I'd tried to get to know him the honest way – but he wouldn't talk. He shut my questions down. He had left me no choice.

And perhaps – I justified my actions, as I began to pull things out of the first box – perhaps Caden *wanted* me to look at her things. I sometimes had the feeling that he wished he could tell me more about her, but that he couldn't bring himself to talk about their relationship. And Caden and I had so little in common intellectually, so few shared interests. Perhaps she was like Ji-woo's Great Attractor, her invisible presence pulling us together, keeping us moving in the same direction.

I found a black drawstring jewellery pouch. *Earrings*, I thought. I unfastened the pouch, letting its contents fall into my palm.

Vicky screamed.

At least ten of them: some black, some covered in dried blood. Long roots like malformed mushrooms. Teeth. I felt hot, and something heavy rose like mercury from my stomach to my chest.

'Oh my GOD. What is it?!' she said, taking a step away from me.

'Milk teeth.'

She gave a look of such consternation that I burst out laughing. I put the teeth back into the pouch and went to wash my hands. I found myself gripping the sink and staring at my warped reflection in the chrome tap. *Grandma, what pointed teeth you have! All the better to eat you with, my child.*

When I returned, Vicky had made a start on the second box. But she was pulling things out haphazardly – more tomb raider than archaeologist. She threw a pair of football boots over her shoulder, tried on a grey Lululemon headband and left it on the floor. She held up a miniskirt against her waist and made a funny jiggle with her hips, then screamed.

'Ow!'

She lifted her bare foot. She had stood on one of the teeth. She laughed; a strange, storybook villain *muahahaha* so comical that we burst out laughing all over again. We dropped to our knees, she grabbed my arm, our eyes bored into each other, and we shook until we were crying.

'So fucking weird, dude.'

I looked closer at the whitish nub. A child's tooth. What a strange thing for her to leave behind; what a bizarre thing for him to hold on to.

Still wiping her tears, she tried to wriggle into the miniskirt. 'Too small for me,' she said, leaving the skirt half undone. She opened the third box; this one contained a large, suede chocolate-brown handbag. She unzipped it and pulled out a dark purple square.

'Oh my GOD, Anna, it's a *passport*!'

I tore it from her hands and flicked through it to the photo page.

Camille Giselle Chayette. 30 January 1995.

'Vicky.' I grabbed her arm. 'Why would she have left her *passport* behind? Do you think he's *done* something to her?'

'It's expired.' She pointed to the date. 'I don't think he murdered her, if that's what you mean.'

'Oh.'

'Don't look so disappointed.'

I looked at the photo. Lovely little quirk in her upper lip. A sly expression in the mouth. Like she was laughing at something.

'So that's why I haven't found any stuff about her online,' I said. 'She goes by her middle name.'

'She's an idiot. Camille's much better. Giselle's kind of a stripper name,' Vicky replied. She dug further into the bag, pulled out a jewellery case. She opened it, and from her face I knew what it was.

'A ring?'

She turned it towards me.

I took it from her. The cold glitter of diamonds. I swallowed, plucked it out of its casing, weighed it in my hand.

'Do you think it's real?' she said, unable to keep the awe out of her voice.

'I think so,' I said.

I took a photo and sent it to my brother. He'd be able to tell me.

'So I guess they were engaged at some point,' I wondered out loud.

She snapped the case shut, dropped it into the bag. 'What happened between them?'

'She did something to him,' I said, 'but I don't know what. Something awful.' I sat on the floor, watched her trawl through the last box. The shock was replaced by a quiet but absolute despair. They had been engaged to be married. What was he doing with me?

I imagined how he would have looked. Solemn expression. Down on one knee, probably. He wasn't a cliché sort of man, but he would have made the gesture. His face upturned. *Will you?*

My phone chirped, and I felt a wave of panic. I had completely forgotten the time.

'Caden's on his way home,' I said, getting to my feet. 'We need to put all this stuff back.'

'Why don't we just confront him?' she said, still digging. 'We could be wearing her clothes when he comes in. He deserves to be freaked out.'

'Vicky, please. I'm begging you.'

Struck by the urgency in my voice, she straightened up and struggled out of the skirt.

'Ow!'

The zip caught and left a puzzle-shaped mark on her thigh. I repacked the boxes as she changed, organized the contents of the brown suede bag.

The passport and the jewellery case were there, but the ring was missing. I unpacked the box I'd just filled, and then the second one, emptying the contents on to the floor.

'Vicky, where did you put the ring?'

She continued to massage her thigh. 'Back in the box?'

'It's empty.' I held it up to her. 'Where is it?'

'No idea, dude.'

I was perspiring, beads of sweat trickling down my face. I opened and closed the jewellery case again, hoping it would appear, that I'd be snapped out of this nightmare. I turned the suede bag inside out, ran my hands over the carpet to check it wasn't there. I was frantic now.

'Vicky,' I said, 'have you taken it?'

She was on her knees now, helping me pack up, but at the question she became quite still, and then threw me a sideways glance. 'What?'

'I know you. I know what you do! I know you took my earrings!' My voice was trembling, and I was close to tears. 'I don't care. I love you, Vicky. But please, just give this back to me.'

'I don't have it.'

I shook my head.

'You're confused,' she said. 'Confused. You need help. I think it's living here with Caden. It's making you crazy.' I recoiled, as if she'd slapped me. And that's when I heard the key in the lock and Caden appeared in the entrance, just as I dragged Vicky on to the landing and shut the door behind us.

'You girls having fun?' He smiled up at us, all long lashes and big brown eyes. As mild and clueless as one of the cows on Midsummer Common.

'Yes!' we said, in unison.

I laid the table in the garden and set about making dinner. I cut up the chicken with scissors, enjoyed the pink elastic texture beneath my fingers. I covered the chunks in buttermilk and dipped each of them in cornflour mixed with cayenne pepper, before dropping them in the pan. Then I sliced onions for frying. I watched them from the kitchen window. At first Caden and Vicky circled each other in the garden like wary dogs, but after a while they both relaxed. He was teaching her how to pass a football, pointing to the part of the foot she ought to use.

'Aim your standing leg in the direction you want the ball to go. That's right! You're a natural.'

He ran after all her wonky passes. I strained to hear what they were talking about. She kept laughing, and I saw him checking her out surreptitiously. Men notice attractive women; that's only normal, isn't it? I thought about what my mother always said about my dad: the arc of his gaze was like a rainbow, with a beautiful woman at its end. The rings of wood on the chopping board looked like tiny eyes, gaping mouths. I shifted my gaze and the patterns disappeared.

I turned the pieces of chicken as they browned, the oil spitting at my fingers. I took the blisters as punishment deserved. Caden would surely realize that somebody had been into the boxes, and that the ring was missing. It would be the end of mine and Vicky's friendship. She was my only friend left in Cambridge, and I would be even more alone.

'The thing with the mice though,' he said. They were passing the ball back and forth, closer to the house now. 'I could never do that. Like, I'm not a total wuss.' He lunged for the ball. 'Lock your ankle when you pass. That's right. I'm not a total wuss, but decapitating live animals . . .'

I ran into the bathroom and let myself sob for a few minutes, running the taps so I wouldn't be overheard.

They were standing in the kitchen when I came out. Vicky was snatching up tiny pieces of chicken from the pan, wincing at the heat, while Caden was rummaging in the fridge. He stopped when he saw my expression.

'You OK?' he said.

I wiped my face with the back of my hand. 'Yeah.' I tried to smile. 'It's nothing. Cutting onions.'

Caden laid the table while I mixed a vinaigrette for the salad then placed the chicken on a paper towel, trying to ignore the blisters on my fingers. I gave Vicky the choicest pieces; a fried peace dove which she seemed to accept, as she hugged me with what seemed like real warmth after we'd finished, and I'd scooped her a bowl of ice cream and covered it with some of his ex's hundreds-and-thousands.

'You're lucky,' she said, pointing her spoon at Caden. 'I hope you deserve this.'

A little while later, he called her an Uber home, insisting that he was happy to pay. After she left, we sat on the sofa. Caden seemed pleased with me, and gave me long tender kisses, cupping my chin in his hand.

'I like her,' he said. 'You know you can have whoever you want over whenever, right?'

'Thanks.'

'It's nice to get to meet your friends, Pudding.'
*Subtext: he never met his ex's friends.*

'YEAH BABY,' he shouted, as the breeze from the revolving fan hit him. 'I never met my ex's female friends.'

'Oh?'

'Yeah, I dunno why. She had trouble making friends.'
*Subtext: she was too beautiful for other women to want to be her friend.*

'Yeah. She was a really jealous person actually. Kinda crazy. Like, she was always watching me to make sure I didn't check out other women. She actually made me stop talking to all my female friends. That's what I like about you. You're not a jealous person. YEAH BABY!'

He pulled me on to the sofa, wrapped his arms around me.

I felt my breath quicken. However much I took in, I still felt like it wasn't enough air, the oxygen slipping through my lungs like a fish evading a net. Who was he, really? I didn't know a thing about him. I knew nothing of his family, his past, his plans for the future. What was it, then, that I was so attached to?

I wriggled out of his arms and crept into the bathroom. My pulse was strong, a throbbing wound. I smiled at myself in the mirror, and my mask of make-up cracked. *Not a jealous person.* My smile widened. I almost laughed.

# 4

## A Polite Understatement

T HAT SAME NIGHT I had an awful dream.
I'm leaning against a fence, watching a racetrack.
Strange, granular quality, like a home movie from the
1990s. People crowd all around me, craning their necks to
get a good view. No faces at all, only top hats, ribboned
straw boaters, fascinators perched at hazardous angles.

A country-club atmosphere; a feeling of Charles, of
Pimm's and cucumber sandwiches. A champagne-cork
*pop* startles me, and then a much louder bang. A single
racehorse gunshots out of the starting gate. Black Beauty
wearing a purple blinker hood. Sprinting in a peal of
muscle on bone and a spray of white foam, green furlongs
shrunk into milliseconds. Here she is!

A gasp from the faceless crowd; she stumbles, and at
first it looks like a glitch in the tape, like she might recover.
But she falls; something snaps and my stomach lurches.
She stays down, her legs twitching in the grass, as if trying
to finish her race. A man climbs over the gate and makes
his way towards her. 'Sad, that,' someone says. 'She had so
much promise.' I know what's coming. A shot so loud it
seems to have gone off in my ear.

I woke in a twist of sweaty sheets. I reached over to the

other side of the bed, but it was empty. Caden had already left for work. My heart was still beating in my ears.

I went down to the kitchen, flicked on the kettle, dropped two crumpets into the toaster. *God, that was horrible.* I went to the sink, scrubbed at the frying pan I'd used for the chicken the night before. The dream was like a puzzle piece handed straight from my unconscious. Butter and Marmite on one crumpet, the last of the Bonne Maman jam on the other. No prizes for guessing where that came from. Mouthful of tart sweetness; crackle of raspberry seeds between my teeth. Already the dream was fading, its meaning draining like sand through the sieve of my waking thoughts. But its dark atmosphere was still present, unpleasant as old cigarette smoke.

My phone chirped. A message from my brother: *Looks like a princess-cut diamond. Hi, by the way.*

I went outside. Last Judgement clouds, volcanic bronze billows, the shade they cast so cold and deep it felt as if they must be made of ash. The first grey day in ages, it was a relief. So, they had been engaged. I tried to laugh. What kind of people in their early twenties get *engaged*? But I was crushed. People who are in love get engaged. People who would like to spend the rest of their lives together. Obviously.

It started to rain, and I went back into the kitchen to finish my breakfast. I sat on the floor by the back door, looking out at the shivering trees. Pringle came running, her paws swimming on the pane of glass.

'Come in, little one.' She dodged my outstretched hand, and ran past me and up the stairs.

'Well, fuck you then.'

A peal of thunder, loud as the sonic boom of a fighter jet. What would happen if Caden found out the ring was missing? It must have been worth thousands. I'd have had to take the blame. I couldn't tell him it was Vicky, admit that I had let her dig through his ex's things. My spying was bad enough, but hers would be unforgivable. He might go to the police. I picked up my phone reflexively, scrolled through my contacts. Vicky had written to thank me for dinner, but her message was brief and polite. She was still upset.

'I'm lonely,' I said to the empty room. It was so obvious. Too much time on my own in that house. Too little to do, my whole mind focused on Caden and his ex.

That was the problem. All the analytic thought I should have been applying to my work had been misdirected. Like a machine gone haywire, my brain was applying scientific scrutiny to my environment, searching for hidden meanings behind Caden's most innocent pronouncements, looking for patterns, formulating endless research questions. Did he mean to upset me? Was I overacting? Was he lying? There were no limits to the hypothesis I could posit, no rules about what counted as data. It all counted. And it was driving me crazy.

I filled the cat's bowl with kibble, shook the pack to summon her. She ignored me, so I brought the bowl up to the bedroom. The pink orchids on the windowsill seemed to expand and contract with each beat of my heart. Pringle was hiding, but she came out when she saw the food.

Caden's computer was on his bed, the power light blinking at me. I flipped it open. Password protected. *Fuck.* I could see that it contained seven digits.

G-I-S-E-L-L-E, I typed.

PASSWORD INCORRECT.

L-A-M-P-A-R-D, I tried, knowing it was wrong as I typed it.

I had one more try before the computer locked.

P-R-I-N-G-L-E.

I was in.

This was not the first time I'd snooped. I had once looked at my dad's phone, when I suspected he was seeing his fancy woman again. Going through a person's devices is probably the closest you'll ever come to being inside their mind. You see what they want, what they think; even more than that, you see the structure of their thinking, the connections between things in their mind. If you break into someone's phone or computer, the curtain which usually prevents you from seeing the most intimate and mysterious parts of another person's life is lifted. It's delicious and dangerous.

I was right about the hunch I had about my dad, yet still surprised by how deeply boring the texts he sent the woman were. (*You all right?/Yes, just at supermarket./What you buying?/Stuff for our tea later.*) I'd found out the predictable stuff I had no business knowing – Pornhub, etc. – but also far more vulnerable things I felt ashamed of having read. 'Hands shaking medical cause' he'd googled. 'Symptoms of early onset Parkinson's'. Poor Dad. It was disturbing to think he was frightened of anything.

The inside of Caden's computer was far sparser, like a crime scene that had been given a thorough clean-up: fingerprints wiped, blood stains bleached away. His work files were manically well organized. He had deleted his search history, logged out of all his social media without saving his passwords. There was nothing at all. A big fat question mark.

I went into the spare room and searched again through the boxes. But I didn't find the ring, nor the memory stick. Only her clothes, her passport, a red-and-blue Paris Saint-Germain shirt, make-up. I looked her up online. Even now that I knew her first name was really Camille, my search came up with surprisingly little: no Instagram under her real name, no Facebook. Not even a LinkedIn account.

There was, however, a photo of a younger version of her playing for PSG. And *Championnat de France D1 2016–2017*: an out-of-date, incomplete Wikipedia page in French. I copied and pasted it into Google Translate.

Camille Chayette grew up in the Paris suburb of Nogent-Sur-Marne. In 2014 Chayette was scouted by FCF Juvisy football academy, and signed with first-division club Paris Saint-Germain in 2016. There, she evolved in the first team while playing occasionally with the U21s. She was let go early from her contract following a violent altercation involving one of her teammates.

Half listening to the rain beating down on the house, I read the page over and over, refreshed it as if expecting more information to appear. *A violent altercation.* The words seemed to pulse on the screen. I wasn't even sure what that meant. A fight? I searched 'Women PSG altercation' but nothing came up apart from stadium violence with Marseille fans. I remembered what Caden's teammate had said about her being sent off the pitch. And Caden's words to me: *She was truly crazy. No woman will ever be able to hurt me as badly as she did.*

I ought perhaps to have been cheered by this information. She did not sound like a good person. But it impressed me. I didn't know many violent people, but the few I had come across were men. And while I didn't admire that quality in a man, in a woman I found it remarkable. She could stick up for herself. Whereas I couldn't. I couldn't defend myself against Vicky's stealing. I couldn't even confront Caden about the memory stick. I was so feeble compared to her.

I managed to fall asleep, and when I woke I was happy to find out I'd managed to use up almost half the day. Another one nearly over. It was still raining, but I was desperate to get out of the house. 'A walk,' I said to myself, shouldering on my yellow raincoat and patting my pocket for my key. 'No one has ever felt worse after a walk.'

There were worms all over the place, twisting pink on the tarmac. I picked a few of them up, threw them on to the grass, but there were so many that I gave up. As I was passing the Golden Hind, I felt a horrible gritty squelch under my shoe. I walked on, dragging my foot to wipe it clean of the worm, until I reached the river.

The rain was falling hard, making patterns on the surface of the river, and the footpath was already partially flooded. I'd rowed in worse than this. Kayla had insisted on us going out in all weather, even when it didn't seem safe.

'You won't drown on the river, but I will personally hunt you down and kill you if you don't show up to practice,' she'd threaten, whenever anyone got shifty about the forecast. I missed that. I missed rowing, missed the lab, missed having something to do.

I walked south towards Goldie Boathouse. It was close to the time Caden would be finishing work; I texted him to say I was waiting outside. I sheltered under the awning, watched the gusts of rain make tornado shapes in the dirt. The door opened. It was Kieran, wearing a mask, but he tore it off when he saw it was me.

'What's up?' He'd let his hair grow long, and the shadows under his blue eyes had deepened, so that he looked more like a bloodhound than ever.

'Waiting for Caden.'

'Well, you can come in.'

'I don't think I can,' I said. I knew the physiotherapy practices were strict about Covid regulations.

'Don't worry,' he said.

I followed him in and let him squirt some gel into my hands. The weights room was empty, but three enormous fans were whirring. I was soaked from the rain and I shivered.

'Caden's upstairs,' he said. 'Must be seeing someone. He'll be down in a minute.'

He lifted his T-shirt to wipe his face, revealing the deep V of muscle in his groin. For some reason I felt furious with him; something about his expression made me want to explore those furrows with a knife.

I turned away and walked towards the entrance. 'Tell him I'm outside.'

'He's not here!' he called. I turned around.

'What?'

'He's not here.' He rubbed his eyes with his thumb and forefinger. 'He left ages ago. You can go check upstairs, if you don't believe me.'

I suspected Kieran was trying to get me to burst in on Caden with a client. But as I reached the landing, I saw that the door to his office was open. I stepped inside and flicked on the light. The skeleton beamed at me with its orthodontic grin, but there was no one in there.

'Why did you say he was here in the first place?' I said, annoyed.

He shrugged. 'Thought it was funny. And I fancied a chat. I don't see many people these days, and as you're probably aware, Cade's not much of a talker. Does he seem off to you, by the way?'

I looked at him. The bags beneath his eyes gave him a haunted, alcoholic look. His arms were crossed, and he was running his fingers up and down his biceps a little nervously, a little manically. *I guess I could stay*, I thought. *I could put on the Anna Show, cheer him up, try to make him my friend. Ask him about Caden.*

'Where is he?'

'I don't keep tabs on him.'

I went out into the rain, letting the door slam behind me. Kieran had made fun of me one too many times.

*

I walked along the river, my eyes fixed on the ground ahead of me to make sure I didn't squash any more worms. I tried to call Caden, but my reception was dodgy and it didn't go through. Where was he? He couldn't have gone home, as I would have run into him on the way there.

He was meeting a girl. I threaded through a group of men smoking outside the Golden Hind, and their cigarette smell clung to my wet clothes, my wet hair. I was hot, but I was shivering, too. A sick feeling of conviction. If Caden was hiding something from me, it would explain why I felt so paranoid. There were rivulets of rain travelling down the red-and-blue striped front door. I went to put my key in the lock, but the door swung open when I touched it.

The front room was in total chaos. Books pulled off the shelves; the neat row of shoes turned up and thrown on to the sofa. *We've been burgled*, I thought, and I took a step back, terrified the intruder might still be in the house.

But then I heard music coming from upstairs. His national anthem playlist. I climbed the stairs, still wary. He was in the bedroom with his back to me. He was ripping the sheets off the bed.

'What are you doing?'

He jumped and turned around, his hand on his chest. 'Fuck. You scared me.'

'Where were you?' I asked.

'At work. I got home twenty minutes ago.' He looked harried; his hair was wild and disordered.

'But Kieran said you left ages ago. Where have you been?'

'I had to take the long way back because the river path was shut. They found another grenade in the Cam.'

'But that's not true,' I said, trying to swallow down the anxiety bobbing in my throat. 'I just came from Goldie along the river path.'

He stopped what he was doing. 'I wanted some time alone, OK? Is that allowed? Should I ask permission first?'

'No,' I said, mortified. 'Of course not. But what the hell are you doing?' It suddenly registered with me that the room was in a terrible state; he had emptied his drawers, torn the duvet from the bed.

'Lost something.'

'Oh.'

I tried to appear calm, to ask in a voice as casual as possible: 'What did you lose?'

He evaded my gaze. 'Nothing important.'

*He's lying*, I thought. *He's lying to me. He's looking for the engagement ring.* My eyes roved over the room in complete confusion. How could he have noticed it was missing so quickly?

'If it isn't important, why have you made such a mess?' I looked around the room. 'Do you know how much time I've spent tidying up after you?'

'I've never asked you to do that,' he snapped.

Suddenly I was shouting: 'It was a fucking mess when I came here. It was disgusting.'

'If you don't like it, you can leave.'

He looked at me and then away, at the floor. I burst into tears.

'Fine,' I choked. 'Fine.' I went into the spare room, only to see that he had emptied all the boxes there, and that my clothes were mixed with all his ex's things. I sank down on to my knees. Caden came after me.

'Anna.' He tried to put his arm around me, but I shrugged it off. 'Anna, I didn't mean it.'

I couldn't answer. My chest was convulsing.

'I'm so sorry,' he said. He cupped my chin, turned it so I faced him.

'I'll leave,' I said. 'I just need to pack.'

'Anna, please.' He took my hand, kissed it. 'Please

don't. I didn't mean it like that. I want you to stay.' He was almost begging.

'Are you seeing someone else?'

'What?' Soulful eyes, as blameless as a child. 'No. I love you, Anna.'

He had not said that to me before. I felt dizzy, a bit sick. I wished he had chosen another time. I didn't want to associate his love with my suspicion and despair. I wiped my face with my sleeve.

'You're exhausted,' he said. 'Let me do dinner.'

He made spaghetti with an insipid tomato sauce and far too much parmesan. But we were both hungry and concentrated on the cold tangles of cheese and pasta.

'Have you ever been engaged?' The question shot out of me.

His mouth was full, and he took a sip of water before answering. 'No. Why?'

There was something satisfying about catching him out in such an obvious lie, and I stabbed my fork into my plate with a grim kind of triumph.

'You're lying. I know you were.'

He put down his fork, ran his fingers through his hair. 'If you already know, then why are you asking? Because you want to catch me out?'

'No,' I said defensively, though this was exactly what I had wanted to do.

'Who told you anyway, Kieran?' I shrugged, which he interpreted to mean yes. 'That guy can't shut his fucking mouth.' He picked up his fork again, tapped it distractedly on his plate. 'Yes. I was engaged once. But that's not any of your business.' He raised his voice, noticing I was about to interrupt. 'I know that you like talking about everything. About your feelings and all that. But that's just not my style. There are things I don't like about you, you know. Like your brutal fucking animal research. But

199

I accept it. If you want to be with me, you have to accept me as I am.'

'Accept that you're still not over your ex, you mean?'

That seemed to me like a polite understatement, but he looked as if I'd slapped him. His face tightened.

'This again?' He put his tray aside and began to scratch at a stain on the sofa.

'All her stuff is still here.'

'You mean the boxes in the spare room? I can move them if they're in your way.'

He wouldn't look at me, his gaze intent on the stain, the action of his fingers.

'But why do you even still have them?'

'Because she didn't answer my text when I asked her to come pick them up.'

'It's not only the boxes.' My stomach coiled tight as a rope. 'It's the way you've compared us.'

'How have I compared you?' he said.

'Telling me.' I hated how my voice sounded; high-pitched, plaintive. 'Telling me how much more put-together she was, how beautiful she was . . .' I trailed off.

'I don't think I ever said that.' His tone was measured, infuriatingly reasonable. 'The whole point I was making was that I like how you are. *Way* more natural. I love that you aren't obsessed with your appearance. You're so much kinder. And smarter.'

'The only reason you think I'm intelligent is because I'm at Cambridge. You don't have a clue about my research. You don't care about it.'

He drew his breath through his lips in a savage kind of way. 'I can't win with you. If I say you're smart, you get angry, and if I say anything about your looks, you cringe. You won't even let me take your picture. I'm always walk-ing on eggshells around you. I can't win.'

He got up from the sofa and went to fetch himself another beer from the fridge.

'Look,' he said, cracking it open, sitting beside me. 'Maybe I made some mistakes when we first got together. I'm sorry about that. I really am. But you have some serious insecurities, Anna. I think you need help.'

He reached for my hand, but I snatched it away. I took the blanket from the armrest and wrapped myself in it. He tidied the food away and I lay perfectly still, pretending I'd fallen asleep. He continued to talk to me and shook me once or twice, trying to get me to go up to bed with him, but I ignored him and eventually he left me alone. Pringle jumped up on to the sofa and purred into my side. I was surprised, as she usually stayed away from me. But she lay there, her elastic back kneading warmth into my body as she breathed. My anger was abating. He had lied about being engaged, that was true. But maybe it wasn't any of my business. Didn't he have the right to privacy? He had mentioned his ex a few too many times, made clumsy comparisons that were meant to flatter me. Maybe I was overreacting. I was insecure, jealous of her looks and her power over him. It was me who had it all wrong. It was me who wasn't right.

The light from the window crept inch by bright inch into the room, rising like a waterline until I felt the heat on my face, the sun shine red through my eyelids. I opened my eyes and went up the stairs, cradling Pringle, who let herself be carried, in my arms. Caden was still asleep. I dropped the cat on the pillow above his head, and then curled up to him, wedging my knees into the back of his legs, his hair tickling my cheek.

'Caden?' I whispered.

'Mmm?'

'I love you.'

He rolled over, his eyes still closed. 'Ten more minutes of sleep. Ten more.'

I lay there, watching him. An angel. Really, you can't imagine. Incredible to think of the dreaming universe within him. At what point did undifferentiated matter become this perfect complex coil of consciousness, this particular man? Helixes of DNA winding and unwinding, proteins knitting together, the membranes of every cell opening and closing: all of it to make this, my love. My heart was fluttering in my chest, my body coursing with adrenaline. He was so alien to me. I was not at ease with him. But I can't tell you how right he smelled, how right his body felt, as if the grain of his skin slotted into mine. It was an attachment so deeply encoded that my brain – my good sense – could not resist it.

# 5

## Dirty Laundry

'THIS IS PROPER SUMMER, Pudding!'
The sun shone like a stemless solar flower, watching itself unblinking in the flat green surface of the river. Though it was still morning, it was hot, and I was uncomfortable in my miniskirt, the tight polo neck which exaggerated the size of my chest. I had borrowed his ex's hoop earrings and tied my hair in a bun, using some of her bobby pins to catch the strays. I had no clue how to do it; the pins dangled like dumb windchimes and knocked against my neck.

I didn't know how to dress to please myself any more. My old garb – corduroy dungarees, my comfy knitted jumpers, leggings and boots – seemed frumpy and awful to me now. But in his ex's things I felt like an imposter, felt I was in disguise.

It was the fifteenth of June, my birthday, and Caden cared about birthdays. He had woken me up with flowers, planned a breakfast picnic, and was being secretive about the present he'd bought me. It was his idea to go for a stroll along the Cam to see the ducklings. We'd counted eight so far; fuzzy yellow balls wobbling in a line behind their mothers.

'What did you do last year?' he asked.

'I had an exam for my finals, and then my boyfriend and I went skydiving,' I said. It seemed impossibly remote.

'No!'

'It's true, we did!' It had been Jamie's idea, but he'd been terrified. He'd bitten a chunk of flesh out of his cheek and spat blood the whole way down.

We were in the Gut now, the sinewy part of the river, the bank narrow and simmering with insects in the gorse bushes. The air was musty with the rotten-wood smell from the houseboats.

'My present is definitely not going to beat that.'

I took his hand. 'This is better. What did you do for yours?'

He didn't answer, but his gaze darted over my shoulder, towards the river. I followed his line of sight to the moored boats.

The *Rise and Shine*, painted in proud curly letters on the prow.

'We're not in a rush,' he said, checking his watch, tugging on my hand, 'but if we want to make it to the lock, we have to hurry.'

My mouth opened, but no words came out.

'Anna?'

'Sure,' I said. 'Sorry.'

I loosened his grip on my fingers, felt for my keys in my pocket, traced the letters embossed on the keyring he had given me. The *Rise and Shine*. The shutters were painted in red-and-blue stripes.


A sky-blue canal boat was passing through Baits Bite Lock. A woman stood on the bank, using a long metal rod to crack open the lock.

The gates parted dramatically, a slit of light flashing in the gap before the river rushed through. The water level rose, lifting the boat with a speed and ease that seemed miraculous. I stared through the porticos. Upholstered moss-green chairs, a table covered with newspapers and teacups, and in the bow a tiny spaniel puppy with a little girl, sitting cross-legged, fondling its ears and smiling.

'She's a beauty!' Caden shouted over the rush of water to the woman, as she leapt from the bank into the bow. 'That's my dream life.'

'Oh, love.' She smiled at us, the ribbons of her white hair flying all over her face. 'It's the closest thing to heaven.'

They passed through the gate, and the water in the boat's wake rolled in on itself to form fluted cylinders that shone in the buttery sunshine for an instant, before coiling back into the water.

We sat on a patch of grass outside the old lock keeper's house. Caden unpacked his picnic bag; croissants, pains au chocolat, orange juice. He must have sneaked away while I was still sleeping to buy it all. I took a bite of a pain au chocolat; it tasted like recycled paper.

'Good?' he said eagerly, raising his voice over the rush of water flowing into the lock.

'So-so,' I said, hating myself for how like my dad I sounded. We ate for a while in silence. The water was full of green lily pads, so wide and robust looking that it was tempting to test them with my weight. I did not spot the water lilies at first, as they were still submerged. But then I noticed them, unfurling slowly, like pale hands clutching for the surface. Caden pulled out a neatly wrapped present from his backpack.

'Open it!' he urged.

'I'll open it tonight. I'll save it for later!' I didn't feel like I could pretend to be excited, and I didn't want to spoil the illusion that he was making me happy.

'Now! Please.' He gave me a doe-like look, batting his lashes, and I gave in. I ripped open the paper.

It was a brown suede handbag. He looked at me, trying to gauge my reaction.

'I love it,' I said. It was a beautiful bag, as beautiful as the identical one I'd found in the box in the spare room.

He left for work and I went home, stopping in at Tesco to buy the ingredients for my birthday cake, some laundry detergent and cat food. Pringle's wants and needs had become part of my subconscious, and I had already filled her bowl and opened the garden door to let her in when my phone rang.

'Hi, Mum.'

'Happy birthday, darling!'

'Thanks.' I cradled the phone on my shoulder and began washing up the mess Caden had made preparing my birthday breakfast.

'Twenty-three today!' The phone purred as she blew smoke into the receiver. 'It will be your best year!'

'I hope so.' Pringle was rubbing herself on my shins, and arched her back when I leant over to stroke her.

'Is your boyfriend spoiling you?'

'He gave me a handbag.'

'Ha! You'll never use it.'

'Ha-ha.' It irritated my mother that I kept my cards and ID in the case of my phone, that I was not more ladylike.

'What are you up to, Mum?'

'In the garden, transplanting hyacinths.'

I looked through the window. The neighbour was peering over the fence, looking for the cat no doubt. I checked the front room, but Pringle had disappeared off somewhere.

'You know I wanted to call you Hyacinth?'

'You never told me that.'

'But your dad was really keen on the name Anna. Said it was the name of a childhood friend of his.' I heard her taking a drag of her cigarette. 'I found out later that she wasn't exactly a friend, if you know what I mean.' She gave a hollow, tinkling laugh.

'Oh, Mum.' I switched the phone to my other shoulder and transferred the wet clothes from the washing machine to the dryer.

'Hyacinth would have suited you better, with your curls,' she said. 'But don't worry, I love you anyway, birthday girl.'

We said goodbye, and I looked up the recipe for devil's food cake, hoping that baking would cheer me up. But by then the housewife game was losing its appeal. The way I obediently followed each step in the recipe; sifted the flour, snapped the squares of chocolate. Everything felt like a fat cliché.

I abandoned my birthday cake preparations and went upstairs into the spare room. The brown suede bag was missing.

Why would he give me something that belonged to her as a birthday present? And take me past her houseboat? The *Rise and Shine*. I felt the outline of the keyring in my pocket. This man took me for a complete idiot. Did he think I wouldn't figure it out?

I wished I could call Vicky, but it seemed impossible to mention the diamond. She was clearly still angry at me, as she hadn't even texted me a happy birthday. I felt like crying as I combed through the boxes. No ring, no memory stick. I went into the bedroom, searched the pockets of his trousers, his shoes, and untwisted all his socks. Nothing.

My phone rang and I jumped in alarm.

'ANNA! How ARE you?' It was Charles. I could hear a dog barking in the background. 'HAPPY BIRTHDAY!'

'Thank you!'

'How are things? Are you and Vicky driving each other bonkers yet?'

'I'm not living with her. I've moved in with a man.' I don't know why I told him, given I'd kept this knowledge from him for so long. I think I knew it would hurt him, and I wanted to feel like I had power over someone, though I regretted it immediately, especially after hearing the hurt in his voice.

'A man?' he answered, after a slight pause. 'What man?'

'A physiotherapist. The one who helped me with my wrist.'

'Oh?'

There was a long silence.

'I hope he's been giving you free physical therapy.'

I forced a laugh.

'Are you happy?'

'Not particularly.' I found myself telling him about the recycled birthday present.

'That's perverse! Move back to Newnham! Immediately. I don't like the sound of this chap.'

'It's not that bad. I'm OK,' I said, enjoying his sympathy.

'You don't sound OK. He sounds like an arsehole, if you'll pardon my French. Move back to Newnham!'

We hung up, and I began to pack up my clothes. I took Mango Bango Jambo Banana off the bed. Most of my things were still piled up in the spare room, so it didn't take long to stuff them into my suitcase. I did not know whether Caden had meant to hurt me or I was just paranoid, but the effect was the same. I was not doing well. I needed to get out of there.

Home wouldn't be so bad, I thought as I zipped up my bags. I could create a kind of work schedule and make a detailed plan for what to do when the lab reopened. And I could pretend my mother was not related to me, like some kind of crazy landlady.

I went downstairs and started emptying the dryer. I

grabbed something matted and white and fuzzy, and my first thought was *Fuck, I've shrunk Caden's fleece*, but then I realized the jumper had a tail.

'No! Oh no!'

I dropped the cat and made it to the garden just in time. Mysterious coloured substances spilled out of me, things I couldn't remember having eaten – blue and green and brown things, the colour of earth. Her tender prawn-pink paws – which Caden had often kissed – were completely black. Her cream fur had shrivelled into dark, clotted wisps. My head felt hot, heavy with a magnetic keening for the ground, as if the grass were made of iron filings.

What had happened to her eyes?

The planetary green glimmers – boiled into rubbery blind eggs. The fine gossamer whiskers, shrouding her face like a white mist, were gone. Her little face was contorted. She had suffered.

I heard the neighbour shuffling on her side of the fence.

'Kitty kitty kitty!' she called.

I huddled against it as she peered over, looking for the source of the noise. She must have heard my retching.

'Kitty kitty kitty kitty!'

I watched her shadow shift on the grass, and when I was sure she had gone, I crawled back into the kitchen on my hands and knees. The cat was definitely dead.

I thought about trying resuscitation – mouth to mouth, CPR? – but I couldn't bring myself to touch Pringle. She smelled like a damp barbecue.

Poor creature. She looked so lonely on the cold kitchen tiles.

*Caden, something terrible happened*, I texted.

*I'm sure the cake is perfect, no stress x*

*I was doing laundry and I didn't realize Pringle was in the dryer. She's dead. I am so, so, so sorry. I understand if you want me to leave.*

But I couldn't bring myself to send the message. He would be devastated. How could it have happened? I'd never noticed her climb into the dryer before. I guess it must have made a cosy nook, before I'd pressed the Synthetics setting and turned it into Hiroshima.

*No, I burnt it Caden, it's inedible :(*

*No problem*, he replied. *I'll buy one on the way home.*

I had to get rid of her. The neighbour might see me if I tried to bury her in the garden; that was too risky. I had to dump her somewhere. I considered putting her in a bin bag, but for some reason that felt too horrible. Instead I wrapped her body in a tea-towel, and then dropped it into my birthday present, the brown suede bag. It was the perfect size for her.

I crushed my feet into my shoes and walked down the street, my eyes fixed on the pavement, convinced I'd run into Kieran or one of Caden's football friends, or that he himself would come home early to surprise me. I turned right and passed the Golden Hind. There were large industrial bins close to its entrance. A few people were having a picnic lunch on the benches nearby, but I approached with confidence and in one smooth motion flipped open the lid, and swung the handbag up and inside.

'Hey! You!'

I looked up. A squat, tanned woman was walking towards me. She wore a large pink T-shirt that read 'Needs Salt'.

'You talking to me?'

'Yes, I'm talking to you. What did you just put in our bin?'

'I'm sorry. I just found that bag on the road and I didn't know what to do with it. It's not mine.'

'I don't care. That's our recycling. Take it out!'

I didn't argue. I fished the bag out from among the

cardboard boxes and walked on. *I'm going to be sick*, I thought. *I'm going to pass out, and someone will find me with a dead cat in a handbag and call the police.* It was hot, and the cars and the bins and the people were ringed in dark distorted halos of shadow, and everything looked bigger than it should, more sinister. I reached the river and, looking over my shoulder, dropped the bag into one of the bins a few metres away from the Green Dragon. It gave a soft thud as it hit the bottom. I thought of her little body there, cooking amongst the latte cups and lurid orange skins, and I felt I was betraying her again by leaving her, far from the people who loved her.

Still, that malicious little voice in me spoke up in sick, sick triumph: was this worse than whatever Giselle had done to him?

'Birthday girl! Get down here.'

I walked down the stairs slowly, sluggishly, unwilling to face him. He was in the kitchen, drinking from the tap. He'd bought champagne and a green caterpillar cake in a box. I helped him light the candles and smiled thinly as he sang 'Happy Birthday' in a surprisingly sweet voice.

'The candles are dripping! Blow them out! Make a wish!' he said.

His face was radiant in the birthday-cake candle glow. I couldn't leave him now. If I did, he would think that I had stolen the diamond ring, and he would know I had something to do with Pringle's disappearance. And I couldn't bear the idea of him sitting all alone, calling and calling for a cat that would never come.

He cut two huge wedges of cake and carried them with the drinks into the garden. I'd forgotten to clean up the sick. It had dried in the sun.

'What's that?' Caden said.

'I have no clue.'

He picked up a stick and scratched its crusty white corner. 'It looks like a giant bird shit. Or a beached jellyfish.'

'It must have been a fox.'

'More likely Pringle.'

We moved the garden chairs from the shade and sat in a fat square of sun. Usually it was me who made conversation. I would ask him about Chelsea transfer news, about his day, his patients. But now I couldn't bring myself to say anything.

I kept catching sight of my reflection in the kitchen window. The icing on the cake was as thick and solid as plaster. I mushed it around a bit, then passed my plate to Caden.

'You don't have to eat all of it,' I said. 'It's not that good.'

He put down his fork. 'You're in a bad mood. Don't tell me you're one of these women who hates her birthday?'

'I'm not in a bad mood.'

'I know how to cheer you up.'

He took my hand and led me into the front room. He pulled down my shorts and pushed me on to the sofa. He was hurried, holding my wrist in a rigor mortis grip.

'Hey!' I grabbed his arm. He had never been so rough. 'What's the rush?'

He gave me a reproachful stare and hitched my T-shirt to my shoulders, then pushed up my bra so that my breasts fell out. I watched the milk-drunk stupidity of his face when he took them in his hands. That was the first time I thought, *You're an idiot. You're a tool.* He turned me over on to my stomach and we had sex in that position. It was humiliating, but I deserved it. A breeze from the garden blew into my face as Caden's knees stuck to the back of my thighs. My mind became blank, my attention constricted to the squeaking of the fake leather and Caden's laboured breath in my ear.

'Pringle! Kitty kitty kitty!'

I tried to concentrate on Caden's breath. I began counting up to one hundred, counting every thrust, whispering to myself, 'One, two, three.' The neighbour went on calling. She rattled the tin of treats. God, why had I left the cat in a handbag? Someone might see it, check if anything valuable was inside, hand it in to the police.

'Pringle! Pringle! Where are you?'

Then a much louder metallic ringing, as she bashed the side of the tin with a spoon and the sound rang out mournfully, like a bell tolling.

The squeaking of the sofa; Caden sighing rhythmically. 'Eighty-one, eighty-two.' The empty picture frame that seemed to wink as Caden pushed me down. *Can you go to jail for the accidental killing of a cat?*

'Pringle! Pringle! Pringle!' And then an empty silence.

Caden ploughed on, undeterred.

# 6

## The Female Suárez

FROM THAT DAY ONWARDS, I stopped thinking of myself as a good person And instead of trying to atone for my wrongdoings, I developed a vindictive need to prove that I was right about myself. Lying, snooping, spying. All of it was just more evidence that confirmed I was rotten, morally bankrupt. I gave up on self-respect. Now there was nothing to stop my behaviour from escalating. And that was dangerous.

The day after my birthday, I told Caden I was going for a run. I was careful to avoid the bin where I'd left Pringle. I didn't want to go near it, in case someone had seen me the day before and would associate me with the handbag. I ran under the Sunshine Posho bridge, down the Reach, round Grassy Corner. I wasn't wearing proper running shoes, only thin-soled Converse, and the high tops rubbed against my shins. Insects flew into my face. I passed a man in army fatigues magnet-fishing right beside a sign that said 'NO DREDGING. DANGER'. The surface of the water wrinkled and puckered in the breeze.

I passed the first narrowboats, their occupants barely visible through the porticos: an old man reading a paper at his kitchen table; someone cooking breakfast, a curtain drawn against prying eyes. There it was, the *Rise and Shine*.

I slowed my pace. The mooring ropes were tied into knots, and it was hard to figure out the logic of their binding. There were flowerpots on the windowsill, but I couldn't tell whether or not they were orchids because I didn't want her to catch me peering inside.

I ran past her narrowboat, then turned back. I walked because I was out of breath. She climbed out when I was only a few metres away. She had her back to me and stopped in the middle of the path to tie her laces. I felt a brief, intense rush of delight. For a moment I thought I was going to go right up to her and start a conversation, saying, 'I love your boat,' or something like that. But then my courage failed me. I looked down at my feet, a searing excited shame coursing through me. The front flap of one of my Converse was stained with blood. It didn't matter if she saw me. As far as she was concerned, I didn't exist. I watched her straighten up, walk on in the direction of the Green Dragon.

I followed her. My heart was in my mouth; I was scared, almost panicking. But the analytical part of my brain was gathering information, collecting data. Blue Adidas shorts, white T-shirt, tote bag. AirPods, which meant she wouldn't hear my footsteps. That was good.

She was small, much shorter than me. This surprised me; she loomed so large in my imagination. After all, she had been involved in a 'violent altercation' with a team-mate. And been sent off during men's games for aggressive play. It was hard to square that with the person in front of me. Her hair, tied in two French braids, looked childish, as did the iPhone cord slung across her torso like a beauty pageant sash. I wiped my sweaty palms on my shorts, tried to calm my breathing. I was stronger than she was, there was no doubt about that.

She crossed the Sunshine Posho bridge and then turned right in the direction of Midsummer Common, and I went after her. Her head would feel small between my hands. I didn't necessarily want to hurt her, but I liked knowing I could master her in a fight if it came to it.

There were lots of people along the river path, so I was relatively inconspicuous. Still, she turned around and looked at me, twice. People always know when they're being followed. But she seemed reassured when she saw it was a woman.

She veered off the path and walked a few metres onto Midsummer Common, towards a huddle of men in football kit, half of them wearing black-and-yellow Cambridge United shirts.

'Hi!' I heard, and then a few words I didn't catch. She sat down, pulled on a pair of long blue socks and laced up her football boots. I sank into the grass near a couple having a picnic. I wished I had brought my phone, as that would have given me something natural to do. I started pulling the laces out of my shoes, glancing up from time to time.

Still sitting, she began to bounce the ball from one shin to the other, ignoring the other players, big bruiser-types with tattooed forearms. A few of them plunged their hands down the front of their shorts, rummaging in their crotches to rearrange themselves before play, and then went around shaking hands. She stayed where she was, intent on the ball.

What had she done to Caden? I wondered. He couldn't have let her go easily. Someone like her.

The wind had picked up and the sky was now completely overcast, so there were no shadows, no haziness; everything was crisply outlined. I had a sense of intensified perception. Things came into focus; I saw them as they really were. I could make out every nuance in the shades of green; the rich buttery green of the grass, the olive of the dry trees, the blue-green of the ferns. I noticed how the wind's invisible equations furrowed and segmented the grass; the corn-husk geometry of her plaited hair.

The players divided themselves into teams. I felt nervous for her because of the sheer physical contrast between her and the men. Giselle took the kick-off, dribbling the ball up the wing, her chin high as she looked for support. She crossed it, but her teammate was too slow and she shook her head at him, gave him a slight smile. My anxiety faded as I became absorbed in the game. She was more skilled than many of the others, who kicked ugly toe-balls and threw their weight around. She had so much acceleration and confidence that it was hard for the defenders to get in her way.

An indescribable feeling was welling up in me. Not jealousy, as I'd expected. An aching, sweet sort of grief. There was something factual about her beauty and her skill that touched me. It was so undeniable that I couldn't resent her for it, couldn't even hate myself. The pace was relentless, the ball pinging over the grass so fast it was hard for me to follow. She was always in flux, woven into the fabric of the game. She commanded respect. She was sweating now, wiping her face with her shirt. She drove forward and scored, and then a few minutes later she scored again. She cheered for herself, pumping her firsts in the air, ostentatious in her joy. I would never have acted like that, even if I were as skilled as her. I would have held back, passed to someone else maybe – but she took all the goals herself. It was selfish and showy. She was perfect.

I left after half an hour, worried that Caden would come looking for me. As I walked away, I found myself choking down a sob. After all the lies and evasions, this felt like a blessed truth. *This is beauty. This is true mastery.* For a while it carried me, and I felt buoyant and far removed from all my cares; from the sordid fact of Pringle's body, and my own mediocrity.

I opened the front door and found the sitting room in complete disarray; books were strewn everywhere, Caden's sports bag emptied out on to the sofa. He had torn the place apart again. *For God's sake*, I thought. *Why won't he just ask me about the ring? Let's get this over with.*

He was in the kitchen, pulling out something white from the dryer; *God, he's found Pringle's body.*

'Caden!'

He jumped.

'Christ, Pudding! You scared me!'

It was his white fleece. The surreal lurch of horror receded. 'What are you doing?'

'Sorting out my laundry. Is that allowed?'

'Why did you make such a mess?' I said, gesturing to the front room. 'It was perfect when I left.'

'No nagging.' He wagged his finger in mock disapproval.

'But what are you looking for?'

He did not answer.

I went over to the sink and gulped water from the tap.

'Did you have a good run? You were gone for ages.'

'It was OK,' I said. The water was ice in my stomach.

He came over to the sink and put his arms around me, squeezed and tried to lift me from the floor. I fought to get free.

'Don't.'

His eyes searched my face. *He knows I'm hiding something. He must be able to tell I've seen her.*

'You look a bit tired.'

'Out of shape.'

'Why don't we go upstairs?' He gave a secretive smile. The skin of his arm was cool beneath my fingers.

'I can't.' I stepped away. 'It's my turn to check on the guinea-pigs.'

I expected him to make a cutting remark about my

work, but instead he stepped towards me. 'Half an hour, then I'll drive you. I have Kieran's keys.'

I let him drag me upstairs. It was awful. I wasn't even able to pretend that I was enjoying it. Caden was frantic and hurried, and everything he said – 'I want to fuck you, you like that, don't you?' – seemed so ridiculous and porno-graphic that I wanted to scream at him. *Shut the fuck up. Of course it's not good. How could it possibly ever be good between us ever again? I killed your cat and it's rotting in a bin.* I was in pain, so I rolled out from underneath him and started to give him head instead. But he wouldn't let me set the rhythm, kept ramming himself into my face. Had he been like this with her? I felt seasick, as if the bed was tilting.

'Just a second,' I said, moving back, wiping my mouth with the back of my hand. 'I just need a minute.' But he was already standing, pulling up his boxer shorts.

'Wait,' I said, putting my hand on his thigh. 'Let me do it!'

'It's fine,' he said, pushing past me. I heard the door slam as he left the house. I took a shower and used the last of his ex's Pantene Pro-V conditioner. I'd never failed to make Caden climax before, and I felt irritated with myself for caring so much. But the realm of my power felt very small, and after watching the football game, I was con-fronted by my own impotence. A big pointless intellect. I could cook and clean. I was more or less able to satisfy him, for now. What else was I good for?

I heard Caden beep the car horn, and I went outside with my hair still wet and clinging to my neck. The sky was lead-grey, but the clouds – like those bell-shaped silver covers they put over your plate in expensive restaurants – seemed to trap the heat, to concentrate the humidity and the smell.

'What is that?' I said, as we pulled off and I rolled up the car window.

'Sewage treatment plant in Milton. Have you never noticed it before? It's always like this when the wind blows the wrong way.'

'It wasn't like this while I was running.' I felt sick, sicker still at the idea of going into the over air-conditioned lab. I tried to breathe through my mouth.

'Are you excited about seeing the guinea-pigs?' he said, as we turned into Chesterton Road.

'Not really.'

'Why don't you rescue one?' he said.

I held my hand to the air vent. It was so hot in that car.

'And do what with it?'

'Bring it home.'

'I can't. I'll be kicked out.'

He turned towards me.

'No, you won't. How will they know it's you?'

'There are only a few people on the rota, Caden. It'll take them about ten minutes to figure it out.'

We had arrived at the lab, and he pulled over. He unfastened his seatbelt and turned towards me.

'It's not that big a deal. No one will really care anyway. What's the difference between killing one of them for science and taking one to make me happy?' Big beseeching eyes. He moved his face towards mine very, very slowly, so slowly that I jumped when I felt the pressure of his lips against my ear. 'I've been pretty stressed out lately. A lot on my mind. This will help.'

'A guinea-pig will help?'

He leant over me and unclicked my seatbelt. 'Go on. Do it for me.'

The lab was cold and silent except for the squeaks of the rodents, the rattle of the air-conditioner. I went into the fridge and got out the cucumber, the radish tops and the grain mix. The guinea-pigs jumped up on to their hind legs when they saw me approach with the food, their front paws waggling in the air. Somebody must have forgotten to replenish their water bottles as they rushed to drink while I filled them, licking the end of the nozzles.

I watched them eat.

I didn't really pause here, didn't wring my hands and gnash my teeth and agonize. I became calm and cool and efficient. I reached down into the cage. A guinea-pig approached my hand and began to nuzzle it. It was black, apart from bright white circles around each eye, which made it look as if it were wearing pilot's goggles. I picked it up and slipped it into my tote bag. Then I remembered that guinea-pigs get lonely, so I would need more than one. I picked up a tiny one with spiky ginger hair, like tusks all over his body.

I watched the rest of them in despair and went to fetch more cucumber from the fridge. 'I'm sorry,' I said, as I sliced slivers into their cage. 'I'm sorry.'

Caden was where I'd left him, the engine idling.

'I did it,' I said in a low voice, getting into the passenger seat. I thought I might feel triumphant, but I felt a strange hot-faced shame, a dreadful feeling that was beyond tears.

'Well done,' Caden said, peeking into the bag. 'What shall we call them?' He leant over to kiss me when he saw the look on my face. 'It's going to be fine, don't worry.'

But I knew that it wouldn't be fine.

# 7

## Rosquettes

THE FIRST THING MY dad ever taught me to bake was a type of biscuit called a *rosquette*. I asked him a few times if the recipe was French, but he evaded the question. He was often like that: distressingly mysterious about things for no good reason. I had a feeling it was a family recipe, but he rarely spoke about his parents, and the few things he'd told me about his dad sounded like complete lies. Never mind their origin story, I loved *rosquettes*, and I made them the morning after we rescued Bubble and Squeak.

You need plain flour, sugar, an egg, good peppery olive oil and an unwaxed lemon. Thanks to me, Caden had all these ingredients in his pantry. After making myself a coffee so strong that it would have raised even Pringle from the dead, I turned the oven on high and mixed all the ingredients together in a bowl. This time I remembered to sift the flour. I had forgotten to do that when I'd made these biscuits for Ji-woo and Vicky, and they had come out all grotesque and lumpy. They had eaten them anyway.

I interrupted my dough mixing to go and check on the guinea-pigs. Caden had built them an enclosure out of pallets and plywood in the front room, and I had stopped in at the Woofmeister pet shop to buy them some pellets and sawdust. Bubble – the black one with the white goggles – was shy, and had burrowed into a corner, but the little orange one – Squeak – ran towards me, and butted his head against my fingers when I crouched down to stroke him.

'I hope you're grateful,' I said.

I went back to my dough. You have to roll it into a long thin snake shape, and then you slice it with a sharp knife. The pieces should be the length of your pinky. Bring the two ends together to make a circular biscuit. They should be sticky, but if they ooze oil it means you've added too little flour. Put them in the oven for twelve minutes. There will be a warm yellowy waft of lemon. Not an appetizing smell really, more like the smell of something clean.

The scent was what woke Caden, and he padded down the stairs in time to eat them warm from the oven.

'Wait!' I said, as he went to dip them in his tea. These biscuits are better when dipped in Greek yoghurt.

'No, really, they are!' I said when Caden lifted an eyebrow.

'I like them,' he said, dipping the last of his biscuit into the bowl. 'Not so sickly-sweet as your usual stuff.'

We spent the morning with the guinea-pigs. I'm almost embarrassed to say how touched I was by the way Caden was with them. He started building them an outdoor cage so that they could 'play in the fresh air', and he cuddled them and spoke to them:

'You're going to have a good life now,' he said, as they squeaked happily. 'No more experiments.'

Perhaps they would compensate for the pain of the lost cat, and we could put all that behind us. We made an odd kind of family: me, Caden and the guinea-pigs. I imagined what he would be like as a real dad, our child a mini Caden, like the photo of him in the sunflower picture frame. His beauty and my brains. *Even if he leaves me,* I thought, *I'd like to have his son. A beautiful boy all of my own.*

My happiness was short-lived.

*It has come to our attention,* Crabwell wrote in an email to our lab group, *that two of the guinea-pigs are missing. I cannot overemphasize the gravity of this theft. I'm going to have to inform AWERB, and this may result in the suspension of our ASPA licence. I have handed the matter over to the police.*

I passed the phone to Caden, and he laughed at Crabwell's melodramatic message. 'They're not going to prosecute you for taking animals they were going to kill anyway. Don't worry. It'll be fine.'

I tried to seem unconcerned, but privately, the mention of the police terrified me. I did not know if there was CCTV anywhere in the building, but I had used my ID card to get in and it would be easy for them to narrow the suspects down to me.

*I have to return them. I have to return them.*

I paced round and round the front room, shaking my hands to try to rid myself of the adrenaline, and when Caden complained that I was making him dizzy, I went out into the garden and continued my pacing there. The weather was wonderful, but the great goofy blue sky disturbed me still more, because I did not believe its happy promise. It had all the menace of a grinning clown hiding a leer behind its mask, and after a few minutes I went back inside.

What would happen to me if I was found out?

I felt the waterline of my terror rise with every passing second. I tried to reassure myself that I hadn't done anything wrong, remembering the two dissections I had botched that winter, the tiny corpses thrown out in sandwich bags – *This waste of life happens all the time.*

Somehow returning the guinea-pigs and confessing to Caden that I'd killed Pringle became irrevocably linked in my mind. I was in a bind: unless I confessed to him, I could not save myself from the consequences of taking the guinea-pigs. And I was too weak to come clean. I couldn't bear to see him suffer, nor to endure the pain of him breaking up with me. But I wish I had told him then. Grief and heartbreak are nothing compared to the long-term harm my weakness caused.

And that same weakness is what made me text Charles a few days after the theft. It was early morning; the shadows scurried across the room as the sun rose. I had not slept and I needed someone to talk to.

*I have a problem*, I said, and sent him a picture of the guinea-pigs.

He rang me at once, but I rejected the call. Caden was still asleep in bed beside me, and I thought that if I spoke to Charles, I might break down and start crying.

*Answer me*, Charles texted.

*Sorry. Just feeling a bit shit.*

*I'm really worried about you. You don't seem OK.*

His concern irritated me.

*I don't need you to worry about me*, I replied.

*Bring them back to the lab! I think you can still do it and it will be fine.*

*I can't.*

*Why? What's going on?*

Caden groaned. The vibration from my phone had woken him. I switched it to silent, watched a barrage of texts come in from Charles.

*Did that guy make you do this?*

This irritated me even more.

*No one made me do anything, Charles. I'm a big girl.*

He rang again, but I rejected the phone call.

*Are you still living with him?* he messaged.

*How is that even relevant?* I replied, and turned my phone off.

It took Caden ten whole days to acknowledge that Pringle was missing. I think he sensed her absence from the first evening, but for some reason, he pretended not to have noticed. I followed his lead and said nothing. It was hard though, because the neighbour called for her every morning and every night. 'Here, kitty kitty kitty. Here, kitty.'

Caden and I ignored the pitiful, longing cries, though his mouth seemed to tighten every time she rattled her tin of treats. He always found an excuse to turn the volume up on the TV or to close the window on to the garden when she called for Pringle. We sat in silence while my conscience shrieked. Why wasn't he saying anything? Wouldn't it seem suspicious if I didn't mention the cat's absence? I'd have to bring it up myself. But I might break down in the process; the truth might come out.

'I'm worried about Pringle,' he finally admitted, to my immense relief. 'The neighbour says . . .' He swallowed, took a breath. 'The neighbour says she hasn't seen her for a week.'

'Oh, Caden.' I put my hand on his thigh. 'I'm sure she'll turn up.'

'I don't know. She's never been gone this long.' He squeezed my fingers very tight as he spoke.

'Don't cats do that all the time?'

'Not Pringle. Yeah baby,' he murmured in a diminished voice, as the stream of the fan hit him. 'Would you mind maybe putting up some posters while I'm at work?'

'Of course not,' I said, despising myself.

I made the posters using a picture Caden sent me. He said I could print them at Goldie, but when we got there the printer was broken. So Caden suggested that Kieran could drive me to Newnham, where I could print them for free.

'Are you all dolled up for my sake?' Kieran asked, as I got into his car. It smelled of hangover, like sourdough and sea-brine. 'How've you been?' he tried again.

'Fine and yourself?' I watched his hands on the steering wheel. His fingers, yellow and calloused, reminded me of the claws on a chicken's leg.

'Very well. And Caden? Are you making him a happy man?' The seat burned against my thighs.

'I hope so.'

He smiled. He looked like a kind of sex wolf. I imagined that, up close, his breath would be foul and hot.

Vicky was waiting for us outside Newnham, wearing a skirt and polka-dot bikini top. Her skin against mine felt warm when I hugged her, as if she'd been lying in the sun. I was irritated that she was wearing so little. Why did she have to show off all the time?

Kieran gazed at her with a look that might have been desire or hatred or both.

We passed Stan in the Porters' Lodge. His moustache stuck out from his mask, and he let out a bark of laughter as Vicky and I saluted him.

'No visitors in your room,' he warned Vicky. 'Covid rules. He has to stick to the gardens!'

I went to the library to print the one hundred PRINGLE MISSING posters. The room was empty, and the wooden desks had been covered with white sheets and bottles of disinfectant. It looked grimly sterile, like an operating theatre. I realized too late that I had printed them in black and white. It was hard to recognize Pringle; her green eyes and creamy coat had been her most distinctive features. I reprinted another fifty posters in colour.

I found Kieran and Vicky in the garden, sitting in the

shade of a bed of delphiniums. They were the most beautiful I'd ever seen; spurts of purple, deep red and orange, the colours of magma and volcanoes.

Kieran had taken his shirt off; the twist of black hair beneath his navel looked obscene against his white skin. I sat beside Vicky, letting the posters fan across the grass. She laid her silky head in my lap, smiled up at me.

'Did you manage?'

She was wearing diamond earrings, each a tiny hall of mirrors only a fraction lighter than her silver-blonde hair. I took one of her earlobes between my fingers.

'Vicky,' I said. 'You're wearing my earrings.' Only once I had spoken did I realize how outrageous it was – she was wearing my brother's earrings in front of me, with no shame.

'Oh yeah!' she said, sitting up. She sounded taken aback. Perhaps she had expected me to say nothing, to let her get away with it. 'I know. You left them in my room ages ago. Are you bummed that I borrowed them? I should have asked.'

'Can I have them back now?' My voice was still low, but there must have been an edge to it because Kieran turned to look at me.

'Sure,' she said, going to unfasten them, but then paused. 'Those hoops you're wearing. Are they new?'

My hand shot to my ear.

'Are they *Giselle's*?' she asked, laughing.

'What?' Kieran straightened up. 'Footballer Giselle? As in, Caden's ex?'

I shook my head, but I knew my face was flushed. I had forgotten that I was wearing them. Of course Vicky would notice.

'You're wearing Giselle's earrings?' The corners of his mouth twisted upwards in a cruel smile. 'It's so weird.' He added, when I didn't reply: 'You're so weird.'

I wanted to burst into tears.

'No, she isn't.' Vicky shifted, lay down on her side. 'I'm wearing Anna's. Women do that kind of thing all the time. Borrow each other's stuff. For bonding purposes. It's a known sociological phenomenon.' She tried to catch my eye, but I was burning with humiliation.

'Are you taking the piss?' He looked genuinely perplexed.

'No.' She smiled at me. 'Anyway, go on with what you were saying. We were just talking about her. Tell Anna what you were telling me.'

'I don't want to know anything Caden hasn't told me himself,' I said, my eyes warning Vicky to stop.

'She means the opposite of that,' Vicky said, winking at me. 'Go on.'

'Well, they were engaged.'

'Yeah, I knew that,' I said.

'He made such a big deal out of it,' he said. 'Went down on his knee at sunset by the Cam.'

'Of course he did,' Vicky said.

'And one week later she copped off with Jack.'

I tried to keep my expression neutral. But inside I was ransacking my memory. Jack. I couldn't remember if I'd heard the name before. Someone he played football with? I don't know why I didn't just ask. I think I didn't want to admit that Caden had never told me this story. So I tried not to react, dug my fingers into the grass, tried to concentrate on Kieran's monologue.

'We had a party on her boat. For his birthday, in September. And we all went mental. Caden was drinking a fuck-ton.' He nodded at his own assertion. 'He's drunk way too much since his dad topped himself. I guess he wasn't really with it that night. Neither was I, to be fair. My ex had just moved out, and I think someone had bought a bottle of tequila. I went fucking nuts after that.'

He looked sternly at both of us and frowned, as if to emphasize just how fucking nuts he had been.

'Anyway, at some point Caden figures out that Jack and Giselle have locked themselves in the bathroom. He pounds on the door, but they won't open up. It was crazy. She comes out and goes for Caden – we had to pull her off him. And Jack drives away – he was absolutely fucked, mind, we'd been doing coke as well. Not that I make a habit of it.' He gave Vicky a long lazy playboy smile. 'Blow's not my thing, I just do it when—'

'Then what happened?' I said, interrupting him.

'Caden goes after him. He never told me what happened, but I think he beat the shit out of Jack. Totalled his car. It was so fucked up.'

There was a pause.

'But I mean, Caden was naive. I could have seen it coming.'

'Why?' Vicky said.

'She was the kind of girl you have to keep tabs on. It was a nightmare. My ex *hated* Giselle. I don't think Jack stood a chance. I blame her more than him, to be honest.'

'That figures,' Vicky said, giving me a wry smile.

He was combing the grass with his fingers. *This is doing me harm*, I thought. His words were working their way deeper and deeper into me, from skin to flesh to my insides, a scalpel to the very core, until I felt it nick the bone. *It's a bad idea for me to hear this.*

'So then what happened?' Vicky asked. 'They broke up?'

'Yeah. And I'm the only one he still speaks to who was at that party. Him and Jack haven't spoken at all, far as I know. It's so fucked. She was such a bitch. Smoking hot, though.'

Vicky shrugged. 'You can't really judge from the outside, though. I mean, you call her a bitch, but who knows? He might have been abusing her. Or gaslighting her.' She threw me a sideways look.

'Why?' I said. 'Why does it have to be his fault? Why does there always need to be a man behind a woman's actions? Maybe she's just a terrible person.'

There was a silence. The electronic chirping of the birds in the bushes irritated me.

Kieran turned to me then.

'I guess you're good for him, Anna. You're nice. You're a good girlfriend.'

I wondered if there was any stage in my life when being told I was a good girlfriend would have felt like a compliment, rather than an insult, as it did now. I was sick of being perceived as kind. I was sick of being the person who put on the Anna Show.

Kieran was leaning close to Vicky, the shadows of the flowers trembling over her back, his arm. His lids were low, his voice gravelly, close to a whisper. So this was what Giselle had done. *How disappointing*, I thought. *How utterly banal and un-epic.* Infidelity. Surely I was capable of that.

I said that I had to leave, to go and put up the posters. I was halfway across the garden when Vicky caught up with me.

'Wait!' she said, fiddling with her earlobes. She dropped the earrings in the palm of my hand.

'I—' She swallowed. 'I—' She shook her head, smiled a close-lipped smile. She put her hand around my fist, closing it over the diamonds.

'Don't worry,' I said, realizing that she couldn't bring herself to speak. I wasn't angry, only relieved that she was finally admitting that she had stolen from me. Proof that my suspicion was justified.

'It doesn't matter. Thanks for looking after them.' I turned to walk off, but she called after me again.

'And there's this.' She rummaged in her bag. I expected her to pull out the engagement ring. But she tugged on the red lanyard, and held it out to me hooked on her hand. The memory stick hung from it.

'Where did you find it?'

It swung very slightly in the breezeless day.

'Hanging on the back of the door. In the spare room.' She seemed to hesitate, but then she reached over and hooked it around my neck affectionately, carefully.

'It's really bad, dude. You should dump him.'

# 8

## Social Realism

I LEFT THE MEMORY stick hanging from my neck, my heart beating fast and shallow. The face of the devil would have frightened me less. It felt intensely animate – a darkly enchanted object, like the blood-encrusted milk teeth.

I found the river and followed it north. So this was what Caden had been looking for. This was why he'd turned the house upside down. Vicky had taken his memory stick as well as the ring. And now she was telling me to break up with him.

The path was lined by obscenely early poppies, little fires that produced no warmth. Haemoglobin red, a smell of metal that reminded me of dissection days. A jogger coming down the river path pushed past me, and I felt a flick of his sweat on my legs. I hurried home, blinking as I let myself into the dark room. A zoo pong: the guinea-pigs.

I went over to the cage and gave Bubble a cuddle. He purred with pleasure. I checked the time. Caden would not be home for an hour. I had time to sort out the guinea-pigs and cook us a nice dinner. But I also had time to check what was on the memory stick.

Carrying Bubble in my arms, I made my way up the stairs.

I sat on the bed, the guinea-pig nestled between my legs. I plugged the memory stick into my laptop.

There were hundreds of folders, all of which seemed related to Caden's work. There was one called 'Physiotherapy Practice 2: Acute and Emergency Care' and 'Professionalism and team working'. I stroked Bubble with my left hand, and with my right hand I clicked on each file. I felt a ridiculous suspense as each of them loaded, and a desperate relief when they revealed themselves to contain only the documents they described. Patient files, rehab protocols. My nervous excitement lessened with each click, and I entered a meditative state that was almost tranquil.

Then I clicked on 'Work Stuff' and I was jerked out of my peaceful flow.

The folder was full of videos: and from the screen previews, I saw that they were not 'Work Stuff' at all.

I clicked on the first one. I recognized the bathroom mirror: the sink; Caden's razor and toothbrush in their familiar places. A lot of moving around, bobbing up and down as if the room were shaking. Perhaps he hadn't meant to record this; perhaps it had been captured by accident. But then the camera was stilled; its gaze became fixed, deliberate. It pointed downwards. I saw a woman bent over the sink, naked apart from a blue skirt rolled up over her waist, her lower back dimpled and arching. A man's hand on her hip, holding her in place. There was no sound, though I knew the sounds Caden made, something like pent-up anger. He reached over and pulled her hair. And that's when she raised her head, so that her face swam into view in the mirror. Her chin raised proudly, her eyes both vague and intent with pleasure. She was watching her reflection.

I clicked on the next video. It was also filmed in the bathroom. The camera was on her face. She stared into it. She didn't smile. The camera travelled down, followed her fingers as she dipped them into his boxer shorts. She was wearing a few bangle bracelets, and I could imagine the noise they would make, clicking together as she worked her hand. Her hair was threaded through his fingers, very black against his skin. I didn't like how Caden grabbed it so hard.

I held my breath as if they might be able to hear me, realize they were being watched. I was doing myself harm, I knew it. But I couldn't stop. I felt sick and turned on. A flaring feeling in my stomach. Like I'd swallowed something bad, a rotten oyster whose pearl began to beat inside me like a second heart. I clicked on the next video. It was filmed in the bedroom where I was sitting. I could tell, because the orchids were shivering pinkly on the windowsill. Again it was Caden who held the camera. She stood by the edge of the bed. Her body was segmented by tan lines, her hair falling in a thick sweeping line just above her breasts. A dark triangle of hair flared between her legs, which shocked me. Caden had asked me to shave.

I felt something funny happen to my vision. A distorting effect, like rainbows in slick motor oil pooling on water. I couldn't even see the video any more. Something was wrong with my eyes, and in my stomach.

I gave a start. I had gripped Bubble too tightly, and he squeaked from fear. I nearly wept as his warm pee soaked my shorts. He was like a child, with his big front teeth and chubby body shivering under my fingers.

'I'm so sorry.'

I pulled the memory stick out and went to the kitchen. I tried to slice some strawberries for the guinea-pigs' dessert but my fingers were numb, and the engorged organ-shaped berries eluded my grasp, rolling on to the floor.

I caught sight of myself in the metallic countertop I'd so carefully cleaned. Tears and Snoopy-nose running, red-faced like a distraught toddler. I'd believed Caden. Part of me had hung on to some hope that I was being paranoid; that all of this was in my head, that I just had problems with low self-esteem. That he loved me. I thought of all the things I'd done for him. The hours cleaning, folding blueberries into muffin trays, the endless exhausting blow jobs; all of it rose like bile in my throat. I was such an idiot.

The worst thing about all this was that I knew exactly what I would find on that memory stick. I knew exactly how this story would unfold; I had known it from the moment Caden mentioned his ex on our first date in the Maypole. I knew what was coming but I stayed with him anyway. Why? A sick compulsion to see the car-crash unfold? Perhaps fate is just the inability to act on one's intuition.

I gave up on the strawberries, went into the bathroom. I'd always found myself ugly in that room; the lights were like luminol on the crime scene of my face and body, letting everything show; the blackheads and freak hairs on my chin and cheeks. I put my hand between my legs and watched myself. It felt good, satisfyingly vicious, to force pleasure on myself on top of the pain. I wanted to know what she saw in the mirror when she watched herself being filmed. She hadn't looked at the camera; she was looking at her reflection. What registered at that moment?

I pulled off my clothes, got into the shower. I shivered beneath the hot water. I was the one who was degraded by watching these videos, not her. I didn't know the etiquette around this kind of material. But it couldn't be right that Caden was still looking at them. Surely she would be upset if she knew. Still more if she were to find out that other people had seen them.

I got out of the shower, dressed, hooked the memory stick over my neck. Without thinking, I started cooking. I peeled some potatoes, sliced them thin as coins, and dropped them into a pan. To think Caden had let me believe there was some flaw in my character. That I needed help. *Are those my self-esteem issues, Caden, or are these videos of you and your ex?*

The thin white discs were stiffening into golden and orange crisps, brittle autumn leaves.

I heard Caden outside, calling something to the neighbour. I took off the lanyard and stuffed it into my bra.

A knob of butter; salt.

The keys turned.

'What is that smell?' He came bounding into the kitchen, flushed from exercise, his black hair plastered to his forehead.

'It's not done yet!' I said, as he reached over my shoulder.

'Tastes done to me,' he said, his mouth half full, all smiles and goodwill. 'Did you have a fun day with Vicky? Good to see one of the girls?'

He leant in to kiss me, pressed his forehead against mine. We stood there for a while, head to head. From that perspective, his eyes seemed to revolve to the sides of his face, and his nose grew long and equine. He was an idiot. He was so clueless. Even as my skull was pressed against his, he didn't have a clue about the kind of images that were dancing behind the bone. I almost felt sorry for him. Almost.

A bad night. The moon shining closer and closer as the night wore on, like a white-robed nurse approaching from a great distance to deliver bad news. Caden cried out in his sleep, but the rattle of the fan drowned out the sound of his nightmares.

He coaxed me into the day with a warm guinea-pig, a strong coffee and a slice of impeccably buttered toast. As soon as he left for work, I went to fetch my computer. I spent the morning watching the videos in bed. *Just one last time*, I told myself. Repetitive cycles of pleasure. Holding my breath, my whole body stiffening, my legs rigid beneath the sweaty sheets. I watched the same scenes several times and felt the images layer one on top of the other, the sediment accumulating and hardening in me as they became my own memories.

Finally I managed to pull myself away. I would throw the memory stick into the river. Not for Caden's sake, but for my own. And for his ex's. I couldn't hold on to this. It would drive me crazy.

I dressed quickly, gulping the now-cold coffee Caden had brought me, and left the house with the remaining cat posters under my arm, the lanyard around my neck. I took a meandering path to the river. The pavement seemed to buck and sag beneath my feet, distorted by tree roots.

I was fastidious about sticking up the posters. Perhaps if I made a really good job of it, I might succeed in convincing myself that nothing had happened to Pringle. She might even come home. I put them in all the obvious places – outside the Golden Hind, the working men's club, the Green Dragon pub – even though I knew my imaginary non-dead cat was unlikely ever to stray that far.

As I approached the spot where I had dumped her body, I saw a group of workmen clustered around the bin. The rush of terror was so intense that I almost groaned aloud. There was an awful fishy smell; surely they'd noticed it, surely they had found her.

But then the details of the scene began to fill in: cigarettes, coffee, fragments of laughter. They were having a break, enjoying the sun. Nothing to worry about.

I crossed over Green Dragon Bridge, turned right

towards Midsummer Common and Jesus Green; the opposite direction to the narrowboats, away from the *Rise and Shine*. I could not cope with seeing her. I wouldn't be able to pretend I didn't know who she was, to act normally. Not after what I had seen. I needed to throw the memory stick in the water. I couldn't believe how green it was on the river path – ludicrously green, out of control, ferns and grasses and stinging nettles staggering beneath their own weight.

My phone rang as I reached Midsummer Common. It was an unknown number. I answered warily, frightened it might be the NHS Test and Trace service informing me I'd been in contact with someone with Covid.

'Anna?'

It was Rosa. I felt a wonderful relief, followed by a sharp stab of fear. *Oh no.*

'Yes. Hello?' My voice sounded steady enough.

'Are you free to speak right now?'

'Yes.' I looked around for somewhere to sit, but then decided against it. There were too many cows, and I was scared they would come near me. I kept walking in the direction of Jesus Green.

'Crabwell found out that it was you who took the guinea-pigs.'

I had a feeling of reality slipping rope-like through my fingers, like I was falling, or that the ground was receding beneath my feet.

'Hello? Did you hear me?'

'Yes.' I didn't even try to deny it.

'Why didn't you tell me you were traumatized by the dissections?'

I could barely bring myself to answer. 'I don't know.'

'Was it because it was an all-male environment? Were you uncomfortable?'

'Yes,' I said. I knew it was a lie, but I made a feeble

attempt to save my skin, grabbing on to the lifeline she'd thrown me. 'It was the men. And the dissections. I was traumatized.'

'I wish you had told me, Anna. I could have helped you. It's too late now.'

There was silence. I was vaguely aware of a large brown cow on my periphery. But I could not move.

'Crabwell wanted to tell the police. But I spoke to him. He agreed not to press charges against you. If you withdraw from the PhD.'

I swallowed. 'I understand.'

'So you can't return. To the lab.'

I couldn't answer. I just breathed in and out, making the phone speaker whistle.

'I'm sorry, but he also asked me to recoup the funding you received for the Easter Term. Are you in a position to do that?'

She talked on and on, but I wasn't listening. It must have been Charles. He was the only person who knew in the lab group. I'd sent him that picture, trying to get his attention. My heart expanded and contracted, propelling itself from chest to stomach to throat, its jellyfish tentacles reaching my toes, stinging the tips of my fingers which pulsed against the phone.

'Stay in touch,' she said, and I hung up without answering.

I sunk down on to my knees. The grass was full of daisies, and it was like being ankle-deep in the purest, truest light.

I was being kicked out of Cambridge. I had to repay all the money. Five thousand pounds. Where would I get it from? Certainly not from my parents. I didn't have nearly enough money saved up. Perhaps my brother could lend it to me, until I worked to pay it back.

I messaged Vicky. *CAN YOU TALK?*

*I'm with Kieran.*

That was bound to happen. I put my phone down, looked up at the sky. An unfocused blue eye. The lanyard was too tight around my neck and the memory stick dug into my back, but I did not move. What would happen to all my data? All that work gone to waste. Perhaps they'd give it to Charles. My papers would be published under his name. It wasn't the first time he'd betrayed me to Crabwell. It had been crazy to send him the photo. No one came near me, apart from a few dogs, their cold questing noses kissing my neck and face. I straightened to stroke one and heard someone call my name.

'Anna.'

I put my hand to my brow, shielding my eyes from the sun.

'Ian?'

Charles's friend, my old crush. He had grown a moustache, like a hot-chocolate stain on his upper lip, and he had an old-fashioned camera slung around his neck. I'd only ever seen him in winter clothes, and I was surprised by the spareness of his legs and arms. The same Humpty Dumpty egg head; the same luminescent white skin.

I stood up, went in for a hug, but then hesitated.

'Oh, don't worry,' he said, throwing an arm around me. 'I've already had Covid.'

'God. Were you OK?'

'It was pretty bad. Angus had it as well, and he got so ill he tried to call an ambulance. The A&E people talked him down, though.'

'That's terrible.'

'And what about you? What did the workhorse do when she was set free?'

'Uhm. I guess it has been an unprecedented time,' I said.

He laughed. 'What are you doing here, anyway?'

'Communing with nature. What about you?'

He tapped the camera. 'I was just taking some shots of the Travellers in Fen Road.'

'Why?'

'Social realism.'

'You know how that makes you sound?'

He got defensive immediately. 'Look, there are only so many pictures I can take of King's Parade,' he said. 'People complain about class privilege, but they also complain if you try to take pictures of the deprived. It's annoying.' I didn't answer, and he took my silence as a sign that I was chastened by his impeccable reasoning.

'What are you doing right now?'

I hesitated. What the hell was I doing?

'Do you want to come over?' he asked. 'Have some tea?'

'Sure.'

Ian lived in one of the brutalist buildings of Jesus College. A strange wet-cardboard smell hung in the entrance, something close to turmeric. His 'rooms', as he called his en-suite, were on the ground floor, with green, fuzzy felt carpet and the strangest yellow wallpaper, covered in large dragonflies with diamanté eyes.

'I added those rhinestones,' he said, when I looked closer, 'when I was bored. Sort of scary, isn't it?'

'Terrifying.'

There were no chairs in his room, so I sat on a low stool while he disappeared into the kitchen to make tea.

My phone buzzed. Caden: *Kieran coming over later, that OK? Was thinking of making a bonfire?*

A bonfire with Kieran sounded about as appealing as doing a dissection with my mouth. I didn't answer, but returned to inspecting the books on Ian's shelf. Norton's Shakespeare; a large compendium of Nietzsche's works. All of them dog-eared, heavily annotated. I opened a page at random, fell on one in *Thus Spoke Zarathustra*:

'Two different things wanteth the true man: danger

and play. Therefore he wants woman, as the most dangerous plaything.'

Ian had underlined this so many times he'd nearly torn
through the paper. I slapped the book shut as he returned
with a tray, trying to look like the most dangerous
plaything.

'You can borrow that, if you want.'

'It'll go totally over my head.'

'I can explain it, if you want.'

'Thanks, Ian.'

He poured the milk and nudged a plate of biscuits
towards me. My phone vibrated. I pushed it away.

'Here,' he said, 'let me dip a biscuit for you.'

He lowered the shortbread into the tea, and I watched
the sugar crystals darkening as the liquid spread like a
stain. Before I could protest, he pressed the sodden biscuit
to my lips. I swallowed. He stared at my mouth as I
chewed.

'You look different, Anna. Really good.'

'I'm wearing make-up, Ian.'

He shook his head, smiled. He reached over and
touched my face, running his fingers over my eyes, my
lips. My phone buzzed again, and the thought of Caden
waiting for me alone at home spurred me on. He kissed
my knuckles, my neck. He unbuttoned my shirt very
carefully, folded it before laying it down, and then took
off the lanyard around my neck, placed it on the table as
if he understood that it and I were precious, to be handled
with care.

He was slow, tremulous. There was none of Caden's
urgency, none of his dirty talk. Deep sighs. The taste of his
black tea; a smell of sweat, but not unpleasant. A little
musky, like ferns. The tips of his fingers damp and hot on
my skin. His chest pale, his heart beating like an echo of
mine. I thought about Giselle. The images from the video

flashed in my mind: her face looking at its own reflection; Caden's white-knuckled grip in her hair.

'I'm sorry.' Ian broke away. He was kneading his crotch with one hand, stroking my arm with the other. 'This never usually happens.'

'Don't worry.'

He continued his furious movements; I pretended to be absorbed in his kisses but sent surreptitious glances to his lap. He looked as if he were hurting himself.

'We don't have to do this,' I said. 'I don't mind.'

'This never happens. I don't get it. You have to believe me, this has never happened.'

I took his hand, tried to get him to meet my eye. 'It's really not a big deal. Please don't worry.'

We returned to the cold tea. I tried to put on the Anna Show, to cheer him up, but he had gone deep within himself. He looked hurt, though I suppose I was the one who'd been insulted. An erection could not be forced or faked. It was an objective measure. I was almost grateful for the honesty.

# 9

## Lonesome Cowboy

T HE COWS STOOD BEFORE me in a semi-circle, their elastic jaws chewing in unison. Snakes of grass hung in festoons from their open mouths, each face a long sha-manic mask looming out of the night, and an ayahuasca smell of purge all about them.

I broke into a run, hoping they'd scatter, but they held their ground. I searched for a way through but they closed ranks, eyeing me as if they knew I'd done something bad. Their soft lowing had a warning note to it. I tried to calm down. Of course the cows weren't menacing me. They were dairy cows, I told myself. Milky mothery beasts. I looked up at the sky, took a deep breath. *Pull yourself together. Don't let what you've done show on your face. Caden will kick you out and you have no money now. Hold it together.*

I saw an opening and ran through, fearing one would charge and knock me over, but I slipped past them and onto Midsummer Common, and suddenly I thought of his ex on the football pitch, how deftly she wove her way through the other players, and what that must feel like. I'll never know what it's like to be her; I'm stuck in the confines of this body and brain. As much as I strain and strain against them, nothing happens. It's as futile as bang-ing my head against the wall; though Ji-woo once said that if you did that an infinite number of times, your head would pass through – something about the vacuum in the atoms and molecules in your head lining up perfectly with the wall.

I suppose there is a universe amongst the infinite universes out there where she envies me, where I play football and live in a houseboat and accept the mantle of femininity with ease, and there is a universe where Charles hasn't betrayed me – and perhaps even one where he has, but Crabwell has taken my side – but I am stuck in this one: the one where I have a memory stick full of pornography in my pocket, and where Caden is still up, sitting alone beside the dying embers of a fire.

He was smoking an actual cigarette, narrowing his eyes against the smoke, looking like the lonesome cowboy.

'Where've you been?' He sounded drunk.

'Out.'

'With who?'

'Ian.'

He reached for my hand and I waited for him to confront me, but he remained silent. He was so impassive, so blank. It was a provocation. It made me want to force a reaction, to shock him out of this equanimity.

'Caden?' The fire was clicking mechanically in the background. 'I have to tell you something.'

He turned towards me, and the cone of light from the outside lamp hit his face. His pupils contracted, like a lemoned oyster. His beauty was always a surprise, always a shock.

'What is it?' he said.

And just as I had been unable to tell him the awful news about Pringle, I couldn't tell him about Ian.

'I've been kicked out of Cambridge,' I said instead. 'Because of the guinea-pigs. Crabwell found out we took them.'

From his expression, I knew he had no clue who I was talking about.

'My supervisor. At the university! I've literally told you about him millions of times.'

'Oh shit,' he said. He was slurring his words a bit. 'That's not good.'

'No, it's not.'

I thought he might apologize for the part he'd played in the whole thing – he was the one who suggested I take them, who insisted I didn't return them. But he didn't.

'I'm sure you will think of a solution,' Caden said. His tone was too casual. He didn't seem to think it was a big deal. 'You got into Cambridge – you could go anywhere.'

'But I need references, Caden. Who the hell is going to write a reference once they know I've stolen from a lab? I'll never get a job in academia again.' The fire glittered hotly in the background.

'Well . . .' Palms facing the black sky. 'Then you can get another job. Like everyone else. I know it's a step down for you after Cambridge.'

'What kind of job can I do?' I said. 'Cleaner? Sex worker? I guess I've had enough work experience at your house.'

'Maybe,' he said. His tone strained with dislike. 'Don't know if you're good enough to charge.'

'Fuck you.'

He went to fetch a cup of water and poured it on to the hot ash, then tipped the cold slather of the fire pit on to the grass. He was right. I had thought I was so smart. But my supposedly superior brain had got me nowhere.

Caden was unwell in the night. He threw the blankets off himself and then snatched them back, before bolting from the bed. I followed him downstairs to the bathroom. His arms encircled the toilet bowl. He was sick, again and again. Each retch sounded like a ripping sheet, as if he were tearing the lining of his stomach. I offered towels and water, but he wanted to be left alone.

'Please. Just go away.'

He kicked the door shut behind me.

It began to rain; the gutter was gurgling, refluxing. The sound reminded me of Crabwell clearing his throat. The enormity of what Charles had done washed over me. The hours spent on western blots, on organ staining, dissections – all of that hard work. So much wasted effort, not only at Cambridge but at Exeter, at school. All those breaks spent in the library, swotting away while my friends had fun, had been for nothing.

My phone buzzed.

It was Vicky, sending me another Spareroom.co.uk ad.

*1£/2br/Arbury*
*FREE CRAB*
*Want a friendly woman of any age. Nothing weird about this ad, I'd just like a woman's company. You have your own room and wardrobe. Text if interested.*
*P.S. There is some leftover crab meat in the freezer and I can throw that in for free.*

Anna: *Are you still looking for a place? What about Kieran's?*

Vicky: *Awful sex.*

Anna: *Explain.*

Vicky: *It's just British men. Bland/bestial/uncircumcised.*

Caden came back to bed, but neither of us slept. When he heard the neighbour dragging her bin over the gravel, Caden started to dress for work.

'You're not well. What if it's Covid?'

'It isn't that. I get stomach aches like this sometimes, when I'm stressed.'

248

Stressed. He had never admitted to having an interior state of being before. I hurried to make him something to eat. Toast, butter, dribble of honey, excised crusts.

He held the bread sacramentally on his tongue. He couldn't swallow, so I passed him some kitchen roll and he spat it out, and I remembered the cows chewing on their spit-up, and thought maybe they'd been prophesying this scene, this unhappy breakfast.

'*Please* don't go to work today. I'm begging you. Just stay.'

'I can't.'

'I'll put on clean sheets and you can go back to bed.'

'I've got this girl from the Boat Race coming in. She's rowed with Team GB. I can't just cancel.'

'Right, can't pass up massaging the young Olympian!'

His toast fell face-down on to the sofa as he pushed his plate away.

'You sold yourself as someone who *wasn't* jealous, Anna.'

'I didn't *sell myself* at all.'

But he was already halfway out of the door. I followed him outside to fetch the bins and noticed – too late – that the neighbour was standing on her doorstep.

'You seen the cat?' she said, rattling her can of treats like a beggar's collection box.

'No.'

'I'm sure the people down Fen Road got her. Do you think she's dead?'

I bobbed my head, neither a yes nor a no, and went back inside. I cleaned up the kitchen counter and the still-warm package of spit-up Caden had left me to take care of, then changed the sawdust in the guinea-pigs' cage, marvelling at the number of torpedo-shaped droppings they produced.

'You guys have got me into a lot of trouble,' I told them, as they nibbled at my fingers. 'Not sure you were worth it.'

I considered calling home. My mum enjoyed a good

disaster, even when she was in one of her low phases. She might even send me the money. She was good at self-sacrifice. I think that's why she stayed married to my dad. Everyone felt sorry for her, including her. The poor, long-suffering wife. Putting up with him. Marrying a bastard is the fastest way to sainthood.

I would have to apply for a job. I had no idea where to even start. I guessed I could try to be a lab technician. I was good at killing mice. But it would be better to do something normal. The kind of job Caden's ex might do. I had no idea at all what she did for a living. I sat on the sofa, thinking I might look up a few possible job options on my laptop, but I ended up returning to the memory stick.

I chose one of her in the bedroom. The camera followed the door swinging open, and she was standing beside the bed, getting dressed. At first she looked surprised, but then gave a superior kind of smile, reacting to Caden's expression which I could not see, and to the camera that trembled up and down her body, like the roaming eyes of a flustered teenage boy. Caden took her wrist and had her turn around.

I felt like I was on the inside of Caden's perception, attuned to exactly what pleased him. I *was* him now, filled by a desire that was not my own. But it wasn't her that I lusted after. I didn't even want to be her. It was still all about Caden. While I watched the videos of the person he desired, I was inside his thoughts, inside his body. And I felt I knew him more intimately than I ever had. For the first time, I truly understood him. And isn't that a form of empathy? Putting yourself in someone else's skin. Isn't that a form of love?

I could hear the neighbour. She was still outside, each rattle a tiny pulse in my stomach, an umbilical wrench. Was she talking to herself? The rattle grew more persistent, and now it seemed she was knocking on the door. I ignored her and continued to watch the video, but the knocking went on, and this created an excited tension in me. The woman on the other side of the door searching for an animal only I knew was dead. I wouldn't let her in. The power felt delicious. I looked at the clock above to see how long she'd keep knocking, knowing I was in there. I was still watching the video, and I loved the feeling of almost being caught in the act of doing something so repulsive. The hands of the clock seemed to be tightening around my abdomen and throat, tighter and tighter, until the coil seemed to snap in me and I found myself rushing to the door, my heartbeat in my ears. I twisted the key and let the door swing open.

Giselle stood on the doorstep. The poster of Pringle was in her hand.

She had come to me.

## 10

# The Most Dangerous Plaything

S HE LOOKED SO UNCOMFORTABLE standing on the doorstep, back at the house she thought she had left behind for ever, and there I was, towering over her, with my aquiline-not-hooked nose – and a look in my eyes she couldn't quite figure out. She shrunk back a little, taking in my height, my broad shoulders.

'I'm here about Pringle,' she said in accented English, and held up one of the posters.

*What to do*, I asked myself. *Admit that I know who she is and know her intimately, that videos of her having sex are on the lanyard dangling from my neck?*

'Ah, right,' I said. 'Well, we haven't seen the cat for a while. We—I put up the posters.'

I didn't dare claim him as mine; not to her face, anyway.

I recognized her so exactly, it was almost like watching myself in a dream mirror. Liquid brown hair tied in an intricate knot; lustrous skin that glistened like something anointed. Her eyes were more animated than I'd imagined. Always moving, but not in a nervous, darting manner. A lazy, slow roll, like an incurious, sated jaguar.

And features that the videos had not captured; she had freckles at the inner and outer corners of both of her eyes. So symmetrical, in the exact same spot on either side, as if she had drawn them on with a pen. But they were real freckles and there were some on her eyelids, too. I noticed them when she blinked. They looked like tiny planets orbiting her irises, which were the exact same dark brown shade. It was easy to stare, to become mesmerized by the constellation of freckles, to try to find the key to the system of her beauty.

She looked up at me. She must have already known who I was, or at least have guessed. I leant against the door frame. I didn't want my height to intimidate her.

'Do you want to come in?' I said.

'Uhm.' Her eyes glanced over my shoulder to the room beyond, questioning.

I shook my head. 'He's at work.'

She followed me in, shrugging off her bag and letting it drop on to the floor in the entrance. I shut the door behind us. I wondered if she felt locked in.

She looked around the front room. I wondered what she saw, what string of associations were tugging at her mind. I saw her take in the changes I'd made. The reorganized shoe rack, the books arranged in order of size. And then her eyes lifted; she saw the picture frame, and the empty space where her photo had once been. She turned to me.

'You know who I am, right?'

'He mentioned you, yeah.'

'Do you mind if I have some water? The heat is terrible.'

'Sure.'

I followed her into the kitchen, and she went to help herself from what was once the glassware cupboard; but I'd moved everything around. She stood, disoriented, while I reached above her into the cabinet and filled two glasses.

'You spend a lot of time cleaning for him?'

I bristled: 'No, he does his share.'

'Pfffff!' she laughed, showing the gap between her front teeth. 'Come on!'

I was unsettled by a feeling of déjà vu. I remembered that I'd heard her laugh in one of the videos. I made myself join in.

'Yes. I clean up after him all the fucking time.'

Her eyes rose from her glass and travelled to the hole in the wall.

'We had a big dispute here once,' she said, punching her fist into her palm, as if to show me what had happened.

'He punched it? Caden?'

'Who do you think?' she said, her eyes still fixed on the wall. I didn't know if that meant it was him or her.

'What was the fight about?'

She gave a shrug.

'Stuff.'

I thought of the closed smile Caden had given me when I'd asked him about this same incident. She too seemed to enjoy the sweet superiority of dangling a secret in front of me. Let her look smug; I knew far more about her than she imagined.

She sipped the water. I wondered if her nails – emerald, sparkling – were real or fake. I thought about asking her. My hands ran a sponge over the countertop.

'She used to sleep here.' She pointed to the corner, by the door to the garden.

I nodded.

'We adored that cat.'

I felt uncomfortable. There was something indecent about that entity, the two of them together in one word: 'we', like one beast with two backs.

'I loved her too.'

There was a pause. *She knows I'm lying*, I thought, panicked. *She knows.*

'Do you want a drink?' I asked.

She shook her head and placed the glass face-down on the counter.

'I meant a proper drink.' I pointed to the liquor bottles on top of the fridge.

I didn't wait for her reply; I went ahead and poured us two glasses of white wine. I dropped an ice cube into my drink and went to add one to hers, but she snatched the glass away.

'Not in wine, thanks.'

I wanted to say, *I fucking know you're not meant to put ice in wine, you stuck-up French bitch, but it's hot today.* She followed me into the garden.

The grass was littered with the silver discs of crushed beer cans from the bonfire the night before. She took Caden's usual chair, and we sat beside the ashes of the fire.

It was so unlikely: the two of us, having drinks together. That appeared to be a thought we shared, as we suddenly grinned at each other.

'When did you meet?' she asked, pointing at the beer cans.

'A while ago,' I said vaguely. I wanted her to think I might have been with him before they broke up.

'What's your job?'

'I'm a PhD student. I study physiology.'

She didn't react.

'I'm studying how diabetes affects gestation. There's this hormone that shuttles glucose between the placenta and the womb, and I think I've managed to figure out how it contributes to the inflammation mechanism in pregnant women.'

I went on and on, even though I knew this couldn't possibly interest her, and had never interested Caden one bit. But it interested me. It interested me so much, and my enthusiasm for research I was no longer involved in made me feel sorry for myself. I was no longer at the university. I was doing nothing of worth, and much of ill-worth. And she wasn't even listening. She drained her glass and shifted in her chair as if readying to leave, but I filled it again, talking rapidly so that she wouldn't be able to interrupt to refuse another drink.

'Cheers,' I said. The fingers clasped around my own glass met as strangers, as if they belonged to two different people. She lifted her glass with mine, but didn't drink.

*So*, I thought, *this is how she looks when she is bored, or wary.*

If I could only slow time, observe the most minor detail, carefully record every inhalation and exhalation. But time did not slow down, or fan out into a series of distinct moments. It compressed itself; every one of her gestures and movements merged together, became simultaneous.

'It's a shame about the cat,' she said, bringing matters back to the motive for her visit.

I took another sip. The clear liquid glittered in the glass. Like a sunbeam shining through a prism, the alcohol distilled the emotions within me and produced a rainbow of distinct feelings. I felt so profoundly jealous of her beauty, and of how this beauty would give her access to a world I'd never know. But I felt great compassion for her too, because she had no idea what I had dangling from my neck. Her ignorance moved me. I felt guilty: for all I'd done to her and to Caden. And I felt pure-hearted admiration. The female Suárez, in the flesh.

'I actually really don't give a fuck about the cat,' I said.

She burst out laughing, showing the gap in her teeth again. *So*, I thought. *This is how she looks when she's amused.*

'It drove me crazy,' I said. 'It was here all the time, and it was so high maintenance.'

She laughed again, and once more I felt the involuntary

memory, the echo from the sex video. *God. I ought to give it back to her, the memory stick.*

'*She*, not it!' she corrected me. 'I really did love her, but yeah, she was always here.'

'It feels like you've always been here too.'

'What do you mean?'

'He never stops talking about you.'

She crossed her legs, scratched at a smudge on her shorts with a long nail. Real, definitely.

'Well, the break-up was really bad.'

Her phone beeped, and she pulled it out of her pocket. There was a Hello Kitty sticker on the case. The stupid, cute cat with the big red bow, smiling at me. *It might be a coincidence*, I told myself, attempting to tame the rage that was now purring in my chest. But another, more sanguine part of me drew the link between the bloody plaster and the phone case and came to a reasonable conclusion. She had betrayed him. They had broken up. They had continued to sleep together, even after he and I met. She was that kind of woman.

I felt an odd jolt of unreality, a green-screen flicker. What was I doing there? I didn't have anything bigger than a walk-on part in Caden and Giselle's love story, not really. It was like I'd stumbled on to the wrong set. And I was ruining it for everyone. They were meant to be together; I was meant to be solitary and brilliant. But for some reason I was still there. Loitering, interfering, messing everything up. No one wanted me in this movie. Why couldn't I just leave?

She was still staring into the face of her phone. It buzzed again with another message. She gave a secret smile and started typing while I watched, wondering who she was talking to. She looked rapt, as if she were in love. She had her whole life elsewhere; she did not realize that she was the centre of mine.

I finished my drink. She got up to leave, her glass of wine untouched.

'Don't you want your stuff back?' I said, straining to hide the emotion from my voice. I wanted every trace of her purged from the house. First the clothes, then the memory stick.

She looked up from her phone.

'What?'

'Your stuff. He has loads of it here.'

'What stuff?'

'Like your shoes, your make-up, some bags – loads of it.'

'I told him to get rid of it.' Her phone pinged again, and she looked at it longingly.

'Don't you wanna see it?'

'Where is it?'

'In boxes upstairs,' I replied.

I went up ahead of her. I felt her eyes on me. I felt so unprepared, so frumpy. Always the same thoughts, the same drumbeat for months on months. My self-hatred bored even me.

I opened the door of the spare room. 'Here,' I said. 'All of this is yours.'

'Oh God,' she said, surveying the stacks of boxes. She unclicked the lid of the one on top and began to rummage. The football boots, transparent bags of make-up, the mini-skirt. Her back was turned to me. We were so close I could smell her. Two competing scents: synthetic strawberry – which I thought belonged to her hairspray – and something else more fundamental; a tart, unplaceable sweet something that I already knew. I had smelt it a long time ago, and I experienced a wonderful relief at finding its source. It was like suddenly being able to identify the source of a ringing I'd heard for months, or remembering a word that had been on the tip of my tongue. *Ah, here it is! That's it!*

She sifted through the box and moved to the side, so I

could see her profile. She was frowning, but smiling too – an enigmatic smile that might have been evidence of the memories the objects triggered, or her embarrassment that I was so close to her. The braid in her hair was more convoluted than I'd thought at first glance. The strands twisted together: A over B then through C, B under D, C looped through E, but then I lost track. I couldn't see any pattern; it seemed unsolvable.

She turned to face me.

'It's so weird he kept all this. I don't know why he didn't get rid of it.'

It was obvious to me why, but I felt she was goading me to say what we both knew.

'Because he still loves you.'

She looked up at me, considered me with those slow smoky eyes. But then she shrugged, went back to rummaging through the things I'd treasured for months.

'You know,' she said, breaking the silence, 'Caden has a side that isn't so nice.' She paused, as if searching for the right word. 'He provokes you, then when you get mad, he pretends he doesn't know what you're talking about. Plays the innocent. He made me feel crazy, sometimes.'

My hand fluttered to my throat. I touched my finger to the pulse there, and felt the lanyard. I should have given it to her. I should have given it to her right then, and said, 'I found this, I think you should have it.'

I cleared my throat. 'Did you and Caden sleep together? When he was seeing me?'

Her lips parted a little. She met my gaze, unblinking. Just when I thought she had been quiet for a beat too long, she shook her head.

'No,' she said, in a voice so light, so casual, that it was as if I had asked her if she fancied a sausage roll. Her nonchalance might have been proof of her guilt, or proof of her innocence. There was no way of knowing.

259

'I wasn't that into him,' she added. She returned to her things. She fingered the Lululemon headband, her old passport, and then she found the jewellery box. My heart began lurching in my chest as she opened it.

'What did he do with the ring?'

My turn to shrug.

'Did he give it to *you*?'

I shook my head. I thought I detected a hint of derision in her voice.

She began hooking items out of the boxes like fish with her long nails and then dropping them on the floor. The room felt stifling; my mouth gaped but the air refused to yield its oxygen. I couldn't say it. *The memory stick, the memory stick.*

She paused for an instance, surveying the mess. 'I don't want any of it.' She picked up the box that had housed the ring, and she snapped it in two, letting the halves fall on the floor.

'This fucking shit.'

She trampled one of the make-up bags. The plastic splintered and popped, and I took a step back, alarmed by her sudden fury. She was kicking the boxes now, knocking them over. Her mouth was a tight white line. I was scared, as I remembered what I knew about her temper. But then she stopped. Something had caught her attention. She bent over and picked up the jewellery pouch. She started fiddling with the string, and I wondered if she remembered what was in it. The milk teeth fell into her palm.

'Oh, *putain*.' She spat the words out, flinging the milk teeth away from her. But then she began to laugh, shaking her head from side to side, her hair following in replay.

'Crazy!' she said. 'The fuck!' And I laughed with her at the Black Mass weirdness of those teeth, and the absurd fact of her physical presence in this room after her long intensive tenancy in my mind. Now she was within arm's reach, smiling at me as we tried to regain our composure, but as I fixed on her laughing mouth, something flicked in me like a switch, mirth turning to anger. Who was she laughing at? I wanted to reach over and crush her face in my hands, grab her bottom lip and twist it and see how pretty she'd look then.

I took a step towards her. She met my gaze, straightened herself. I'd never squared myself up to anyone before. I felt the full breadth of my shoulders. She might be tougher, but I was bigger. I thought of the Hello Kitty plaster, felt my resolve harden.

My phone buzzed.

*I'm sick, coming home early.*

She watched me read the message.

'Is it him?'

'Yes. He's coming home.'

She walked out of the spare room, and I hurried to follow her down the stairs. Her eyes jerked over the hallway, looking for her bag.

*The memory stick!* But it was as if I were watching a film; I couldn't interrupt the flow of events, couldn't do anything.

'I don't want to see him. I'm scared he's . . .' She didn't finish her sentence, instead made a circling motion with her finger near her temple.

'He's not that bad,' I said, showing some too-late-in-the-day loyalty.

She looked as if she were about to say something, but then she opened the door.

I tugged at the lanyard around my neck. 'Wait,' I said.

She turned to look at me over her shoulder, her hand resting on the door frame. Mouth slightly parted, white teeth glinting.

Something flashed across her face; a strange, grinning distortion. I took a step back. I was scared.

'Be careful.'

She left without closing the door behind her.

I went into the kitchen, took a sip of crème de cassis straight from the bottle. I felt dizzy, but I continued to gulp it down. What had she meant by 'be careful'? That I should watch myself around Caden, or that I should stay away from her? It was hard to tell if it was a warning or a threat.

# 11

## Too Bloody Sane

'HONEY MILK OR CHOCCY milk?'
Like many children, I loved being ill. School, homework, bedtime – all the constraints of my ordinary life vanished, and I wondered how I had ever endured such a rigid existence. What was more, my mother – usually busy with her therapy practice, unwilling to play– turned the full light of her attention on me, and for once, she would let me choose what I wanted for breakfast.

I'd agonize over the pros and cons of honey or chocolate milk, convinced there must be a right decision if I knew what I truly wanted. Eventually my mother would grow impatient and decide for me, and I was never happy with her choice. I've always been a passive person. Not fighting back against Nate, Crabwell and Charles. Not confronting Caden about my birthday present or the memory stick. Not giving it back to Giselle. I've always been like this.

'Honey milk or choccy milk?' I asked Caden, my hand on his forehead, comparing it to mine.

It was the morning after Giselle's visit. Caden was no longer vomiting, but he had a sore throat and a fever. We did a test.

'It's negative.'

It wasn't Covid, but I was still nervous; the anticipation of the second red line appearing reminded me of the anxiety of waiting for a pregnancy test the week after Jamie and I first slept together. I had read the result for Jamie, as he was too scared to look.

'It's negative.'

'Oh, thank God. Look, I don't think we should do it again. It was fun, but it wasn't worth all that.'

Caden sat up to drink the milk and complained that it burnt his lips. He went to shower, leaving his sweat shadow behind on the sheets. I stripped the bed, and when he returned, I held him against me to calm his shivers.

'I'm not really ill, am I?'

'I'm not even a tiny bit worried.'

He had incredibly dark shadows under his eyes, and when he looked at me, it seemed he was staring up out of a well of terror. 'It's not Covid?'

'No, Caden! Drink this.'

He laid his head on my arm. His wet curls left fern patterns on the sheets.

'I'm scared.'

'Because you're ill. You're going to be fine. You know how paranoid I am usually.'

'Your arm's going to die.'

But I did not move my arm. I wanted him to be as comfortable as possible. It was easy to be kind to him in this way, when he seemed so childlike. I watched him frowning at something, a dream he would not tell me about. He never told me anything. My arm felt like a heavy bundle of silver needles beneath his head.

I shifted to free myself, ignoring his protesting groans, and went downstairs to the front room, where I drank the tepid chocolate milk beneath the white Cyclops eye of the picture frame.

Pringle had liked milk. The licking lap, she'd made it

look so delicious. That beautiful bundle of consciousness wrung out of existence by my mistake. I would have liked her to be here still, to see my movements reflected in the little planetary mirrors of her eyes.

Vicky was calling. It was far too early to call on a Saturday, but I answered anyway.

'Where are you right now?'

'Why?' I asked. I had the feeling she wanted to come over.

'Are you at Caden's? I'm coming over!'

'Not now, Vicky, I can't. Caden's sick and . . . am I on speaker?'

'Yeah. But listen, someone wants to talk to you.'

A scramble of the phone being handed over.

'Ohmygod hiiiiiiiii!'

'Ji-woo?'

'I'm baaaa-ack,' she sang. 'The bitch is back!'

My heart sank. I didn't feel like seeing anyone. 'That's amazing!' I managed. 'How come they let you?'

'My lab opened up! And my supervisor, like, wrote to the college and they were like, yah cool no problem. Has yours opened yet? Are you back at work?'

I ignored the question.

'So you're in Cambridge?'

'Yeah. Kieran's just driving us to drop my bags in Newnham, and then we're gonna come and see you!'

'Right now?'

'Is that a problem?'

'No,' I said.

'Great. Shall we meet at the river? Vicky says the pub's open today!'

I was so out of touch with the outside world that I'd had no idea. But it was the fourth of July; she was right.

I wore jeans with one of Giselle's oversized white sailor's T-shirts, and applied some mascara, foundation and aubergine-coloured lipstick. I retrieved the memory stick from where I'd hidden it in the sofa before Caden had got home, and hung it around my neck.

It was the earliest I'd left the house in a long time. The pavement and the trees and the leaves were glazed with dew, and as I rounded the corner of Sherwood Close, they caught the sun and everything shone together in golden-honey harmony, and for a moment it lifted my heart.

I went up to the Hot Sausage van that was parked outside the Green Dragon, which was not yet open.

'What'll it be, love?'

'Three Lincolnshires, please.'

The man behind the counter used plastic tongs to pick them up, three shiny brownish links, and he snipped each one with his scissors, dropping them deftly into the splayed bread rolls.

He studded ketchup along the slit in the sandwiches. 'Have a good one.'

I walked to the river and waited on the pavement, clutching the hot greasy packages against my chest. The young ducklings were canoodling happily, and there were a few moorhens making hasty circulations. How could I tell Ji-woo I'd been kicked out, when our thing had always been nerding out over our PhDs?

Kieran's car pulled up, and before it had even come to a full stop, the back door swung open and Ji-woo jumped out.

'Can I hug you?'

I nodded. Same glistening black hair, same cuddly, soft torso, and the laughing, high-voltage energy. *Oh, YOU*, I thought, closing my eyes, inhaling a smell that I wished I could follow back into the past.

'Oh my god.' She tried to lift me in her arms but failed, screaming as the hot sandwiches pressed into her chest. 'I missed you so much!' She stepped away, dabbed at her eyes with her silver-fingered nails while I pressed the palms of my hands into my eyelids, smearing my make-up in the process.

Vicky got out of the passenger seat, while Kieran – still in the car – lowered his window.

'Hello,' he said, looking up at me.

'Hi.'

'You look rough.'

'Stayed up late having sex with your dad.'

'He's eighty.'

He gave me a lopsided smile and a wave before driving off. The pub was still closed, so we walked northwards along the river. I was scared of running into Giselle, but Vicky insisted we go that way, so that Ji-woo could see the wilder side of the river.

There were splashes in the water under the Sunshine Posho bridge, and at first I thought they must be from jumping fish. But then I realized that the group of boys sitting on the bank had a slingshot. The swans were moving swiftly away from the stones, but the ducks were thrown into confusion, criss-crossing in the water in panicked little surges, unable to locate the source of the danger. I thought of saying something, but the boys – though they were only children – frightened me. The others seemed intimidated too, and we hurried on in silence until we found a patch of grass opposite some willow trees.

'How was home?' I asked. 'How's your family?'

Vicky winced, and I looked from her to Ji-woo, not understanding.

'My grandpa. He died.'

'Oh, Ji-woo. I'm so sorry. Was it Covid?'

She nodded grimly. 'We brought him home from the nursing facility. But we did it too late. He went into the ICU at the end of April. He died at the start of May.'

'I'm so sorry,' I repeated. 'And I'm sorry I wasn't in touch more.'

'That's OK,' she said. She was staring at the foil package in her lap. 'You're in love. People in love are selfish.' There was no anger in her voice, no reproach. But the words stung, all the same. *Don't cry*, I thought. *Don't cry. Her grandfather died. Don't make this about you.*

For a moment we were quiet, focusing on the food, though I had no appetite and had to force myself to eat. While Ji-woo and I ate our hot dogs from one end to the other, Vicky chewed hers through the middle so that it fell into two parts. She scrutinized the contents, pinching up the translucent onions. She only ate half, and threw the rest into the river.

'Are you back at work yet, Anna?' Ji-woo asked.

'No,' I said, a sick, unhappy feeling riding up my chest.

'Are they gonna open soon?'

I couldn't hold it in any more. I told them everything – everything apart from what I had found on the memory stick, though I knew Vicky had seen the videos. I felt her eyes rest heavy on my face. My mouth was trembling, and I had to press my lips together to smother my sobs. All the while, the river lapped at the bank, a slow slapping sound that punctuated my story at odd moments, giving emphasis to all the wrong things and making me feel like I wasn't telling it right. They gave me looks of such tender compassion I could hardly bear to make eye contact.

I hated myself for not having the courage to tell them what I had done in a more sober way. I felt that I was manipulating them with my tears. The thought made me cry even more.

I fell silent at the sound of approaching hooves. A stout, glossy horse, with feathered bell-bottomed forelegs and the broad, indelicate hooves of a working animal, was pulling a trap, its driver leaning so far back on his seat he was almost horizontal. He nodded at us as he passed, leaving a bloom of vape smoke in his wake.

'So, like . . . what does this mean for your PhD?' Ji-woo asked, as my sobs subsided.

'It means I can't do it.'

'And they won't give you the rest of your scholarship?'

'That's right.'

'And your research? They're going to just trash it?'

'I don't know,' I said. 'I can't handle these questions. Everything bad you're imagining right now is actually happening.' While I wasn't speaking loudly, my tone was so bitter that it seemed to poison the air. As in protest, a bird let out a harsh cry and flew up out of the willows on the opposite bank.

'You should complain about your supervisor,' Vicky said. 'Remember what he called you when you went to complain about your workload?'

'Damsel in distress,' I said, 'but I mean, that's not really that bad.'

'It's totally that bad!' Ji-woo said. 'If anything, you're in denial about how bad it was. You're gaslighting yourself.'

'I'm just putting it into perspective. He was right – I should be able to stick up for myself.'

'Why is it, Anna, that it's always your fault, never anyone else's?' Ji-woo was fiddling with her rings, and their reflection in the sun sent glimmers into her hair. 'Caden basically made you steal from the lab. He's ruined your life. And *you* feel guilty?'

'I killed his cat!' I said. 'And dumped it in a bin!'

'You didn't kill it.' I could tell from Vicky's expression that I was irritating her. 'It climbed into the dryer. Do you know the number of people who must have accidentally killed their cats that way? Do you think they think they're Satan? No. They have self-respect. Which you are sorely'– she pointed her finger at me – 'sorely lacking, ever since you got together with fucking Al Pacino. He's ruined your career, Anna. Do you understand? You need to move out.'

I didn't reply.

'Do what you want,' she said. She was no longer looking at me, but wiping her fingers on her napkin with meticulous care. 'But that beautiful dashing piece of shit is going to do something bad. It's not going to end well. I'm telling you.'

Ji-woo complained that she was getting sunburnt, so we went for pints at the Green Dragon. It was already packed with people, red-faced from the sun or drink. The carnival atmosphere was odd – because hadn't a lot of people died? Hadn't lives been ruined? People were excited and chatty, looking around them at all the other tables, raising their glasses to other pub-goers. *We've made it! The disaster has passed!* But I was silent, distracted by my reflection in the mirror opposite our table.

I watched myself swallow thick mouthfuls of black Guinness, sucking the liquid through its foamy white head. I looked so unfamiliar and felt entirely cut off from myself. The shadows under my eyes were so dark they looked crevice-like, as if they had depth.

I watched myself take another pull of beer. How could Caden not have noticed how sad I had been? I could not imagine that I would ever let him look so unhappy. Vicky and Ji-woo were right; he didn't love me. My friends loved me, and the glow of their affection made me feel safe in a way I had never felt with him.

But even as I sat there, only a few minutes from home, I kept thinking of him. Not fondly, not really. I just wanted to make sure he was really ill and in bed, that he hadn't lied. I had never thought I'd be capable of such wretched obsession.

I watched myself reach under my shirt to make sure the

270

lanyard was still there. I had to get rid of the memory stick. Otherwise I would rewatch the videos again and again, and the wound would be opened afresh, and I would never heal.

But when I tried to leave, the girls resisted.

'Stay,' Vicky purred, hanging on to my arm. I shrugged her off.

'I need to go.'

'Why?' She eyed me suspiciously. 'You're going to see Caden, aren't you?'

'No,' I said. 'I'm going for a walk.' I was irritated by the disbelief on their faces.

'What about hoes before bros?' Vicky said.

Eventually they let me go.

As the door closed behind me, I saw that two police cars were blocking the river path leading north. I asked a man what was going on.

'Magnet fisherman dragged up a bomb,' he said. 'They've blocked the road.'

People were filtering over Green Dragon Bridge. I tried to take shallow breaths, to focus on my own shadow. I felt uncomfortable being so close to so many people, but I wasn't able to resist the swift motion of the crowd, which carried me all the way to Stourbridge Common. *Throw it in the river*, I thought. *Just do it now*. But as I approached the bank, I noticed that the group of boys I'd seen earlier had come south down the river. They were close to the water, and one of them was aiming his slingshot at a family of geese. I tutted loudly and shook my head at them. 'Cunt!' one of the boys shouted, and a couple of them began to follow me.

I hurried my footsteps. I felt ridiculous – I was an adult; I should face up to them. I glanced over my shoulder a few times, hoping they'd drop off, but they seemed to follow me all along the stretch of Midsummer Common.

It wasn't until I broke into a full-out run that the boys gave up, their laughter and shouts still stalking me. I sat on a bench in the shade of an oak tree, trying to seem nonchalant rather than terrified. That's when I saw her. Giselle playing with her team. Players in yellow and orange bibs weaved in and out, shouting and laughing.

I sat facing the game, my back to the river. Someone took a corner; Giselle missed the header. The shadows of the leaves were shaped like puzzle pieces, and they interlocked and separated on my lap as the wind rose and fell. The thwack of the ball as someone went for goal, but they missed, and it rolled towards me. Giselle ran to retrieve it. She was breathing hard. Her eyes were on the ball, but as she reached it she glanced up for an instant and met my gaze. Something seemed to leap from her eyes to mine. I felt a heat and smiled, but she was already returning to the pitch. A few minutes later, the game ended.

The men went around shaking hands, but Giselle sat on the grass and fussed with her shin pads, peeled off her long red socks one by one before putting on her trainers. *If she looks in my direction again, I'll say hi*, I thought.

But when she stood up, she did not look over. She was bent over her phone. The sun was behind us now and hit her silhouette, casting such a precise shadow that she looked like a sundial. I got up and dusted off my clothes. I realized that I'd half squashed an earthworm with my shoe – it looked so awful, one half flat with the other red and engorged. I stamped on it so that it wouldn't suffer any more, shivered at the horrible pulping sensation under my foot. When I glanced up, Giselle was looking over her shoulder. Following her line of vision, I noticed a man walking towards her. Caden.

The distance and perspective confused me for a second. I thought he might have been coming to find me with that smile, the bonfire heat of it. Perhaps he felt better. I hadn't checked my phone in a while. He might have been trying to call.

But then why wasn't he coming my way?

He cut across the grass, walking towards Giselle, and she turned to him. He reached her and for a second he hesitated, as if unsure what to do. She took a step forward, tilted her chin up, her lips pursed. His mouth was only halfway closed by the time it met hers; an ugly kiss. They separated and she opened her mouth to smile; all of her was shining. Uneven segments of white sunlight reflected off her damp forehead and her bare shoulders. She reached up for another kiss, a look of private amusement on her face. This one was the kind you give when you know you are being watched, like a perfectly staged cam-kiss.

'Caden!'

I couldn't form the shape of the word properly because the shock had winded me. 'Caden,' I repeated, but I said it as if his name meant 'please'. The plea shot across the field towards them, but by some miracle or curse they didn't hear. They didn't even look in my direction.

I started to run back towards the river, knowing they were bound to see me. But I did not try to hide. My stomach climbed into my throat and I tasted wet dirt, as if Caden's name had turned to mould in my mouth. I walked through Midsummer Common. It looked ugly. The grasses and bushes and brambles, all of it looked like pollution; weeds asphyxiating the river like plastic bags in a whale's lung, and the dark brown cows oozing over the green field like puddles of crude oil.

Stourbridge Common had been closed off because of the bomb, so I walked over the suspension bridge and took a right towards Church Street. I did not look back. The road seemed to move beneath my feet, to shrivel and blacken and spit like singed hair. I tried to steady myself by thinking of what I should do next. But there was no place to retreat within myself, no safe nook of secret hopes, of sweetheart longings. The past was a reproach to my present failure, the thread to the future crumbling in my hands. No way out of this, no way out.

And I was howling now, like an animal having its throat cut, because I'll say this, I'll admit it now: the mice and the guinea-pigs knew what we were doing to them. Because those creatures are as alive as you and me; their eyes are as deep with meaning. However much I had tried to underplay it and be the professional scientist, killing those animals tore at my heart. And now I was getting my comeuppance. After what I had inflicted on them – and on Pringle – it was the natural order of things that Caden should leave me for someone better. I deserved it.

I turned on to the High Street; the pavement was busy with pedestrians and kids on electric scooters, hooting with laughter. I stood back to let them pass and didn't smile as they rang their bells to thank me.

He must have felt some power, manipulating a person who thought she was so smart, so intellectual. *You have some serious insecurities, Anna. I think you need help.* He must have enjoyed watching me trying to figure it out. Now I didn't even have a Cambridge PhD to plump up my ego. He had ruined that as well. If I was at all arrogant at the beginning of our relationship, Caden had been meticulous in making sure I was thoroughly humbled by the end.

And Giselle. I thought of how I'd droned on about my research, wanting to impress her, all breathless and excited. How she must have been laughing at me trying to ingratiate myself, offering her a drink, confessing that Caden was still obsessed with her, showing her all the things of hers that he had kept. And had she compared herself to me? She had seen my nose, my broad shoulders, how ungroomed and frumpy I am. Maybe she felt sorry for me. But it was far more likely that she did not think about me at all.

Suddenly my mood changed. The yawning expanse of uncertainty in my mind contracted and cleared. After months of trembling on the brink, I felt the final puzzle piece slide into the jigsaw. I had doubted myself, hated my obsessive paranoia about the ex. But I was vindicated. I was perceptive, I was smart. And I was right.

I looked up at the sky: shadowless, galactic blue, as neutral as a fact. I saw now, very clearly, that he had never wanted me. Gone was all the postulating about the multiplicity of perspectives, the attempt to find the just median between what he said and what I suspected. I was fizzing with a kind of lucid ecstasy. I had never been crazy. If anything, I was too bloody sane.

The pleasure of being right was so overwhelming that I felt a smile play on my lips, and when I caught my reflection in the Tesco window I tried to swallow it down because it looked a little mad, the knowing bitter smirk of someone who has been proven right yet again.

I was halfway down the High Street and passed a gang of grandpas on the benches outside the working men's club. They were intent on the parcels of newspaper that contained their dinners, their wrinkly fingers browsing for the white flakes of fish through the chips and batter. One of them looked at me enquiringly, returning my teary smile with a fragile twinkle of his own before lowering his eyes to his food again.

I hesitated on the corner of Water Lane and Green End Road. Right would lead me back to the Green Dragon, where Vicky and Ji-woo must still be where I had left them not twenty minutes ago. I couldn't face them. I didn't want Ji-woo's well-meaning 'Sometimes you have to lose your way to find yourself,' or 'Find the love you seek inside yourself.' Vicky, who'd be all philosophical about it, would give me Kierkegaard's take on infidelity and Feyerabend's refutation thereof. And maybe they'd exchange a few sly smiles because, dude, weren't we right about Caden all along?

I turned left, walked down Green End Road until it became Kings Hedges Road, passed the Golden Hind pub.

*No woman will ever be able to hurt me as badly as she did.*

The memory stick tucked against my chest was damp from my own sweat. The light seemed turned up to maximum brightness; everything in Sherwood Close suddenly came into microscopic focus. The St George's Cross had been taken down from the neighbours' front window. Perhaps there were new tenants; I hadn't noticed. The abandoned supermarket trolley cast a grid-like shadow on to the tarmac, like an ecologist's quadrant, dividing the ground into squares that could be divided into smaller constituent squares, like the tiniest atom-shaped gravel on the path to Caden's front door. Tiny staring stone eyes. I unlocked the door. Red-and-blue stripes. Of course no one was home.

*No woman will ever be able to hurt me as badly as she did.*

We'd see about that.

# 12

# Parasite

**M**Y HEART WAS RACING but my hand was steady. That's one thing I learnt about myself in all this. My hand never shakes. Not when I slit the throat of a live mouse. Not when I walk into my boyfriend's house, bolt the door behind me to make sure he can't come in and stop me. Not as I go up the stairs, unhook the memory stick from my neck. My hand was perfectly still as I opened his laptop, typed in his password, logged into his email, and it remained still as I uploaded the videos and sent them in blind copy to every person on his contact list, including his patients and the director of Goldie Boathouse and Kieran and Giselle.

It wasn't a burst pipe of fury and vindictive rage; I didn't cry as I did it. I was cold and calm and precise. I suppose it was my experience in the lab that taught me how to see an action all the way through to its brutal end.

The feeling: not gleeful, not triumphant, but sober and profound. Until then I had thought it was better to forgive people, to turn the other cheek. But I realized in that moment that forgiveness is just an excuse for feeble people to let life roll over them. And I felt instantly better the minute I sent the videos. As if the wall of glass that had come down between me and my self when I first met Caden had at last been shattered.

I slapped the computer shut without bothering to hide the memory stick. Then I walked out of the house, leaving the front door ajar.

I wanted to laugh. I wanted to laugh because I realized that my perception of myself as a passive, sweet-natured person was a lie that had fooled me my whole life and would go on fooling all the people around me. Caden would be blamed. No one would think me capable of doing what I had done. Because nice, smart girls do not behave like that, do they? And if they do, then it's a boyfriend making them do it, or it's an abusive daddy behind it all. Then I laughed again, because my boyfriend and my father fitted perfectly into this narrative as they truly were such terrible people. *Thank you, boys. You've made it all so easy.*

All the pain I had felt on my walk to the house was transformed as I left it. I thought about the kiss. Caden telling me to work on my self-esteem. Giselle's cruelly enigmatic parting remark: 'Be careful.' *Well, I have taken care of myself this time*, I thought, smiling grimly. The glance she'd given me on the Common didn't hurt me any more. The image of them together did not hurt me any more. It was like reliving the memory of a danger that has long passed. *Remember when we drove to Cambridge and saw that terrible fight? I was sure we were going to die.* The danger can no longer touch you; only you can touch it. Revenge gave me the same distance, the same control that time does. I thought about trivial things, petty insults: Angus's comment about my nose; my father's remark as I doubled up in pain – *Come on, Sporty Spice, you've only bruised it* – Giselle stopping me from dropping ice into her wine. And I watched those moments through the prism of my revenge, feeling all the small humiliations of my life crumple and recede, like a vampire fleeing before a crucifix.

I reached the Green Dragon and found my friends slumped in front of the aftermath of a boozy roast; greasy balled-up napkins beside fat-ringed slices of beef. Both had their hair tied back, and their faces were flushed, as if eating had been strenuous exercise.

They could see immediately that something was wrong with me.

'What's happened?'

I just said 'Caden' and 'Giselle', and the story of his infidelity told itself.

I didn't tell them what I had done. They would have been appalled. Not for Caden, but for what I'd done to another woman. That's when I thought about it for the first time. The reality was starting to dawn on me.

'Where is that piece of shit?' Vicky said, sidling out from the bench seat. 'Where is he?'

'Do you want us to go over there?' Ji-woo asked. 'We can pack up your stuff. You don't need to come!' she added, when she saw my face. 'We'll take care of it.'

'No,' I said. 'We should stay away. He's dangerous.'

And then – suddenly – my hands were shaking, but not just my hands; the chair, the table, and Ji-woo's eyes were wide and terrified, and Vicky was clutching me, and then there was a roaring sound, an explosion so loud that it seemed its centre was everywhere: in my stomach, the grip of fingers on my wrist. The windows rattled as they bellied in. My first thought was that one of the fighter planes from the nearby base had crashed, that we were all about to die. But then things steadied themselves. A few people laughed nervously.

'It's the bomb! They've defused it!'

This got everyone excited; there was a general rush towards the bar. But I didn't feel like drinking. My body was vibrating like a struck bell. Vicky offered to ask Kieran to drive us back to Newnham, but I did not want to see him.

'I'm sure he knew Caden was seeing her,' I said. 'He probably egged him on. He was probably laughing at me, Vicky.'

'Don't let your imagination take this turn,' she said, looking at me with a pained expression.

'I know it's true,' I said, my voice sharp and bitter. 'I know they've all been laughing at me for months.'

We walked all the way to Newnham, and I did not say anything to them. They were quiet too, shaken up by the sound of the explosion. Vicky's room was the messiest I'd ever seen it; mossy plates and black banana skins, tampons peeking out of wads of toilet paper in her overflowing bin. She and Ji-woo offered to order me Uber Eats.

I was about to thank them, but felt my phone vibrate in my pocket.

*Where are you? Went to chemist. Took some meds. Feeling much better. x*

I let out an audible whimper. I hadn't accounted for him sending me such a tender message. I thought he'd see the memory stick and understand at once. I had steeled myself for fury, but not kindness.

'Oh, Anna.' Ji-woo sat beside me on the floor. 'Don't text him back.'

'Why would he do this?' I shook my head. 'Why didn't he just break up with me, if he wanted her? I tried to make it easy for him to break up with me.'

I looked at Vicky, searching for an answer in her face. 'I kept asking if he was sure he was over her. I offered to move back to Dorset, but he said he didn't want me to. I don't get it; I just don't understand.'

'There's no answer I or anyone else could give you that would make any of this feel better,' she replied.

Her phone started to ring, and from her expression I knew it was Caden trying to call her.

'Don't answer!' I shouted, and Vicky looked taken aback.

'It's my mom!'

'You're lying.'

She held out the phone and I saw that it was her mother.

'Please don't speak to Caden,' I said, wiping my sweaty face with my T-shirt. 'Promise me you won't talk to him. Don't tell anyone where I am.'

Ji-woo nodded slowly, as Vicky went outside to take the call. Ji-woo looked at me, fiddled with her rings.

'Would you consider talking to a therapist? It could . . .' She made a vague gesture with her hands.

'What, pay someone to tell me how badly I fucked up everything?'

'No,' she said, her voice low and steady, as if I were a child who needed some facts of life explained. 'Just to understand, you know, why this happened to you. So you don't carry the trauma of this with you and manifest another toxic relationship.'

I didn't answer. Classic Ji-woo. I deserved to be arrested, and she wanted me to get help. After a while, Vicky returned, and they put on a film. It was the Korean movie *Parasite*. The violence disturbed me. I couldn't focus, and my friends were not paying attention either. They were on their phones, and I tried to get a glimpse of their screens so that I might see who they were texting. I had a feeling they were messaging each other about me. Or perhaps they were messaging Caden; maybe he had told them what I'd done, and they were debating whether or not to turn me in. The room got dark, but none of us moved to turn on the light. Ji-woo and Vicky's faces were pale and flickering in the light of the computer screen.

A string of messages from Caden. What about dinner?

Hey, he was worried; was I OK? Then he began to call me, and I knew from the way the phone rang – knew it in my stomach – that he'd found out what I had done. It rang and rang in my pocket, each vibration like an electric shock. I was going to get caught. He was going to tell the police.

'I want to be alone,' I said, my voice strange, rising in the silent room like a helium balloon.

Vicky packed an overnight bag for Kieran's, and Ji-woo promised to bring me breakfast in the morning.

'Just cry it out, Anna,' she said. 'And remember. The best revenge is happiness. Ed Sheeran's words, not mine,' she added as she left me.

I regretted driving them away, because being on my own was worse. I felt an iron grip of fear on my heart, the kind of terror I'd felt as a child when I'd call out to my parents at night knowing they wouldn't hear me; the kind that knows there is no hope of it ending. What if Caden came after me?

I didn't have my laptop so I couldn't distract myself with a Netflix series, and I didn't even want to touch my phone. Ordinarily I would have tidied Vicky's room for her, but I felt too nervous to organize the chaos. So I got into her bed, breathed in her familiar smell. But then I thought of her lying there with Kieran. The idea of them together, his yellowed gym-bro hands touching her, gripping her blonde hair – it made me sick.

The shadows contracted as the moon whitened. I dozed off, then jerked awake abruptly. I checked my phone but it was out of battery, and I had not thought to bring my charger.

I looked in Vicky's bedside table and found her long rattling tubes of American Ambien. I swallowed two. The bed was uncomfortable. It was horrible not having my phone, not being able to check the time. I fell asleep again but woke up to the sound of myself whimpering. I put my fingers in my mouth, trying to stop myself from crying out. I took a third pill, and fell into a poppy-field *Wizard of Oz* sleep.

I woke up at what must have been dawn. A film of dew lay over the gardens, like the skin that forms over hot milk left to cool. I didn't fall asleep again until late morning, and then I clung to it as best I could. I had strange dreams; the moon was a pill I was meant to dissolve in some water, and then she was my nurse, always too far away to hear my cries. I reached from dream fragment to dream fragment like tree vines, and every time I drifted towards consciousness it felt like I was falling through the jungle canopy, plummeting to my death.

I came to, my gums creaking against my teeth, desperate for a drink of water. I got up from the bed, easing my weight from it bit by bit so as not to disturb Caden, who was still asleep. I loved the sight of him; the disordered hair that twisted in different directions, no discernible pattern that I could make out, just a lovely chaos. The curtains were glowing, and I drew them back. All the seeds and bulbs I'd planted over the spring had suddenly come up: golden, velvety swirls of honeysuckle unfurling before my eyes; karma dahlias, like blood-red lotuses, carrying all the sweetness and hope I had dug into them.

'Look!' I said to Caden, but even though I tried to shake him awake, he slept on. I bent to kiss him, but as I approached he took a sudden gulp of air, as if to speak; but he made no sound. Something was scratching at the door.

'Pringle!'

The scratching intensified, and then suddenly I was awake. It was not scratching, it was knocking. There were voices behind it calling my name. I got up from the bed and crossed the room to open the door.

A man in uniform stood in the doorway.

## 13

## The Lock

I PRESSED THE PALMS of my hands hard into my eyes, and my vision speckled with black spots and then resolved itself. It wasn't the police; it was Stan, the porter, wearing a mask embroidered with the Newnham crest.

'Sorry to disturb you.' He stood aside to let Vicky, Ji-woo and Kieran enter the room, all of them wearing the same Newnham-issued masks.

'We've been trying to call you. And we've been knocking. We couldn't get you to come to the door,' Vicky said. 'So we went to fetch the key from Stan.'

My mouth was dry, and I swallowed with difficulty.

'What's going on?'

I felt strange, but not as in a dream. Instead I found myself in a state of hyper-realism, my mind a million bulbs flashing on surfeit details: the zodiac of moles on Stan's neck; the elliptical wet patch on the front of his mask.

'We have bad news,' Vicky said.

Stan took it as his cue to leave, and as soon as he was out of sight they removed their masks. None of them said anything, just stared fixedly at me. They looked as though they were high, and I almost laughed, but something about Vicky's gaze stopped me.

'What's wrong?'

She took a step towards me.

'You're gonna have to be strong.' She gazed at me. Her eyes were liquid, glistening – so kind that I was frightened.

I stood there, waiting for her to elaborate. It was agony, an endless wait for the curtain to rise on something awful, for the starting gun to go off. I was about to scream at her to spit it out when she finally spoke.

'It's Caden.'

I turned around again, reached for the duvet and pulled it off the bed. The remnants of my dream were fading, but I was muddled from the sleeping pills and it took me a second to realize that I was not in his room, in his house.

'Caden passed away,' she said, her voice quiet, barely above a whisper.

There was no moment of incomprehension or disbelief. Her words passed seamlessly into fact, and I understood. I looked from Vicky to Kieran.

'He died,' he said. I nodded to make it clear I understood, but he said it again. 'He died.'

Kieran's red-rimmed eyes strained blue as he tried to contain his tears. Vicky hugged him and he held her, his big hands threading up from the base of her neck through her blonde hair. I sat on the bed, not trusting my legs to support me.

'What happened?' I asked, when it became evident that no one apart from me felt the question hanging over the room.

Kieran pulled away from Vicky and wiped his face with his T-shirt.

'He killed himself.'

'He died by suicide,' Ji-woo corrected. Her black hair was piled on top of her head in a messy bun, the tips waving whenever she moved, ridiculous as a peacock's crest. She had clearly been crying.

'Is it because of what I did?'

'What?' Kieran said, drawing away from Vicky.

I spoke slowly, as if to a dim-witted child. 'Did he kill himself because of what I did to him?'

'Anna, don't,' Vicky replied, in a voice so firm that it seemed she had already played out this exchange in her mind, and anticipated I would blame myself. She sat next to me on the bed, too close. She smelled of her own familiar lemony bourbon, but also of Kieran. I felt sick.

'You're not listening to me. I'm telling you, this happened because of me.'

'Anna.' She looked at Kieran, a wordless appeal for him to say something.

'I've been blaming myself too, Anna,' he said, his voice breaking. His knees sagged beneath him. Ji-woo and Vicky guided him to sit beside me on the bed.

'He was my best friend.' He hid his purple, wretched face in his hands. 'I'm never, ever going to see him again.' His sobs drowned out my own thoughts, and before I knew it I was crying too.

Kieran threw his arms around me, and I fell into his weight. *God*, I thought. *This can't be happening.* His skin was hot, and he cried into my hair, holding me tight, just as I'd longed to be held all night. His chest convulsed against mine, and each of his sobs seemed to hit me with a bludgeoning force, because I'd done this to him. I had killed his friend.

'It was me, Kieran,' I managed, speaking into his chest. 'I did this to him. It was me.'

He held me tighter, shushed me, until we were both trembling and silent. He let me go and we parted, our faces red and tender.

'It's not you, mate,' he said, running his hand over his face and giving a weak, watery-eyed smile. 'I wasn't the perfect friend. I coulda been there more for him. Asked him about his dad. But I just felt he never wanted to talk about anything. I tried to get him to talk after what happened with his ex, but he just shut it down. I should have tried harder.'

'Kieran, it wasn't you. It's my fault he died. It is. Listen to me! It's my fault. I should be in prison—'

'Stop it, Anna!' Ji-woo interrupted, her voice loud and earnest. 'Survivor's guilt is REAL. You can't blame yourself like this!'

'Ji-woo, you're not listening.'

'Honey, it's very common to experience guilt as part of grief. But you're not responsible. It's. Not. Your. Fault.' She squeezed my hand with each syllable, as if to underscore her words. 'You're blaming yourself because it makes you feel in control of the situation.'

'She's right' – Kieran hugged me again – 'we can't blame ourselves.' He went out to wash his face in the bathroom.

'You guys know this is really my fault, right?' I whispered.

I searched my friends' faces for a sign they understood, but they only stared at me, and we were silent until Kieran returned, his shirt drenched with water, his hair smoothed back from his face. He gave me a small, reassuring smile, genuine enough, but it reminded me of the other smiles: the sardonic, mocking grins he'd given me on the sideline of the football game; in Goldie Boathouse.

*Stop talking*, I told myself. *Stop talking.*

'Have you – have you checked your messages recently?' he asked me, taking a seat beside Vicky on the bed, which let out a familiar moan from his weight.

'My phone's not working,' I said. I tried to make it sound like I wasn't making excuses. 'I haven't looked at my emails in ages. Why?' The word slipped out of my mouth before I could stop it, and when I heard it in my own voice – *email* – a kind of seized me. Kieran and Ji-woo did not seem to notice, but Vicky turned her head abruptly towards me. I stared helplessly into her face, completely unmasked for a second, and felt a plea bubbling up my throat. *She knows; she's seen the videos. She's going to tell them. Don't do it. God, please don't.* But she cut her eyes away. I swallowed, shook my head from side to side. *Hold it together, hold it together.*

Kieran was scrolling through his apps. He clicked on the email I had sent from Caden's address and opened one of the files. Ji-woo got down on to her knees, propped her elbows on my legs, while Vicky got up and went to the window.

I looked down at Kieran's phone screen but was distracted by my own reflection. I saw Giselle projected through me. The dancing glances, the ironic downward quirk of her mouth, as if she were laughing at us. I could hear Ji-woo and Kieran swallowing on either side of me. The fist clutching at her brown hair, and turning slowly outwards, the strands sticking through his fingers.

I couldn't breathe. I tugged my T-shirt from my chest; it was soaked through with sweat.

'We shouldn't watch this,' Ji-woo said, her voice a little hoarse. 'Let's stop.'

Vicky was still staring out of the window. The mirror above the sink reflected her back.

Kieran closed the video. 'He sent it to everyone.'

'Poor Giselle,' Ji-woo said. 'She must be absolutely devastated. I can't imagine how this must feel.'

'Fuck her,' Kieran said. 'Don't feel bad for her. I'd say if anyone's to blame for him killing himself, it's her.'

'Vicky,' I whispered, but they all heard. She didn't move. 'Vicky!' I said. 'Can I talk to you alone?'

She turned around. Her eyes were dancing, following some invisible gossamer in the air.

'You want us to leave?' Ji-woo asked, sounding a bit hurt.

Vicky wasn't saying anything. She was just staring at me, her face blank and expressionless. Something wrenched in my chest. *She's going to tell them.* I covered my face with my hands.

'Oh, honey.' Ji-woo reached over and took my hand. My fingers felt cold and rigid. I had a sudden horrible thought.

'Where is he right now?'

'At the morgue.'

'In a bag?' I thought of the mice and guinea-pigs, how we threw them away in sealed sandwich baggies. And Pringle, how I had dumped her in the public bin. How utterly alone and helpless she had seemed.

'I guess I should have seen this coming,' Kieran said, breaking the silence. 'Did he tell you his dad killed himself? That can be a genetic thing, depression and stuff. *Right?*' he added, patting my knee, trying to force me to return his gaze. 'You're the scientist. Depression can be genetic, right?'

'Right . . .' I nodded slowly, trying to make it seem like I was reluctantly accepting the truth of what he said.

'And the stuff Giselle did with Jack. That fucked him up properly. Really cut him up. I'm sure you noticed he wasn't himself since then.'

The comment made no sense, because I'd only known Caden after he and Giselle had broken up, but I went along with it anyway.

'I never thought he'd do something like this though.' He held up his phone. 'Cos he was so private, you know? But I guess you never know. He might have just reached his limit. He lost it.'

I glanced up and caught Vicky's eye. She gave a slight, almost imperceptible nod. But it was enough. *She knows,* I thought. *She knows, but she isn't going to say anything.*

'Did he seem weird, or off, to you?' Kieran asked.

With effort, I managed a shrug. 'He was obsessed with Giselle. He kept all her stuff. He had this weird shrine to her in the house.'

'I saw it,' Vicky said. 'It was pretty fucked up.' She came over and put her hand on my shoulder, and my heart lifted, just a little.

'And he compared her with me all the time,' I continued. 'Like, all the time. He took me to all the places they'd been together. Literally, everywhere. He even gave me the same gift he'd bought for her birthday.'

'What?' Kieran said.

'He gave us exactly the same handbag. Maybe—' The thought occurred to me for the first time. 'Maybe I should have told him to get professional help, or something? I knew it wasn't normal. But he made it very clear that he didn't want to talk about it. About his feelings. So we never did.'

'He was a tough nut to crack,' Kieran agreed.

I started to cry again. I was losing control of what I was saying. I confessed that I'd encouraged him to drink, because it was only when he was drunk that he would talk to me about himself, and I told them about my obsession with Giselle. But they didn't really listen, didn't seem to take in the gravity of what I was admitting. Ji-woo put her arms around me, swaddled me, until I was crying so much I couldn't speak, my sobs gagging the truth.

'Honey,' she purred. 'You can't internalize this. Anna, I'm sure Caden wouldn't want you to blame yourself.'

My thoughts were so dark, so confused. Who knew what Caden wanted? I'd never really understood him. But I found it impossible to imagine him harming himself. 'How did it happen?' I asked.

'He drowned,' Kieran replied.

'He drowned? Where?'

'Baits Bite Lock.'

'But the water isn't even that deep there. How could he have drowned?'

They were silent; shocked, perhaps, by the gruesome specificity of the question.

'I mean, couldn't this be an accident?' I went on.

'A fisherman found him this morning,' Kieran said, matter-of-factly. 'They're waiting for the coroner's report. But they're saying there was no foul play. I guess they're pretty sure it was suicide.'

'What should we do now?' Vicky asked.

'Not sure,' Kieran replied. 'I guess we wait for the funeral.'

I imagined going, all of us there. Vicky and Ji-woo helping me dress, doing my make-up; an echo of the night they had readied me for the spring-themed formal. That had been in the middle of March. Less than four months ago. It seemed so remote, a completely different existence.

'So does the family know?' Vicky asked. 'His mum? Is anyone supporting her?' She addressed her questions to Kieran, who knew him so much better than I ever had.

'Yeah, the police told her first . . .'

Drowned, drowning. I kept thinking of the lock, and the woman we had seen crossing it in her narrowboat on my birthday.

*Oh, love*, she'd said, her white hair blowing into her face, her hand cupping her eyes to shield them from the sun. *It's the closest thing to heaven.* The little dog in the bow. The water lilies that were just coming through might have broken the surface by now. I saw Caden there, his hands white and outstretched like stars, his clothes billowing out all around him, buoying him up for a while, until they drank up the water. I imagined his face and body changed by the river, the lines softened, more womanly.

They were still discussing the details of the funeral.

'Probably Torquay,' Kieran said. 'But I guess his—'

'Guys.' I spoke over them and pressed the palms of my hands into my eyes again, wishing I could escape into the black spots that sprung up in my vision. 'I want to go home,' I said. 'I need to go home now.'

## 14

## The Cyclops

PEOPLE SAY THAT GRIEF is unpredictable; it follows its own inscrutable logic. Loss has a different effect on us all, they say, and we cannot predict – still less judge – how others mourn.

I think this is all nonsense, but on that day, this popular wisdom served me well. No one seemed to think it odd that I wanted to get out of town as fast as possible, and no one commented on the fact that after the initial shock, I didn't look sad. It was impossible to go on crying because what I felt most of all was indescribable relief. They were blaming Caden for the videos. Vicky was on my side. Things were going according to plan.

'Grieving doesn't make you imperfect,' Ji-woo assured me, as I borrowed her phone to call Jamie. 'It makes you human.'

'Hel-*lo*?' he said cautiously, not recognizing Ji-woo's number.

I cleared my throat. 'It's Anna. It's me.'

'Baby A!' he screamed excitedly. 'How are you?'

'I can't,' I said to Ji-woo, shaking my head. She took the phone from me.

I went to the bathroom. I gulped some water from the

tap and then hid in the cubicle. I stared at the tiled floor. I could not believe how badly things had turned out for Caden. And for me. Both of us had become caught in the web of our obsessions, the sticky filaments of his lies and my insecurities tightening around us over the months. Caden had been the first to die. I might still escape it. If I was careful.

I went back to the room to find Kieran and Vicky sitting on the floor. He was crying again, and she was stroking his hair. Ji-woo was making the bed.

'Jamie is on his way. He'll be here in a few hours,' she said. 'Is any of your stuff still in college?'

'No,' I said. 'Everything's at Caden's.'

'We can go over there now,' Vicky said. 'Kieran will drive us.'

'Are we allowed in there?' I said. 'I mean, isn't it a crime scene or something? Won't the police need to go there first?'

Vicky shook her head. 'Suicide isn't a crime.'

We went out into the gardens. The grass was yellow, fidgeting and sick from too much sun. Even the Michaelmas daisies were looking wan, the purple petals folding in on themselves like the legs of an injured insect. No scent, only an antiseptic heat and a burning neutrality.

As we were about to go into the Porters' Lodge, Ji-woo stopped me.

'I need to go back to my room,' she said. 'I'm so tired. I haven't slept. It's jet lag.' She hugged me. 'I'm so sorry this has happened. I'm here for you 24/7. I just need to crash for a bit.' It was only a day ago that we'd been joyfully reunited. I couldn't make sense of it, couldn't really do justice to the moment. I stood stiffly as she squeezed me then let go.

'Bye,' I said rather absently, and then followed Vicky and Kieran to the car. It was even worse than usual; the smell of old peanuts, their softness squishing beneath my feet like damp acorns.

We pulled out and along Queen's Road, the Backs visible in the distance. Vicky was talking to me, but I was finding it hard to concentrate. I felt sick again. To our right, the ribbon of the river glistened, and the glossy canal boats looked like multi-coloured beads in a child's necklace. Kieran kept glancing at me in the rear-view mirror. Perhaps he was just checking I was all right, but I was wary of those eyes. The bloodhound quality was too pronounced. 'Anna,' he said, 'if you're gonna be sick, let me know. I'll pull over.'

'I won't.' I gritted my teeth, fixed my eyes on the road in front of us, but it seemed to me that Kieran drove in a jerky, stop-start way which made me feel even worse.

'What about Giselle?' I blurted it out. I felt his eyes on me in the rear-view mirror again.

'What about her?'

'Is she OK?'

Kieran shrugged. 'Fuck her. She's a bitch.'

I was worried about what Giselle would do when she saw the video. She would most likely think Caden had done it, as payback for her infidelity. Revenge porn is a man's thing. She would never suspect me.

Unless she had checked her email when she was still with him. Then she would know I had done it. She would tell the police, or come after me herself. *Be careful*, she had said. A threat, or a warning?

I rolled down the window but the air smelled of petrol, and I felt sicker still.

'Stop!' I clapped my hand over my mouth. He pulled over on Chesterton Road, and I scrambled out. I bent over a street bin and my stomach convulsed, but nothing came out. My toes spread wide and pink on the tarmac, reminding me of the drive to Cambridge with Jamie and how we'd run barefoot down the road to help the injured man. Nobody had been there to help Caden in the river, choking amongst the green weeds.

Giselle must have been desperate. I almost felt sorry for her. Almost. But then I thought about her, the glance she'd given me while I watched her play. She would have enjoyed me seeing them together. They must have gone to her boat after the game. I pictured him kissing the russet-brown freckles at the corners of her eyes, on her eyelids. Her salt-sweat taste from playing football. The soft sway of the water lapping. *The closest thing to heaven*; *oh, love*. My stomach convulsed again, and the water I had gulped from the tap spewed out on to the pavement.

*I don't need to ask myself anything, any more*, I thought. I didn't need to know why he'd taken me to the same places he took her, why he'd kept all her things. I didn't have to figure out whether he was still in love with her, whether he was hurting me as punishment for what she had done, or if he didn't mean to do it. I didn't need to figure out if he was an evil manipulative bastard or only a fool. He was gone; the black box of his mind was irretrievable. The mystery was no longer there to poison my life.

'Sorry,' I said, climbing back into the car. 'I feel better now. We can go.'

He put the car in gear, but did not drive. His hands were enormous and bone-white, gripping the steering wheel.

'This is a nightmare,' he said, his voice trembling. 'I feel like I'm in a nightmare.' And suddenly, unexpectedly, he started banging his head on the steering wheel, hard.

'Kieran!' Vicky grabbed his arm but he was too strong for her, kept smacking his head so hard that I was sure he would knock himself out.

'He was my best friend.' He was sobbing now. 'Cade.

What the fuck happened to you?' With each hit, I felt like someone was bludgeoning me.

'Oh God. Kieran, I'm so sorry. I didn't mean, Vicky, I—'

BEEEEP!

Kieran had managed to hit the horn. We jumped, and Vicky burst out laughing, a high-pitched baboon giggle so ludicrous that I couldn't help smiling, and even Kieran snorted.

'How can such a beautiful girl have such an ugly laugh?'

She fake-punched his arm. He cleared his throat, wiped his eyes with the back of his hand.

'I'm sorry, guys,' he said.

'Don't apologize,' we replied in unison.

He pulled out past Tesco, the fish and chip van, the Golden Hind. People were eating on benches outside, soaking up the afternoon sun. I hadn't eaten for ages and was starving. But I couldn't tell them I was hungry. Not when Kieran was crying his guts out.

We pulled into the drive. Kieran said he couldn't bring himself to go inside, that he would stay in the car. 'But it's too hot,' Vicky argued, as I unlocked the front door. 'At least park it in the shade.'

It was cool inside. The objects in the front room seemed to flare suddenly out of the darkness as my vision adjusted. The fake leather sofa, the picture frame, an inside-out fleece jumper hanging from the banister. The shoes kicked off in the entrance, the ironing board, a half-full smoothie; things I would have tidied away in a second but which now looked as inviolable as museum exhibits, their everlasting allure guaranteed by their connection to a dead man.

I heard a squeak, and I hurried to check on the guinea-pigs. They chirped at me happily, their tiny chicken feet trotting towards me. Their water bottle was half empty, but there was another bowl of water near it, and an enormous pile of pellets. Caden must have emptied the whole bag for them. He hadn't wanted them to go hungry.

I sank to my knees and covered my face with my hands. Vicky came across and bent over me.

'But they're all right!' she said, reaching down towards Bubble, who was standing on his hind legs, squeaking interrogatively. 'They're fine!'

'I know. I know. He gave' – I fought to get the words out – 'he gave them. Extra food.'

'I'm so sorry,' she said, stroking my hair. 'I'm so, so sorry.'

'He didn't deserve this,' I said. 'He didn't deserve this.'

She crouched down beside me, peeled my hands from my face.

'He's at peace now,' she said, looking into my eyes. 'He's with his maker.'

'I don't believe in all that,' I replied, shaking my head.

'It doesn't matter. I can believe for both of us.'

We went upstairs. She got started on my clothes in the spare room while I went into the bedroom. The bed, still as I'd left it, was perfectly made, Mango Bango Jumbo Banana propped on the cushions. The laptop was on the floor, closed. There was no sign of the memory stick.

I backed out of the room, spooked, and went to join Vicky. She helped me pack in a chaotic, emergency kind of way, mixing dirty and clean clothes together, stuffing in a single muddy Converse when I couldn't find its pair. I wondered if I dared take any of Caden's things. His white Patagonia fleece jumper, his green beanies, his New Balance shoes – could these fragments stand for the whole? Would they offer me any comfort? But I couldn't take them. They seemed to belong to a world that was vast and now forever lost to me.

What I really wanted was to burn everything. Giselle's make-up, her stupid herbal teas, their clothes, books, the picture frame. Make a huge crackling pyre. Douse it in petrol. Watch the objects shrivelling in on themselves. That's what I wanted.

Kieran, presumably cooking in the heat of the car, came into the front room and sat on the sofa. He kept his eyes fixed narrowly on his phone, and stared at it in a way I recognized. That longing to escape into the moment between this tab and the next, the second between this image and the next, that kind of hopeful reaching for nothingness.

I filled a pint glass with water and held it out to him. He murmured a thank you and gulped most of it down, before having second thoughts and offering the last few drops to Vicky, who was staring at the sunflower-shaped frame. I came and stood by her, and side by side we looked at it: the bald white eye of the missing photo in the middle, the other smaller ones around its perimeter; the white cat; teenage Caden in his Chelsea blue, and the man with two little boys holding hands.

'Who's that?' Vicky said, pointing to the cat.

'I dunno,' I answered, shrugging. 'His childhood cat, I guess.'

'And them?' She pointed to the two little boys.

'His dad, Caden and Jack,' Kieran supplied, when I didn't answer.

Vicky peered at them, frowning slightly.

'That's Jack? They're identical.'

Kieran shrugged. 'Well, they're brothers.'

'He has a brother?'

Kieran looked at me as if I were an idiot. 'Yes. Jack. His little brother.'

'Oh, right,' I said reflexively. And all at once I understood.

The pint glass escaped from Vicky's hand and smashed at our feet.

'Fuck's sake!' Kieran shouted, getting to his feet. But

Vicky and I just stood there, jagged bloody slashes appearing as if by miracle on our ankles, calves, blood unspooling itself into the fringe of my white socks.

'Why are neither of you wearing shoes? Are you hurt?' he asked, checking Vicky's face for signs of pain. 'Put your arm around my neck.' He whisked her off her feet, one arm under her shoulders, the other under her knees. He carried her to the sofa, laid her down carefully. She looked over her shoulder towards me. Her eyes, like crushed diamonds, were glittering with pain.

She, too, understood. It had not been Caden I'd seen with Giselle. It had been Jack. The truth was terrible.

'You're bleeding everywhere,' Kieran said, turning to me. 'Holy shit.'

It was dusk by the time Jamie pulled up outside Caden's house. We hugged and his body against mine was yielding, offering no resistance, only soft flesh. He seemed so upset for me I almost felt sorry for him. Vicky and Kieran helped Jamie load up the car. I lined a cardboard box with sawdust for the guinea-pigs, put them in the back seat with a head of lettuce.

Kieran was silent but Vicky talked a lot, and I recognized she was putting on her own version of the Anna Show – asking Jamie all kinds of questions, offering to make us a thermos of coffee for the road, forgetting she'd already asked how many hours it would take – well, it's getting late, better hurry, you're sure you don't want any coffee? You're really sure?

There were tiny glitches in the night around us, ripples in the sea-dark fabric of the sky.

'Bats!' Jamie pointed, but I couldn't see them if I tried to focus. They danced at the corner of my vision.

We stood by the car readying to say goodbye, but Jamie had us look at the sky. It was early July, a little early for meteor showers, but it was worth a try, he said. We looked up, squinted into the sky littered with stars and planets, waiting for something to stir; but they were stubborn, nails hammered hard into place. Once or twice, I thought I saw something, but Jamie said they were satellites, not comets.

'Starlink,' he said. 'Elon Musk.'

I felt there was some kind of wisdom to be gleaned from that: you look up hoping for some kind of escape, but all you find is some tycoon's litter, like an eye turned inside-out, staring back into its own socket. Something about the inability to see what is right in front of you, to look at the right things. But whatever it was, the lesson to be learnt was lost on me. I was looking up at the sky but thinking about Vicky.

Should I say something to her? Try to get her on her own, maybe? She must be thinking so badly of me: that I was an idiot for not knowing Caden had a brother, for confusing them. But I wanted to explain myself, to tell her it wasn't my fault, Caden was so secretive. It was unbearable not to have her on my side. I wanted to remind her that I'd forgiven her stealing, and never made her feel ashamed. But I knew this was not comparable.

Jamie was anxious about the drive home; he wanted to make a start on it. I hugged Vicky goodbye but she held herself back, and her body felt like a cluster of angles in my arms. I held her a little tighter, but I sensed her recoil and I let go.

'Take care of yourself,' she said. Her voice was impersonal. I felt a flare of anger. I felt terribly let down by her. *You think it's bad for you*, I thought, as I climbed into the passenger seat. *You're just the witness. I'm the one who has to live with it.* I slammed the door shut. But my anger quickly gave way to a desperate, hopeless sadness as we reversed, getting ready to pull away.

I jumped as I heard something bang against the car. I turned around and felt the blood drain from my face.

'Wait!'

It was Kieran. He stared at me through the glass window, almost pressing his face against it. He looked shocked, as if he couldn't quite believe it. *Oh God*, I thought, *he knows. He's figured it out.* I tried to tell Jamie to drive, but I couldn't speak. I sat there helplessly, even as Kieran opened the passenger's door.

'You're leaving already?' He moved towards me and I drew back, flinching, terrified. He was confused at my reaction. 'I just want to hug you, Anna,' he said, in a slow, even voice, as if I were a child. 'Is that OK?' I nodded mutely, held myself still as he leant into me. 'Look after yourself,' he mumbled into my hair, and I felt a tremor in his voice, like he was about to cry again. He shut the passenger door and gave the side of the car a friendly little tap.

Vicky and Kieran stood outside the red-and-blue painted door, his arm slung protectively around her waist. She did not meet my gaze.

The A10 was deserted, but Jamie drove as he always did; slowing for stop signs, using his indicators even though there was no one behind us. That was the difference between Jamie and me. He always did the right thing, even when no one was watching. I could still feel Kieran's sob in my scalp. If only I had befriended him. He was the person who could have told me everything I needed to know.

The moon was a slim curved blade, slicing clouds into Gothic wisps that stretched and yawned over the sky. I realized with a pang that I'd forgotten Mango Bango Jambo Banana. I'd left him on Caden's bed. *Well*, I thought sadly, *time I grew out of him.*

I kicked off my shoes, put my cut-up feet on the dashboard. Jamie glanced at me from time to time, his hand fluttering over his chest as if his heart ached for me. Sensing I didn't want to speak, he put on the radio. It was the *Shipping News*.

'Today, Sunday the fifth of July. The general synopsis at 21.48. Low, north-west Malin at 10.02, losing its identity by 18.00.'

I had always loved hearing about the wild weather lashing the coasts, thinking of all the sailors and fishermen to whom this language actually made sense. Caden was from the coast; he might have understood it. He'd loved water, and the river. I switched stations. Leonard Cohen came on, and Jamie started singing along.

'Didn't we listen to this on the way up?' Jamie asked, catching his breath as the song ended.

'Maybe.' A van whooshed past us, and Jamie slowed down.

'I think we're near where that accident happened,' he said, leaning forwards, peering through the windshield at the fields that we knew from memory were there, but that we couldn't really see in the dark. 'Wasn't it outside Royston?'

'I don't remember,' I lied.

I saw him glance up to check the rear-view mirror.

'Did you ever follow up on that? I didn't find anything about it in the news.'

'No,' I said. 'I never did.' I rolled down the window and my hair flew into my face, gagging my mouth. I tied it back in a high bun, the way I used to wear it before I met Caden.

'But I do sort of know what happened.'

'Yeah?'

'It's a story about two brothers who were very alike. And a woman. A great beauty.'

That's how it began.

# 15

# Eternal Recurrence

THE HOUSE WAS IN darkness when we arrived, my mother asleep in her therapist's chair in the front room. It had been years since I'd been in her office, and I was surprised by how lovely she had made it. A hanging mobile of squares, circles and triangles in yellow and purple and red were dangling overhead, like a moving Kandinsky painting. Blue walls, interrupted with framed Rothko blocks of green and black, and a tall bookcase. *Games People Play: The Basic Handbook of Transactional Analysis*; *Clean: Overcoming Addiction*; *Cognitive Behavioural Therapy of Addiction*. Two velvet armchairs facing each other, as if in amiable conversation.

There she was, head thrown back over the headrest, throat white as a fish's belly.

'Do you want me to stay?' Jamie whispered. I shook my head, plucking the charred cigarette stub from between her fingers.

The next morning, I showed my mother the article that had appeared in the *Cambridge News*: 'Body of a man found in Cam near Baits Bite Lock', the title ran. Beneath, a picture of the lock, and then a short paragraph.

*Emergency services attended the scene, and the man was*

*declared dead a short while later. The death is not being treated as suspicious. His next of kin have been informed.*

'Is that all?' she asked, sounding disappointed.

It would have been a bigger story if Caden had been a student at the university. 'Death of brilliant Cambridge student; tragic waste of potential.' There might have been a more thorough investigation. If anyone had done any digging, they would have found the videos. I would have been caught. But no one was asking the right questions.

Apart from my mother. She was a little too interested.

'Had he been drinking too much?' She was in the bath, and I was sitting on the tiled floor waiting for my turn.

'Yes.'

She asked me a string of questions: did he have a family risk of suicide or depression (yes); did he talk about feelings of shame or guilt (no); oh, but did he repress his feelings, as that's also a sign (yes); had he gone through a stressful life event recently (yes, but I didn't tell her what).

'I know it's my fault. I know I should have stopped him.'

'No one knows what's going on in someone else's mind,' she said, using her foot to turn on the hot water tap. 'Thank God we don't.'

'Isn't that the whole point of therapy? To figure that out?'

'No. It's to make people feel better about all the dark stuff that's going on in there. But I don't need to know about it. I would rather not.'

I spent the rest of July lying around in my bedroom. Sometimes the cracks in the ceiling seemed to widen as I watched. The Howling Woman was still there, cackling at me. At the start of August, my mother put me to work. She had me organize the bookshelf in her office, help her sort through her cupboards, and when that was done we went out into our tiny garden. We weeded the flowerbed and planted kale and spinach for the guinea-pigs. Then I finally unpacked. But my boxes were like a minefield; I had taken some of Giselle's things, and touching them made me feel sick. And there was all my rowing stuff, my lab stuff. One day as I was cleaning, a note fell out of one of my folders.

*I hope you slept well. Green Dragon, tomorrow night, at seven? X*

I sank to the floor. I wasn't even able to miss him. All the sadness I felt – the longing – was obliterated by the power of my self-hatred.

*I want to die* was the refrain of my heart, something I said to myself whenever I cast my mind back, whenever I did something stupid or clumsy. 'I want to die,' I said aloud, when I knocked over the glass of water my mother had just set down on the table.

'You will,' she said, stooping over the mess, picking up the clear shards with her hands. 'You will, soon enough. But not before your old mum.'

She'd stopped asking me questions when she understood that talking about Caden upset me, but she kept on at me to reach out to my department.

'Have you told your professor about Caleb?'

'Caden,' I corrected.

'Tell him. Say that you were grieving when you stole the guinea-pigs. Your boyfriend died by suicide. Just try,' she said, when I shook my head. 'Traumatic response to loss happens all the time. I can get a colleague to write you a note.'

She set up a Zoom consultation with a woman she'd qualified with at Bristol. I dreaded the meeting intensely. I had never spoken to a therapist before, and I feared she might have methods to extract information, that I would tell her everything and end up in prison.

The woman wore a white embroidered shirt, her blonde

hair styled in a braided coronet around her head. *Not fright-ening*, I thought. *More Heidi than Gestapo interrogator.* But she was disarmingly quiet. She didn't ask questions, and just sat there so still that I sometimes thought the screen of my computer had frozen. Had she tried to prise things out of me, I would have resisted. But my resolve was sucked into the vacuum of silence.

I talked. It was a relief at first, to be wholly honest with someone, but then I became frustrated. No matter what I said to her, she did not react. Her face was blanker than a white page, offering no judgement.

Even when I told her about hiding Pringle's body, she fixed me with the zen forbearance of a yogi.

'I have the feeling I'm telling this wrong,' I said. 'I'm trying to get you on my side.'

'It's impossible to be objective about your own life,' she replied.

'Then what's the point of therapy?' I said. 'What am I paying you for? To make me feel better? What if I don't deserve it?'

I could tell that had annoyed her. 'Well, don't you think everyone deserves to feel better? What about your boy-friend? Did he deserve to feel better?'

I ended the session early that day. But I met her again the next week, on my mother's insistence. She was wear-ing an even more elaborately embroidered top.

'Sorry about last time,' I said.

She didn't acknowledge my apology. 'You were telling me about the videos.'

I went on with the story, about the memory stick and the diamond ring, how Vicky had stolen it. She remained largely silent. *I'm boring her*, I thought. *I should spice up the story a bit. Put on the Anna Show.* But I continued to relay all the events in a neurotically pedantic way. It was almost compulsive, the need to tell her about every detail.

Then, just as I was describing returning to Caden's house after seeing Jack and Giselle on Midsummer Common, she cut me off abruptly.

'I'm going to stop you there, Anna. I have a good idea of what you're about to say, but you shouldn't. Because there are some things – including image-based sexual abuse – that I would have to report to the police.'

Image-based sexual abuse. The words made me want to drive a knife into my stomach. But she was right. That's what I'd done. I waited for her to speak. I felt the walls close in around me; it was as if I were being clasped in a pair of tweezers, held up to the light.

The silence grew unbearable.

'Aren't you going to say anything?' I burst out.

She didn't blink.

'You find silence distressing,' she said, making a note.

'I find it useless,' I said. 'It's not profound. Sitting there in silence. I want to know what's wrong with me. If this was all my fault. I want your professional opinion.'

She put down her pen, pushed her glasses against the bridge of her nose.

'I'd challenge any woman who was in the situation you were in – with those kinds of comments and comparisons – not to have had a strong reaction.'

'Even now,' I said, 'after everything that's happened, the thing I keep thinking about is how jealous he made me.' My face flushed; it pained me to admit it. 'That upsets me more than his death. Isn't that terrible? The ex.'

'Use her name,' she said.

'Giselle.'

She looked at me, clearly expecting me to elaborate. But I remained silent.

'People often pretend not to care about beauty when it is often the very thing affecting them most deeply.' She frowned, leaning close to the screen. 'Beauty is still the main form of power that women possess, or do not, as the case may be. It gives them power over men, and other women.'

There was a pause. 'Well,' she went on. 'The distribution of beauty is deeply unfair, as life tends to be.' She looked down at her notes. 'But we all have to play the hand we've been given. So what' – she looked at me straight on – 'are you going to do now?'

'I don't know.' My hands fidgeted in my lap, pulled and jerked as if tied to puppet strings.

'You do know.' She reached for her pen. 'I'll write what you need for your supervisor. Just give me their contact details.'

I gave her Crabwell's email address. A few days later, he wrote to me.

Dear Anna,

I am writing to offer my most sincere condolences for your loss. My son died under similar circumstances two years ago. The world has always seemed so sweet, so full of possibility and love to me, that it was impossible for me to understand such an act. But I have found solace in accepting there are some things in this life we are not meant to understand. And that unknown nebulous thing hovering at the centre of our lives is what makes us human.

Do let me know if you would like to return to Cambridge. I have a good vision of where your research could lead you, and exciting new possibilities are arising.

Sincerely,

Colton

And I was grateful for this miraculous reprieve. But I was not particularly surprised. So much had happened which ought not to have. I accepted Crabwell's invitation with an apathetic fatalism that was almost like serenity.

*

A few weeks later, I packed my things and appointed Jamie *in loco parentis* for Bubble and Squeak.

'But they're still mine,' I said, as he cooed over them while they nosed excitedly around his garden. 'I want them back during the holidays.'

He drove me, and this time my mother insisted on coming with us. She had made a whole loaf's worth of egg and cress, and I chewed through the mushy clumps until I thought I might be sick. I watched the road, the tarmac stretching out into the distance. I was anticipating Jamie pointing out the spot where we'd seen the accident, and I was dreading it. *What if it starts all over again*, I thought. *What if I'm in an infinite loop of eternal recurrence, and it's all about to kick off again.*

But we passed by without comment, and before I knew it we were right in the centre, driving along the Backs, the trees melting red and purple into the river; the buildings of Trinity and King's seeming to float above the lawns, white and bright as the moon.

We made a right on to Sidgwick Avenue and pulled up outside Newnham, went into the Porters' Lodge. Stan's smile widened as I approached. I saluted him, and he rose from his chair to offer me his own standing salute.

'Good to see you, Anna.'

Moustache upturned at the corners. Familiar gentle eyes. He handed me the key to my new room. 'And when you see Vicky, tell her there are nearly twenty letters waiting for her here. This isn't a concierge service.'

'I will,' I said, not wanting to admit that I had written to her many times over the summer, but there was never any reply. A whistling silence.

I showed them the gardens. It was dusk; that brief, most beautiful moment when night and day collide. The sun had set, but everything possessed a rosy-red luminescence, a beautifying night-dew that made my mother's face shine.

'You're such a lucky girl,' she said, bending over the flowerbed. Tall purple foxgloves, bumblebees creeping around inside their thimble-shaped flowers. A huge orange spicebush on the lawn, the leaves trembling like a bonfire. 'This is heaven.' She smiled up at me. 'I would have killed to go here.'

They helped me move into my room in Rosalind Franklin, a modern block of flats right next to the Porters' Lodge. This time I was not surprised by the interior; I was used to the Cambridge illusion.

'Well,' my mother said, examining the mustard-yellow wall-to-wall carpet, the squeaky mattress covered in plastic. 'You'll just have to pretend you're a hooker in a Las Vegas motel.'

'Or like you're that guy in *Psycho*,' Jamie said, struggling through the door with my big duffle bag. 'The one who keeps his mother mummified in the basement.'

# Epilogue

S O THAT'S WHERE I live now. I've pushed the desk up against the window, and I've bought a quilt for my bed, and it isn't bad at all. I like the girls who live on either side of me. A German doing an MA in gender studies and a shy film student from Lebanon. They're young, and I've taken them both under my wing – introduced them to Stan, explained the rules of Formal Hall; when to stand, when to sit.

Early in October, I took them into town to buy their academic gowns. We took the scenic route – through Sheep's Green, down Laundress Lane and up Silver Street. And I saw it all afresh through their eyes: the luminous river that seemed to coax the morning into life; the contrast between the dark narrow lanes and the gasp of space and light as we stepped out on to King's Parade. The buildings jostling for attention like showy beauty queens. The girls took pictures, as chirpy and happy as sparrows.

We were about to turn right on to Market Square, when I saw Vicky. She was wearing a long silk dress with a high slit up to her pale thigh, barefoot, high heels hanging from the tips of her fingers. Clearly returning from an all-nighter. I ducked into the entrance of the Copper Kettle cafe just in time. She passed without noticing me.

Her blonde hair was pinned up. Glitter on her face, plum-purple lipstick. I wondered where she'd been, whose party. That life in Cambridge is closed to me now. I will never be at the glowing centre of things.

'I think it's that boyfriend of hers,' Ji-woo had said, when I'd asked her if she had seen Vicky over the summer. 'She moved into his place a few days after you left, and since then she's never around. Kieran has the worst vibes.'

I wonder why Vicky is still with him. At first, I'd been anxious that she might tell him what I'd done. But if she ever betrays me, I will tell the college that she's a thief. I'll tell them she stole my earrings, Caden's diamond ring. So she keeps my secret and I keep hers, in a precarious acknowledgment of our mutually assured destruction.

I'm still close to Ji-woo who, for all her brilliance, has not figured out the part I played in Caden's death. We have breakfast together every morning in Newnham, steeling ourselves for long days in the lab. She's busy finishing the Great Attractor thesis, which is due in a few months. Already I sense her thoughts have turned to home, to academic jobs in the US.

I don't see much of the old group. Angus finished his PhD in September and was offered a job teaching at the London School of Economics. Ian has published an anthology of poetry with Faber, and is one of the organizers of the Cambridge Literary Festival. He sometimes invites me to incredibly crappy poetry readings. I always sit in the back, wishing Vicky was there so I'd have someone to laugh at it all with.

Leonid and I are good friends now. I helped him re-extract all his RNA so that he could start the sequencing again, and I often find his samples when he can't locate them in the fridge; the kind of thing I used to do for Charles. He has never apologized for betraying me, and we don't talk to each other any more. He cuts his eyes away from me, looking aggrieved, especially when I chat and joke with Leonid. He goes on struggling with his guinea-pig dissections, while I'm making excellent progress with my own research.

I don't work with rodents any more. Crabwell reached an agreement with Addenbrooke's Hospital. They donate placentas from C-sections for my research. I pick them up from the maternity ward and then run tests on them, trying to understand which pro-inflammatory proteins affect the health of newborn babies. I'm applying everything I learnt from my mouse models on these human cells. None of it went to waste. It is terrible that the tragedy of Caden's death was the bargaining chip that got me back into the lab. But I try to focus on the work I'm doing. Helping women. Helping babies. It's a form of atonement.

Crabwell has promised to write me a recommendation for his old lab at UC Berkeley once I finish the PhD. Jiwoo and I fantasize about living together on the West Coast.

'It's so much better than here,' she tells me. 'Berkeley is way nicer than Cambridge.'

You could say that after that first disastrous year, I'm making a success of it. But I'm not a psychopath; I'm not happy. The city is not alive to me any more; it is a museum of my past. I'll be doing something normal like baking *rosquettes* or eating tomato pasta, and I'll suddenly think of Caden. The memory is illuminated with forensic precision: his reaching over to grab a biscuit, his black hair falling over his face; the feel of the cold cocktail mixer in my hand. In those moments, I'm filled with such intense self-hatred that I am scared I will do something drastic.

The only time it feels safe to think about him is at dawn rowing practice. In the boat, my thoughts last only the length of the inhalation of air between two strokes. In that exhausted state of semi-consciousness – my thighs burning, my wrist stiff from feathering – I palp my memories of him.

Sometimes I feel like someone is watching us from the bank, but when I turn to look, Kayla screams at me to keep my eyes facing forward. Every morning we row past the *Rise and Shine*. The porticos are shuttered against the sunrise, but on some days I think I can see a faint light emanating from inside, can smell coffee and toast. Imagine waking up to her every single day. Imagine waking up to him. The same dark hair and eyes as Caden. The strong, elegant fingers tracing a line from her lips down to her abdomen. I imagine him monitoring her progress, watching her face. I like to pretend that the breathing of the girls in the boat behind me is coming from inside the *Rise and Shine*. Jack and Giselle together.

A few times, I've grazed the side of their boat with my oar. It makes a loud scraping noise, and flakes of red-and-blue paint break off into the water. I don't do this on purpose, but it's not exactly an accident either. The other rowers don't notice. To them it's just another obstacle we don't want to crash into. Something to navigate around. No one knows the exhilaration and despair I feel. I hide it well. I keep my stroke steady and my blade-work exact.

This morning, though, something happened to my wrist during the session. Maybe the cold made me tense up – it's below freezing today. The fields are white, and the river is steaming like a tired animal. I must have gripped the oar too tight. It feels like I'm giving myself an electric shock every time I move my thumb or index finger. I try to hide it, but Kayla must have noticed, as she calls me over after the post-outing talk.

'Let me see,' she says. She takes my hand and moves my fingers carefully, as if testing the wings of an injured bird.

'Is this the same one you injured last time?'

I nod.

'You have to go and see someone. Go to Goldie. Do you still have the number?'

At those words, my heart begins to beat against my ribs like a monkey rattling its cage. *It's happening again*, I think. *It's the eternally recurring nightmare.*

But I nod, and agree to let her know what the physio says. My wrist hurts too much to cycle home, so I leave my bike locked at the boathouse, struggling with the chain.

I don't have too much to do today for once, only to check my write-up from last week's ELISA protocols. So I decide to save the cab fare and walk, crossing over the bridge to Midsummer Common, moving aside to let the other rowers pass me on their bicycles.

'Feel better, Anna!' they shout.

I don't answer. I don't want to wake the people in the riverboats; it's still so early. The sound of the rowers' voices and their pedalling fades away as they're sucked into the fog. It is eerily silent, but perhaps the fog increases the illusion of unnatural stillness. Perhaps the confluence of blankness and quiet is what makes me uneasy. I look up. The bare branches above me are twisted and forked, like white lightning bolts lancing up to the sky.

I cross Stourbridge Common. The mist is denser over the fields than it was over the river. Perhaps I should go to Goldie. There's no harm in going to say hello to Kieran. He might think it's a bit suspicious that I haven't even tried to get in touch with him yet. I hear a crack and jerk my head over my shoulder to see what it is. But there's no one there.

I stuff my hands in my pockets. God, it's bloody freezing. It's not even December yet and I'm already sick of winter. I can only see a few metres in front of me through the drifting veil of fog. I have to be careful where I walk, as the path is uneven. The roots forcing their way up under the concrete split and fissure the pavement into all kinds of patterns and skewed faces. Some funny, some scary. I hear another noise, but it sounds like a lowing. It's just the cows, I tell myself. But then it seems too late in the year for them still to be out for pasture.

Still following the river path, I hurry my steps a little, and as I reach Midsummer Common, my heart lightens. Yes, I was right; there are cows up ahead. Big brown paperweights holding down the low-anchored clouds.

That's when I hear something behind me, and this time it's definite. I glance over my shoulder, and I see someone walking at some distance behind me. My stomach lurches, but then I notice they are wearing pink leggings. It's a woman. I relax. Cambridge is safe.

I'm shivering now. The sweat from the outing has cooled, and my muscles are stiff. I should have called an Uber; I'm dying for a hot shower and an aspirin for my wrist. But I'm almost there – I might as well walk the rest. I sense something moving nearby and glance to my right, but the river is empty, and I glance to my left towards the field and see that it's a cow. A beautiful reddish-brown animal, nosing the frozen grass. She looks up at me, sweet breath steaming in the cold, and gives a soft lowing. A warning, maybe, but it is so bland as to be almost friendly. I walk on, realizing that I'm starving. They'd better have porridge at breakfast, or I'll be grumpy all day. That's what I'll have, a big bowl of porridge smothered in golden syrup.

I'm approaching the cows now, and annoyingly there are several of them right on the path in front of me. Perhaps I can go around them on the grass, but it's white with the first frost of the year, and my shoes are not waterproof. I slow down a bit more. There is a snap behind me, and I turn around.

It's the same woman as before, but she's closer now and I can see her more clearly. Dark plaited hair. A familiar figure.

No, it can't be her. Why would Giselle be up so early? It doesn't make sense. I squint through the fog.

The mirage hardens into fact as she approaches. Her face is shining. There's something shiny in her hand; it gives off a pretty glimmer. I turn around, but the cows are blocking my way now. I can't even go around them through the field. Hindquarters and faces in an arcing line across the path. The barrage of sound is more frightening than their bodies.

Something comes into my mind. Too late to be of any use. But I know I'm right. Caden never drowned himself. He was pushed. It wasn't my fault. The truth feels like mercy.

I glance back over my shoulder. She's so close that I can see the funny quirk of her upper lip. I look to my right, at the river. It is nearly completely still; there are only a few tiny ripples and shapes plucking at the surface. One with a nose and mouth that seems to expand, as if the cows' lowing is tearing a hole in the water. It widens and widens. It's the Howling Woman.

I can see the freckles on her eyelids, I can make out a pattern.

She has come for me.

# Acknowledgements

With thanks to: Cindy Xin Wen Zhang for sharing her research, teaching me about ELISA sandwich protocols, and helping me develop my character's scientific mind; Arjun Ashoka for sharing his vast knowledge of physics, and Great Attractors.

Gratitude to Jean McNeil, Elle Hunt and Amy Hughes for their excellent feedback on early drafts. Claire Gatzen and Isabella Ghaffari-Parker for all their hard work on *Plaything*. Charlotte Seymour for her faith and support, and the unholy trinity of editors at Doubleday: Alice Youell, Charlotte Trumble and Bobby Mostyn-Owen.

Noa, the Chief Biscuit Handler. Sally, who taught me how to chill like a legend. Islington Borough Ladies' Football Club and Belsize Square Synagogue; for getting me through a dreary autumn. Thanks to Newnham Boat Club. The early mornings were real.

For all of you who bought my first novel, *Berlin*, and wrote to tell me you loved it. I am so grateful for your encouragement.

To Bobbot, for all you've done. Credit to my big brother, who allows me to steal his odd linguistic 'isms'. My father, for teaching me to pay attention to the world around me, to really *look* at things. And finally thank you to my mother, Catherine, who is my first reader and most exacting editor.